PRAISE FOR
Love Warps the Mind a Little

"Lively reading . . . an enormously funny writer with
a rich, expansive vision."
—*Miami Herald*

"Dufresne manages to meld comedy and tragedy in the
story of a maniacally humorous, willfully unenlightened
fellow from Worcester who must learn the hard way
where to find love."
—*Boston Globe*

"Dufresne takes on the most elemental stuff in the human
universe, our radical hunger for affection, and catches
our ear and holds it."
—*Chicago Tribune*

"Dufresne's characters are charming and absurd
and perfectly believable."
—*The New Yorker*

JOHN DUFRESNE attended Worcester State College and had a
seven-year career as a social worker in drug-prevention and cri-
sis-intervention programs. He also drove a cab, tended bar, did
landscaping, painted houses, and hitchhiked across the country
with $27. His first novel, *Louisiana Power & Light*, was a Barnes &
Noble Discover Great Writers selection and a *New York Times*
Notable Book of the Year. It and his short-story collection, *The
Way That Water Enters Stone*, are available in Plume editions.
Dufresne teaches at Florida International University and lives in
Dania, Florida, with his wife and son.

ALSO BY JOHN DUFRESNE

The Way That Water Enters Stone
Louisiana Power & Light

Love Warps

the Mind

a Little

JOHN DUFRESNE

A PLUME BOOK

PLUME
Published by the Penguin Group
Penguin Putnam Inc., 375 Hudson Street, New York, New York 10014, U.S.A.
Penguin Books Ltd, 27 Wrights Lane, London W8 5TZ, England
Penguin Books Australia Ltd, Ringwood, Victoria, Australia
Penguin Books Canada Ltd, 10 Alcorn Avenue, Toronto, Ontario, Canada M4V 3B2
Penguin Books (N.Z.) Ltd, 182–190 Wairau Road, Auckland 10, New Zealand

Penguin Books Ltd, Registered Offices: Harmondsworth, Middlesex, England

Published by Plume, an imprint of Dutton Signet,
a member of Penguin Putnam Inc.
This is an authorized reprint of a hardcover edition published by
W.W. Norton & Company, Inc. For information address
W.W. Norton & Company, Inc., 500 Fifth Avenue, New York, NY 10110.

First Plume Printing, February, 1998
10 9 8 7 6 5 4 3 2 1

Ⓟ REGISTERED TRADEMARK—MARCA REGISTRADA

Library of Congress Cataloging-in-Publication Data is available.
ISBN: 0-452-27898-8

Original hardcover design by Susan Hood
Printed in the United States of America

PUBLISHER'S NOTE
This is a work of fiction. Names, characters, places, and incidents either are the
products of the author's imagination or are used fictitiously, and any resemblance
to actual persons, living or dead, events, or locales is entirely coincidental.

BOOKS ARE AVAILABLE AT QUANTITY DISCOUNTS WHEN USED TO PROMOTE PRODUCTS OR
SERVICES. FOR INFORMATION PLEASE WRITE TO PREMIUM MARKETING DIVISION,
PENGUIN PUTNAM INC., 375 HUDSON STREET, NEW YORK, NY 10014.

This book is for my sisters, Paula Sullivan and Cindy Wondolowski,
and for my brother, Mark Dufresne,

and in memory of my friends
Francis Bartlett, Ethel Berard, and Meg O'Brien.

Acknowledgments

I want to thank those people who helped make this novel possible, some who read the early drafts, some who encouraged, offered expertise and insight, some who listened to me talk: Jack and Barbara Bell, Pamela Paquette, Flo LeClair, Walter Chao, Dan Whatley, Lydia Webster, Leo Stouder, Ellen Wehle, Maureen Powers, Eve Richardson, Betty Sosnin, and Garry Kravit. Thanks also to my students and colleagues at Florida International University and to the Friday Night Writers who've been sharing their work and enthusiasm with me and each other for more than six years now; to Dick McDonough and Leslie Arnold, friends; to Steve Barthelme, who accepted one of Lafayette's stories for the Mississippi Review. I am indebted to Jill Bialosky, my editor, as always, for asking the right questions and getting to the heart of the matter. I am especially thankful once again to Florida International University for a faculty research grant which facilitated the writing of the book. And thanks, Worcester. My love and appreciation to Cindy and Tristan, without whom any book would be inconceivable.

"But is there any comfort to be found?
Man is in love and loves what vanishes,
What more is there to say?"

—WILLIAM BUTLER YEATS
  "Nineteen Hundred and Nineteen"

1.

Love Without Its Wings

THE DAY I FINISHED MY BEST STORY YET—ABOUT A social WORKER WHOSE CHILD gets Lyme disease, slips into a coma, suffers brain damage, becomes a burden to his father—after I typed it, retyped it, and mailed it off to the *Timber Wolf Review,* my wife, Martha, came home from work and, just like that, asked me to leave our apartment forever. What's with you? I said, as if I didn't know. She packed my green plaid suitcase, threw toiletries in an overnight bag, and set it all by the kitchen door.

A month earlier, Martha and I had gone on a couples retreat with some other folks from the parish out at the Trappist monastery in Spencer. The idea of the weekend was to reinvigorate your marriage, renew your vows, and rededicate your life to Jesus. I should tell you I'm not a religious person, and I was more than a little skeptical about the efficacy of this therapeutic undertaking. I doubted that a gang of cloistered celibates would have much to offer us struggling spouses other than the customary Pauline counsel. But then we all got to sharing our feelings so openly, talking about our hopes and fears, and we got so honest and nonjudgmental and everything, and the truth is such a dangerous drug and all, and I was feeling splendid, feeling like the world was pure, refreshing, like some god had created it with humor and generosity, that I was regrettably moved to reveal to Martha the unpleasant truth of my infidelity. I told her about Judi Dubey. But I said, Martha, I'm finished with all that, I promise. That last part was a lie, it turns out.

So as I stood there in the kitchen, my back to the door, hand on my suitcase, I could see that my disclosure had been festering inside Martha all these weeks and had turned her hateful. I told her I loved her. She jabbed me in the stomach with my typewriter. You don't know what love is, she told me, which is probably true. I mean, who does? I asked if we could talk about this. I said, Forgiveness is divine, isn't it? She said, You got what you wanted. Which was also probably true, though I didn't understand it then. I took my last look around the kitchen, trying to secure the details: the cast iron skillet on the stove, the yellow dish towel folded over the handle on the oven door, the crucifix, the wall calendar from Moore's Pharmacy. I knew they'd all wind up in a story some day. A guy like me, who had just given up a career in order to write stories, would be the central character. A story about love and anxiety.

Martha told me to take the goddamn dog and get the hell out. Spot heard the jingle of his leash and came blasting into the kitchen from the parlor and slid right past me into the door. He started barking. I cuffed him one.

Martha shook her head, called me pathetic. "You're thirty-six years old. You're working part-time in a fish-and-chips store, and you're breaking my heart."

Sure, the job thing again. I said, "Martha, you knew I was a writer when you married me."

She laughed. "You haven't published a damn thing in your life."

I said, "Neither did Emily Dickinson."

Spot grabbed his leash and tugged. I told Martha we should talk about this.

She pulled a book of matches from the El Morocco out of her pocket. "Found them in your shirt this morning."

I don't smoke. I lied and said my friend Francis X. had asked me to hold them for him.

"Your shirt smelled like that slut."

When I think about that afternoon now, I wonder if I had acted purposefully, if, in fact, I wanted to get caught, wanted to hurt Martha so badly that she would never take me back. At the time, I imagined I was acting spontaneously, if recklessly, a slave to my late-blooming libido. But infidelity, as you know, is anything but spontaneous. You can't possibly conduct a proper affair without a lot of deliberating, scheming, speculating, and conniving. It's a delicate balance where the excitement must equal the guilt and the sex must be as bright as the future you gamble. Was I no longer in love with Martha? Had I allowed her to become a stranger? If I sound disingenuous, I don't mean to.

"We'll talk about this when you've calmed down," I said. "In the meantime, what about my mail?"

"I'll forward it to you."

I gave her Judi Dubey's address, but not her name.

2.

Feeling Around for My Shoes

JUDI SAID I COULD STAY AT HER HOUSE UNTIL I GOT BACK ON MY FEET. MY EMO-
tional feet, she said she meant. That didn't sound like sweetheart talk to
me. We sat at her kitchen table. She lit a cigarette, exhaled, waved the
match like a wand. She said Spot could sleep in the cellar tonight. Spot
raised his chin from the floor. But tomorrow I'd have to buy him a doghouse for the backyard. I'm allergic, she said. She sneezed, in case I didn't
believe her. There I was, in need of consolation and comfort, but all I
was getting were more problems. Spot won't like that, I told her. Spot
doesn't have to like it, she said.

To be honest, I had hoped for a warmer reception, more cordial and
enthusiastic. This was the same woman who, when I was supposed to
be home with my wife, but was here romancing her instead, wouldn't
want me to leave, would lock her legs around my waist so I couldn't get
up, tell me just ten more minutes, baby, or one more quick one, or whatever. And I'd be reaching over the edge of the bed, feeling around for
my shorts and my shoes, saying, Honey, come on. You know what time
it is? So this evening's formality made me feel vulnerable.

I drummed my fingers on my typewriter case. I got up. I said, Maybe
this is a bad idea; I should just go. But who was I kidding? Where was
I going on foot with a suitcase, an overnight bag, a Royal portable, a
twenty-pound bag of dog chow, and a drooling Irish setter? I'd walked
enough for one day. I was being petulant. Still, I lifted the suitcase. I'd
figure something out by the time I reached the back door. Judi could see

right through me, though. She smiled. She's a psychotherapist. Laf, she said, sit. Spot sat. He looked at Judi, looked at me. Woofed. I sat down. Judi stood and went to the sink, ran the water over her cigarette, tossed the butt into the wastebasket. She told me how my arrival, while not unwelcomed, was a big change in her life.

I could understand that.

She said she enjoyed living alone, was a creature of habit, and wasn't sure she wanted to live with anyone else right now, even someone she cared about, like me. She sat down again, with her back away from the chair.

I apologized for my irritability. I explained how it had been a trying day. I smiled. I said, "What are you doing?"

Judi kept her eyes closed. She said, "Pulling a ball of mercury up through my spine." She held her breath. "And now," she said, "I'm letting it drift and settle." She exhaled slowly. "What were you saying?" She opened her eyes.

I thanked her for letting me crash. I said, So why don't we make love. She told me to first get Spot situated down cellar while she made room in her closet for my stuff.

"Can I leave the typewriter on the table?" I like to work at the kitchen table.

"Put it in the mud room."

Judi was very expressive in bed. She choreographed every move. She liked to make it last forever. And she liked to talk about it, check on my progress, my response to her maneuvers. Me, I'd just as soon concentrate on what I was doing and feeling. Sometimes I think she made a bigger deal of it than necessary. I also think she lied about her dreams. Each was loaded with prescience and significance, with archetypes and allegorical figures. She never just dreamed about missing a history test or going bald. She was after coherence, even in sleep.

And there's a connection there with why she didn't like my stories. She wanted to know what the hidden meaning was. I told her, There isn't one. Why would I hide it? I told her, It's just a story about a woman who loves her husband to death but realizes that she can't live with him. Or whatever it happened to be. Judi asked me why I wanted to write about made-up people. She said truth was more interesting.

I told her truth is imagined, not absolute. It used to be true that the earth revolved around the sun, that an imbalance of humors caused disease, that gods walked among us. For some folks today it's true that the earth is six thousand years old and dinosaurs never existed. Truth is fiction, I said. She wasn't buying it. She gave me one of those glassy-eyed, indulgent, therapeutic nods that say, Why don't you go with that thought while I plan tonight's dinner menu.

So after we made love, Judi told me she'd been expecting me for a week. She took her journal out of the night table drawer and read me the dream that foretold my coming. In the dream, a woman dressed in a fleece jacket ties me to a sled and starts me speeding down a mountain. Just as I am about to fly off a ledge, I scream Judi's name, and she wakes up.

I asked Judi if she saw herself in the dream. Me, I've never had a dream that I wasn't in.

I was the snow you fell into, she said.

I asked her what kind of sled it was. She smiled and said I asked the silliest questions. She kissed me on the nose, gave my dick a little squeeze. She put on her headphones, listened to the sounds of the rain forest until she fell asleep.

I had a Speedway sled when I was four. That's why I asked. On the bottom my mother had written my name and address with red nail polish: Lafayette Proulx, 16 Security Road, Worcester, Mass. My first home. But I couldn't use that address in a story. Irony needs to present itself more subtly than that. Security Road was in the Lincolnwood Housing Project and got leveled in a tornado.

I heard Spot barking, scratching at the cellar door. I looked at Judi. With her eyes closed she reminded me of Martha, which is odd, I thought, because they don't look alike. Sure, they're both slim, both have dimples, both are about five feet six. But Martha's blond and has these guileless blue, almost silver, eyes that are impossible not to stare at. Judi's hair is auburn and her eyes are a greenish brown. I thought about where I could buy a doghouse. I thought about my fourteen stories out there in the mail and how they'd all be coming back to the wrong address. Or not coming back. I could hope. Just maybe at that precise moment in Vermont, an editor is sitting at his desk, reading my manuscript, shaking his head, thinking he's discovered the next John Cheever. He's so excited he has to go for a walk. He comes back and wakes his significant other and tells her that she has to read the story immediately. While she reads, he writes me a letter: *Dear Mr. Proulx: We here at* Pond Apple *are happy to accept your miraculous and devastating short story, "Someone Winds*

LOVE WARPS THE MIND A LITTLE | 19

Up Dead," for publication in our Winter/Spring issue. Payment is two copies. Please send more. The significant other calls from the bedroom. Hurry, she says, I need you now.

Then I imagined Martha getting this letter of acceptance, staring at the envelope, tossing it in the trash. I hoped she wasn't swallowing Percodans and wine like last time. I hoped she was sleeping. I was ashamed of my cynicism. That night I dreamed Ed McMahon accepted my story for the Publishers' Clearinghouse Literary Review.

3.

Fly Away Home

JUDI DID LIKE ONE STORY I WROTE AND SOME POEMS. SHE LIKED THE POEM THAT ended, "I want to dance the poozle/ with you all night long./ I want to infiltrate your everything." She didn't know I changed the title from "Martha" to "Choreography" before I read it to her.

The story she liked is called "We Are Unable to Come to the Phone Right Now," and it's about a guy who grows up in a family of sociopaths but seems wholly unaffected by their depravity. He becomes a successful and contented dispensing optician. I wrote the story to try to figure out how lunacy can just slide off someone's back like that. Judi found the story's incongruities amusing and provocative. She was reminded, she said, of her clients' troubled lives. But in real life, she told me, the suppressed emotional trauma of such a childhood would necessarily manifest itself in disabling and destructive behaviors. Here's the thing: The story's about her. I switched genders, occupations, changed the names to protect the guilty. Goes to show you, I guess, how the mind doesn't always see what the eyes see. It sees what it needs to see.

Judge for yourself. Judi's family lived (and still lives) in a Quonset hut out in Millbury by the Blackstone Valley Rod & Gun Club. In their gravel yard they had a twenty-four-foot travel trailer stabilized with leveling jacks. Judi's mom, Trixie, lived in the hut with her second husband, Hervey Jolicoeur. Her ex-boyfriend, Noel Prefontaine, lived in the trailer with his son, Edmund. Judi's sister, Stoni, lived at home. She was a nurse at Memorial and a two-hundred-pound junkie. Stoni's boyfriend, Arthur

Bositis, worked in the kill room at Boston Beef and was at the house all the time except when Stoni's fiancé, Richie Muneyhun, was furloughed from the Worcester County House of Correction. When he was fourteen, Judi's brother, George, hanged himself from an exposed joist in the bathroom because, his note said, the house was so dark, the rain so loud. Trixie told me that. Judi never mentioned a brother. Sometimes I had the alarming notion that maybe I was the sanest person Judi had ever been with.

I got the idea for my actual story at Judi's thirtieth birthday party. We had finished the three tubs of fried chicken from Chicken Delight and the Carvel birthday cake. Judi had opened her gifts—a bottle of Giorgio, a savings bond, an electric curling iron—and was sitting in the living room talking to her fourteen-year-old cousin, Layla, who was Edmund's date. Edmund was with me and the others at the kitchen table. He told me he was entering divinity school that fall in West Virginia. "Going to be a preacher in the International Foursquare Gospel Church."

"You're Catholic," I said.

"Don't get me wrong," he said. "I'd rather be a priest. Just that priests don't get to do the wild thing."

Hervey handed me a bottle of warm ale from the case on the floor. He told me about the bandage on his head, his shaved scalp. Said on his last job he pissed off some Puerto Rican drywaller, who then fired a two-inch nail into Hervey's head with a nail gun. "I thought the spic just punched me. I didn't know about the nail till later when I tried to take off my hat. Doctors told me I was lucky to be alive." I thought, You should have asked for a second opinion, but I didn't say anything. Then he asked me was Judi any good in the sack. I told him it was none of his business. I said it nicely, with a smile. He said, Hey, don't get all worked up, my friend. I excused myself, went to the bathroom where George had hanged himself, and wrote down what I had just heard. I made a note to ask Arthur more about the sounds and smells in the kill room.

When I came out, Trixie asked me did I think everything was going swell. I said yes. She told me she was so stressed, being the hostess and all. "Stoni," she said, "where are the roofies?" They were in the sugar bowl on the table. Trixie took two. Noel took a few. Arthur said he'd had enough for now. All of this, by the way, is in my story about James the dispensing optician.

A while later Stoni lifted her head from the table, looked across at her mom, who was sitting now on Noel's lap, and said, "You fucking bitch.

I ought to kick your ass. You drove Daddy away, and now you're driving Hervey away."

Noel said, "Hey now, Stoni, just hold on. She ain't no fucking bitch. She's your mother, for Christ's sake. Don't forget that, you trashy little whore. Look at you, you're a goddamn mess, your own self."

Arthur said, "Who you think you're talking to, asshole?" He came around the table after Noel. Trixie was crying by now and she slipped right off Noel's lap like a fried egg off a Teflon pan, ended up puddled on the floor. Arthur grabbed Noel by the throat, put his other thumb in Noel's eye socket. "One more word and you lose the eye, motherfucker."

I woke Judi on the couch, and we said good night to everyone. I had to get home before Martha started worrying, making phone calls. No one got hurt until later. That's when Edmund and Layla stopped by a bungalow on Eddy Pond. Layla waited in the car, listened to Little Walter on 'BCN. Edmund went into the house through the window. Someone in the neighborhood called the police. The old woman inside startled Edmund. He shot her dead.

4.

Difficulty Worth Living For

WHEN I WOKE THE NEXT MORNING, JUDI WAS GONE AND SPOT WAS BARKING at the cellar door. I let him out in the backyard to do his business, and I made coffee. I called Petland and ordered a doghouse. They could deliver it in an hour. I sat down to write. In a high school algebra class, Brother Doherty once told me that what I didn't know would make a good book. I always hated that son of a bitch, but I've let his wisdom guide me ever since. I write about what I don't know. I figure if I know it already, what's the point of writing about it?

All right then, here's a guy. He's thirty-seven and lives alone in an eight-room adobe house in Hobbs, New Mexico. His name's Dale. He teaches at the junior college. Wait, he doesn't live alone. He has a poodle, no, a Shih Tzu, with a slipped disk and a food allergy. Dale teaches . . . I'm a moron about economics, so he teaches economics. The Shih Tzu's name is Keynes. Dale owns several handguns, collects presidential campaign buttons, and watches a big-screen TV. He eats breakfast every morning before school at Furr's Cafeteria. He's a Baptist, but he used to be a Catholic.

Dale teaches with a 9-mm. Ruger automatic in a shoulder holster. He doesn't mind if, once in a while, the students get a glimpse of the leather strap beneath his sport coat. Some days he looks over the class, at the rows of oil-field trash, and imagines drawing his weapon and firing a round into the forehead of one of those dumb, smart-assed ones in the back of the room.

Dale has a new girlfriend, Theresa Plotczik, who's a nurse at the regional hospital. Theresa says she's never been to Ruidoso, which she pronounces "Riodosa." Dale says they should go skiing for the weekend. When he picks her up Friday evening, Theresa hops into the cab of the truck, says, I hope you don't mind. I brought along a bottle of Jack Daniel's. I know you don't drink. Dale checks the rearview mirror, says, I hope you don't mind. I brought along a loaded .357 magnum. This makes Theresa laugh.

Three miles east of Maljamar, Dale pulls off the highway and onto an oil-field road. He pulls over by a pump jack and parks. Theresa wants to know what's going on. Thought we might go for a walk, he says. He leaves the headlights on, and they walk ahead in the river of light. There are a million stars in the sky. Dale runs his hand through a low sagebrush and tells Theresa to smell his fingers. She wants to go back to the truck. It's cold. He says, I think this would be a good time to get a few things straight between us. I wondered what the hell Dale was up to.

Spot started to bark like crazy. I went to the window and saw the truck from Petland, the two workers standing in the driveway with the doghouse. I had them set the doghouse near the back fence, and I signed off on the delivery. The doghouse was unfinished pine, cedar shingles on the roof. It smelled sweet and resinous. Spot barked at it. The word *trousseau* came to me and the image of my aunt Emma's bone-white linens, starched and folded, my mother's giggle. *Theresa thinks of her two kids. She says, I'm not sure what you mean, Dale.* I grabbed Spot's collar. He growled. I shoved him inside the house and told him to stay. I could see he was panicked, but I figured he'd calm down with my petting and my baby talk. He snapped at me and lunged out. He ran a circle around the yard. *Dale just stands there, not saying anything.*

I chained Spot to the fence with enough lead so he could get in his house. I begged him to please stop barking. I brought out bowls of water and chow. I went inside the house. I found a Post-It note, wrote, *Dale stares into the headlights until he's blind,* and stuck it on my story-so-far. The phone rang, the machine answered. A neighbor, Mr. Lesperence, complaining about the barking. I took a shower. Martha hadn't packed my razor. I shaved with Judi's.

I walked downtown to Judi's building. I thought I'd meet her for lunch, then go to the library to write, maybe do a little reading on New Mexico. There are three other therapists in Judi's building, an old brownstone on Irving Street. The offices are upstairs. Mr. Natural's Health Food Store is on the first floor, which is where Judi told me to meet her in ten minutes.

A bell jingled when I opened the door. I smiled at the woman there arranging a display of banana chips. She smiled back, said, Let me know if I can help you. I read somewhere that you get a warning before you're hit by lightning. Your hair feels like it's standing on edge and your skin tingles. That's what her voice did to me. I had that chill in my neck and shoulders. I wanted her to say something else. Anything else.

"Is there something wrong?" she said.

"Nothing," I told her. "I'm just waiting for Ms. Dubey." I pointed to the ceiling. "You have a lovely voice." Her eyes were gray. God, gray eyes.

"Judi's nice," she said. "Should quit smoking, though."

I had to stop staring at her, so I looked at the wheatgrass, the watercress. Dale might be into health food. Makes his own bread with—I looked at the barrels of flour—stone-ground rye. He has a juicer. Grinds lamb and bulgur for the dog. I pretended to be reading a can of Pritikin barley soup, and I watched her. I could see only parts of her at a time. The eyes and cheekbones, the top of an ear poking out of her brown hair. Her collarbones and the hollow at her throat. Her lips. I asked myself what I thought I was doing. I already had a wife and a girlfriend. I should get out of there. I stopped at the counter on my way out. She was on the phone explaining to whomever that watermelon juice would cleanse the kidney and bladder. I nodded. She smiled, gave me a tiny wave. She smelled like vanilla. I wanted to rest my face on her neck and leave it there and breathe her in. I was staring again. I smiled. I could tell she noticed my tooth.

All my life I've had trouble with my teeth—soft enamel, spongy gums. Fillings, bondings, extractions, root canals, bridges, scalings. I don't even want to talk about it. Anyway, my last dental adventure a week earlier had been this crown on my front tooth—upper-right central incisor. The cap looked lovely in the dentist's hand, white and flawless. Looks good, I said. So Dr. Shimkoski cemented it to a post drilled into my gum. He handed me the mirror. It looks like a white picket in a gray fence, I said. You'll get used to it, he said. It's just the novelty of the thing.

We had lunch, Judi and I, at Kalil's, a Lebanese place with four tables. Judi finished her salad and spinach pie and picked at my tabbouleh. She said I seemed distracted, did I want to talk about it? I told her about the doghouse. She said avoidance won't make it go away.

"What's that?" I said.

Judi smiled. "You're going to have to talk to Martha sometime."

I nodded, sipped my coffee, thought about Dale talking to Theresa. They haven't moved. Right now he's smiling like everything's a big joke. *"Don't play games with me, Theresa. Okay?" Dale steps toward Theresa, takes her hand in his, snuggles his cheek into her neck.*

"Did you ever consider marriage counseling?" Judi said. She put down her fork and wiped her mouth with a napkin.

"We talked about it."

Judi fished through her purse. I told her lunch was on me. I said, "Do you think we should?"

"What?"

"Go to counseling."

"Do you love her?"

I swept crumbs of cracked wheat into a pile with my hand. "I don't know." I shook my head. "It's not that simple."

"Isn't it?"

"Maybe I love Martha but not marriage."

"Or vice versa."

"But if I love her, why aren't I happy?"

"So *maybe* you love her."

"Even if I'm really in love with her, but I think I'm not, then I feel like I'm not. That's the way with emotions—even if the source is fake, the feeling is true. And if I can doubt my love, can imagine not being in love, then maybe that's proof I'm not. Does this make sense?"

"What *do* you feel?"

"Like I've quietly lost my life. It's the awareness of that. Like I woke from a nap and realized I wasn't who I dreamed I was. Whatever you call that is how I feel. Scared, maybe."

Judi looked at me. My eyes dropped to the table, to my little mound of crumbs. I blew on them. I said, "You lose a wallet or keys or something and you notice in a second. But your life can go missing and you don't even know it."

Judi put her elbows on the table, rested her chin on her folded hands. "Does turbulence make you feel more creative?"

"Tranquillity. But you might be on to something," I told her. "Maybe that's why I don't want to wrestle with problems. Too much turmoil. I'll have to think about that." I thought about my characters, how their troubles were more interesting than my own. Then something occurred to me, and I said, "Some problems are worth intensifying, you know. The more you worry, the harder you struggle, or choose not to, the more you learn about yourself."

"Sounds self-destructive to me," Judi said. "And self-centered." She grabbed her purse, stood. "Anyway, I've got to run. Grief group at two." She checked her watch, kissed me on the cheek. "I've got tennis after work. Be home around eight."

"You play tennis?" I said. What kind of world had I walked into?

5.

Whose Dog Are You?

I was on the phone trying to explain to Judi why I had to tie Spot to the deck—that way he can sleep under it. She said, What do you mean he ate the doghouse? I heard the doorbell, checked the time. This would be the mailman's signal. I said, He's been munching on it right along, but that thunderstorm last night must have made him crazy. Judi said, That's the most bizarre thing I've ever heard. I told her that's nothing, told her how one time Spot chased a Jeep up Blossom Street, caught hold of the vinyl fender, yanked it off, ran to the park, and ate it. I didn't tell her how he'd chewed up and splintered most of a wicker ottoman that first lonely night in her cellar. Judi said, Well, what if he eats the deck? I said, He can't. It's redwood. She said, That dog needs help. I knew that. I also knew it would do no good. I'd already got my money back from K-9 Kollege. One of their obedience counselors had wired a cordovan house slipper so that every time Spot chewed on it, he'd get a shock. Turns out that Spot kind of liked the jolt. The guy turned up the juice, said he'd never seen anything like it. Now you couldn't get the damn slipper away from the dog. The counselor said any more voltage would just fry old Spot, so we stopped. Judi said she'd be home after step-aerobics.

I found two manila envelopes in the mail addressed to me in my handwriting. I could feel my manuscripts inside, but I told myself that maybe the editors wanted some small changes before they published the stories. I set the envelopes on the kitchen table beside the typewriter and perked another pot of coffee. I ate an apple. I called Our Lady of the Sea Fish & Chips to get my hours for the weekend. I don't know why I do this, why I refuse to open the mail, I mean. It used to drive Martha nuts, the way I'd leave a letter from my brother, say, sitting on my dresser for days. She'd say, What if something terrible happened? I'd say, Then he would have called. I took a tennis ball from the top of the fridge and went outside to play fetch with Spot. He ate the ball on the first toss. I went back to the kitchen, sat down, and opened the envelope.

The editor of *Rick Rack* thanked me for letting him read "The Soft Hiss of Vinyl," which he found "well-crafted" and "a delight to read," but not quite what he was looking for. Try us again, he wrote. The second response was less encouraging. It read, "Please read *Incomplete Flower* before submitting! The literary arts have been reduced to imploding pus with material rewards reserved for vapid stylists and collegiate pud suckers. We publish writing that counts, friend, that redefines and reshapes the world. Too much of what we receive appears to have been submitted after getting a *B* in Professor Scribbles Creative Writing Workshop. Your story, 'Hammered to Smithereens,' is maybe a *C+*." The letter was signed, "The *Incomplete Flower* Collective." I looked at the address—a P.O. box in Cambridge.

Now I was too agitated to write. If I had tried to do a scene now, Dale would just end up drilling three bullets into Theresa's forehead or something, and I didn't want that responsibility. I called Martha at the Chancery. She's the bishop's administrative assistant. I left a message on her machine, thanked her for sending along the mail. I asked her did she want to get together to talk, have a drink, or whatever. I waited a second. I said she could call me at Our Lady of the Sea all day Friday, nine to nine. If you're there, Martha, please pick up.

I put my two stories into new envelopes with SASEs and addressed the envelopes to the next two magazines on my list, the *New Hampshire Review* and *Raw Material*, and headed downtown to the post office. I was trying not to think about my fantasy of pummeling the Collective's minister of communication with a Louisville Slugger. I thought about Martha instead, how I knew her better than she knew me. I knew she didn't always mean what she said. Or, let's say, she meant what she said, it just wasn't true. Not that she was a liar. I'm the duplicitous one. Just that she didn't know herself any better than she knew me.

Martha and I had graduated from Worcester State College with our education degrees. We got married and made a deal: I'd work until she got her master's, and then she'd work while I wrote my novel. It took Martha a year to get her master's, and me twelve years to get out of the classroom. Twelve years teaching English at South High. The only good that came of that time was my friendship with Francis X. Harvey. He taught history. Twelve freaking years.

Every April I'd tell Martha I was going to quit, and every April she'd cry and tell me all the practical reasons why I couldn't—car payments, rent, retirement. Retirement? Jesus, Martha, I haven't started living yet. She'd tell me to grow up. And every year, I'd give in. So then two years ago, I just didn't tell her until after I'd quit. You've ruined our old age, she said. Better than our middle age, I said. Things were pretty tense from then on. And then, as you know, I went and took up with Judi.

I mailed the stories and walked to the Jersey Bar for coffee. C+, my ass. They keep the story six months, and they don't have the time to justify their goddamn grade. If you're going to be nasty, have the decency to be specific. Write, *Dear Lafayette Proulx, We don't understand the central character's motivation at all, nor were we impressed with the puzzling and unedifying shifts in viewpoint. Though your grammar, usage, and spelling in this Joycean pastiche are impeccable, we find little else to recommend this plotless, pointless piece of trash, and we humbly suggest you find yourself an entry-level position in the food-services industry, where we're certain you'll be jolly and prosperous. Yours truly, The Collective Unconscious.* At least then I could respect them.

Well, this was getting me nowhere. I took the notes to my story out of my overnight bag, got another coffee. Let's see, Dale's staring into the headlights. Theresa takes a step back. So there are the lights, high beams flooding Dale's eyes, so bright and painful that Theresa thinks she sees a tear in his eye. He can't hear what she says. She wonders why he won't look away from the light. He says, I love you, Theresa. But he doesn't look at her. Dale had thought this could be romantic, alone at night with Theresa in the desert, all the quiet. But it's not, is it? He doesn't know how to act. He's never been in love, never tried to be tender to a human being. Theresa says, Are you all right, Dale? I don't know, he tells her. Theresa touches his arm. Say it, Dale, she says. He says, I love you, Theresa, and turns to her, but he is blinded and cannot see her smile. Let's get in the car, she says. She slips her arm around his waist and leads him.

I cracked my knuckles, flexed my hands. I liked the turn the story had taken. I liked Dale and Theresa, and I was sure other people would.

But suddenly, I was back to editors and feeling steamed again. Then I wished I was going to Ruidoso with Dale and Theresa tonight. We could sit around the Horsemen's Lounge and shoot the breeze. I'd know when to make myself scarce. Well, I could do that—be with them, I mean—right there in Judi's kitchen tonight, but, then, it wouldn't be polite to ignore my hostess when she got home.

What was I doing with Judi anyway? I didn't love her even though I told her I did. She didn't love me and never bothered to lie about it. I could see that my life was a mess in many ways. I was living out of a suitcase, working part-time with no benefits. I had no home. An uncertain future. I had hurt my wife. I was a mess, sure, but I was writing.

6.

Echo

I sat in Dentaland's waiting room at the Greendale Mall and stared at the framed print of an amaryllis that looked more like a red machine or a horsey fungus than a flower. I planned my strategy for Shimkoski. I'd be reasonable, tell him I deserved matching teeth. If he put up a fuss, I'd go to Plan B, which included threats—letters to the Better Business Bureau, the newspaper, the attorney general, and the ADA; an informational picket line outside his office; calls to radio talk shows and to my lawyer, as if I had one.

A woman with pearl-gray hair sat across from me, an issue of *Time* open on her lap. Her eyes were closed. The man beside her, fiftyish, thin red hair, rosy-cheeked, soft of flesh, held her hand and jabbered away a mile a minute. In a single breathless sentence, he mentioned television, a bus ride, Indians, a flashlight, a sore toe, and sunglasses. Then he talked about a photograph that had something to do with his uncle William, who was trying to trick him. "I know he is. I know he's trying to fool me. I know that. I know his tricks. Uncle William is." And then he said he wanted a blue toothbrush today. Not a green one. Blue. He said this to his left hand.

He is her son, I realized. I saw the resemblance now in the pinched lips, the snubbed noses. And I knew that he'd been chattering like this, nonstop, since he first learned to speak. His mother has never gotten used to the noise, but she understands that this is how her boy makes sense of his world, that he cannot think without talking, that he lacks a silent dialogue with himself. She has sacrificed everything for her son—her marriage, her career, her dreams, her friends—and she resents him for it. Resents him because there is no one else. He has driven them away. She loves him. She wants what's best for him. She knows what it's like to love someone who cannot love you back. Someone who needs you, holds you, yes, but someone who will never know that love is the knife in your heart, that it moves the sun, that love exalts the lover and the beloved, and that it vanishes. All she receives is the resonance of the love she gives, the familiar and unsubstantiated echo of her own dire passion. Nothing fresh, nothing she can embosom or taste.

She wishes he would die. Not always, but at times like these, when their lives are public. She wants relief. She's not yet seventy. She could still have a life, she thinks, a bit of one anyway. She could travel, eat at restaurants with men who would talk about books and ideas. She could sleep at last without the interruption of her son's tears or his footsteps on the landing outside her door.

The receptionist slid open the pebbled-glass window and said, "Mrs. Diggins."

The woman opened her eyes for the first time since she'd sat down. "Take Charlie first," she said.

Her son said, "Charlie first." He stood and looked at the receptionist, then at his mother.

"Go ahead," his mother said. "I'll be right here."

"Right here," he said.

I took out my pen. I balanced my tablet on my knee and wrote as fast as I could. I described Charlie's plaid shirt and his chino slacks, the eczema on his forehead, and his long fingernails, his mother's navy blue shoes and white patent leather handbag. I wondered why she'd never called a nursing home. I wrote about that and about what she might do if she got sick. Did she have a plan? I mean terminally sick. Would she just refuse to die until he did?

A hygienist opened the door to the waiting room and told Mrs. Diggins that Charlie wanted her. She stood, Mrs. Diggins did, draped her purse over her arm. She looked at me doing my job. She said, "Okay, Charlie." I wrote that she limped when she walked. I wondered about Uncle William and that trick.

I didn't want to deal with Shimkoski just then, so I told the receptionist that I felt like I was coming down with the grippe, and I resceduled the appointment. She told me there was a twenty-four-hour virus going around. I smiled like it hurt. She said the tooth didn't look all that bad. I walked out into the mall and stood outside the yogurt place. I thought I'd wait for Charlie Diggins and his mother, and then I'd follow them. See if they sat down somewhere, so I could eavesdrop. And I would have done it, too, except that I saw Judi arm-in-arm with a guy wearing a Greek sailor's cap. I thought, She's dating Stanley Kunitz? They had just walked out of Le Bon Pain, and when they turned to admire something in Zales's window, I saw that the man was young, in his twenties, it looked like.

I left the mall without buying Spot a treat at the Pet Supermarket. I figured Judi would be expecting me on my feet rather sooner than later. I wondered how the imminent upheaval was going to affect Dale and Theresa. Their weekend was over. Dale was just then standing in front of his Eco 101 class trying to remember the point he was making about supply and demand. Theresa's in her bathroom brushing the little one's teeth, telling him to hold still, it doesn't hurt.

At Mr. Natural's, I picked up a block of feta cheese and a pint of hummus, put them on the counter, smiled with my mouth closed, and introduced myself. She said she remembered me from the other day. Said her name was Pauline. She asked me how Judi was doing. I said, Fine, now that she's got the cute boyfriend. The one with the cap? she said. Yes. I found out that Pauline had two boys in grade school, Mick and Keith, and an ex-husband who still comes around. I wanted her to whisper her entire life's story into my ear. I steadied myself on the counter. My bones hummed her name. I wondered if she could hear it. I wondered what "comes around" meant. She told me I looked wan. She used that word. I wanted to hug her, take her away from all this nutrition. I was getting stupider, giddier, by the second. She said, It comes to $8.34 with the tax.

7.

She's Married—She's Happy—
She Drives a Mercury!

WHEN I STEPPED OUT OF THE SHOWER, I SAW HER NOTE ON MY BATH TOWEL, written on "From the Desk of Judi Dubey" stationery. "Laf, Here's # of a really terrific marriage counselor. Name's Terry Cundall; she's a friend, and she's expecting your call. Kindly scoop up dog shit in backyard— Please!!! Judi. PS: Won't be home for supper—golf lessons." I dripped a little water on the phone number until it was illegible.

I set the typewriter on the kitchen table and rolled in a blank sheet of paper. I cleared away Judi's cereal bowl and her juice glass. I sat and read the *Telegram & Gazette* while I made coffee. Edmund's murder trial was finally under way, and Edmund, through his public defender, had entered a plea of not guilty by reason of insanity. I was disappointed, wished Edmund had done the decent thing and accepted responsibility for the killing. So I reminded him. I said, You were trying to rob the house, Edmund. You did shoot a .38-caliber bullet into Lena Tremblay's neck after Judi's party, remember? On page three was a photo of Edmund sitting at the defense table with a trim little haircut and a baggy suit. You could even make out the Quonset-hut people behind him in the spectators' gallery, Edmund's dad, Noel, blowing his nose. I wondered, Is this what got Judi's day off to a contentious start?

Spot must have heard the clacking typewriter keys because he started to bark. I sent him a telepathic message to shut up. I typed: *Dale phoned Theresa from Furr's and asked could he swing by before work. Just because, he said. Just to say hi.* Spot kept up his racket. *Dale stuffed a finger into his left ear, told Theresa she'd need to speak up. "There's a screaming baby about ten feet away from me."* And then Mr. Lesperence, next door, fired up his weed whacker and let it whine outside our opened living room window.

Usually I can write no matter what. When I taught school, not even all the wheezing, snorting, and barking by the hormone cases in the back of study hall could keep me from working on my story. But on this morning, two weeks after I had left home, the real noise was not outside. It was this persistent and distracting rattle in my head. The commotion of what I had done and what I was not doing kept me from my work. And if I couldn't even hear what Theresa was saying, how ever would Dale?

My fingers rested on the keys. Spot quit yelping. Mr. Lesperence idled, then shut off, his weed whacker. I heard a ringing in my ears. I closed my eyes and pictured Martha at our table, eating supper by herself, chewing the pasta wearily, staring out the window. I opened my eyes and saw Pauline standing at the sink, smiling at me over her coffee cup. This was a complicated business. I reminded myself that you can't have everything, but I kept my eyes on the phantom Pauline. I thought if Martha would just let me write, not pester me about what she called "a real job," then maybe I could live with her and be faithful. But could she live with the *me* I turned out to be?

The phone chirped. I listened to the caller leave his message after the beep. It was a guy named David with a Scandinavian accent, or Baltic, or Wisconsin. Who knows? Judi's cap boy, I figured. He apologized for spoiling (only he said "shpoilink") last evening's dinner at the El Morocco. He hoped she could forgive him. I erased the message and dialed Martha's work number. I told her machine that I was calling to see how she was doing, how she was feeling. Maybe we ought to talk sometime, Martha, I said.

First the doorbell chimed, then Spot barked, then the weed whacker droned. I answered the door. The delivery woman from Avant Gardens looked at her card. "Judi Dubey?" she said. "Jody," I said. "They're lovely. Thank you." I brought the dozen scarlet roses to the kitchen. I tore David's card into six pieces and threw them in the trash. I sneezed. I put the roses in the fridge. That's when I remembered the dog shit. I grabbed a snow shovel out of the garage and went to the backyard. Spot was so happy to see me, he grabbed a wallpaper brush in his mouth, ran from me as far as his leash would go, then made an arc around the yard. Ran into the apricot tree. He picked up the brush and shook the life out of it. Then he jumped straight up in the air. I love that dog. I waved to Mr. Lesperence. He hates me.

Mr. Lesperence is a doll wigs hackler. I didn't know what it meant either. One morning I watched him heave junk over the fence at Spot. Apparently, he had noticed that Spot was omnivorous. The wallpaper brush was Mr. Lesperence's. Since that morning, I'd seen him toss dowels, magazines, shoes, a birdhouse, a picnic basket, a folding chair, and plastic flowerpots into the yard. He was cleaning out his garage. Spot ate most of the stuff. Another morning I found five baby-doll torsos lying in the grass by the deck. No heads or limbs, just the buttery little bodies. I did see a gnarled leg by Spot's tail. Very interesting. Perhaps Mr. Lesperence hoped that Spot would choke on an arm or something.

I asked Judi that night what exactly she knew about her neighbor. She told me that Mr. Lesperence was a widower, worked at Capital Toy, and she didn't blame him a single bit for complaining about Spot. This has always been a quiet neighborhood, she said, and she gave me a look. Do you know his first name? I said. I called Capital Toy, told them I was David Crockett from American Express, and I was calling to verify the employment of Mr. Barry Lesperence. He's applying for our platinum card. Yes, that's right, like the guy at the Alamo.

He's a what? I said. Madeline from personnel explained that Barry Lesperence pulled synthetic hair through a hackler—a cylinder kind of gizmo with teeth. It softens the hair, she said. We make the Fretty Betty doll. You've probably seen it in the stores. He's been hackling for sixteen years.

I kept my eye on Mr. Lesperence, just so he didn't lob over any light bulbs or tin-can lids or anything. I didn't think he would. He was not a vicious man, just an angry one. Mr. Lesperence's jetsam actually kept Spot from gnawing at the redwood joist under the deck that he was halfway through already.

I shoveled the dog shit and dumped it behind the laurel bushes up against the foundation of the house. I took the mighty Spot for a stroll around the neighborhood. Checked the mail. Nothing for me. I walked to the library, sat in the periodicals room, browsed through old *Life* magazines looking for Dale and Theresa. I found Theresa's face in an automobile ad from 1954. The woman in the ad is smiling up a storm in the upholstered front seat of her Mercury. Her scruffy, adorable Little Leaguer sits beside her, and you can tell he's just scored his team's winning run. Mom is thrilled with the gas mileage, the ad tells us, and with the ample space in the glove compartment. I stared at her face. Pert blue eyes, thin lips, mahogany hair. I heard Theresa tell Dale, "Sure, come over. I'm getting the kids dressed for preschool, but stop in for a cup of coffee." I wrote that down in my notebook. Her kids are that young. I quietly tore the ad from the magazine, folded it, and put it in my shirt pocket.

That night when Judi got home, I gave her the flowers. She looked stunned, perplexed. I said it was my way of thanking her for her gracious hospitality, that's all. The least I could do. I told her I knew I was intruding, was in the way. She didn't deny it. I sneezed. "So I'll be looking for another place ASAP," I said.

"Laf, this is so sweet," she said. She looked at the roses. "I want to trim these, put them in a vase," she said. "Why don't you make us a couple of martinis."

8.

Having Been Gertrude
of Helfta

THIS IS HOW I FOUND MYSELF IN BED WITH A THIRTEENTH-CENTURY SAXON MYS-
tic, an unsettling business that began with the roses. The roses bought
me time. Judi backed off her passively aggressive insistence that I leave
the house. Young David the cap boy was now, evidently, on her shit list.
She invited me and not him to an upcoming psychotherapists' party. I
had continued to erase David's several daily phone messages asking
"Chewdi" why she would not return his calls. I left classified rental ads
by the phone along with a business card from Jack Bell Leasing. I jotted
notes on the "While You Were Out" memo pad, like "no pets," "call back
at six," and "one-year lease required." Judi and I were back to spirited
lovemaking. I was writing eleven hours a day. And I was, of course, de-
laying the inevitable.

Who was going to take me in? Not Martha. I was kaput with her, at
least for now. Not my best friend, Francis X., who, though he did have
a spare room over his garage, also had six kids, two Siamese cats, and a
wife, Sandy, who despised me with a vengeance. Not any landlord of any
decent apartment, not with Spot the Destroyer by my side. I could buy
a tent at Spag's and pitch camp at Rutland State Park. I could live there
till the fall, at least.

Nicky Kargeopoulos said Spot and I could stay with him as long as
we wanted. He understood about women, he said. Nicky's my pal from
the fish-and-chips store. A sweet, funny, and generous man. But here's
the thing. Nicky lives kind of like Balzac in a room on Harding Street

over a Vietnamese restaurant. I told him, Thanks, Nicky, that's nice of you, but I don't think so. It's not just that Nicky's is one especially cluttered room and not even that it reeks of *nuoc cham* sauce. It's the televisions. He's got three of them in that tiny room, and at least one of them is always on. By the bathroom door, he's got a black and white Philco console with a round screen. There's a Sony portable attached to a VCR and a cable box on the table and a four-inch bonsai TV that he sleeps with.

I admire the intensity of Nicky's obsession with television. It's breathtaking, really. He has tapes of all fifty-eight episodes of *Boston Blackie*. He can recite entire segments of *The Prisoner*. He knows the name of every Ernest Flatt Dancer on *The Carol Burnett Show*. What kind of writing could I get done in that room? I said, I'd love to, Nicky, but Spot would have your Philco for lunch.

Judi rubbed my leg with her foot. She laid her book on her chest, rubbed her eyes, and yawned. "I'm getting tired," she said. I told her I wanted to finish reading the draft-so-far of the Dale and Theresa story. Then I'd put out the light.

She said, "Why don't you quit this fantasy?"

I looked at her. What did she mean?

"This writing business," she said. "You gave it a try. So it didn't work out for you. You've got nothing to regret."

I didn't say anything. Dale and Theresa and I just stared at this woman beside us in the bed.

She scratched her nose, looked up at the mirror. I read her the scene where Dale comes by Theresa's for coffee. Peter, the little one, won't come out from behind his mother's leg. Dale thinks there's something about the boy that's different. Before he can put his finger on what it is, the girl, who's four (for now her name is Caroline), tells Dale he has yellow teeth. Theresa says enough of that now and scoots the kids into the back hall to put on their shoes and watch for the Kinder-Kare van. Dale looks around Theresa's kitchen, at the yellow dish towel folded over the handle on the oven door, the cast iron skillet on the stove, the white plastic crucifix with the gold Jesus over the pantry door.

Judi said, "You're never going to make a living at this, you know that."

"Because people like you would rather read trash like this." I picked up the paperback she had been reading, *Finding Yourselves: A Practical Guide to Past Life Regressions*.

She said, "Don't lose my place."

I said, "Do you really believe in this crap?"

"Don't dismiss what you can't understand, Laf. It's childish."

I read the jacket. "By the author of *Color Me Love* and the best-selling *Self-actualization Through Hypnosis.*"

She said, All right, I'll prove it to you. Judi sat up, leaned back against her pillow, shut her eyes. I guessed she was toying with the ball of mercury. A minute later she told me that in one of her past lives she had been a woman named Gertrude who was born in 1256 at Helfta. At five years old, she was entrusted to the nuns at a local convent. She never saw her mother or father again. A woman named Mechtilde cared for her.

She told me that as Gertrude she began having visions when she was twelve years old. "I saw myself covered with ashes, and I was on my knees before our Lord, Jesus Christ. His loins were girded with Justice, and blood bubbled from His brow and ran like oily pellets down His face. And then my ashes were gone, and I was shining, and then Jesus touched my breasts with the wounds in His hands, and I burned, and I melted and liquefied into Him. And I was like a dish of beaten gold. And I heard His voice say, "Thank you, sister, for your service. You will live a hundred lives in me." Judi smiled and opened her eyes.

All I could do was look at her.

"How could I know all that stuff," she said, "if it didn't happen to me?"

"What did Justice look like?" I said.

She closed her eyes. "It's like this . . . this . . . I don't know, this drapey kind of garment, but it's not." She looked at me. "It's ineffable. You need other eyes to see it."

"I didn't realize you had such a vivid imagination."

She shook her head. "Memory," she said. She yawned. "I'm exhausted."

I said, "Well, you've been awake for seven hundred years."

She put her book on the night table. "Very funny," she said.

I remembered my future, bleak and undefined. Wifelessness, joblessness, a cloud of unknowing, love uncreated, an unbridled wound. I remembered everything—my unwanted stories, my beguiled wife, my homelessness, my manic dog. I realized I could end up like one of my characters—smoking clinched cigarettes on the front porch of a halfway house, talking back to the radio.

"I wrote a book, too," she said.

"What?"

"When I was Gertrude. *The Herald of God's Loving Kindness.* You should read it."

"Okay," I said.

"And I meant to tell you. Now that Edmund's going to prison in Wal-pole, Noel's moving to be closer to him. You can have the trailer for one hundred dollars a month, my mother says."

I'd have to do something fast. Call the florist or something. And then I had a brainstorm. I'll ask Pauline if she knows of any apartments in her neighborhood. I put out the light. And then I imagined she'd say, Well, I don't, but I do have a spare bedroom in my apartment you could have for like fifteen dollars a week. Is that fair? I could use the money. Really, you'd be doing me a favor. And the kids would adore a pet. Yes, I tell her. Yes, yes! Christ, I don't know what gets into me sometimes.

9.

Married to My Conscience

A. "CLINGING TO THE WRECKAGE"

In my dream, Martha and I sat in a small boat, a twelve-foot tender. Martha wore a yellow slicker and a sou'wester. First we sat side by side on the rowing thwart, the way I like it, then face-to-face, the way Martha likes it. She told me that it did not depend on logic, reason, or material evidence. It's ineffable, she said, a belief, not a thought. It is willed, not anticipated. I thought she was talking about faith. Not faith, she said. Love. Now our little boat lifted in the swelling sea, and I could make out the silhouette of shore, and then I couldn't; now a glimpse of dense forest, and then not. We were without oars or life jackets. Not smart of us. I gripped the gunwales. Martha said, It's a public admission of abject failure, an absolute loss of hope, a profound disgrace, a deadly shame. I thought she was talking about divorce. Not divorce, she said. Suicide. Our cradle rocked in the waves. Martha said, But at least with suicide you don't have to live through it. And then our tender swamped and battered against a reef. When the bow broke, Martha tumbled to the ocean and vanished. I gripped the floating transom. I thought, If you cling to the wreckage, you might be saved; you might not drown.

B. "HYPNOPOMPIA"

A door clicked shut somewhere in the house, and I woke, but not completely. I didn't know where I was, and I didn't want to know. I closed my eyes. The dream was gone. I'd drowned my wife. A door opened, this time in my head. A globe rolled through the doorway and stopped at my feet. I saw it wasn't a globe at all, but a glove. Well, not a glove so much as a pleasant grove of shade trees, if you looked real close. And nestled within the grove, a single grave. You don't expect this, word games first thing in the morning. Always a surprise. This is something I try to do every day, linger here between sleep and sentience in this curious and effortless country. Marvelous things happen here. One morning I suddenly understood what it was the universe was expanding into, and the explanation was breathtakingly simple and elegant. But by the time I'd snapped on the bathroom light, I'd forgotten it. On other mornings, characters from my stories appear and tell me what they'd like to say in the next scene. This morning a guy, who doesn't really have a face yet, tells me he's lost. I notice his hair is wet, his clothes are dripping, he's standing in a puddle where a grove of trees once stood. I think I know him. I ask him where he lives. He says, Home is where your family is. He's being cute. I hear Spot barking outside, try to ignore him. He keeps it up, and I wake. I'm at Judi's. What am I doing here? There's something compelling about the dripping man. I want to know how he got lost, why he came to me, things like that. I'll get up and write about him.

C. "DECONSTRUCTION"

I wrote: *Should love be allowed to interfere with the continuity of marriage?* I wrote it, but the narrator said it. Who was he? And where did he get the line? Now my homeless man had a face, and it was, of course, a lot like mine. I gave him a name. *John* will do for now. I sat him down on a wicker chair in an otherwise empty room. I wrote down what John told me: *All the mystery is gone, all the love loved away, all the passion expired, all the happiness deflated.* He was talking about his marriage. I needed someone to walk into the room and talk to him, ask him what he wanted to do now. At least that. Someone to tell him, This is the woman you loved, who loved you and your sadness and loved your joy and your dark moods. John said, *Marriage may exist for love, but also for safety, for punishment, for comfort. Any number of immaculate reasons.* What was he driving at? No one entered the room, so I asked him myself. I said, How do you feel now that you're alone? He just sat there all wretched and hunched, his face buried in his fists. I answered for both of us, wrote this down: *I feel like my wife and I, we've been disassembled from each other,*

piece by piece. My arm from her shoulder. Her lips from my cheek. Decon-
structed. Her smile from my eyes. My face from her breast. Where do all these
parts fit now?

D. "FEAR IS A WAKING DREAM"

I didn't know why I had done this to Martha, broke her heart, I mean.
What was I doing walking away from my wife and my past and myself?
Why was I leaving a woman who needed me for one who did not? If
that is what I was doing. I told myself that by staying away like I was, I
would be saving my life or starting it over or something. Maybe I was
temporarily insane or chemically imbalanced, or this was an inevitable,
if unflattering, biological craving for sexual variety—a genetic com-
mand, simple as that. I didn't believe any of this, but didn't want to believe either that I was capable of battering Martha with infidelity, of
abandoning her to panic and depression, of behaving like some jaded
libertine. I was a stranger to myself.

I detested this banal and reprehensible behavior, but I also hated who
I had become with Martha. I would be nasty for no reason. Often when
she would speak, I'd respond with sarcasm. Even when I knew I was
doing this, I couldn't stop myself. It was like she could say nothing right.
I was hurting her, and resenting her for somehow making me hurt her,
and so I'd lash out again. It was crazy. What did I mean I couldn't stop
myself? Something had gone wrong in the marriage. Maybe what went
wrong was me. Whatever it was, we were in trouble, and I did something about it. I took a risk and I left, so to speak. I let myself be tempted
away. This was courageous or foolish or both. It was not heroic. I could
have waited until we punished each other more, I suppose, until Martha
caught on and left me. Or maybe this was all just the normal course of
intimacy, like the falling away of physical love. This is what happens
when two people are so close over so long a time. Just a bump in the
road.

I imagined Martha waking up from a fitful sleep and realizing that for
sixteen-plus years she had loved a man who was selfish and who returned
her passion with the semblance of love only. And now, I thought, there
will be no growing old together, no more lying together beneath layers
of blankets and books, no more talking in bed.

I knew I could have gone on for the rest of my life with Martha and
been happy. Maybe not ecstatic, but content, not fulfilled, maybe, but
satisfied, secure, benevolent. Instead, I chose to humiliate the one I

loved. Still the easiest thing for me to do now was to go home, back to Martha. Would this be fair if there was even a chance I might leave again? Martha would take me back if I promised to change my ways, talk about what bothered me, not keep it all bottled up like I do, be more patient, more considerate, help out more around the house. And everything would be fine for a while, but you know how long promises last. Soon we'd find ourselves alone in a quiet room, and we'd be uncomfortable. Martha might recall her recent anguish, feel the swell of resentment, might wonder. I'd breathe the perfume of her indignation. We might distract ourselves by cleaning out the pantry or inviting friends over. We might turn on the television. She'd yawn, complain about an early meeting, kiss my forehead, go to bed. Me, I'd stay up so late I'd fall asleep on the sofa. Maybe I'd realize in the morning that I'd been aloof, cold, and I'd try to be more loving. But if you have to attempt love, can you be in love?

The difference between fiction and life is that fiction makes sense. Problems in stories get resolved. All day I sat at a typewriter and tried to order the universe. All day I paid attention to the troubles of made-up people. Meanwhile my own life was at stake, my wife was in peril, my future was black. I should have moved, but I was still. I should have attended to Martha, but I did not.

10.

Love-Lies-Bleeding

ON THE SATURDAY MORNING OF THE PSYCHOTHERAPIST PARTY, I GOT BACK TWO more form rejections on my stories. First, I felt deflated. What the hell do they want anyway? And would they know it if they saw it? Does it go in one eye and out the other? My limbs were like pig iron. I couldn't move. I just sat there on the couch, staring at my pages, sluggish and thickheaded. The *Wyoming Review* didn't want "Shufflebrain," and *Southside* said no to "Steak and Shake." I got angry. Judi was gone, and it was just as well. I wasn't fit to talk to. She and Trixie were over at Elements of Style getting their hair done. I felt like calling in sick to work, but that would leave Nicky on his own till three. I needed to break something, and I usually regret when that happens. I took a pound of tub butter out of the fridge, slammed it on the counter, and hammered it with the side of my hand. I scooped up what I could of the mess, shaped it into a butter ball, and carried it out to Spot. He was eating a turkey baster. He sniffed my hands. I set the butter in Spot's water bowl and told him to eat it before the ants come. He woofed out the side of his muzzle.

I sat down at the kitchen table with my story. Dale and I found out that the boy, Peter, was retarded. He's teachable, Theresa told us, but only so far. She kept her hands on her knees when she said this, her eyes on Dale. Dale didn't know what to say. He'll always need help, she told him. She looked at her hands. Always. On his drive home that night, Dale couldn't shake the image of the boy on Theresa's couch, sucking his thumb, holding his Fretty Betty, rubbing the doll's hair against his cheek.

On the bus to work, I noticed a gym bag from St. John's High under the seat in front of me. No one around. I opened it. Bus tickets, a pack of Camel Lights, a ninth-grade algebra text, and a pornographic comic book. Dagwood and Blondie going at it. Dagwood and Daisy. Blondie and the boy, whatever his name is. This was very depressing. I thought about the guys who write this stuff and about what must be festering in their ulcerous little brains. I tossed the bag and everything into the Dumpster behind Our Lady of the Sea.

Nicky poured oil into the Fryolator, his long black hair tied up in a hairnet. "Nicholas," I said. He said, "Who was the Tsar of Russia who suppresseed the Decembrist Movement?" These days Nicky responded to everything in the form of a question. He was trying to get on *Jeopardy!*

I played along. "All right, Nick Kargeopoulos, tell us a little about yourself. It says here that you sleep with your TV set."

"That's correct, Alex. I'd like to say hi to—"

The phone rang. I took an order for a pint of scallops, haddock and chips, a large Moxie. I handed the slip to Nicky and went to the fridge. "American Indians called it *manninose*. In England it's known as the sand-gaper."

Nicky said, "What is the soft-shell clam, Alex?"

"Is correct."

"Gourmet Foods for two hundred."

The phone rang again. I handed Nicky the bucket of scallops and answered. Judi wanted to know if she should pick me up at five. We could swing by her mom's and take a look at the trailer. I thought fast. I told her I wanted to walk home, check the three-deckers by Hope Cemetery for FOR RENT signs. *Hope* Cemetery—I'm not making that up. The poet Elizabeth Bishop's buried there, as a matter of fact. So's my aunt Emma.

Before I left work, Nicky told me a joke I could use at the party, about how it took six psychotherapists to screw in a light bulb. One to turn the bulb, five to share his feelings.

I told him, "Good night."

He said, "What did Guinevere say to Lancelot?"

Judi and the other Irving Street psychotherapists, Mark, Josh, and Ron, were about to launch a new business, Holistic Mental Health Associates, and tonight's party was a celebration of their venture and a publicity event. The party was at Josh Wolfson's, and everyone Judi knew in the profession would be there. Judi was so nervous, she let me drive her Miata. She couldn't stop smoking. What's to be nervous about? I asked her. She said, A lot of unfinished business with some people. I let that drop. She looked at her reflection in the side window. She practiced a smile.

Josh's house was a two-story stone-and-stucco on the west side. Walnut-paneled doors with glass doorknobs, raised paneling on the wainscoting, brass and crystal chandeliers, oak herringbone plank floors, blue tile trimming around the fireplace. Gregorian chants played on the stereo. I felt like I was in church. I wondered what Stoni and Arthur would do at a place like this where every handshake was firm, every smile eager, and eye contact seemed to be an art form. I told Judi, See, I'm not the only one here wearing jeans. I pointed to a couple of older gentlemen by the buffet table. But, yes, I was the only one wearing a T-shirt.

I was introduced to the other associates. I left them talking networking strategies. I wandered through the house checking titles in the bookcase, photos on the wall, cracks in the ceilings. The party spilled out of the house and into the floodlit backyard, where I spied the wet bar. I loaded up at the buffet—smoked salmon spread and stone-ground wheat wafers, rillettes of smoked trout, artichoke fritters, curried peanut chicken nuggets with a hot mustard sauce—and sat outside on a wrought iron lawn chair. I nibbled and watched the guests. I eavesdropped when I could. I heard two women talking about Judi, how she did such a terrific job with what's-his-face, the manic-depressive. David, the other one said. David Michelak.

I went to the bar for a drink. I ordered a Hennessey martini because I'd seen it advertised on the back cover of *The New Yorker.* Behind the bar were several large plants, maybe four feet tall, with these hanging clusters of long, crimson flowering stalks. I'd never seen anything like them. The bartender caught me admiring them. She handed me my drink, looked at the plants. She said, "Love lies bleeding."

"Excuse me?"

"The common name for the plant. Love-lies-bleeding."

"You're making that up."

"*Amaranthus caudatus.*"

She told me she used to be a botanist at the Worcester Horticultural Society, and now she ran a software consulting business out of her house and tends bar once in a while for her friend, a caterer.

She handed me a business card from *Creative Affairs: Environmentally Friendly Caterers.* She jotted down her home address. I turned the card

over and borrowed her pen. I asked her to spell that Latin name for me.
I told her I was a writer and introduced myself. Her name was Daphne
Engdahl. She mixed me another cognac martini. I watched her wait on
Josh, who couldn't decide what he wanted. He scratched his beard,
squinted at the bottles of liquor, ordered a Cape Codder. Daphne had
straight, thick dirty-blond hair, blue eyes, and a dimple on her chin. Her
nose turned up a little. Josh tested his drink, pronounced it scrumptious.
Daphne thanked him. God, I just love women.

She asked me what my stories were about. I said love and death, which
is what I always say, because what else can you say? I didn't ask Daphne
what she read because I was afraid of what I might hear: Danielle Steele,
Rush Limbaugh, Robert Fulghum, the Madison County guy. Daphne
waited on one of the older gentlemen in jeans. I thought I'd better find
Judi.

She was not in the den or the living room. Before I searched farther,
though, I had to change the music. If I heard one more minute of *Cats*
I'd go crazy. While I was flipping through Josh's CDs, looking for Elvis
Costello or Van Morrison, I heard Judi's voice coming from the kitchen.
She was telling someone that she had a completely different recollection
of a certain evening. He said, That's your choice. That seemed a little ar-
rogant to me. No Costello, no Morrison, no Marley, no Al Green, no Bon-
nie Raitt. Judi said, And I'll bet you're still screwing around on your wife.
He asked her to kindly keep her voice down. No Mavis Staples, no
Clash, no Kate Bush. I heard Judi say, Open marriage, my ass. No Bobby
Bland, no Lyle Lovett. Judi said, Why don't we just go and tell your dear
wife that she's been living a lie for ten years. Or has it been longer? James
Taylor he's got. Christ, might as well let the cats sing. I thought I'd drift
into the kitchen to see who might need to be rescued.

I could see that Judi and her pal were not pulling balls of mercury
up through their spines. They were not visualizing harmony. They were
not centered. I introduced myself, shook hands with Sam, his name
turned out to be. And then nobody said anything. Judi inhaled her cigarette, leaned against the fridge; Sam looked at the floor; and me, I kept
nodding my head. Judi said to me, "If you don't mind, we have some
issues."

An hour or so later I was talking with Ron about whatever happened
to transactional analysis when Judi found me. Ron was sitting in an overstuffed mohair chair with an inflated plastic doll—the screaming figure
in the Edvard Munch painting. Ron told me that the real money was in

real estate. He asked me what I did. I write, I told him. Oh, you're the one, he said. And that's when Judi sat down on the arm of the sofa, told me she was ready to go.

We tried to find Josh to thank him and say good night. A woman named Claire told us that Josh and Albert had a tiff earlier on the front porch. Josh got one of his migraines, Albert got frantic about that, and then they said their good-nights and went up to bed. I think Josh left Mark in charge, Claire said. Have you seen Mark? Judi said. Claire said, He's out in the gazebo smoking dope with the bartender. Have either of you seen Sam? she said.

I thought I'd just drive, so I got on the expressway and headed east away from Judi's. She didn't say anything. I put on a Philip Glass tape, turned it low. Judi said she wished we had some toot. I told her I knew a guidance counselor who kept his friends supplied. I could call. We decided on beer, and I stopped at an after-hours place on West Boylston Street. We ended up with the six-pack out at Hot Dog Annie's. We bought some dogs and sat out back at a picnic table.

"We should talk about this, Judi."

"About what?"

We heard a giggle. I saw over Judi's shoulder the silhouette of a young couple at another table. I watched moths swoop around the light that illuminated the menu painted on Annie's wall.

"You don't see anything odd—maybe that's the wrong word—anything curious, interesting, about going out with married men?"

"No, please tell me, Dr. Proulx."

"Dating your patients."

"What are you talking about?"

"David," I said.

She folded her hands on the table.

"You cooled off to me when I left Martha." I took a sip of beer. "Maybe you don't want to give up your independence or you don't want a long-term relationship."

"Maybe I don't," she said. "Want either."

"But then you get upset about it, which is what you and Sam were discussing, I guess."

"You don't know anything about me and Sam or me and anyone else."

I heard the girl tell the boy to stop what he was doing. She was laughing. I heard Judi crying. I got up and walked around the table to her side, sat down. I put a napkin in her hand. She wiped her cheeks. I told her,

Don't listen to anything I say. She said, We're both of us fucked up. How could I disagree? I held her while she cried. I kept hearing that awful *Cats* music. Finally, Judi took some deep, slow breaths and sat up. She said she was okay now. She said, Thanks. She smiled, said she must look awful. She looked young, actually. And frightened.

"So, who else were you?"

It took her a second to see what I was driving at. "You'll make fun of me."

"I won't." I swung my leg over the bench, sat facing her. I put my elbow on the table. "I'm all ears."

Judi drank some beer, sized me up. "Really?"

"Really."

She said, "This was in Russia. A little village. Obruchanovo or something like that. I don't know exactly when yet. I'm just beginning to recall. My name was Marya Dolzhikov. There were many of us children. I think ten. No mother—she died giving birth to me, they say. I am the smallest. Papa's name was Matvei. I remember him holding me by the neck, whipping me with a willow branch—my legs were full of sores from scratching. I remember playing with bits of broken pottery on a path to where the cattle grazed. I think there was a factory in the village. We ate black bread. You would have to sweep the roaches off the loaf first. We dipped the bread in water to soften it. My sister Katya was in charge of our samovar, but the tea smelled like cheese and the sugar was gray and infested with weevils. I died in a fire on my name day. I remember it was dark, and I was shoved to the floor. It must have been my brothers and sisters running over me. I can remember the sting in my eyes, how my chest hurt, how I lay there waiting. I heard the crackle of flames."

"That's sad."

"But you don't believe all this, do you?"

I didn't believe she had lived before. I told her that. How could I? "But something's going on," I said. "How do you remember?"

Judi shook her head. "My memories are like dreams," she said. "They just come."

I left it at that. We drove home. Judi took a shower. I went outside to talk to Spot. I took him for a walk. I did send a story to Daphne Engdahl that Monday, by the way. Sent her "Change of Plans," a story that begins with a child riding his Big Wheel up and down the walkway of the motel where he lives—the City Squire in De Ridder, Louisiana. (Later

I revised it, put the family up in Monroe, got rid of the ugly business where the husband beats the wife, locks her out of the motel room, added other characters, called it "Splice of Life.") Twice in that time I drove past the house she gave me as her address. It's out in Barre—a two-story Victorian with a hipped roof and cross gables. White with green shutters. A blue minivan in the gravel driveway.

11.

My White Bear

I GOT AN UNEXPECTED BUT MUCH APPRECIATED REPRIEVE ON THIS MOVING BUSI-
ness. It seemed that Stoni's beau, Richie, aka Attila the Muneyhun, would
be paroled at the end of the summer, and that meant that I would not
be immediately sentenced to solitary confinement in the trailer. Richie
might want it. Stoni would want to offer it to him at least. Fine with me.
But I was not to breathe a word of this to Arthur Bositis. Arthur's such
a high-strung fellow, Judi said.

She told me not to worry, even if Richie took the trailer, he wasn't
likely to have it long. Why's that? I said. Judi said the last time he got
out of jail, Richie wasn't on the streets seventy-two hours when he tried
to hold up Iandoli's Package Store on Grafton Street. He waved a pistol
over his head, but he was so messed up on heroin he couldn't find the
trigger. The guy behind the counter had a baseball bat and broke both
of Richie's arms in several places. His kneecaps, and then his jaw and
his teeth.

Judi and I were sitting on the deck. It was dusk. We could hear Spot
beneath us chomping away on his Te Amo balsa wood cigar boxes. Judi
shook her head, looked at me, and smiled. Good thing I like you, she
said. I like you too, Spot. Spot woofed. We were into our third or fourth
gin and tonic. Judi laughed, said she was just picturing Stoni and Richie
making love on the fold-out bed in that cramped trailer. She said Richie
was twice Stoni's size. I found that hard to believe.

"You know how big Arthur Bositis is," she said.

"Real big," I said. Arthur's at least six feet three, probably 220 pounds, and solid.

Judi said, "One time Richie hung Arthur out a third-floor window by his ankles. Dangled him over the sidewalk. Richie told him if he even so much as looked at Stoni again, he'd toss him into the blast furnace at Wyman-Gordon."

Judi went inside to freshen our drinks and returned with them—the glasses garnished with fresh crescents of lime—and with a snapshot of Richie and Stoni. Richie had thin, brown, straight hair that reached nearly to his waist. He wore a sleeveless black T-shirt that said, "Instant Asshole—Just Add Beer," and large turquoise rings on every finger. Stoni sat on his shoulders with a can of Bud. She looked like a party hat.

"He wears spurs on his boots," Judi said.

"And your sister goes out with this guy."

"He carved that scar on his face himself."

"Do you know if he's ever killed anyone?" I said. I figured he might have.

Judi told me that, in fact, Richie did kill this biker one time, but it was accidental, sort of. "Accidental" reminded me of my tooth. I put my tongue over it. I'd have to call Shimkoski before he forgot who I was. Richie and this other guy—his name was Himmler—were finalists in a head-butting contest at some Labor Day picnic. Himmler collapsed and died of a brain hemorrhage after losing the match.

The phone chirped. Judi said, Your turn. I stood, told her I just remembered that Dr. Stouder called with a date for her appointment. "I marked it on your calendar." I went inside. I put my hand on my forehead, imagined slamming my head onto the edge of a toilet bowl, saw the skull plate crack, the porcelain drive the sharp bone into the gray matter. Jesus. "Hello."

It was my brother, Edgar. The last time I saw Edgar was at my wedding fourteen years ago. Edgar followed my parents to *"La Florida,"* as they like to call it. Edgar lives in Miramar with his wife, his two boys, Matthew Mark and Luke John. Usually, Edgar makes his annual phone call in January when it's ten below here, and he acts like he hasn't been watching the Weather Channel. He'll tell me he's sitting by the pool. Anyway, I figure this call can only mean trouble.

"Is that you, Laf? What's going on up there, bro? Just talked to Marsha—"

"Martha."

"She tells me you're living with some world-class bimbo. Says you quit teaching and everything. She gave me this number."

"That's right," I said. "That I quit my job." So Martha knows the number. She's on to me.

"What's this all about, Laf?" He began to speak quietly. "Why can't you just have an affair like every other normal human being? Why do you have to make such a big hairy deal out of it? You think you're better than everyone else? Is that it?"

"So, what's up, Edgar?"

"Jesus loves the fornicator, Laf. Hates the sin, loves the sinner."

I should tell you that Edgar and family are Charismatic Catholics, which means, as near as I can tell, that they can speak in tongues when they are slain in the spirit and occasionally will become enraptured and collapse during Mass. Edgar's other fascination is with professional wrestling. He and the boys go to all the matches they can. At the time of this call, Edgar was managing a NAPA Auto Parts store and was president of the Miramar Optimists Club. Now he's bought himself a Pollo Tropical franchise and runs that. Anyway, all of this depresses me. I could hear Edgar's wife yelling at her kids to "Get down off the g.d. washing machine."

"Why did you call, Edgar?"

"Delores," he said. "I'm trying to talk here. I'm on long-distance." She said something I couldn't make out. "Is that all right with you, Delores? Is it all right if I talk to my brother?" I heard a dog yip. Edgar said, "Shut up, Tin-Tin." And then, "I called 'cause Dad's sick."

I didn't say anything.

"He needs a triple bypass."

"I'll send him a card."

"He might not make it. You really ought to see him."

"I can't do that right now."

"It might be your last chance."

"I'll call him."

It's not that I disliked my father, although Judi thought I had some volatile unfinished business with both parents. They pulled out of my life in 1979. I was twenty-one and a senior in college. Blaise and Eudine sold the house I grew up in and moved to Hollywood, Florida. They bought a motel on the beach, the Maravista, and they'd been running it ever since. For a while we talked on Easter, Christmas, and my birthday. Then just Christmas. They were always very much in love with each other, I thought. They seemed to resent Edgar and me. Like we had intruded on their romance. I know that doesn't seem probable, but there, it's what I believe. Like I said, Edgar went after them when they moved away. He says they're terrific grandparents. They're nice people. The world is full of nice people I don't know.

"Are you still there, Laf?"

"I was thinking about Dad."

"What about him?"

"How he always stopped talking to Mom when I walked into the room."

" 'A foolish son is a grief to his father, and bitterness to her that bare him.' Proverbs 17:25."

"Is he still at the motel?"

"Yes. They're not going to admit him till Thursday."

"Anything else, Edgar?"

"Why are you tormenting those that love you?"

"Good night, Edgar."

"I'll pray for you, Laf. We all will."

When I was around seven or eight, my father came into my room to tell me to turn out the light, bedtime. I was reading *First Down Showdown*. He snapped off the light. He said, "Try not to think of a white bear." And, of course, I thought of a white bear. I said, "Why did you say that, Dad?" He closed the door. First it was the cute bear on the Polar soda bottle, then it was a lumbering hunter on an Arctic snowfield. He'd stop, sniff the air. This was the first of my obsessive images, but not the last and not the worst. For the first time in my life I realized my brain has a mind of its own, and there was very little I could do to control it. Soon, I found I could no longer read my Chip Hilton high school football hero books because whenever I thought of a football, it changed shape—the ends became tubes, and soon the football would look like a broomstick with a lump in the middle. And so for nearly thirty years I have been unable to imagine a football as a football.

Another time Dad woke me up early. I thought maybe I had to serve Mass or maybe we were going fishing. He shook my knee. He asked me was I awake. I nodded. He said, I'm going to sing a song and you're not going to be able to get it out of your head for the rest of the day. And then he sang "I Fall to Pieces" in a nasally whine. Of course, I found myself humming the song everywhere I was for several days. I asked him, Do you do this to Edgar, too? He smiled. "Do what, darling?"

And so now every night that I've been here at Judi's, just before I fall asleep, when I can't read one more word or keep my eyes open, I see Martha at our table at home, and she's got a thread of spaghetti in her mouth that reaches to the dish. She's sucking on it absentmindedly. The thread never shortens. Then I can't sleep. So I watch her to see what she'll do next. Just the way I might watch Theresa in her living room. Theresa would say something, do something, and then I might write that down. See what she does next. But Martha never moves, not even to look at her watch.

12.

Communicants

I WENT TO SEVEN O'CLOCK MASS SUNDAY MORNING AT ST. STEPHEN'S. I SAT IN the back of the church on the right beneath the stained-glass window of St. Anthony, one of the Fourteen Holy Helpers, the hammer of heretics. This St. Anthony was a pasty-looking young man with a tonsured head and a brown robe. He held a lily in one arm and the child Jesus in the other. I sat here, away from the faithful, because what I dislike most about the service is the handshake of peace, or whatever they call it. It has long seemed to me that the Church took a wrong turn on the liturgical high-way sometime in my childhood. Martha and I argued about this often. She accused me of being ritually conservative, hopelessly medieval. She said, What about community? I said, What's the neighborhood have to do with my soul, if I've got one? Fellowship, she said. Fellowship of the workplace, I said.

My idea of the religious experience is that it should be private, first of all. It should not be the social event it has become for Catholics: let's respond in unison like we're reciting the times tables; let's all warble a tuneless song; let's shake our neighbors' hands, wish them eternal peace and Godspeed; let's get together Thursday night for bingo. I used to tell her religion's become a substitute for living a spiritual life. That drove her crazy.

The religious experience should be private and it should aspire to ec-stasy. Worship should not restrain you, keep you standing/kneeling/sit-ting in your pew, should not secure you to earth. It ought to take you out of yourself, the way reading Tolstoy does. At least that. It ought to lift you, set your feet on higher ground. And it should disturb you, bewilder you, confront you with the reality of your condition. I was beginning to understand why Dale may have gone Baptist. They have to have better music, for one thing.

The mystery had once meant something to me, the incense, the hypnotic cadence of Latin, the tangerine and wine-dark light pouring through the clerestory windows, the entrancing hymns, the priest, his back to me mumbling the incantation that would transubstantiate the bread to flesh. Now the Mass is all so clear, so forthright, so shared, so rote, and all the mystery is gone.

I had come to Mass to see Martha, and perhaps, though I wasn't yet certain, to speak with her. A young priest I didn't recognize—it's been a while—introduced himself as Father Bob and began his homily on the subject of "The Word of God Across the Ages." I drifted away. I wondered who the patron saint of writers was. I figured since I was here, it couldn't hurt to put in a prayer for some editorial intervention.

I noticed Francis X. up front with his scary wife and the six little Harveys. Eight redheads, all in a row. I was reminded of teaching and of how a job is incompatible with writing. So are a marriage, kids, religion, a bowling team. Probably everything is. And why is it called writing when the words are only a part of it? How do you explain to someone that your eyes are drifting up and to the left because you're trying to watch this actual person you made up cross the room and close the blinds, and that this is your job?

I looked to the wall at the eighth Station of the Cross, where Jesus tells the woman of Jerusalem not to weep for him. He's fallen twice. He'll fall again. This is the culmination of his father's work. I hear the Sanctus bell, and I kneel like everyone else. I realize that coming up are the last two weeks in July, when Martha and I have always taken our vacation in Wellfleet. For the last dozen years we've rented the same cabin from Edith and Ray Fortin above the beach at Lecount's Hollow. Maybe that's why this Sunday, some internal alarm went off, but I hadn't told myself I'd heard it.

There was Martha. She was wearing a calf-length black and tan print dress and running shoes. Her hair was clipped short. I thought she looked like a nun. She was a Eucharistic minister this morning. She stood beside Father Bob, handing out communion. I walked to the center aisle, got in Martha's communion line, winked at Francis X. when I shuffled by. The guy in front of me smelled like yeast. It looked like I had a choice. I could take the host in my hands or on my tongue. And I was supposed to say something, but I didn't know what. They used to do this differently, simply, quietly. I decided on the hands. What I said was, "Thank you, Martha." Her glance fell to the chalice.

After Mass, I waited at the bottom of the steps. Homer Donais was there selling the Sunday papers like he'd been doing since I was a child. Homer had large teeth and kept his jaw slack. His glasses were thick and opaque. My father used to tease him, I remember. He'd say, Homer, I gave you a five. Francis X. said something to Sandy. She pointed her chin at me and turned. She corralled the children ahead of her. Francis X. gave me a hug, called me a stuck-up son of a bitch. He looked around. He said, Where the hell have you been? I told him. He said, Jesus Christ, then it's true. He told me he had to run—taking the kids swimming at Howe Pond. Little cookout, you know. We made a date for Wednesday night at Moynihan's.

I waited for Martha to come out. Figured she might be telling Father Bob what a swell job he did with the sermon, how he certainly could hold a congregation's attention. Pretty soon it was just me and Homer out there on the sidewalk. She must have ducked out a side door or something. It looked like rain. The little Harveys would end up crying in the station wagon. I told Homer hi and bought a *Herald*. He told me his name's not Homer. "I changed it."

"When?"

"Twice," he said. He straightened out his piles of *Globes*, *Telegrams*, *Heralds*, *Times*. "I was Virgil for six years."

"Now you're Dante?"

"Azad Chaparian. Went all the way this time. I like the sound." He looked at his watch. "Next Mass at ten-fifteen."

I said, "Do you know me? Remember me?"

He looked at my face. "I seen you around."

I smiled. "So, Azad, how have you been?"

"Loosey-goosey," he said.

13.

Lemonade and Paris Buns

IF I HAD ONLY LISTENED TO PAULINE, TAKEN THE FOOD SUPPLEMENTS SHE'D SOLD me, eaten the flounder and buckwheat pâté she'd made, maybe I would not have been sitting there on the divan in the dark with a palmful of crumbled teeth and old fillings. Pauline had said she could tell from my fingernails (powdery, gray) and my hair (limp, lusterless) that I was desperately deficient in calcium and selenium. She was right about that but wrong about how the symptoms would manifest themselves. It was not gradual like she said, but all at once.

I had been chewing on my pen when I cracked a tooth on the upper right side of my mouth. The crack opened a fault line, and one tooth after another fissured and splintered at the poke of my tongue. And then the gum bone shattered, and the gum itself went slushy. The teeth lost purchase, slipped away from the cementum. I had to spit them out before I swallowed them. My first thought was, I can't afford this—the surgery, the upper plate, the whatever else. I felt no pain, but how would I be able to eat? How would I talk? I ran to the bathroom mirror. Not only was my mouth a dark and bloody pulp (save the reinforced, bleach-white crown, front and center), but my cheeks were sunken, and my jaw had assumed a novel and unflattering configuration. I looked like my great-uncle Telesphore just before he died.

So there I stood, a philanderer in cotton briefs, toothless, penniless, and a soon-to-be charity case at City Hospital, if I was lucky. I noticed clumps of my hair at my bare feet, on the sink, on my shoulders. Must have been, I thought, the shock of the fractured teeth. My fingers felt brittle, like if I touched anything, they would break off. All I could do was cry.

Judi shook me awake. Laf, you okay? she said. I touched my head, clicked my teeth. I thanked Judi. Do I look all right? I said. You look like you always do, she said, which was good enough for me. I nuzzled into Judi's back. She said, You're drenched. Actually, this is a dream that I pull on myself with some regularity, and I always fall for it. Judi had explained lucid dreaming to me once, showed me how I could take control of the imagery if I wanted to. It didn't work for me. Here I was, manipulated yet again by my unconscious. It made me feel better to speculate that Kafka rattled himself awake with cockroach and secret police dreams. Still, maybe if I called the 1-800-ROGAINE number, I'd have one less anxiety to torment myself with. And then phone Dentaland.

At breakfast I finished Judi's poached egg for her. Said she felt bloated. She took Pepto-Bismol with her orange juice. She reminded me to call my father, and would I do a load of wash? Whites, she said. She left for work. I poured myself a cup of coffee and called Florida.

My mother answered. "Maravista, could you hold, please." I heard a click and then Glen Campbell singing "Wichita Lineman." I considered hanging up. When I was young, my father would pretend not to know me. He thought this was funny. We'd be at Spag's buying nails and batteries, and he'd turn to me and say, Who's little boy are you, handsome? I'm yours, Daddy, I'm Laf. He'd smile and say, Have you seen my little boy? I know he's here somewhere. He'd keep this up until I cried.

"Thank you for holding. How may I help you?"

"Mom. It's Laf."

"Laf, is that you? Edgar tells me you're out of your mind."

"How's Dad?"

"Did you leave that lovely girl you married?"

"Martha."

"For a dying man, your father's doing remarkably well. You know how he is, always philosophical about everything."

"Can I talk with him?"

"He's sleeping."

"So how are you doing?" I heard a click.

"Laf, hold on a sec."

My mother came back on the line to tell me she couldn't talk right now. I gave her Judi's phone number. She said she'd call if she could find a second. Tell Dad I called, I said.

I got to work. Theresa's kids were with their grandmother for the night. Theresa and Dale were at the Cattle Baron for steaks. This was their one-month anniversary. Theresa smiles at the waitress and orders a vodka martini. Dale says he'll have an unsweetened iced tea. With lemon, please. The waitress, Tammy, says, Thank you, Mr. Evans. She was a student in his microeconomics class last semester. His name's Dale Evans, like the cowgirl. I wasn't sure if I liked that. I know he doesn't, has had to put up with too many jokes in his life. I was still a bit addled from the dream and the parental conversation. Dale and Theresa sat for several minutes without talking, fiddling with menus, looking for some insight into the entrées, I suppose. I was having trouble concentrating. I have mornings like that. Finally, Dale says, The prime rib looks good.

Theresa says, It's not enough that you love me, Dale. You have to love the children, too. Dale wishes he did. He nods. The kids treat him like an ogre, won't come near him. He figures he's just unnerved by them, and he'll eventually relax into a nice easy relationship with them. Theresa says, You know, you could spend the day with Caitlin (the girl's new, tentative name). Peter might be too much to handle right now, she says. Dale says, Maybe a movie to start. Take her to Mladinic's Bakery for lemonade and Paris buns. The phone rings. Not in the restaurant, but in the living room.

Judi told me she was going to Provincetown for two days. The Associates had scheduled an appointment with a really hot consultant/psychologist who was going to help them with their counseling model. She told me the four of them were right then into a heavy brainstorming session and could I please call Dr. Stouder for her and reschedule her pelvic exam. I said I'd be happy to perform the exam and I could fit her in today and I would accept co-payments. Funny, Laf, she said. Did you start the laundry? Next thing on my list, I said. Do you want to come to P-town with us? Of course I do. Wednesday and Thursday, she said. I said, I'll put Spot in a kennel. He'll probably enjoy the company.

I called Stouder and got Judi an appointment in three weeks. Then I called Dentaland. They told me that Shimkoski was no longer affiliated with their practice. What was I supposed to do? Well, we can set you up with Dr. Calcagni or Dr. Vigeant. The receptionist wouldn't state her preference. I want someone good at repairing shoddy crowns. Is this Mr. Proulx? Yes, it is. We went with Vigeant. I thought I heard someone talking to Spot. Mr. Lesperence, I figured, trying to convince Spot that vinyl was better than candy. I dumped the whites into the washer, poured in the Tide, set the timer.

14.

Down the Cape

Judi's consultation was scheduled for ten at the psychologist's East End home in Provincetown. We left at six A.M. Judi drove. I remembered this was Wednesday, and I was supposed to be meeting Francis X. at Moynihan's tonight. Shit! I remembered my father and his impending operation and his possible, though unlikely, phone call. Martha would want to know that he's sick and all. I should tell her. And then I remembered the doleful look in Spot's eyes when I dropped him last night at Aesop's Fabled Animal Hospital.

Judi said, "I have a story you can write."

"Say what?"

Judi turned the radio down, then off. "Two guys, lovers, and one of them has the AIDS virus and the other doesn't." She looked at me. "They are the same as married," she said. "They're monogamous, live together, joint bank account, the works."

I waited to hear about the trouble, which I assumed would be dreadful.

"The one who is not HIV-positive wants to be infected by the other."

My first thought was, Why? But first, the plot. I said, "And the lover doesn't want to do that."

Judi nodded, raised her eyebrows. "And it's causing problems. They fight about it all the time. It's jeopardizing the relationship."

I said, "The one thinks it would be murder. How could you kill someone you love?" And the other? I thought.

"The uninfected one thinks it would be romantic," Judi said. "Eventually they would be sick together, he figures. 'Poisoned by love,' he calls it. He told me, 'What's to live for after forty anyway? You're not pretty anymore. Your body's lost its buff.' "

I supposed it could be romantic in a *Sorrows of Young Werther* way, but Jesus Christ! I shook my head. There's so much of the world I know nothing about. I told Judi she was right. This would make a strong story. I'd have to think about it.

Judi and I checked into a B&B on Shankpainter Road. Josh, Ron, and Mark had already arrived. Albert was due this evening—couldn't get out of work. The consultation sessions were scheduled for ten to five today and tomorrow. We'd party Thursday night and stay over till checkout on Friday. When they all headed off for work, I walked down Commercial Street. I stopped at Spiritus Pizza for a cappuccino, sat on the sidewalk and drank. Watched the people drift along. Stanley Kunitz walked by, I swear to God. Black sailor's cap, Birkenstocks with black socks, a leather bag over his shoulder, smoothing his mustache with his thumb and index finger. I love Provincetown.

I wound up in the Fo'c'sle at a quiet table. I ordered a draft and called Francis X. One of his kids answered. I said, Hi, is this Kevin? He said, No. Timothy? No. Who is this? I said. This is Eamon. I asked Eamon if his daddy was home. He wasn't. I told him to give his dad a message that Laf would not be able to meet him at Moynihan's tonight. Okay? Okay. I said, Did you write it down, Eamon? No. I said, Who am I, Eamon? When he didn't answer, I said, I'm Laf, a friend of your dad's. Yes, Laf, like ha-ha-ha. I made him repeat the message.

Someone played Neil Young on the jukebox. "Helpless." I looked over at the window booth and saw Martha and I at twenty-three. We're sitting there, sunburned, shoeless, dreamy. I shook away the image. My story: All Dale can think about these days is Peter at thirty still in the room upstairs, still rolling toy trucks along the floor, making engine and brake noises, still spitting up his vegetables. I make him think about Theresa and how she's made him feel like a kind and generous loving person. She's made him better than he is. What if she weren't in your life, Dale? Dale thinks maybe Peter should be institutionalized. They could find a real good place, the best doctors. I tell Dale not to bring this up to Theresa. I know what will happen if he does. Whose story is this, anyway? Mine or theirs?

I ordered another draft and called my father. While I waited for the answer it occurred to me that maybe my father was not sick at all, that this was another one of his jokes. My mother transferred me to my father's extension. His voice was reedy, shrill almost. He told me he was happy I called. He asked where I was calling from. Do you remember, he said, when we fished off the pier in P-town and you caught a sea robin? Ugly little fish. I didn't remember, but I told him I did. We had a great time that vacation, he said.

"How are you feeling, Dad?"

"Temporary," he said.

"Are you in pain at all?"

"More weak than hurt."

I asked him about the weather down there. He said it was a furnace. I listened to his breathing.

He said, "You and Martha having trouble?"

I told him we were.

"Those things happen," he said. "Do what's best."

My mother cut in on the line. "That's enough, you two," she said. "Your father needs his rest."

I wished him good luck, and said I'd call late tomorrow to see how things were going. "So long, Dad."

"I love you, boy."

Judi woke me around six. You're doing a lot of sleeping today, she said. I blamed it on afternoon beers. She told me they were all going to Ciro and Sal's for supper with Lodi and did I want to come.

"That's a city in New Jersey."

"Lodivicius Puusepp," she said. He was born in Estonia, for your information. Get dressed," she said. "You'll really like him. He fills a room."

I knew I wouldn't like him, and I was right again. Lodi looked like a wolf—icy blue eyes, luxuriant gray hair and gray beard. White, collarless dress shirt, white slacks, huaraches. Manicured nails. Judi couldn't take her eyes off him. She hardly touched her *abbàcchio brodettato*. Albert entertained us with stories from the Worcester Housing Court, where he worked as a clerk. Tenants raising livestock in their kitchen, landlords dousing back porches with gasoline, and so on. Josh suggested we all go dancing at Piggy's. Albert voted for the Atlantic House. Lodi excused himself and said he had reading to do. Judi and I walked back to the B&B in silence.

In bed, I tried to imagine just what a bypass operation might look like. I tried hard to remember ever being with my parents in Provincetown.

Was I blocking it out and maybe any other warm memory of my father with it? Or was he lying about it? Or maybe not lying, but confused. Maybe Edgar caught the fish and it was at Nantasket. I remember going there for the day, getting sunstroke on the beach and sick on the rides. Judi, Martha, Dad, and Guilt were all in bed with me.

15.

To the Lighthouse

I ASKED JUDI IF I COULD USE THE CAR, TOOL AROUND A LITTLE. I WAS NOT INTO sunbathing the day away with Albert. That was fine with her. Meet us at The Moors if you want to eat supper with us. Around six, she said. I drove by Race Point and Herring Cove, reminding myself of past visits, of camping out in the dunes along the bike path for a week, of sleeping in culverts to stay out of the rain. I headed south through Truro to Wellfleet. I was on my way to find Martha, to speak with her if I could. I wanted to know if she was all right, if she was getting along. And what would that mean if she were? That I wouldn't have to worry about her anymore? And if I learned that she was not okay, what then? I hadn't thought this out.

It was close to noon. I figured my father was lying on an operating table with his sternum cracked open. How could I do this anyway? Talk to Martha, I mean. Walk up to the cabin, pound on the door like the person from Porlock, rouse her from her reverie, say, Martha, it's me, open up? Martha, I'd say, my father is dying, and me, I don't know what I'm feeling. Scared, maybe. How are you?

I pulled off Ocean View into the dirt road and idled by the scrub pines. I saw our Impala in the driveway alongside a second car, a boxy, brown Japanese model. A woman's bathing suit and several beach towels hung drying on the clothesline that ran from the house to the white pine. A clutch of rocks and shells lay by the outside shower. The hammock was empty. I wondered who these visitors in the brown car might be. I heard no voices through the opened windows. What to do? I hadn't expected company. At that moment the German shepherd from next door came tearing out of his yard. He charged the car, growled, bared his teeth by my door. I should have killed him when I had the chance two years ago, that time he went after Martha's niece Lexie. I had the Alpo, the strychnine, everything. Now I was unnerved. I backed the car up a bit, cut the wheel, and floored it at Baron. He dove into the pines, the bastard. I backed out onto Ocean View.

I parked in the beach lot and walked down the dune to the shore. I looked around. No Martha. I walked a quarter mile north and back along the surf, but couldn't find her. I did see the family from Connecticut that comes every year—the Belinkys. Etai, Sheila, and their fat little twin daughters. Etai waved, but I pretended I was someone else, and I was beachcombing, and I dared not look up from the sand and chance missing the perfect sinistral whelk. I didn't want the senior Belinkys walking over to Martha's saying, We saw the son of a bitch on the beach just as big as life. And he waves to us like we're on his side, you poor dear. Better they say: Strange, we saw this shell collector at the beach who looked kind of like what's-his-face.

I drove into town and sat on a bench in front of the Lighthouse. I saw Mary Oliver buying *The New York Times* at the News Store. I saw Howard Zinn scraping gum off the sole of his Teva with a Popsicle stick. I saw Sylvia Plath's mother walking a calico cat on a leash. I saw Perry Como smoking a cigarette. You wouldn't expect that, would you? I saw Larry Bird duck his head and walk into a gift shop. I saw John Kennedy, Jr., and Daryl Hannah sharing a pistachio ice cream cone on the Town Hall lawn. I saw Peter Jennings check his reflection in the ice cream shop window. Norman Mailer drove by in a Range Rover and honked at two kids rollerblading in the street. They gave him the finger. The bass player from J. Geils walked his kids into the bakery. He'd put on a lot of weight.

I poked around town. I did not buy saltwater taffy or postcards of the National Seashore or a T-shirt with "Wellfleet" across the front. I didn't buy varnished seashells or a plastic lobster. I didn't buy sunglasses or sunscreen or temporary tattoos or a whale-watch video or a New Age audio tape or a stuffed puffin. At five o'clock I went into the Lighthouse, sat down at a small corner table, and ordered a pint of Bass ale and oysters rancheros. Thursday night is Mexican Night at the Lighthouse.

I tried calling Florida while I waited for my food. I got the night clerk at the Maravista, a guy named Guy Duplessis. I explained who I was. He hadn't heard any news. I told him to be sure to tell my parents that I called. I ate, drank a couple more drafts, took out my notebook. Marty Robbins played on the stereo. Dale liked Marty Robbins, Ferlin Husky, Kitty Wells, the Sons of the Pioneers, George Jones. Obviously, I was not meeting Lodi and the Holistics for supper. Just when I was trying to decide my strategy vis-à-vis Martha, Martha herself walked into the Lighthouse alone, spotted me, said something to the hostess, and came over to my table. I capped my pen. I said, Hello.

"You've got your goddamn nerve," she said.

In a fraction of a second, I was able to take offense, feign innocence, create excuses, drop the charade, relax, and offer Martha a seat. She looked at the chair. I told her I was there alone. I ordered her a drink, a Midori sour. One summer that's all she drank. The summer we went to the Wellfleet drive-in about every night, the summer she threw the sea-gull salt shaker at me because she wanted help cleaning the kitchen and I wouldn't stop doing the crossword puzzle. Caught me on the cheek-bone. Instead of flying into a rage, I let the blood drip onto the news-paper and blossom there like little rosettes. Martha told the waitress that she wasn't hungry. She sat, held her purse on her lap with both hands, like maybe it was helium-filled and would float away if she let go. I wanted to ask her who owned the brown car.

On the only camping trip we ever took together, Martha and I drove to a state park in the White Mountains. I'd borrowed a tent and a propane stove from Francis X. I was hoping that a weekend in the forest primeval might awaken a pastoral urge in Martha, and this might lead to a consideration of living the simple life, quitting work, moving north to some farmland near a lake or the ocean, do some simple farming, work enough to stay alive. We would be like Helen and Scott Nearing, I figured. Well, I pitched the camp. I cooked Spam and eggs, hot dogs, pancakes, and hamburgs on the stove and ate them alone. I built a campfire and roasted marshmallows. I slept in the tent. Martha stayed in the car and read *Vogue* and *Middlemarch* that first day. At ten, she started the engine and drove away. She checked into a motel for the rest of the weekend. Martha had taken her stand against nature and the simple life. And now she had that same combative look on her face.

"So where do we stand?" I said.

She opened her purse and took out a Kleenex. "You're killing me," she said.

"Martha, I'm sorry—"

"Like hell you are."

I looked at her trembling hands. They were chapped and raw, like she had been washing dishes in very hot water for months. I knew that anything I said now would elicit a hostile response. I saw the Belinkys take a table by the window.

Martha said, "The day you left me I took twenty-seven Valium and drank a bottle of wine. I wanted to die." She closed her eyes. "Father Bob saved my life." She was crying.

I wanted to remind her that I didn't exactly leave, I was thrown out, but that was beside the point, given the circumstances. Then and now. I wanted to ask her where she got the Valium and how was it that Father Bob got himself involved in our business. And what kind of car does he drive?

I said, "Can we just talk, Martha? Calmly, rationally."

"I've been abandoned," she said. "My life is in turmoil. I'm sick. I can't work. I've been made to feel ugly and useless and dispensable. And I'm not supposed to cry?"

"Martha, you're not—"

"I was raped last week."

"What?"

She took a breath. "Raped."

"By whom? Where? Are you okay?"

Martha shook her head dismissively. "You don't know him. Some guy." She wiped her eyes, bit her lower lip. "I've had dates," she said. This was an accusation.

"Martha, what happened?"

She put her head in her hands.

"Martha, you can't make an announcement like this and then drop it."

I asked her if she wanted to go for a walk. It might be easier to talk in a quiet and private place. She didn't. She took the first sip of her drink. Sheila Belinky walked her two daughters to the ladies' room. Martha said she'd been seeing this guy who was a computer genius at Digital. Someone from the parish council. The guy became obsessed with her. Maybe it wasn't exactly rape, she said, but it felt like it.

"We were kissing on the couch," she said. She looked at me. "Our couch." Martha wiped her eye with the Kleenex. "I told him no. He begged me. He kept at it. I didn't kiss him or anything from then on. I hated it. I haven't seen him again."

"Jesus, Martha," I said. "You should have called the cops or something. You should have called me."

"Called you? What a fucking laugh. You did this to me."

I got back to the B&B around nine-thirty. Judi wasn't there. I went for a walk. I wanted to be alone but not by myself. Martha hadn't said much else except that she would never talk to me as long as I was with Judi. None of my business who owned the brown car. I had a couple of drinks at the Fo'c'sle and then walked out on the wharf. When I got back to the B&B I saw Josh and Albert making out in the parking lot. Albert had Josh pinned against their van. They kissed. Albert put his hand down the front of Josh's basketball shorts. Judi was still out. I didn't wake up until ten. I missed breakfast. Josh, Albert, Ron, and Mark had left already. I showered, packed, and sat on veranda waiting for Judi. My father could be dead for all I knew.

16.

The Lek

I LOOKED AT MY WATCH. JUDI AND LODI, I FIGURED, WOULD BE ABOUT THEN capping off a fascinating evening together with brunch at some sunny café by the water. Portuguese sweet breads, jams, eggs over ever-so-lightly, limber bacon, grapefruit juice, *caffè latte*. Probably telling each other how splendid and meaningful the last twenty-four hours had been. And here I was, antsy, hungry, fidgeting on the veranda of the Fin de Siècle Bed & Breakfast, trying to cultivate an interest in the spring fashion issue of *Esquire*.

A silver Lexus pulled up in front of the B&B. Judi got out carrying her shoes. Lodi gave me a wave and a toothy smile. Judi stopped at his door, and the two of them exchanged a few words. Lodi pulled away with a toot. Oh, Laf, Judi said, I hope you're not too pissed. She asked if I wouldn't mind driving. Fine, I said. And drive to a drugstore, would you.

Judi bought Maalox, Tums, and Pepto-Bismol. I think it's the stress of the job, she said. All this indigestion lately. She chewed a couple of Tums, poured herself a shot of Pepto and drank it.

"So what do you see in this guy?" I said. "He's nothing like me, is he?"

"Well, he's married."

We discussed monogamy for a while. How it was a lovely, uncompli-cated idea, but so unnatural. A prophylactic devoutly to be wished these days, a handy political tool, the way it keeps people settled and preoc-cupied. But a doomed notion. Even in Darwinian terms. A man wants to spread his genes around as much as he can. A woman needs as many

protectors and sustainers as she can get. Judi told me that a female ba-
boon will copulate with every male in her group except for her sons.
With the paternity in question, no male hurts the babies. We said enough
to calm ourselves, to placate our consciences. I mean, we believed what
we said. We just didn't say a whole lot. Not a word about emotion.

I pulled into the Black Duck in South Wellfleet to use the pay phone.
Judi went into the store to nose around. Guy Duplessis told me my father was doing fine. Great news, I said. Great. Your mom's over there at
Hollywood Memorial right now. They figure he should be home in a week.
Course, he's going to have to take it easy for a while. I thanked Guy and
hung up. For some reason, I wanted a Turkish taffy. Bonomo's vanilla. I
don't know where that came from. I hadn't had one in twenty years, I bet.

I couldn't find Turkish taffy in the candy aisle. Judi knew what I was
talking about, but the kid at the counter had never heard of it. I bought
a postcard and a stamp, wrote a note to my father wishing him a speedy
recovery, and dropped it in the mailbox outside. Judi said I'd better get
a present for Spot or he'd be hurt. I went back into the Black Duck and
picked out a plastic pail-and-shovel set. I went next door to the package store and bought a six-pack of Beck's and a church key.

Probably it was the Turkish taffy that got us started on food. Judi remembered how good Sky Bars were before they changed the flavors.
Pretty soon we were talking about foods we liked as kids, and then we
decided to open a restaurant for people who were feeling a little sick or
depressed. We'd call it The Milk Mustache. We'd have a special salon for
those with mild headaches or hurts-all-over. We'd have couches with
afghans. Here you'd drink pale dry ginger ale, nibble on Saltines, and
read comic books.

Our menu: fried baloney with cheese, spaghetti with butter and
ketchup, mayonnaise sandwiches. Stuff like that. You know, Fluffernut-
ters, grilled cheese sandwiches, tuna noodle casserole with a top layer
of potato chips, shepherd's pie, baked beans with salt pork and molasses,
brown bread from the can. For dessert: Creamsicles, peanut butter cups,
Devil Dogs, s'mores, strawberry shortcake with bananas, gingerbread,
and maple syrup apple pie. You could bring your cat or dog to The Milk
Mustache. We'd have a radio going that just played snowstorm warn-
ings and no-school announcements.

After a couple of beers, Judi had to stop for the ladies' room. I pulled
into Frates Fried Clams and waited in the car. When Judi came back,
she had a large order of fried scallops. I asked her what attracted her to

me. At first, I mean. She said, "Your cheekbones and your tattersall shirt." We met at a crowded singles bar in Worcester called The Lek. I may have been there to get out of my marriage. I don't know. It was my first time in the place. The bar was mobbed and the music loud, insistent, and percussive. Like everyone else, it seemed to me, I had staked out a little territory of my own. I occupied a barstool at a shelf along a wall. I felt safer with no one at my back.

All over the place, men in suits were rolling their shoulders, stretching, adjusting their loosened ties, catching glimpses of themselves in mirrors, patting their hair, laughing rousingly with their upper bodies, shooting sidelong glances, bending toward the women they were listening to, turning their ears toward the women's mouths—all the better to hear you with, my dear. This one guy, wearing a Red Sox cap backward, lit a cigarette like he was conducting an orchestra through the *1812 Overture*. None of these men looked like the high school teachers I was used to being with. None, I bet, worked second jobs like Francis X. did, stocking the frozen-food cabinets at the Big D supermarket. I watched a guy across from me become irritated at a hanging Swedish ivy that kept brushing against his bald head. He turned his face up and bit off a leaf.

I thought, What am I doing here? I felt out of place and incompetent. But I didn't move. I watched women smile and flash their eyebrows at these men who, in my opinion, were acting so lame. And there I was, tapping my foot and bopping my head to the Donna Summer song blasting through the sound system. That's when I noticed Judi for the first time. She sat at the bar, smoking, looking right at me. Her gaze was steady, direct, and it lingered for just a moment after I caught her looking. Then she looked away. I stared. She flicked her eyes back. I looked away involuntarily. What was all that? I thought. For just that second, she was the only person in the bar who was not in motion. Elsewhere women were twisting their curls, shifting in their dresses. I watched their heads tilt, their eyes widen. They giggled, flicked their tongues, wet their lips, studied the hairlines of guys they flirted with. I looked back and saw her watching me, giving me the mating gaze.

And then at the bar, I introduced myself. Judi told me I looked famishing. I told her she looked ravished herself. She smiled. I smiled. It's not what you say, but how you say it. Judi swept her hair back with her hand. I rolled up my shirtsleeves. Pretty soon we had a table. And soon after that we were out the door. I put my hand on her waist.

Judi chewed a couple of Tums. She adjusted her seat back and closed her eyes. I turned on the radio, fiddled with it till I heard Jonathan Richman singing "Roadrunner." I thought about Martha and how we met in college. I was crazy for her. If I were at home reading a book, I'd want to call her up and tell her about it. If I saw a movie on TV, I'd wonder if she'd like it as much as I did. Everything I saw reminded me of her. This is how Dale feels about Theresa. The poor guy can't work, can't even relax at home with his hobbies. He is nagged, as I had been, with hope and uncertainty. Martha's flaws were charming and more interesting than other people's. Her orthodox Catholicism, her theatricality, her thumbsucking, her fascination with the literature of her childhood, with *Anne of Green Gables* and C. S. Lewis. What happened to my passion, that fire, that admirable foolishness?

Judi woke from her nap. I told her we were in Upton. I asked her why passion doesn't last. She said that passion in a relationship is all behavioral, emotional. You can regulate it. Said she deals with this all the time in couples counseling. I've had clients married thirty years just as frisky and spellbound as teenagers. You just work at it. It's all up here, she said, and she tapped her forehead. Biological. Your brain simply can't keep up the accelerated metabolism of romantic bliss. Passion has a limited and definite half-life, like nuclear material. That meant someone like Dale had better do something before it was too late.

We pulled into Aesop's parking lot. Judi waited in the car while I went in to fetch Spot. The receptionist asked me to wait a moment. She returned with a vet who told me that Spot would not be welcomed back to their kennel. He'd been a bad influence. He ate his food bowl, for one thing. You'll see the cost reflected on your bill, the vet said. Ten dollars for a bowl? I said. He ate the Reardons' poodle's squeaky toys. He kept running into the electric fence in the exercise yard, and he got the other dogs doing it. Oh, sure, I thought, he twisted their forearms. I could tell that he held me responsible for everything Spot had done. I said, He's never behaved this way before. What have you done to my precious?

17.

Letter from the Editor

I PUT MY NOTES AND MY TYPEWRITER ON THE KITCHEN TABLE, POURED MYSELF a cup of coffee, sat down. The phone rang, Spot barked once for each ring. I heard Lodi's unctuous voice introduce itself. It seems he was missing his favorite watch, a Jaeger-LeCoultre "Grande Taille," and wondered if, perhaps, she might have it, or might remember having seen it. Lodi signed off leaving his phone number, fax number, and e-mail address. I got up and erased his message. I noticed that my props were missing—my scribbled notes, apartment ads, rental agency card. Judi must have cleaned up.

Some days Dale feels on top of the world. Other days, he doesn't know a thing. But you can't push him, exasperating as he might be. So now he's sitting at home. It's Thursday night. Keynes is sitting on his beach towel on his side of the couch. The TV's on to an old *Mary Tyler Moore Show*, but Dale's not paying attention. I'm watching for him to do something. This is like one of my dreams. I can see everything clearly, but I have no control over what happens. I made a list of things that Dale could do: polish his guns; call Theresa and chat; read *Time;* have himself a snack—eat those jalapeño-stuffed olives he bought at Jewel Osco today; go for a drive, maybe to Eunice; give his sister a call up in Lovington. Dale scratches Keynes behind his ears, sees Ted Baxter on his knees, pleading with Lou, but Dale doesn't know why that's happening. He's trying to think of how to proceed with Theresa and the kids. He knows the kids are afraid of him. And he's afraid of them. He thinks about their father, what he might be like. Theresa has told Dale that her husband left after Peter was born. He was repulsed, she said, by his own child. No, she tells him, I don't know where he is.

Theresa is in her kitchen, ironing her uniform, listening to a call-in show on her radio. A woman from Denver wants to know if she should switch her capital from some no-load mutual funds to CDs. Theresa has no idea what they are talking about. When the phone rings, she answers it quickly so it won't wake the kids. She's glad it's Dale and not some bad news at this hour. She thinks it's a great idea—the kids'll love it, she says. Dale's idea is that all four of them will drive up to Capitan and Lincoln next weekend. Smokey the Bear and Billy the Kid all at once, he says.

I figured there'd be some tension on the trip. It's a long drive for kids. Dale and Theresa had thought of that, too. Still this was the right step to take if this love affair were to continue to grow. Dale might not know it yet, but he'd be crazy to give up Theresa. Dale hangs up and smiles. He tells Keynes it's time for bed. Theresa takes the suitcase out of the storage closet and washes it down with Simple Green. She knows she has a week to pack, but she knows how she forgets. She puts Band-Aids, cough medicine, and Tylenol in separate Ziploc bags and puts them all in the fabric pocket of the suitcase. She closes the case, flips the locks, and stands it up beside the stove. She makes a list of what to bring. Mittens, toys, crayons, sweaters. Pick up some ipecac at the hospital. She reminds herself to check the weather forecast before leaving. I heard the mailman's signal.

My story "Figure of Fun" touched an exposed nerve with Mr. Thom Blake, the editor of the *Brooklyn Review*. He took me to task in a noxious and ferocious letter, just bubbling with vitriol. "Please," he wrote, "no more of these insufferable rustic septic tank rural stories. No more grotesque bumpkins or genetically damaged rednecks. Enough of these afflicted, desperate, ugly, indigent freaks, these marginal and insignificant wallowers in misery. These dysfunctional misfits do not represent the way we live now in America. We have indoor plumbing in America and medicines to cure rickets and fathers who are not alcoholic child-abusers." Right there on the classy *Brooklyn Review* stationery was a thick, blotchy period.

Mr. Tom Blake continued: "People want to find themselves and their lives reflected in the stories they read. Is that too difficult to understand? Psychopathology," Mr. Thom Blake wrote, "is not literature. Neurosis is not narrative. Save your ramshackle minimalist puppet show for your buddies in the writing workshop. They probably think you're real clever. If someday you're ready to admit that individuals interact with and are affected by society, by politics, by economics, by culture, then maybe you can dust off that typewriter. Until then why don't you read the newspaper and see what the real world looks like." He signed the letter, "Th. B."

Can't you just see the artery throbbing on Mr. Thom Blake's temple? Son of a bitch was probably seconds away from bursting the walls of that sucker and staining his cortex with blood. I almost killed an editor! When my hand stopped shaking, I wrote this editor of the famous-from-Canarsie-to-Coney-Island *Brooklyn Review* a brief response on my "From the Desk of Judi Dubey" memo pad:

Dear Thom,
I am so grateful for your insightful comments. Thomorrow I will thry to write a story—no, a novel—about the wealthy makers and shakers, the Baptist golfers, the successful guys and gals of Gotham, like yourself and your investment counselor. The tale will be urban; it will be encompassing; it will be topical; it will be about people who read newspapers from the front to back, even the recipes on the Lifestyle page.

I'm pulling your leg, Thom. A fiction writer must make significance, you fool, not borrow it from the six o'clock news or the headlines. Since when is poverty not politics, ignorance not economics, shame not social, crime not cultural, you insipid little camp follower?

Got you that time, Thom! I'm only jerking your chain, amigo. Hey, you're the editor, and I know that just because you can't write a story doesn't mean that you can't recognize one if it bites you on the ass. I think we could be friends, Thom. I mean it. I love every bone in your pointy little head, every sebaceous cyst on your scalp, every synaptic ravine in your gray matter.
                    Your pal,
                    Lafayette Proulx
                    (his mark)

Should I mail this to Thom or would that make me as big a fool as he was? I won't mail it, I decided. I'll call him. I dialed the number on the buff-and-green *Brooklyn Review* stationery.

"Hello," he said.

"This Thom?" I asked, pronouncing the *th* in both words.

"That's Thom," he said, without the dental consonant in the name. "Who, may I ask, is calling?"

I introduced myself. "Lafayette Proulx. 'Figure of Fun.' "

"And the call is in regards to . . . ?"

"Your letter, Thom." I began to read it.

His memory jogged, Thom interrupted. "I don't think I want to speak with you."

I told him, You hang up and I'm on the four-thirty Greyhound with my uncle Tiny. Tiny sits on people, I told Thom. And me, I'm a firebug.

Thom hung up.

I read the story over. It wasn't flawless. I'd need to get back at it. But what I knew was that every objection Thom Blake had to the story, everything he hated, was exactly what made the story honest and worthwhile.

I needed a drink. I got Spot and we walked down to Moynihan's. John Joe drew my draft and told me, Who the hell was it was asking about you? He couldn't remember. He gave Spot a pickled egg. Spot sat under my stool with his lunch. John Joe asked me did I want any action on the Sox game. I thought not. John Joe remembered. Francis X. He was in here Wednesday night, I guess it was, looking for you. I thought, Kids!

18.

For I Have Already Been a Boy and a Girl, a Bush and a Bird and a Leaping Journeying Fish

WE WERE DUE IN MILLBURY AT NOON. TRIXIE WAS HOSTING A COOKOUT IN THE gravelly yard, an all-in-one going-away-to-Walpole party for Noel, wish-you-were-here party for the incarcerated Edmund, and birthday party for Stoni, who was turning thirty. Arthur Bositis was bringing a case of club steaks for the grill. This would be an excellent opportunity for us to check out the trailer, Judi said. I changed the subject. The night before she had started to tell me about this woman in Oakham whom she was seeing about her past lives. I ran my tongue along her breast, and she forgot what she was saying. We were out on the deck now, brunching. I tossed Spot the last of the Paris buns. I said, So who is this lady from Oakham?

Judi said the woman's name was Pamela Bibaud, and she was absolutely the best at regression therapy. Judi said she'd been going to Pamela for only three weeks and had already remembered so much. And it's just the beginning. Besides Gertrude and Marya, Judi had also identified four other incorporations. She remembered herself when she was a man, a stonemason in Arles, France, in the early eighteenth century. Drowned in a boating accident. As far as she knew, that had been her only male embodiment. She said, I was a banker's wife in Connecticut, a pharmacy clerk in Bristol, England, and a teacher in Québec. And that's when I first met you.

"You met me?" I said. "And when was this?"

"The middle of the last century." She told me I had been a priest in

L'Ange-Gardien. "You were my confessor," she said. She smiled. "Actually, you were more than that. We were in love."

"But how do you know it was me, Judi?"

"I look with different eyes." Judi smiled. "It was you, André Berard."

"My name was Berard? So we've really been going out for a long time, then."

"We went for walks to the river. We could see Ile d'Orléans appear out of the fog. You were always ashamed and tender. I lived in a room upstairs in Madame Lussier's house on the *rue de Champignon.*"

Why was I flattered at being ashamed and tender a hundred fifty years ago when I knew this could not have happened? Judi's eyes wandered up and to the left. They narrowed, as though she were trying to focus on the details of an image. I didn't tell her that my grandfather, my mother's father, was in fact born in L'Ange-Gardien. This was too strange just yet. Of course it was an accident, a coincidence, but even accidents need explanations. So I said, "Judi, don't you think it's a little too convenient, in the cosmic scheme of things, that we both meet again out of all the billions of people who've lived in the last hundred years or so? That the two of us from northern Québec just happen to be born in Worcester, Mass., U.S.A., within a few years of each other and then just happen to meet in the city at a bar one night? Isn't it just too contrived or too coincidental?"

"No, it's not," she said. "Not coincidental."

What was fascinating to me about Judi's past-life scenarios was that since I believed they could not be historically based, what the hell were they? Where was she coming up with all these engaging characters and these lovely and persuasive details? I knew she wasn't lying to me, so there must be some channel she'd found for the flow of these worlds.

It was eleven, and Judi wanted to stop off at the office to get her personal organizer. We cleaned up. I kissed Spot on his brown nose. I met Judi in the garage. Let's see, she said, gifts, hot dogs, fruit salad, keys. We're all set. We had pitched in and bought Stoni her own blood pressure cuff and an electric toothbrush. I've never seen such a family for small appliances.

While Judi ran upstairs to her office, I ducked into Mr. Natural's. Pauline wasn't working. Josh was there buying flaxseed oil, and he was surprised to see me. I told him Judi was up getting her appointment book. "What do you do with flaxseed oil?" I said.

"Two tablespoons a day keep your skin creamy and tight."

Josh wore a white tank top with "Man Alive!" in red printed on the front. He told me that was the name of his support group.

"For what?"

"Man Alive! is a place where men can recover their lost identities," he said.

I wondered where they'd lost them. But you can't joke with Josh.

He said, "We talk about our feelings."

I said, "The child inside." I'd read about it in the *TV Guide*.

Josh smiled. He said, "Or the wolf inside."

And then all I could think about was Flannery O'Connor, how she told a friend that the lupus, the wolf, was inside tearing up the place. I told Josh good-bye and went outside to lean on the car. I thought about the secrets our bodies have, what they keep from us. Our bodies have lives of their own. We have nothing to say about what's going on deep in our tissue.

Hervey had a fire going in an inverted and bisected oil drum. I had a feeling our club steaks might have a slight petroleum flavor. But I figured that's what the half-gallon of ketchup was for. I grabbed a bottle of Canadian Mist and poured some over ice in an Archie and Jughead jam jar. I asked Trixie if she wanted some help in the kitchen. She said Judi was all the help she needed right now. I told her she looked alluring.

"Cut the blarney," she said.

"You look like Hedy Lamarr."

"Drinking the high-octane today, Laf?" Noel said.

So that was it, then. Today's theme was gasoline.

I slapped Noel on the shoulder. "We'll miss you, Noel," I said.

"Don't get sappy on me," he said. "Just let's get drunk and stupid."

"We're halfway there already."

Noel's brushy gray eyebrows were as thick and wiry as his mustache. The mustache was stained with nicotine at the lip. He said, "Here's to Edmund!"

We toasted. I said, "Long live Edmund."

Noel and I sat at the picnic table nearest the card table of booze and by the cooler. We watched small balls of flame explode from the barrel. Noel explained it was probably little bits of tar or pitch igniting. When Hervey puts on the charcoal we'll be cooking with gas.

I said, "What's he burning now?"

"Some roofing shingles. Last year's Christmas tree."

Stoni's gone for the charcoal and beer, he said. Arthur's tenderizing the meat in the trailer. That explained the pounding. I looked behind me. Yes, the trailer. This blue and white barge run aground.

And then we suddenly ran out of things to say to each other. Noel blew his nose. I poured another drink. I watched Hervey poke at his inferno with a television aerial.

"I blame myself," Noel said.

I said, "For what?"

"For the boy." He put his head down.

"Well, look, Noel, there's plenty of blame to go around."

He looked at me. He said, "It ain't like it's my fault, though. Edmund and me spent scads of quality time together. We were like this." Noel held up his crossed fingers.

I opened a bottle of Rolling Rock and handed it to Noel. We heard a horn. Stoni was back with the charcoal, several cases of Old Milwaukee, and the night shift from Memorial's emergency ward. Arthur leaned out of the trailer and waved hello with his mallet. Noel and I were introduced to Virginia, Elaine, Raymond, and Netty. They were all dressed in plum-colored scrubs and running shoes, and they were all smoking cigarettes. Layla, Edmund's ex, arrived with her new boyfriend, a kid with a goatee and dreadlocks whom she called Pozzo Beckett. Pozzo didn't talk to strangers, she told me, not even to thank them for a bottle of beer. That's just Pozzo, she said. Pozzo's wallet was attached to a silver chain that arced from his back pocket down below his waist and back up, where it clasped onto a front belt loop. Layla said that Pozzo was the sun and that his brother Lucky was the moon. She meant that literally. She said we shouldn't look directly into Pozzo's eyes. She smiled. We owe them so much, she said of the brothers Beckett.

To call Judi's family dysfunctional would be unfair and not exactly accurate. Judi's family was open to adventure, certainly. *Les Dubeys* were very tolerant of eccentric modes of self-expression. I found that admirable. Just that the family members seemed to define themselves in terms of whom they latched on to. I figured in that case, Layla was likely to become a planet soon. The Dubeys did not believe that life was purposeful. It was, rather, a situation to be endured. It helped if there were clever and/or amusing distractions about, which could take your mind off the emptiness. If they had been born into money, the Dubeys would all be out at the country club this afternoon, diverting themselves with games and chitchat about cars and real estate, and the world would think they were all productive and sensible.

Noel and I watched the nurses jam the cans of beer into two Styrofoam coolers. Raymond brought several gift-wrapped packages from the car to the other picnic table. Then he pulled a tank of nitrous oxide out of the trunk. It was on a bottle cart. He wheeled it over by the table, then attached a hose and mask to the pressure regulator. Noel told me he knew why Edmund did it. How did Judi manage to ignore the turbulence in this extended family?

Myself, I don't know what to make of this crew. Is this what happens when you settle for pleasure? Pointless amusements. You suck on gas to make yourself laugh. Pleasure's such a small achievement. Maybe they know what I don't—that life's too short to get all worked up about or something.

Noel said, "Semigloss paint."

"What's that?"

He said, "When he was a toddler, Edmund was all the time peeling chips of paint off the wall in his bedroom, and eating it. Well, his mother and me didn't see no harm. Turns out lead is no good for babies at all. So Edmund had that poison, you see, in his blood all these years, and I guess it finally worked its way up to his noggin."

I thought about Spot, naturally, and those baby dolls and whatnot he was eating and what manner of poisons might be involved in those inorganic meals. I thought about George, who died, Edmund, who killed, and Richie, who terrified. I suppose there's an essence called human nature, but what is it? For me, incomprehensibility is like water—it's always just below the surface. But why can't life be unreasonable, absurd even, disturbing? And why am I bothered? I looked around me. Here's what I thought. In each of us is a little of all of us. I suppose that should have scared me. I felt comforted by it. Like the idea that you can start anywhere and go anyplace.

Judi joined us, said Trixie was making enough food to fuel an army. I wondered what kind of food. Usually the only thing Trixie made for supper was a phone call to Chicken Delight or to Iago's Pizza and Pasta. I knew that the only cookbook in the house was the one called *Science Experiments You Can Eat*. It was Judi's from junior high. She'd used it to bake hygroscopic cookies for the science fair. Judi grabbed herself a beer, yelled over to Hervey that maybe it was time to put the charcoal on. It's going to take a while, she said.

I asked Judi if she'd met Pozzo the sun. She said she had. And he's so cute, so shy and all, she said. Judi had a blind spot where her family was concerned. Noel said, She's going to break Edmund's heart. I said, Noel, you can't expect the girl to wait sixty-five years for his release.

I had a steak, a ladle full of Trixie's wienies and beanies steamed in beer, several scoops of potato, macaroni, and seafood salads. I ate an ear of corn and a bowl of Trixie's famous secret-recipe green pea soup. At first I thought she'd said Greenpeace soup, and I couldn't imagine— mock dolphin? ersatz hawksbill sea turtle? I passed on the orange Jell-O with the parti-colored minimarshmallows. We were ready for the cake and the presents. Arthur, Stoni, and the nurses were getting pretty silly over at their table. I saw that Pozzo had come out of his shell somewhat. He was talking to the fire. Trixie brought out a cake shaped like a nurse's cap with white frosting and a red cross made with M&M's. She snapped a "Happy Birthday" tape into the boom box and we all sang to Stoni.

Stoni opened Arthur's gift first—a pink teddy that Noel thought was a mosquito net. She held it up for us. A beeper went off, and one of the nurses—Elaine, I think—went into the house to make a call. Raymond showed Hervey how to take a hit off the laughing gas. Stoni opened our gifts and then one from Hervey and Trixie—a jewelry-cleaning machine. Elaine came back. No big deal, she said. The oldest boy sprained an ankle. The emergency ward crew had brought gag gifts. The first was a Klingon phrase book, which Stoni passed along for us to look at. I learned that *Dochvetlh vISoplaHbe* meant "I can't eat that." I committed it to memory. I handed the book to Layla, told her Pozzo might want to look at it. She said, Pozzo doesn't read.

The second gift, a dildo called Wide Willy, made Layla blush. Hervey was back at the gas works. Stoni showed us her new monogrammed proctoscope. Noel said, You do what with that? And then, Why would anyone do that? Then we all got to look at twelve photographs of enormously fat naked women. Stoni held up the "Women at Large" calendar and leafed through the year.

Layla brought Pozzo a piece of cake. Judi went in to help her mother clean up. I listened to the nurses talk shop. The subject was things they'd extracted from rectums. One guy had an alarm clock up there and it was still ticking, Stoni said. They talked about Coke bottles, toothbrushes, spoons, batteries, a computer mouse, and beef jerky. More than I wanted to hear, really. Layla came back. She said she and Pozzo had better be going. If he's not home in an hour, there'll be no dark tonight. Noel said, You got a message you want me to deliver to Edmund? Layla thought a moment. Tell him I got the new Pearl Jam CD. Tell him it's awesome.

Stoni said she'd give Layla and Pozzo Beckett a ride home or wherever. She needed to pick up smokes anyway. She gave Arthur a soul kiss. When they left, I sat with Arthur. I said, Tell me about the kill room—about the smells in there. He told me, Smells like iron tastes, you know? I wasn't sure. He said, Some cattle will be dead before we get to kill them right. You start gutting them dead suckers, and you get a smell like whistles going off in your head. I was thinking of my recent meal. I said, Do you get many dead steers there where you work? He said, More sick than dead. Like they'll have pneumonia or liver abscesses, a lot of them. You won't know that till you shell the guts out of the carcass. You'll see the damage. Ones with abdominal bloat or laminitis you know right from looking at them. Ones with cancers even, you can guess at. Those ones'll roll their tongues upside down all the time. Look demented. Or they'll bite the bars in their pens or they'll just stand there swaying back and forth for hours. We call it the barn dance. That was all I wanted to hear for now. Arthur said, You'll be slicing away for a while and you're spacing out and you'll notice you're standing ankle deep in entrails and mucus and you'll get yourself a whiff of hell.

Hervey said he felt like the back of his head was coming off. I told him he should have kept the nail in it. He told me I was about as funny as a tapeworm, and then he started to laugh and told us about the time his brother Honoré got a tapeworm when he was seven or eight. "My mother starved him for three days. Then Dr. Beaudry came to the house. The doctor stuffed a wooden wedge into Honoré's mouth to keep it open. Then he placed a few drops of milk on the tongue. In a while, up came the worm, sliding over the tongue. The doctor shined his flashlight in Honoré's mouth and let us look. The worm had four holes in its head. The doctor grabbed it with a metal snare and eased it out. Looked like a ten-foot-long ribbon." And then Hervey laughed again, said he had to see a man about a horse, and excused himself.

Arthur said, "You ever been in love?"

I said, "Yes, I have."

He said, "I'm way in love with Stoni. I don't know what I'd do if she left me."

I nodded, smiled.

"I've asked her to marry me."

"Congratulations."

"She won't."

"Maybe she just needs some time."

Arthur shook his head. "It's Muneyhun." Arthur freshened our drinks.

He had peeled the label off the bottle with his thumbnail, but it looked like, tasted like, we were drinking bourbon. "He was her first love back in high school."

I said, "Everyone remembers the kiss that brought them to life." I remembered mine with Midge Martel. I was too stupid then to ask her out again. I had no car, no money, no ideas, no courage. She married a potter and moved to Maine.

Arthur said, "How do I compete with history?"

I said I wished I knew the answer.

An hour or so later, Virginia or Netty—I forgot which nurse was which—put on an Asleep at the Wheel tape and tried to teach us the Texas two-step. By this time Raymond and Hervey were alternating hits off the nitrous and giggling like adolescents. Trixie and Noel wandered over to the side of the trailer and started to smooch. Judi saw this and took my hand. "It's time to see the trailer," she said. When Noel opened the door, we were hit with a putrescent odor that was like a hot spike in the eye. Judi said, Noel, what died in here?

Noel let go of Trixie's hand and leaned in through the door. He took a whiff. Kind of ammonia smell, you mean? He said, That would be your toilet. About every forty-fifty dumps, it needs a recharge. He did a little silent calculation. I'd say we're right at about forty. Judi shut the door.

When we got home, Judi stood beside the car before going in. Spot heard the doors close and began to bark. The lights went on in Mr. Lesperence's living room. Judi said, Look at those stars, all that darkness, Laf. Jesus. What do you suppose it means?

That Pozzo's home in bed, I said.

19.

A Life in Vermilion

I DROPPED JUDI AT THE AIRPORT. SHE WAS OFF TO A WEEK-LONG CONFERENCE in Cleveland on therapeutic modalities or something. It was easier than I thought it would be, asking Pauline for a date. Why I asked, though, is another matter. Maybe I was feeling too attached to Judi or not attached at all now that she was away. I didn't stop to think about it. I walked into Mr. Natural's and waited around until the guy buying buckwheat groats, corn germ, and lentils paid up and left. Must be having a party. Then I told Pauline that I hadn't come to shop, but to ask her out. She smiled. I tried to remember how to do this, I mean how to allure and seduce. I looked at her, cocked my head, raised my eyebrows, blinked—harmless little primate—and smiled. The chase was on. You're making me blush, she said. Then she fixed her eyes on mine, narrowed her gaze, set her jaw, scrutinized me. Sure, she said, okay. I said, You like movies? We'll go to a movie. Get a drink after. Is Wednesday good? Wednesday, then.

So at about six on Wednesday evening I was telling Spot how excited I was, and he was wagging his tail a mile a minute because he figured from the tone of my voice I could only be talking about the beef brisket I had in the oven just for him. The phone rang. I heard Pauline's voice on the machine, and I picked up. I wasn't sure this was the right number, she said. She meant Judi's voice on the tape, I guessed, but I didn't offer any explanation. She asked me if I would stop at 235 Providence Street and pick up Marvin the sitter. Sure. He'll be waiting outside at 6:45, she said. Well, Marvin the sitter turned out to be Marvin the estranged husband. I've heard a lot about you, I said. He shook my hand, said it was a real pleasure. What do you think of these? he said. For the kids. He showed me two neon-colored yo-yos. One green, one orange. They're beauties, I told him.

She probably told you about the drugs and shit, Marvin said. I nodded. A little, I said. He said, I'm off that stuff. Clean as a whistle. He rolled up his sleeves to prove it. Went through rehab at Marathon House. Sometimes you have to hit bottom, Lafayette, he said. He pronounced it "Laugh yet." He told me how he had owned a produce market on Chandler Street and lost it all. My father's business for thirty-eight years, and I pissed it down the drain. I became a total scumbag, he said. I wanted to tell him this was not an AA meeting, but he kept going. One time my buddy Albert Golden keeled right over in that alley behind the Peking Garden. I was so fucked up I pulled the spike out of his arm and fixed myself. Albert died and I wound up in detox. Saved my life.

Was Marvin telling me this, that he probably was HIV-positive, so that I would keep my pecker away from his wife? I wasn't sure, but I was certain that I shouldn't take any chances. I realized I was temporarily unprepared, but how do you tell a guy you're just running into the pharmacy for a pack of rubbers because the one thing you want most in the entire world is to have intercourse with his wife?

Marvin told me he was into kundalini yoga now and meditation. Told me he worked out every morning at Lord's Gym on free weights and the Nautilus. Best shape of my life, he said. I might do a little pot now and then, he said, but never around the kids. He tapped his head. You got to use common sense. He asked me to pull into the next parking lot, and I did. He ran into Iandoli's Package Store, came back with a twelve-pack of Budweiser. Marvin opened a can for himself and offered me one. No, thanks. Then he said, If you store your guns in PVC pipe, they can last forever underground. No rust at all. I don't have any guns, Marvin, I said. He seemed not to want to believe that. What kind of blue-collar philanderer doesn't have himself an equalizer? He looked at me and back out the window, said, I'm going to be ready for the revolution when it comes.

I figured—wouldn't you?—that Marvelous Marvin was some unreconstructed old new lefty who was holding on to the dream of a socialist revolution. Power to the people, and all that. I was afraid I was going to have to like the guy.

"President Clinton's got a black son," Marvin said. "Keeps him hidden away in a private school in Ohio. I bet you didn't know that."

Was he joking? I didn't know if this was some subtle junkie irony that I was just too unhip to pick up on or what.

Then Marvin told me about the Council of the Hundred, headquartered in Zurich, that rules the world. We were stopped at a red light on Belmont Street by Memorial Hospital. You really never heard of this? he said.

I said, No. I didn't say, Because I've been living on this planet the whole time.

He took a breath and explained that the Council was made up of members of the Rockefeller Trilateral Commission, the Yale University Skull and Bones Society, the World Bank, UNESCO, the CIA, the British MI-5 and MI-6 intelligence agencies, the College of Cardinals, the former Politburo, and the Elders of Zion. The light turned green.

I was speechless. I wanted to ask him to write all this down for me. Material like this doesn't step into your life every day. He told me that the NEA's sole purpose was to destroy the minds of the youth of America, turn them against God, liberty, and make them tools of the Council.

I said, "Marvin, do you have many friends?"

"Friends are from the past," he said, "and I don't live in the past. I live in the here and now."

"You know, Marvin, I was a teacher, a card-carrying NEA member, and I never once got instructions to fry anyone's brain. I might have done it on my own, I admit."

He said, "Two plus two equals four." He looked at me. "That's what you teach. Well, what's *two*? How do you know two equals two?"

I took a left onto Everard Street.

"Tenth house up on the left," Marvin said.

Tenth, Marvin? I thought.

Mick and Keith went nuts when they saw their father. Each of them grabbed a leg and hugged it, and then they took turns being lifted for a kiss. Pauline looked on, warily, it seemed to me. Mick and Keith were willowy boys of six and seven, I guessed, with shoulder-length sandy hair, sallow skin, and bruised knees. They were dressed in their Jockey shorts. They wanted their dad to come look at their room. Sure, he said, but first he had a surprise. He pulled out the yo-yos, and the boys whooped. Pauline said, All right now, you know the rules. In bed by eight-thirty. She kissed them good-bye. Be good for your father, she said. And then they noticed the stranger standing by the fridge. Who's he? the younger one said. Pauline introduced me. I smiled, said hi. The older one said I had a dumb name. The younger one said, What happened to your teeth?

We went to see *Elvira Madigan* at the Paris. I hadn't seen it in about fifteen years. I had once cherished the tragic notion that you could pretend the world does not exist if you are in love. Was I wanting to feel that way again? Pia Degermark is beautiful, of course. I tried to imagine what she looked like now, almost thirty years later. More beautiful. But I'm afraid that the story didn't hold up all that well over the years, and I was disappointed. Whenever I could during the movie, I leaned toward Pauline so that our arms might brush each other, or our shoulders. I thought if I could gently press my cheek to hers, I would find bliss. I held her hand.

After the movie, we walked across the street to the Soho Pub. Pauline made a call home while I ordered a pint of Watneys for me and a sparkling water for her. "How's everything?" I said when she sat down.

"Under control," she said.

Pauline thought the movie was sad, their suicides and all, how they both had so much—each other—to live for. But any other ending would have been even sadder. She said, "I always wanted to live in a town where the railroad tracks came right down the main street. I must have read about it as a child or seen some show about a town like that."

"Did it have a name?"

"Vermilion."

Pauline told me about Vermilion. "Well, I have a cozy, white house. It's got a front porch and a gabled roof."

"And a white picket fence?"

"I don't see one," she said. "A catalpa in the front yard. I hang out the morning wash on the clothesline and listen to the wind snap the sheets. I put my baby in her Snugli, and we walk and walk, and I sing to her until she sleeps. At night I watch the moon rise over the town. In winter, the snow drifts against the house, and I have to stay in. Sometimes I walk to a coffee shop that faces the railroad. I go there to hear the dishes clatter in the kitchen."

We drove back to Everard Street. The house was quiet, and we tiptoed across the kitchen. Mick and Keith had fallen asleep on the floor of their room. Pauline put them in bed, tucked them in, closed the door. Marvin had fallen asleep in his wife's bed. Pauline and I sat on the couch in the living room. I drank one of Marvin's Budweisers. I asked Pauline what she thought about Marvin's politics of paranoia. She guessed he needed something to take the place of heroin. He's better off, she told me.

Marvin yelled from the bedroom. "Are you coming to bed, Pauline?"

Pauline looked at her watch, saw that it was nearly midnight. She said she really should get some sleep—work in the morning, day camp for the boys. At the door she kissed me, thanked me. I wanted to touch the small of her back, pull her toward me. I didn't dare. Friday night? I said. She nodded, smiled. She put her finger on my lips. Come by about nine. I'll have the kids in bed, she said.

When I got home, I told Spot the whole story. There was a message on the machine. Judi was checking in to say hi; everything's cool in Cleveland. Bye. No rejections in the mail, at least. I did get this small manila envelope, postmarked Dania, Florida 33004. My father had meant to write "Do not bend" on the envelope, but the "bend" came out "bond." Inside was a photograph of me holding up an ugly-as-sin fish. I'm about six or seven, and I'm standing on the wharf in Provincetown. It's me, all right, I can see that, this figure of shade and light, me staring into the camera, one eye squinted shut, and there's my father the photographer, his long shadow covering me like a blanket. I wondered now if I had been happy that morning. And if I could remember that moment, any bit of the holiday in Provincetown, would I be happy now? Would I even be the same Lafayette Proulx?

Before our second date, I was so tense with the anticipation of making love to Pauline that I nearly deep-fried my hand at work. I told Nicky what was going on. He said, I know that woman. She's a knockout, he said. I was so worked up I thought my nose was going to bleed. Nicky said he used to have a wicked bad crush on Pauline, as bad as the one he'd had on Princess Summerfallwinterspring. But look, he said, do you think you should be doing this?

I showed up at nine. The kids were awake, and they were irascible. I could see that they were trying to protect their mother and their futures from the fishy-smelling guy with the peculiar teeth. I sat on the couch in the living room, reading *Prevention* and listening to Pauline try to reason with her sons. One wanted to call Daddy. The other had a stomachache. One wasn't tired. The other wanted a story. Like that. I read about preventing kidney stones the natural way, about platelets, the little lifesavers that can kill you, about the anticancer vitamin combination. One of the boys began to cry.

In her bedroom, Pauline put the lights out and kept her T-shirt on. Our lovemaking was deliberate and intense. Pauline scratched, writhed, and cried quietly, never spoke. Were the tears about the children down the hall? We finished. I listened for footsteps. I thought I should get up, but I wanted my lips on her neck, my knee between her legs, my hand on her breast forever. We made love again. This wasn't fun for Pauline; this was serious. Her gravity flattered me, but I didn't understand it.

When I dressed to leave, Pauline thanked me and cried. I kissed her eyes. We walked to the back door. The sun bloodied the eastern sky. We heard a whine. One of the boys, his hair bed-tousled, stood in silhouette at the doorway to the kitchen, rubbing his eyes. He cried, said, Ma, I'm all wet. Pauline tapped my hand, turned to her son. I stepped out of his life for the moment and closed the door behind me.

I wanted to believe that if we decided to, Pauline and I could drive off together into the sunset, begin a new life in Vermilion. I wanted to believe that this would not disrupt or destroy anyone's life. That's what Pauline did to me. How can a body have so much power?

20.

Evidence of Things Unseen

On Monday afternoon at the airport, awaiting Judi's arrival from Cleveland via Newark, I held a pair of conflicting images in my head. The boy with the bed-tousled hair, crying, rubbing his eyes, smelling of urine, was one. The second was Pauline's breath on my cheek as we lay in bed, the breath delicate, warm, susurrus, that breath and the heady smell of her dampness, like milk and pears and must. And two emotions: fear and pleasure. And what is the image in this boy's mind as he stands there, shaken from his dreams, scared into incontinence? What does he see in that shadowy kitchen? My overcoat and leather shoe? The steely glint in my eyes? Have I marked my scent on the linoleum? Does he sniff dominance? Does he hear the jays' first squawks outside in the fir tree? And will he always hate those birds? And how does he name this perception? "Mother Leaving with Stranger"? or "Intruder Backs Away from Trouble"? or "I Don't Care; I'd Rather Die Than Ask Them for Help"? When I heard that the Continental flight from Newark was delayed, I went into the lounge, got a coffee, and sat at a table. I opened my notebook.

Theresa was dressing the kids in front of the television, getting them ready for the weekend trip. Dale was dropping Keynes off at his sister's house. She asks him could he change a fuse for her. She's such a klutz. The power's off in the bedrooms and bathroom. He does and kisses his sister Magda on the cheek, thanks her again for watching His Highness. Dale and Theresa were ready for the drive, but I wasn't.

Something was missing, I knew. I know that what's not in a story counts as much as what's in it. And I didn't know clearly enough what I was leaving out. So what I decided was that Dale and Theresa had been holding something back from each other and from me. Well, they could be cautious with each other, as lovers sometimes are, but before we took this trip, they'd each have to tell me one secret about themselves. And the secret would have to do with the first two notions that popped into my head. Dale's secret, then, would pertain to salacious behavior; Theresa's had to do with Peter's birth. At first I thought that maybe Dale kept skin magazines in his room and that Theresa blames herself for Peter's retardation because she smoked and drank alcohol during her pregnancy.

Ten years ago, it turns out, Dale dated a woman who was new to the faculty, fresh out of grad school up in Clovis. She taught ESL. During the course of their semester-long romance, Dale spanked her with a hairbrush during sex because she asked him to. She needed the pain to feel alive, she told him. What Dale is afraid of or ashamed of, or both, is that he enjoyed it. He was relieved when this woman took a job in Fort Collins.

Theresa's revelation was this—that her ex-husband was not Peter's father. She had been having an affair with an intern at the hospital. When her husband became so distraught over the child's condition, she could not bring herself to tell him the truth. She thought she was protecting him. And despite what she told Dale, she does know where Dan is— Odessa—and she would never ask him for child support. She still sees the intern on occasion. She never told him. He has a family practice in town. He's married. Theresa's seen the photos of his baby girl. I wasn't sure how, but I knew this information would make itself felt in Capitan or in Lincoln, and I knew as well it would not appear on the page.

I heard the announcement that Flight 3660 from Newark was arriving at Gate 2. I closed my book. Judi was frantic. She had twenty minutes to make her appointment with Dr. Stouder. She couldn't possibly cancel again. I told her just to drop me near downtown on her way. I told her I'd probably go to the library, and I'd meet her back home for supper.

Of course, I did not go to the library, but trucked right over to Mr. Natural's. Pauline stood behind the counter waiting on an elderly gentleman who wanted something for the constant ringing in his ears. Well, not a ringing, really, more like a buzzing. It's unbearable sometimes, he said. Pauline gave him zinc and chromium supplements and prescribed three ounces of beef a day, liver if he liked it, with sweet potatoes, carrots, or spinach. When the man left, I told Pauline we should get some lunch. She took off her apron, told someone in the office she'd be back in a half-hour.

We went to the common and sat on a bench and watched people. I bought a hot dog and a root beer from Harmonica Hansel's cart. We sat quietly while I ate. Pauline asked me did I want to know what this meal was doing to my body? I don't think so, honey. She took out a squeeze bottle of sunscreen and applied the lotion to her face and arms. She leaned back on the bench and closed her eyes. She smelled like coconut and bananas.

"The other night," I said. "When your boy saw us. Is that what's bothering you?"

She looked at me, squinted. "I'm just letting myself get angry at you," she said. "No reason." She held my hand and then let go. "That way it's easier for me to tell you what I have to tell you. Marvin and I are getting back together." She said she had to be heading back to work. I walked with her.

"Don't go back with Marvin just to get rid of me," I said.

"You flatter yourself," she said.

"Do you love him?"

"My feelings for Marvin are none of your business."

"You know that crazy son of a bitch is going to end up calling in radio talk shows every night, warning Americans of the dangers of fluoride in the water."

She said, "Marvin and I have a history. I'm not even myself without him. I'm just that single mother, you know, who works at the health-food store. That's how you see me. But that's not who I am." Pauline made a fist and put it to her mouth. "Maybe I resent it."

Pauline cried. She let me wipe her eyes, kiss her forehead. She stepped back, took a breath. "I can't be Marvin's friend," she said. "I can only be his wife. I owe it to the family to try this."

We stood there on Elm Street in front of the copy shop. Pauline said, "It seems exciting to reinvent yourself, to become new again for someone else. But in the end it's just hard work." She kissed my cheek, and left me there staring at my reflection in the copy-shop window.

I looked at myself, a wrinkled fish-fryer with crazy hair, pale skin, baggy eyes, a tumor the size of an egg on my wrist, and an incandescent tooth. "You're a glorious piece of work," I said. I walked across the street to the Valhalla, sat at the bar, ordered a pint of Bass, and took out my memo pad. I found the name and phone number. I called Terry Cundall and set up an appointment for Martha and me. I called Martha's machine, left her a message with the time and date, told her I had a lead on a mobile home out in Millbury.

When I got back to Judi's, I thought it was odd that all the lights were off in the house. Judi was lying on the bed, her eyes closed. Are you okay? I said. When she didn't answer, I thought she must be sleeping. I took off my shoes and lay on the bed. I looked up at the two of us in the mirrored ceiling. I said, Judi, I called Terry Cundall and made that appointment. She opened her eyes. "Dr. Stouder said she felt something on my ovary."

21.

A Palpable Mass

I GOT UP AND WENT TO THE KITCHEN. JUDI SAT AT THE TABLE, DRESSED FOR work, drinking coffee and smoking a cigarette. I sat down across from her. Her eyes were red, glazed, and fixed on some wrinkle in the tablecloth. No, she said, she hadn't been crying. Didn't get much sleep. I nodded, looked at the clock, at the sink, at the floor. Was she waiting for me to say something? I got up and poured myself a cup of coffee. I sat, stirred in the cream and sugar.

Judi told me her dream. She's in her office, listening to a client, a woman from Oxford, tell her about the ex-boyfriend who is stalking her, making obscene and threatening phone calls. The client is certain that this boyfriend is going to kill her, and she is panicked. Judi sits behind her desk ("which I never do"), leaning back in her chair, knitting her brow, and she realizes she is naked. The client, though, is so distraught that she hasn't noticed, hasn't even looked up. Judi can feel a tremor inside, and soon she feels her guts losing their hold, settling, sliding toward the seat, and then all this slimy internal business oozes out her vagina and plops to the floor. She tries not to seem alarmed. She doesn't want to spook the client. Judi said to me, I looked down and saw it was all gray and red and slick, and my only thought is, I've been a sausage all my life. And there's the meat, in a pile between my feet, and it's throbbing, steaming, turning blue. And my client is screaming at me to give her some answers. She says, How do I keep this maniac from killing me? Judi looked at me. She said, Cancer is as blue as iodine.

Judi told me that Dr. Stouder had identified an adnexal mass, had a CA 125 blood test and an ultrasound performed, and wanted to go over the results and stuff today in her office. I said I was going with her. She didn't want me to. I didn't care what she wanted. What time is the appointment? Noon. I'll meet you outside your office at eleven-thirty. I said, You shouldn't get all worked up over what is probably nothing. I said that, knowing that in her place I would be hysterical by now. I'd be breaking glass, punching walls, drinking the good stuff. Like when the doctor told me my wrist-egg might be Hodgkin's, and I had to wait the weekend for the results. Are you really sure you want to go to work, Judi? She picked her keyes out of her purse. I've got a session at nine. I looked at her. She said, Don't worry, I won't sit behind the desk.

I called my father. Sometimes he couldn't remember things. Your mother told me that we went to Publix today and to the cardiologist's. I told him I couldn't remember things either. Yeah, he said, but with you it's your—what-do-you-call-it?—your concentration. With me it's the brain damage from the stroke. What stroke? Why didn't you tell me about a stroke? I did tell you. No, you didn't. He said, Did you come to your senses yet? What about? You and Martha, he said. Did you get your ass back home yet? In my day, he said, a man kept his affairs discrete, kept them out of the home. I didn't want to hear what he may or may not have done. I said, Say hi to Mom for me.

Peter and Caitlin (I thought I'd stick with that name) were upset that Smokey the Bear was dead. They were bored by the gardens in the park and by the museum displays. They liked the gift shop. They both got little plastic Smokeys they could talk to. The little Smokeys were in a fight immediately, and Theresa had to threaten to return the toys if the kids didn't behave. The four of them walked across the street to a junk store. Dale noticed how always one of the two kids held on to Theresa's hand while the other got between their mother and him. The old man in the store showed the kids fossilized dinosaur dung and fed everyone from a bowl of piñon nuts.

Dale drove Theresa's car, followed the Rio Bonito east on 380 to Lincoln. They checked into the Wortley Hotel. From the front porch, you could see the whole town, a single street wide. Dale said out loud, I'm standing in the exact spot where Billy the Kid gunned down Sheriff Pat Brady. Theresa took the kids upstairs to their room for a nap before supper. Dale walked to the Historical Center and then from one end of Lincoln to the other. He felt apart, untethered, and yet bound by the emptiness of the valley. He wanted to hurry the day, have supper done with, the kids scrubbed and tucked into their beds, asleep in their room. He wanted to be in bed with Theresa, holding on to her. This weekend had been his idea, but he was unhappy. And he knew he had no control over his happiness in this place where he didn't belong.

At the table in the hotel's restaurant, Dale tries to make Peter laugh. He puts a spoon on his nose and lets it dangle there. Peter decides this is frightening and cries. Theresa hugs him and kisses his head, rocks him in her arms. Now Peter won't look at Dale. This is the first time in his life that Dale has made a child cry.

Theresa asks Dale to pass her a napkin. She wipes Peter's eyes. Whom does this anger belong to? Dale wonders. He remembers when he cried as a boy his mother would tell him to shut up or she'd give him a reason to cry. He cried when he had to go to bed, when some miserable lizard he kept in a popcorn box died, when he couldn't do a multiplication problem. He cried when he scraped a knee or had to eat every bit of his supper.

The kids order cheeseburgers and Cokes. Theresa and Dale order the trout. Now it's Caitlin who's pouting. She's kicking her legs under the table, shaking it, kicking Dale's chair. Peter drinks his Coke in a second and wants more. Dale's stomach is churning. He doesn't know how he'll eat under these circumstances. Caitlin kicks his leg. Theresa tells her to sit up straight, please. In doing so, Caitlin spills her Coke. Dale is about to stand up and leave—it's that or scream at this little shit, tell her to sit still like a human being—when he sees a gentleman a couple of tables over watching him. Theresa picks up the ice from the tablecloth and puts it back in Caitlin's glass. She tells Dale he could help. Dale sops up the Coke with her napkin, gets the attention of the waitress.

When they're settled again, Theresa apologizes for snapping at Dale. Dale says, We're all a little tense. Caitlin says there's nothing to do here. Dale smiles and says, How about we all get ice cream after supper? There's an ice cream store across the street. The kids love the idea, except Peter wants it now. Theresa tries to explain that first we eat our burgers and then we eat our ice cream. Caitlin says, My father is a cowboy and he has a white horse and a blue shirt and the horse's name is Andrew, and I can ride it when my father comes to see me. The man at the other table is still watching them. He's smoking a cigarette now. He seems amused. He nods to Dale when Dale catches his eye. Dale offers a smile and a long-suffering shrug. Theresa's trout is cold by the time she can touch it. She's feeding Peter one French fry at a time. Caitlin takes a bite of her burger and announces she's finished. Dale wants to say, If you don't eat your meal, no dessert. If I was their father, he thinks, they wouldn't get away with this crap. Theresa looks at Dale, raises her eyebrows, says, Maybe this was a bad idea. Dale says, Yes, perhaps it was.

In Dr. Stouder's office, I wanted to hold Judi's hand, but I thought that might make things worse, might make her feel more vulnerable, or it might suggest that I was frightened or something. So we sat like I suppose defendants sit in court waiting to hear the jury's verdict. You can't sit still, and yet you can't exactly move. Dr. Stouder said, We have reason to be optimistic, and I looked at Judi. She hadn't changed expression. Dr. Stouder explained that the pelvic mass was not clinically suspicious. It was mobile, mostly cystic, she thought, unilateral, and of regular contour. This doesn't mean we're out of the woods, she said. But the prognosis is hopeful. I didn't like that word *hopeful*. I didn't know why.

Dr. Stouder flipped through some pages in Judi's file. She said, The blood test was inconclusive. They often are. The ultrasound revealed the mass to be six centimeters. The size works in our favor. Dr. Stouder's inclination was to start Judi on a regimen of hormonal suppression. I made a mental note of that phrase. Taking out my memo pad would seem like bad form, even to me. A regimen of hormonal suppression. Sounded like junior high school. That would simply mean taking oral contraceptives for a couple of months. What we'll do, Dr. Stouder said, is suppress and observe. My guess is that the mass will begin to regress. If it doesn't—and we'll do regular pelvic exams and ultrasound—if it doesn't, then we'll have to consider surgery. Dr. Stouder had already consulted a surgeon and an oncologist, just to be safe, to get them on board, she said.

In the car, Judi said, The only thing worse than having cancer is having it again. You've had it before? I said. Jesus. She said she'd died of it before. I wanted to tell her to stop talking like that. This is the real world, Judi. But I didn't. I said, You don't know you've got cancer. Weren't you listening to Dr. Stouder? If you worry, the stress is only going to make matters worse. We were quiet. I asked Judi how she was feeling. Like stone, she said.

22.

The End Was Still Far, Far Off, and the Hardest and Most Complicated Part Was Only Just Beginning

WHY WAS I SO PISSED WHEN I GOT THE ANNULMENT QUESTIONNAIRE IN THE mail? Wasn't this, after all, the consummation I so devoutly wished for—the end of that married part of my life, the death of Husband Proulx, the repudiation of Teacher Proulx, the disavowal of Sterling Citizen Proulx? Was I upset, then, that Martha had usurped the privilege of making the final decision regarding our marital status while I was off pissing away my time across town? Was I angry at Martha's attempt to void the last dozen years? Or was I angry that Ms. Voice Mail wouldn't respond to my calls, but she could send me this, and just when I make the initial overture at reconciliation? You can see how completely deluded I was. Forget it, I'm not calling her this time. So I walked downtown and went to Martha's office in the Chancery, just as if I had the right to be offended and surprised. I didn't even knock, didn't so much as nod at the receptionist in the outer office. Martha told whomever she was talking to that she'd get back to him or her.

I said, "What the hell is this, Martha?" I held up the questionnaire.

"I think you can read."

"What are you trying to do here? Are you trying to pretend the last twelve years didn't happen? Are you trying to obliterate the past?"

While Martha answered the phone, I took the seat across from her at her desk. She used to keep a photo of the two of us on the desk. We were on the Casco Bay ferry and our hair was blowing across our faces. The photo was gone. She hung up.

"Didn't you get my message?"

"About the marriage counseling? Yes, I did."

"And . . . ?"

"That's my answer in your hand."

Well, that shut me up. She told me she had a job to do, and, more than that, a life to live. I said, "You think I don't?" I couldn't believe the way this was ending. I looked at the papers, at Martha. I said, "This isn't the way a marriage ends."

"It seems to me it ended a while ago, Laf."

"So you don't want to work on this?"

"I will not be your cliché, Laf."

"Fine," I said. "If that's the way you want it. I'll fill out your questionnaire." I stood and walked to the door. I imagined little priestly ears listening at the other side. "Good-bye."

Martha said, "So this is it?" She grinned. "This is all you care about our marriage, is it? You're just going to walk away from . . . everything?" Martha stood at her desk. She put her hands on her hips. "Is that it?" She began to cry.

I held up my walking papers. I shook them. "I'm sick of your fucking games, Martha." I was very close to reaching that delirious point where I start slamming things—a lamp into a wall, my face into a window, my body into a bookcase—when all the words I've ever learned melt down, and I release some bloody scream. I shut the door quietly behind me and ignored the two nuns sitting in the anteroom awaiting their audience with His Excellency, heads buried in *National Geographic,* and thinking, no doubt, that long ago they'd made the right choice in fleeing to the convent.

I went to Moynihan's, bought a beer, took a booth near the window for light, and took out the annulment questionnaire and a pen. Five pages of questions. I began.

Q. *Is there a history of mental illness in your family?*

A. Ample history, indeed, and all of it documented in the two-volume study by Eunice Travers, *Examples of Mental Aberration in the Devolution of a Franco-American Family: A Study in Depravity* (University of Lowell Press, 1989). A more recent example, not included in the book, is a letter my cousin Louie wrote to the Ford Foundation, and which was published in its 1992 annual report:

Dear Sirs and Madams,

I'm not writing to you just on account of you have money to help me out. I'm writing cause God has chosen you to help me out. One night, I made a plucky and selfish prayer. I told God I would discover a live dinosaur, either that or the bones of Pope Joan. For this, God's end of the bargain was he'd force my ex-wife, Baby Jane Proulx, to let me see my kids, Victor, Henri, Little Louie, and Arlene. Well, guess what? Jesus showed me an honest-to-goodness real live young triceratops in answer to my prayer. I have left the dinosaur alone for seven years, thinking it was better off in the wild. But then, you know what? Jesus returned to my dream and told me the dinosaur needed to be discovered, and I must hurry before greedy men (unlike yourselves) find her.

Here's where you come in. I'll need scuba equipment (and diving lessons) and caving gear and a submersible video camera with light collecting lenses of reputable brand (in other words, no knock-offs). And two hundred feet of braided nylon rope. I have priced all the stuff and it runs to like $15,000. Petty cash for you dudes. I'll also need a plane ticket, but I can't tell you to whereto. It will all be written up in my final report.

Now, I could have asked for money for an apartment as I am one of the million of homeless in this country or to see a dentist before my staph infection kills me, but I asked for this instead. Where to mail my check, you might ask. To: Father Peter Barrett, St. Pelagia's Mission, 12 Elm St., Leominster, Mass. 01453. He will hold it for me.

Respectively Yours,
Louis A. Proulx

Q. *What was your mother and father's relationship and how did it affect you?*
A. They were husband and wife. It made me their son.

Q. *Describe the relationship with your former spouse.*
A. If you refer to the plaintiff in this case, the former Martha Williams, I would say that we're not getting along that well.

Q. *What were the main features that attracted you to your former spouse?*
A. Her mind and her breasts.

Q. *How long did you date?*
A. Often till three in the morning.

And so on for eighty-six questions. I could see that question 47 and some of those in the fifties, having to do with procreation, might prove embarrassing to Martha with her boss since we had no kids, and she had been taking precautions. I appended a P.S. to the questionnaire: "Is it true that all shepherds fleece their sheep?" and mailed it off to the Diocesan Council on Matrimony, just like the cleverest of asses.

23

Martha Marie Williams Proulx

A. "A MYSTERY"

Judi once showed my story "All's Hell That Ends Well" to a therapist friend of hers. The story was about a withering marriage. The narrator's wife's name was Marsha Mary Roberts. Judi mentioned Martha's name to her friend, Robert Wigdor. Dr. Wigdor read the story and told Judi that I had raised passive-aggression to a whole new level. I was a retribution artist, he said.

I fell in love with Martha because she was graceful and polite, enthusiastic and kind. She was beautiful, clever, and curious. I'd never met anyone like her. I couldn't believe she'd noticed me, never mind liked me. I loved the way she hopped a bit when she walked, the way she looked at me out of the corner of her eye. I even admired her naïve fidelity to Catholicism, the way she dismissed the hypocrisy and repression as tangential to faith. And I loved her for what I couldn't understand about her. Love searches for the mystery in the beloved, seeks the unknowable. I couldn't feel the attraction to what was hidden in her anymore, and I didn't know why.

B. "MARTHA AND THE CATHOLIC CHURCH"

Martha is the woman in charge of a man's world. As Bishop Hago Harrigan's factotum, she runs the day-to-day operation of the Diocese of Worcester. She handles all personnel matters, and there are many. She sees to it that the alcoholic priests get assigned to the quiet, rural parishes out in Orange and Royalston, where the bingos run themselves and there's not a whole lot of driving to do. The politically ambitious or connected curates get the city's west side parishes, where they can wheedle money out of the professionals. Martha has to be familiar with the personalities of all two hundred or so priests so that when she makes parish assignments, she doesn't sentence one of the aunties to rectory life with a couple of jocks, let's say. And that way she avoids the aggravation of phone calls complaining about Father So-and-so and how he smokes cigars in the TV room—It sinks of the pig farm in there, Mrs. Proulx—and how he hides the remote control, and how his chasuble looks like a tablecloth.

Martha oversees all public relations, youth programs, fund-raising, charity, and education. While Hago visits the Holy Land or the Old Sod, she's in charge. Hago spends his weekends golfing with politicians and undertakers down at Pleasant Valley or at his family's compound in Brewster, and he can relax. So that's one side, the practical side, of Martha's faith. There's another.

When she was thirteen, Martha made a usual daily visit to St. Stephen's Church after school. She knelt in the front pew to pray the rosary. She had it down to four minutes. She saw the statue of the Virgin move. Mary lifted her damp eyes upward toward the frescoed apse, raised her plaster arms in supplication. When Martha told Father Holland what had happened, he told her not to tell anyone else what she had seen, especially any of the nuns. That's all we need. Just keep it between you and the Blessed Mother. Ever since that day, Martha's been a believer in Marian apparitions and miracles and all the rest. She's devoted to the blood, she likes to say. She subscribes, in my name, to a kind of underground tabloid, a Catholic *Enquirer*, if you will, called *The Seven Thunders*, which regularly features photos of apparitions and stories of miracles in everyday life and so on. I remember reading the story of one woman who lived in Westerly, Rhode Island, whose flesh got so hot when she prayed that her clothes would catch fire, so she prayed naked, kneeling on the tile floor of her kitchen. Plenty of stories of flagellants and self-mutilators.

Martha wasn't a disciple of all this neo–Dark Ages stuff exactly, but she was fascinated by it, by women who rub pepper into their faces to prevent vanity, scrub their hands and legs with steel wool, and then rub lime juice into the wounds. Martha thought it was just possible that anorexia was a gift from Jesus, a sign of holiness. One night while we were eating supper, Martha told me about this woman she had visited in Charlton. People in her rooming house wanted the woman, Cecile Blondin, canonized. Cecile was about thirty-five, Martha guessed, lived alone, and kept a dummy of a corpse in her room in a casket. A store mannequin, really. On Fridays, she took out the dummy and lay in the coffin herself. She wore a haircloth blouse and a crown of thorns fashioned from braided rose stems, sometimes draped her limbs in chains, ate a single piece of dry rye bread every day, drank only tap water. I laughed. This is a joke, right? Martha said, Cecile sleeps on the floor, on a bed of uncooked rice. I said, Did you call the hospital, at least? Martha said, Why? I said, This is a sick woman. I think she's blessed, Martha said.

I'd like to think that Martha longed to achieve the fervor in her faith that her zealots seemed to have. But how would that play with Hago Harrigan the Sane? She didn't talk about her faith that much, at least not with me, the lapsed Catholic and apostate whom she prayed for at night. We'd only fight about it. Sometimes I hated that freaking church. Could have been the Silverado Bank for all the time it stole from me.

C. "DOMESTICITY"

Martha would deny this, I'm sure, but she is obsessed with housework. She has three vacuum cleaners: an Electrolux family heirloom that she stores in the front hall and uses on the living room and dining room carpets. She keeps the Hoover upright in the bedroom closet and uses it on the hardwood floors and the kitchen linoleum. The Shop-Vac in the shed is for the big spills. She's got a little portable Dirt Devil, too. I threatened to get her a holster for it. She never laughs at housekeeping jokes. At parties she was right there with her Devil, sucking up crumbs around the guests' feet, or she was snatching up their cocktail glasses as soon as drinkers set them down on the coasters. She didn't understand that this behavior made our guests ill-at-ease. Or she understood it, sympathized, but could do nothing to control herself. All our parties ended around ten-thirty with me at the door saying, *Good-night, glad you could make it, we'll do it again soon, safe home,* and Martha fastened to a roaring canister back in the apartment. I'd say, Martha, now? And she'd say, Unless you're planning to do it in the morning. When I told her she would have "No Dust Bunnies Under This Coffin" carved on her headstone, she said I was raised like a pig, so how could I expect to know what a clean house was. I'd say, I don't want to eat off the floor, Martha. If I'm going to clean the floor, I'll clean it to my standards, not yours. She'd say, That is just your typically male way of shirking housework. I hated being called typically anything.

Martha loved paper products. We used paper towels and paper napkins and paper plates and paper cups and paper trash-can liners and paper placemats and paper doilies under our canisters and fruit bowls. We had boxes of tissues opened in very room. Martha thought the whole idea of handkerchiefs was nauseating. Martha used the same cleaning products her grandmother had used and was fiercely loyal to the brands. She used Ivory Soap for clothes—but only because you couldn't get Rinso Blue anymore—Dutch Cleanser, Octagon all-purpose soap, Red Cap Refresh-R, Brasso on the hardware and Never Dull on the dinnerware, Glass Wax on the windows, a sudsy ammonia for the mirrors, and liquid Joy for the dishes. She washed and ironed our cloth cleaning rags and bought only real sponges, which she trimmed with scissors once a week.

D. "THE GRAND PASSION"

Martha didn't read trash. Her favorite novel, one she read each January, was *Anna Karenina*. Anna followed her heart. Martha was a devotee of the grand passion, the sensual rapture so overwhelming that it sweeps all reason away. There is no fighting the heart. Martha, I believe, desired to live that intensified, unrestrained, tortured life in the same way that she craved the passionate spiritual life. It was clear, however, that she did not wish the same life on me. She talked almost obsessively about unfaithful husbands.

I speculated that to succumb to her passion as Anna had would have been a loss of control that Martha could not tolerate or confront, the surrender to fate, to faith, to love. Our own courtship was theatrical, but reserved. Perhaps she was simply better able than I to make a clear distinction between literature and life, between the spiritual and the histrionic. I do wonder why she would not want for herself what she admired in others. But maybe it's normal to feel that way.

E. "METEOROLOGY"

Martha takes the weather personally. It's too hot for her, or it's too cold or too damp, too cloudy, dry, or bright. She's never dressed appropriately, it seems. Her comfort zone is so minuscule as to be nonexistent. She'll wear a sweater inside the apartment until it's eighty degrees and then immediately close down the windows and doors and switch on the air conditioner, lie on the couch, and lament the insufferable heat. How does one learn to take offense at the weather?

Her entire family was like that, was unable to adjust and enjoy the natural environment. Her parents and her cousin Blondell, who lived with her family while Martha was growing up, all jacked up the heat in winter and wore their knit caps, crocheted slippers, and chenille robes over their sweaters. In winter, it was so dry in their house, you could barely open your eyes. The four of them were forever squirting Nivea cream on their skin, massaging Vaseline on their lips. Then, in the summer, they cranked up the AC and sat in their swimsuits like puddles, mouths open, barely able to whine complaints.

Throughout our marriage, Martha and I fought about the windows. I wanted them open, especially the bedroom windows at night. But Martha thought the draft would cause stiff necks, or it might rain. In the summer she was too sweaty and rashed to be touched. In the winter, my hands and feet were too cold for her. I hope she doesn't find herself dating an outdoorsman. Then again, maybe it was life with me that brought all this on. Or maybe I just like to think she'd be better off without me.

24.

$$2 \text{ Cool}$$
$$\underline{+2 \text{ Be}}$$
$$4 \text{ Gotten}$$

WHAT I SHOULD HAVE KNOWN—IT'S SO OBVIOUS—BUT DIDN'T, AND HAD TO learn from Francis X., was this: that the experience with the most profound impact on a child's life is the unlived life of the parent. But I'm not sure Francis X. understood his own lesson; otherwise, wouldn't he have done something about it?

Our classroom was Moynihan's on a Wednesday night. Francis X. and I had finally managed to get together. I wondered where he told Sandy he was going. I could see early on that Francis X. was on a mission—to talk some sense into me. He held his beer bottle with both hands, only sipped at the Bushmills. My job, then, was to see that he drank enough to forget why he was here and to have some fun—loosen his golden tongue.

"You seem tense, Francis X.," I said.

He denied it, looked up at the Sox game on the TV at the end of the bar. He asked me why I was throwing my life away. His eyes never left the screen. Clemens struck someone out. I said, "Francis X., I'm not a tenth-grader, and I don't need a lecture right now." I ordered another round. Now Francis X. had two shots of whiskey in front of him. He told me that Martha was dating Marty O'Sullivan, who, it turns out, has always been interested in her. Marty taught with us at South. Science.

I said, "Isn't he married?"

Francis X. nodded. "Three boys."

Great, I thought, now I'm responsible for five more miserable lives. "Does his wife know?"

He raised his shoulders, turned his hands palms up. "Well," he said, "I don't know if you'd say they were seeing each other exactly. Let's just say O'Sullivan's been very solicitous, you know what I mean? Always asking Martha if she needs anything. Tuned up her car. Things like that."

"How do you know this?" I said.

"She talks to Sandy."

I said, "Maybe Marty's just being kind."

He said, "Marty?" and laughed.

We weren't having fun yet.

I held up my shot glass. "To your kids," I said. He'd have to drink to that. He did. He bought me another shot. "To Ireland," I said. "One island. One country. Two more shots, John Joe," I said.

I said, "Don't you want to do something spectacular with your life, Francis X.?"

He gave me a look like didn't I think six kids was spectacular.

"You know what I mean. Have you done everything you wanted?"

He said, "I'm a success."

"You're a vice-principal of a public high school."

"And you're a fish-fryer." Francis X. swiveled on his stool so that he faced me. He leaned his left elbow on the bar, struck his chest with his right fist like he was saying the *Confiteor*. "I have a beautiful family, Laf, six wonderful kids." He tossed back his shot. Pretty soon we'd be talking about his mother. "I got security." He tapped his forehead. "Peace of mind." I held up two fingers to John Joe. "I got a home on Beechmont Street. Swell neighborhood. I got a cottage down the Cape." Francis X. paused for effect. "What do you have to show for yourself, Laf?"

I had to admit this was a disconcerting question. We were talking a whole other level of possessions here. Forget peace of mind, too. "A dog."

"You still got that crazy setter?"

"Spot."

"What else you got?"

"I got a good friend sitting beside me."

Francis X. told me to cut the bullshit and get serious. But he smiled. We drank to our friendship.

I said, "One time you told me all you ever wanted to do was move to Maine, get a farm, live off the land. Whatever happened to that?"

"Why don't you grow up, Laf? You're acting like a spoiled child. Your wife's in pain. Go to her. Don't throw your life away."

"I guess you didn't want it bad enough."

We were quiet then. Drank our shots and watched the Dread Sox get shelled by the Indians in the fifth. I said, "You have a home on the Cape and you're in Worcester for the summer?"

"We rent it out except for the last two weeks in August. A gold mine."

I ordered two more shots.

Francis X. said, "Around 1980 I had a chance to buy three hundred fifty acres in Hancock County. Had an old farmhouse, a barn . . . I don't know, some other shit. Near Ellsworth." My friend took a drink and excused himself. He went to the men's room. At the end of the bar under the TV, John Joe was arguing with some older guy about the Sox. The guy wanted the manager fired tomorrow. John Joe wanted the whole team executed in Copley Square.

Francis X. picked up where he'd left off. "Sandy said no way in hell was she living there, raising her kids with the Frenchies in some goddamn bog. No offense, Laf."

I shrugged.

"She thinks your people fuck their children."

"Not as much as we used to."

"So, what was I supposed to do?" Francis X. looked at himself in the mirror behind the bar. "Kids would have had a quality life up there. Fiona, anyway, wouldn't have a goddamn ring in her nose," he said.

We talked about his kids for a while—the eldest with the nose ring and the grunge records; the son who back talks his mother; the boy with strabismus; Kevin, who rides the bench for his Little League team; Timothy, whose life is dinosaurs; and, of course, Eamon, who forgets what he's doing when he walks into a room. Francis X. told me about his dreams for all of them—college, marriage, homes nearby, successful careers, tranquillity, and children. Fiona wants to start a rock 'n' roll band. FX wants to be a doctor, but he can't even pass science. The others are too young, God bless them. How would the kids live their own dreams if their old man hadn't lived his? How do you learn to do that?

When my father came back from Korea, he had one thing in mind—to play professional basketball. He was the best around and had all the clippings to prove it. He took a job at the South Works wire mill and kept playing ball four or five nights a week in parks and industrial leagues. This was all before Edgar and I came along, before he even married Eudine Pelletier. Well, the Celtics called and offered him a tryout. At last, he'd get to play with Cousy and Sharman. He'd have his shot at the bigs. So he showed up at the Garden drunk on his ass. I didn't hear this from him but from a couple of his pals at my wedding. They thought it was a hoot. None of the players would even talk to him. Right after that, he married your old lady, the friends told me.

Francis X. had set us up again. We drank. His mother was a saint, he said. If she hadn't met up with Herc, she could have been a fucking diva, he said. She had a splendid voice, lovely voice. Sang like an angel. You ought to come down the Cape this year, he said. You know where Pocasset is, right? I said, Yeah, I'm sure Sandy would love that. Francis X. became animated. Fuck her, he said. It's my fucking house. I built it with my own frigging hands. If I can't have my friends in my own house . . . Jesus . . . what can I have? Am I right?

And so we got plastered along with the Sox, and soon it was time to leave. I told Francis X. I didn't want him to drive. He was drunk, and I loved him. I gave him a hug out on the sidewalk. I've driven in worse condition than this, he told me. But now you're vice-principal, and you have a, you know, lot to lose. He said, Get in. I'll drive you home. No, not home. Wherever. I said, No way, Francis X. Give me your keys. He shook his head, took a deep breath, made a face like he'd tasted something sour. This was a bad sign. I leaned him up against his Voyager. I told him to wait there a minute. I put my hands on his shoulders, looked him in the eyes. Promise? I said. He nodded. I went back into the bar and had John Joe fix me up two black coffees to go. When I went back outside, Francis X. and his Voyager were gone.

The next morning, when I finally woke up, I checked the *Telegram & Gazette*. Nothing about a minivan wrapped around a light pole. I considered calling the Harvey home, but I imagined things were a little tense for Francis X. already. I could relate. How many times had Martha sobbed and locked herself in the bedroom when I had too much to drink?

I took a shower. I drank coffee and let Dale reminisce about his old man, Les Evans. Dale's at home on Monday night. Just he and Keynes. He's got Bob Wills on the stereo, and he's trying to think of himself as a father to two children. Stepfather, anyway.

Dale remembers his dad coming home from work. He'd park the cruiser in the driveway, peel off his uniform, park himself in front of the tube, and send Dale off to fetch him a beer from the fridge. Most nights he wouldn't even join Dale, his sister, and his mom for supper in the kitchen. The only time they were together as a family was Sunday morning at Mass. When Les died, Dale was ten. Les, himself, only thirty-seven. Dale's age now. Died of a massive cerebral hemorrhage while watching *The Man from U.N.C.L.E.* And that's when Dale found out who his father really was.

Before Les married Dale's mom and they moved out here to Lovington to raise a family, Les Evans had been a nightclub singer in New Jersey, where he'd grown up and where he served on the Newark police force. Dale's mom brought down all the old photo albums and scrapbooks from the attic. There was a poster of Les opening for Frank Fontaine at a club in the Poconos. One newspaper feature called him "Les Evans, the cop with a beat," and said he was the next Sinatra. He was even a local celebrity when he was still in high school. He had his own weekly radio show on a New Milford station.

Dale wonders what the hell went wrong. He never heard his father sing in his life. They never even had a record player in the house. Dale scratches Keynes behind his ears. Keynes lies on Dale's chest and licks his other hand. He does remember when he was in high school himself. He was nothing like a star at all. He was closer to being a mirage. He even felt like an impostor at the graduation party out the highway and down at the pump jacks. He kind of sat on a rock by himself and watched his classmates drink Lone Star and make out. He had had a crush on Elisa Martin since eighth grade, and that night, for the first time, she talked to him. She sat down in the dirt beside him, wiggled his foot, said, Why you being an old mope, Dale Evans?

They talked, and he even tried to drink some of her beer, and she asked him what he was going to do now that it was all over. He said, You really want to know? Yes. He told her that what he wanted to do eventually was to get involved in politics, maybe start out running for office in Lea County and then on to the statehouse, if I'm lucky, and then who knows. She said, Maybe you'll be the President. I think you could do that. Dale blushed. She said, You're not like the others. She looked over at the revelers. Cowboys and roustabouts, she said. He asked her if she'd sign his yearbook. She said, Sure. He ran to his truck and got it. She opened to her picture, made a face, said, I look like a dork. She wrote that Dale was too cool to be forgotten like it was an addition problem. She signed it "Elisa M." and put a heart over the i. She kissed him on the cheek. He asked her what her plans were. She said, You haven't noticed?

What? he said. Elisa stood and pulled down the hem of her T-shirt so that the jersey clung to her body. She took his hand and placed it on her belly. She smiled. I'm going to be a mommy. She gave him back his hand, said she was moving to Las Cruces next week.

Dale thinks how could he have been so stupid—a politician who doesn't speak to people. He thought about Elisa Whatever-her-name-might-be-now, as he had so often over the years. The phone rang. Judi's. Stoni told the answering machine that her Richie Honeybun was sprung from the slammer. She was just too happy. I'll talk to you guys later, she said. Maybe we can all go for a drink.

25.

Dog Days

WHEN THE WEATHER THAT FIRST WEEK OF AUGUST TURNED SWELTRY, DAMP, AND stifling, Judi and Stoni cut themselves a deal. If Stoni would give up pharmaceuticals, then Judi would quit smoking. Judi was now down to two or three cigarettes a day. Stoni was down to just a few over-the-counter substitutes: Percogesic, Afrin, Benzedrex inhalers, NyQuil for sleeping. Judi became flamboyantly annoyed with her sacrifice. I tried to stay out of her way and warned Spot to do the same. Of course, with the oppressive heat and the grim humidity, Spot could barely manage to lie in his scooped-out bed of dirt under the deck and pant. Judi explained to me that the two best cigarettes of her day, the most tempting and delicious, were the one after a big meal and the one after sex. Therefore, until she felt more in control of her habit ("It's not an addiction"), she would have to forego the near occasions to sin. She was also at the doctor's office nearly every other day for one test or another, for consultation, for reassurance. Meanwhile, Mr. Lesperence seemed to have left on vacation. Newspapers littered his front stoop. I gathered them up and fed them to Spot. He did his best to nibble at them. Judi told me that Mr. Lesperence had a son, a Realtor, who lived on a lake in New Hampshire. Mr. Lesperence was likely there fishing as he does every summer.

Trixie cleaned the trailer from stem to stern, she told me. Had it fumigated. Even hosed down the outside, flushed the sewage system, aired out the foam mattresses, and put down new contact paper on the kitchen counter. It looks so festive, she said. Richie Muneyhun had, indeed, moved into the trailer. He'd been out of jail two weeks already and hadn't been arrested yet. Trixie called him a changed man. She reminded me how much good prison had done for Charles Colson. Buckets of good. Same thing with our Richie, she said. And you should catch Stoni now—such a lady she's become. Like Princess What's-her-face. I hear wedding bells, she said. I said, Planet Earth to Trixie Dubey. Come in, Trixie. She slapped my shoulder, told me to peddle my cynicism elsewhere, thank you. Hervey had a different take on Richie. He told me Richie'd been mouthing off about cleaning Arthur Bositis's clock. What he said, actually, was he was going to adjust Arthur's *cojónes* with a strap wrench, put his opened mouth on the edge of a curbstone, and kick in the back of his head.

My father was recovering fairly well considering, though he did have his setbacks—fluid in his lungs, a slight stroke or two, albumin draining to his legs and feet so that they swelled up like melons. He'd spend a day or two at a time in the hospital getting medicated, X-rayed, needled, probed, and whatever else.

While this was going on, my pal Nicky took two weeks' vacation and rode the Amtrak out to Los Angeles so he could appear on *Jeopardy!* And me, whenever I could, I collapsed on the sofa near the window fan and read. When I wasn't doing that, I was lying to people. I had come to the conclusion that lying was the best way to handle some things. Take my father, for instance. When he asked me about the old days, I told him my childhood was sensational. What would be the point of telling him anything else? I can live with the lie easier than I could live with the pain that my truth would have caused him. I lied to Martha. I apologized about the annulment questionnaire, said it just proved how serious I was about the possibility of reconciliation. I told her I had moved out of Judi's and into a sweet little mobile home in Millbury. She said it was about time. She agreed to show up at the marriage counselor's. I lied to Judi. I said she never looked better. Anxiety had drained the blush and the radiance from her face. She was too thin. I figured she'd get back to eating when this medical business resolved itself.

I couldn't wait until the weather broke. I was getting up at six these days, since I couldn't sleep anyway, and writing until ten or when it would just get too hot in the house. And then I got news in the mail. The *St. Alban's Review* said they were much impressed with my story "Married to the Married Life" and would like to publish it if I would make the few changes indicated on the manuscript. I should have been elated, I know, validation of sorts, at long last, but I was depressed. I didn't like the story anymore. It was one of my earlier efforts and certainly the bleakest. It was almost without hope.

The story dealt with a married couple who are both heavy drinkers. He's an engineer at a defense plant, and she's a graduate of Mount Holyoke who doesn't need to work. At first, she is disconcerted by her leisure. Eventually, however, she adjusts to the long hours in the house. She fills the time with shopping trips, dusting, rearranging, preparing elaborate suppers. She thinks of herself as a gourmet cook. She's put away Jane Austen and George Eliot for whatever paperback's on the top of the *Times* best-seller list. She's Tina; he's Paul. They were both the youngest in their families, both brilliant and adventurous kids with luminous futures—they'd be the ones to finally get out of the neighborhood—but terrible, it turns out, disastrous, for each other. She gets fat, wears dark glasses, makes embarrassing pronouncements at family gatherings. He grows ever more condescending. In private, they abuse each other by conducting nasty and senseless affairs with neighbors, by reminding each other what they've given up for this marriage. Publically, they protect each other tenaciously and defend their acquisitive way of life. The story ends with Tina at forty, giving birth to their first child, a daughter they'll name Patricia. I saw this as their chance at redemption. The editors wanted the ending cut. So I took away the couple's child. I felt like a creep and a fraud, but I mailed the story off anyway with a groveling letter of thanks. The happy ending here is that the editors decided that they really didn't like the story after all. And one more thing. Mr. Barry Lesperence was not on vacation. He was dead on his bathroom floor. His shift supervisor at Capital Toys had asked the police to check on Mr. Lesperence when he didn't show for work or answer his phone.

26.

Tic Douloureux

I SENSED THAT TERRY CUNDALL WAS STUDYING US AS WE STEPPED THROUGH THE doorway into her office, Martha first. I nodded, smiled, shook Terry's thin, cool, limp hand. She switched on a white-noise machine by the doorway and closed the door. The drone of the machine would muffle our revelations and not disturb or intrigue anyone in the waiting room. That was the idea, I supposed. Terry was, I could tell, intent upon our entrance, though she remained impassive. Martha had a choice between the gray overstuffed chair and the matching loveseat. She seemed confused. I sat on the loveseat and sank back into the cushions. Martha complained she was cold. She put on the sweater she had carried with her. Terry sat across from me on a leather club chair. She crossed her legs. On the coffee table between us, a box of beige tissues and a small clay statue of a seated American Indian woman with nine Indian babies crawling all over her. Martha sat beside me. I sat forward as she leaned back.

Out the window, I saw the railroad tracks, the abandoned Union Station, the library, and, beyond that, up the hill, St. Casimir's Church and St. Vincent's Hospital. Terry said it was natural for couples to be ill-at-ease on the first visit. Martha was already launched into her reconstruction of our marital collapse. She reached for a tissue. I looked at the framed child's painting on the wall behind Terry. Mostly green and yellow with what could be trees or bombs, and something alive, a bear maybe, a crab, a virus. Martha blew her nose. She told Terry she had no idea why I took up with another woman, why I quit my job, why I abandoned her. I'm sure I rolled my eyes or clenched my fist or sat up straight or something. Terry said, Laf, let's hear Martha out. She had no idea, huh? Where had she been living? When she was finished, and it was, I guessed, my turn to share feelings, Martha started to cry. As I began to speak, I heard her sob. I looked at her. She said, I can't help this, you bastard, I'm in pain. I sat back and looked at the ceiling.

I remembered Spot, how that morning he had sat in the backyard, staring at Mr. Lesperence's fence, howling, cocking his head, listening. Judi was at Dr. Stouder's, getting, I hoped, encouraging news. I wondered what they were doing for a doll wigs hackler over at Capital Toys. How was Nicky doing at the taping out in California?

When Martha stopped crying, I said, I'd like a chance to revise my wife's story. I began with the prenuptial agreement—where Martha gets her degree and I eventually become a writer. Martha made an audible gasp of, I guessed, exasperation. I looked at Terry. I said, Isn't this where you tell Martha to hear me out? Terry said that I seemed angry and did I want to go with that. I said, You bet your ass I do. No, this is a ploy where women get the man irate so they can dismiss whatever he says. I took a breath and apologized for that last vulgarity. I said, I'm okay now. Terry said, Are you stuffing those uncomfortable feelings? She said, I want you to be in touch with the moment. She was getting on my nerves. I didn't care how cute she was.

All right, I said, I'll be here-and-now for you. I considered my mind and my body. In the here and now, I said, I'm numb and confused. But I was seldom ever concerned with the present. It is the least interesting of the places we can be.

I noticed that Terry had this thing she did. She put her left index finger on her lips when she was thinking and about to speak. Her eyes got wide, her mouth tight. She said, Why don't we begin by talking about your expectations of marriage counseling. I didn't wait for Martha. I said, I'd like to be able to have a conversation with Martha in which she did not break down into weeping. I've been listening to her cry for fourteen years, and I'm tired of it.

Terry said, Martha, are you all right? Martha was choking, she was crying so hard. I walked to the window. I thought I'd scream or smash the Indian statue if I didn't. I saw my buddy Alvin, the reference librarian, parking his car, checking his pockets. I wanted to signal Alvin, say, I'm being held captive, come rescue me. I'll buy us drinks over at the Valhalla. We'll talk about Buddhism or the Moody Blues all afternoon. Whatever you want, Alvin. Martha was quiet now. She sniffled. I heard the sigh of leather as Terry sat back in her chair.

I used to have an illness called tic douloureux, where something goes wrong with the trigeminal nerve in the brain, and no one knows why this happens or how. The pain, which came like an excruciating shock to the left side of my face, was so profound and agonizing that I wanted to kill myself. Pain may not be worse than death, but it is more tyrannical. Pain, more than anything, even more than love, traps you in the present, narrows your life to a second. The relief I felt whenever the pain stopped was paradise, but I spent it dreading the next wave of misery. Anything could set off a spasm—a gust of wind against my cheek, a smile, the taste of mint, chewing, the aroma of a flower. Same as in my marriage. Any movement, any word, a look, even, might set off Martha's next convulsion of tears. Better, I thought, not to do anything. Better to watch the shadow of that cloud pass over the face of the hospital.

Terry said, Would you join us, Laf? I sat in the chair this time. I looked at Martha with my jaw set. Martha said, I want our life to be what it was, the two of us on the sofa, nestled under an afghan, sipping coffee, reading the Sunday *Times*. That happened only once that I could recall, down the Cape. At home Martha didn't want the *Times* anywhere near the furniture because of the ink. I said I wasn't so hopeful.

Martha cried. I could see that she was trying to stifle the tears, and I appreciated that. But she couldn't. I looked at Terry. Martha said she felt set up. She felt like the whole reason for this session was so that I could pummel her again. What was I, some kind of rabid animal?

Terry looked at me, asked, Did you hear what Martha said? I said, Yes, Terry, I heard. I said, You may want to die with a tidy sum of money in a bank account downtown, Martha. You might covet that letter from the Pope when you retire. You might want all the talk at your wake to be about how antiseptically clean you kept the apartment. I don't want any of that. I want to work just enough not to worry. I want to work so I can write, and if I die owing Sears and MasterCard a bundle, so what? She looked surprised. I sat back and waited. The thing is, I knew that Judi didn't think much of my philosophy, if you can call it that, either.

This time Terry kept her finger on her lips as she talked. In her opinion, we had made remarkable progress. We had both been able to articulate some difficult and emotionally charged concerns. Change is not comfortable, she reminded us. She smiled. We agreed to meet same time next week. Terry gave us homework. We were to each think about and write down ten things that we liked or appreciated about the other.

I walked out of the office and through the waiting room with Martha. The midget couple sitting there did not look up from their magazines. He and she had identical slick, black hairdos. I had decided that I would walk Martha to her car, make a joke on the way like, Can you believe we even have to pay for this? or something. I didn't. Martha told me she needed to freshen up in the ladies' room. She was going back to work. I said, Would you like to get some lunch? She said she wouldn't. She said, I'm not obsessed with housework, you know.

27.

Staging

I GOT HOME BEFORE JUDI. NO MAIL FOR ME. TWO MESSAGES ON THE MACHINE Stoni asked if we'd be home tonight so she and Richie could stop by. Judi said she was back at her office and would be home at sevenish. I tried to read the diagnosis in her tone. I thought maybe she was just tired. I made a pitcher of martinis, changed into my shorts and T-shirt. I took the phone book and my pen and writing tablet out to the deck. I was going to do my homework and find someone who'd deliver our supper. I kissed Spot, hugged him, tossed him the olives from my drink. I asked him what was going on over at Mr. Lesperence's house. He woofed. Someone had set up scaffolding in the back of the house.

I called Forbidden City and ordered Hunan beef, lotus prawns, and Happy Family to be delivered at seven. Ten things I like about Martha. One: Her feet aren't webbed. Two: She can braid palm fronds into a crucifix, like the one she's got pinned to the visor of the car. Three: She lets me eat the lima beans out of her succotash. Well, I could see I wasn't taking this homework seriously. I was just so ragged from the session, I couldn't think. I needed a laugh, even at Martha's expense. I went in and refilled the glass. Two more olives for Spot. Okay, get serious, Laf. I tore off the facetious page from the tablet, crunched it into a ball, and tossed it to Spot. Sorry, Terry, the dog ate my homework. Okay, get serious.

Martha had told me things about the sun that I didn't know. She told me about the green ray and about the gegenschein. When the sun is setting over the water, she said, just before it slips below the surface, at the last possible moment before it vanishes, you can see the green flash of light—if you're lucky. She saw it only once in her life—on a ferry to Nova Scotia with her aunt Racine. The gegenschein, on the other hand, is a faint, sort of elliptical, glow of light that you can see—and I did when Martha pointed it out to me—in the twilight sky, just opposite the sun.

I remembered the night we saw that counterglow. We were in Chatham, near Monomoy, watching the sunset over a salt marsh, and she took my head in her hands and aimed me at it. And then she told me that what I'd seen wasn't really there. For some reason, we went into town and bought some toys at a children's store, drove back to Wellfleet, and played with them in the cottage. A top, I remember, with a suction cup at the bottom, Chinese checkers, pickup sticks, jacks. They're all still in a box, I think, in our bedroom closet at home.

Okay, then, start over. Martha, my dear, you are: 1. kind; 2. generous; 3. loving; 4. intelligent; 5. honest; 6. sensitive; 7. compassionate; 8. (I got stuck there at eight for a few seconds) beautiful; 9. enthusiastic; 10. hard-working. There. I had finished my assignment. I'd have the whole week to goof off.

Judi stood at the sliding screen door to the deck. I told her where the drinks were, asked her about the doctor's visit. Let me change, she said. I got Judi's drink, brought it out to the deck. The doorbell rang. The man from Forbidden City was here. When I carried the boxes of food outside, Spot perked right up. He loves the chicken in Happy Family. He likes the boxes. Judi said, How was the session? I told her I got homework on the first day. She didn't smile. She sipped her drink. I told her how explosive things had been. She said if I was serious about counseling, I probably shouldn't be living here. I didn't say anything. I asked Judi if she'd listened to Stoni's message. She nodded. She said, I'm not going to toss you out. I guess I've gotten used to you.

It was not encouraging news—what the doctor said. The tumor had not regressed. The pelvic exams and the ultrasound indicated that it may even have grown a centimeter or so. Dr. Stouder was now in favor of more aggressive therapy. The first step would be a staging laparotomy, next week. Judi said, I'm scared, Laf. I got up and hugged her. I squatted by her chair, moved her bangs away from her eyes. I told her not to worry yet. It could still be nothing, right? Judi shook her head. It would have shrunk by now. This is it. I pulled my chair by hers and held her hand. A staging laparotomy. Sounded like someone was putting on a play or setting up scaffolding. Judi said, Don't mention anything to Stoni, okay?

This was a strange moment to feel happy about, but that's how I felt. I felt at home. I felt calm. Judi's eyes were closed. What did this feeling mean? Judi said, Let's eat before this gets any colder. I got the plates and chopsticks and the pitcher. I read the message on the chopsticks' envelope: *Please to try your nice Chinese food with Chopsticks, the traditional and typical of Chinese glorious history and cultural for swallowing clouds, vegetable dried, Buddha jumping over wall, and others.*

Judi said, "Trixie heard from Noel that Edmund was gang-raped at Walpole. He's in the infirmary now."

"Jesus Christ." I thought how Edmund had more of the same to look forward to for the rest of his life. And I thought there were probably people who would think he deserved it. I was pissed off at Noel for what he had let happen to his boy. And I was pissed at Layla. I imagined her right then probably cuddled up in a ratty sleeping bag with Mr. Sun himself. I wanted to call her up and explain to her what she had done to Edmund, but what the hell was I thinking? She hadn't done anything but forget him. Maybe I just wanted her to care. I don't know.

We heard Stoni say, "Hey, you two sure don't seem to be having much fun." She and Richie were coming around the side of the house. "I just love Chink food," she said. "I'm so hungry, I could eat a cat."

Richie Muneyhun was even larger than I could have imagined, biblically large. He was Goliath the Philistine. Six cubits and a span. He was Hoover Dam, a bull mastodon, an armoire, a sequoia, a John Deere harvester, Polyphemus in a sleeveless denim jacket. Richie carried a case of beer under his left arm. He shook my hand, gave Judi a peck on the cheek. He looked at Spot. Spot hid under the deck. Richie had tattooed quotations on each arm. The right one said, *Vengeance is mine; I will repay.* The left: *I have created the waster to destroy.* I said, Let me get you guys some plates, glasses, and stuff. Stoni said, We'll just eat out of the boxes. You'll need forks maybe, or chopsticks, I said. I hoped.

Richie inhaled the prawns. I suspected he didn't get a lot of exotic seafood in jail. I asked him how it felt to be a free man. He said, Are any of us free? Uh-oh, I thought, determinism, Divine foreknowledge, the constraints of Fate. Richie's been reading Aquinas and Descartes in his cell. "Richie," I said, "what about work?" He said he was mulling over a couple of attractive offers. He wasn't at liberty to discuss them.

Stoni had us reach into the bag and pick out our fortune cookies. Stoni read hers first: *Possession is the grave of love.* Richie's was *Street angel, house* devil. Mine: *If you are afraid of loneliness, don't marry.* Now they tell me, I said. That got a laugh. Judi's I liked: *We think in generalities, but we live in detail.*

Judi said it would probably be better if Richie didn't smoke his joint out here on the deck. He said, That's cool, and went out front to sit in Stoni's car. Back in ten, he said. While he was gone, Stoni let us know that poor Arthur Bositis was pining for her. He calls me at work every day. I just hope Richie doesn't find out. Stoni told us about this guy who came into the ward last night complaining of abdominal pains. "First of all, he's got the logo of *The New York Times* tattooed across his chest and under it is the headline MARILYN MONROE FOUND DEAD. Then I notice carrot greens sticking out of his asshole. Turns out someone had rammed a couple of carrots up there. But, of course, the guy who brought him in didn't know anything about it."

I said, "Stoni, why do you want to work in Emergency anyway? It must be so gruesome."

"I don't like sick people. We keep them alive too long, and they're just like babies at the end. It's pathetic."

Richie was back. He thought maybe we should all head out to a club and do some dancing, maybe out to the Blue Plate. The Coyotes are playing. We begged off. Judi said she was exhausted. Stoni thought it was a great idea, but let's stop at Aris's for some baklava on the way. Richie thought about that. Wow, he said. Let's go.

I cleaned up while Judi got ready for bed. I scraped all the sticky rice, sauce, chicken, and beef onto a plate and set it out for Spot. I gave him a box. He got it stuck on his nose. After I did the dishes, I took Spot for a walk. I let him off the leash and he dashed into Mr. Lesperence's yard. He sniffed around the back door, the garage, the front door. Some of Mr. Lesperence's volatile molecules are still around his house. Spot shook his tail adamantly. He woofed. I told him Mr. Lesperence was invisible now.

When I got to bed, Judi was sleeping. I kissed her shoulder, put out the light. I dreamed that I was the Forbidden Boy from Lotus City, and I lived with my Happy Family. In Lotus City you forget about everything as soon as it happens. You could remember facts like the recipe for baklava or carrot cake, but you could not remember sensations or emotions, like how they tasted, or how the fragrance made you feel. In Lotus City, when someone in your family dies, you forget all about them. That's how you stay happy. But I was the Forbidden Boy because I remembered every blessed detail.

28.

Vinegar from Wine

I SAT AT THE KITCHEN TABLE WITH MY COFFEE, MY NOTES, MY TYPEWRITER. DALE and Theresa had reached a crucial and fragile point in their courtship. Dale sat in his office at school, his door closed. He was holding a stapler in his hands and staring at a poster of White Sands on the wall opposite his chair. He had notes for a Personnel Committee meeting to prepare, but he couldn't concentrate. He had tests to grade. He had a long weekend ahead of him unless he called Theresa. I wanted Dale to realize that Theresa was his one chance at love. I needed him to understand that the children were not a liability at all, but a bonus. How would I convince him? I wasn't listening to him tell me what he needed. And that, no doubt, explained why I was presently unable to write about him. Dale's mind was not where I needed it to be—on Theresa and on his future. His thoughts were cluttered with my own aggravations. It has always been easier for me to pour my energies into my characters' problems than into my own. They are more intriguing.

I cleaned the platen, bail rollers, and type guide with alcohol. I sprayed the keys and the type bars with WD-40. I got most of the gunk out of the guts of the thing with a sponge and a damp rag. I oiled the carriage return and wiped down the body with Windex and then lemon Pledge. Nice job. Even got out the Liquid Paper stains. I fed Spot. I poured myself another coffee, sat down, rolled a blank sheet into the typewriter. Dale was still staring at the poster. I called Judi. I said, Let's have lunch, honey bunch. She said, Let's. She had two hours today and didn't want to spend them alone. She thanked me for calling.

At Mr. Natural's, I asked Pauline how she was, how Mick and Keith were doing. How's Marvin? She hesitated. She rubbed her left forearm with her right hand. Marvin's Marvin, she said. I could push this, I thought, or I could let it drop. I said, Nice to see you again. Pauline smiled, but we didn't seem to have anything else to say. I remembered us in bed.

Judi and I drove out to Ronnie's for clams. She was worried about Josh. What's the matter with Josh? I said. She said, Didn't I tell you? He's got AIDS. I didn't want to hear this. The story on the way to the Cape? The one you wanted me to write? She nodded.

We drove to the reservoir in Leicester and walked along the trails. Lady's slippers and laurel everywhere. We sat on an old stone wall that ran through the woods—a Yankee farmer's handiwork two hundred years ago. Glacial deposit pushed here from Hudson Bay, buried eons ago, unearthed by a plow, lifted and fitted here with the others. This is what Judi said:

I see people in this world, like you, and I see people in that world, too, and often at the same time. I know I'm here. I'm not crazy. It's like I have lucid memories, I guess. I don't remember so much as I experience what happened, as if it's happening right now. Every detail comes back and in every sense. I can walk around a room in, you know, France, two hundred and fifty years ago, and I can tell you exactly what's there. I can open a drawer and pull out all of the contents item by item. I can't explain this. Sometimes I'll smell something I've never smelled before, like let's say I smell mold on rye bread—in fact, I've done this—and immediately, even though I'm holding the bread and I'm in my kitchen, and I know I am, I'm also back in Helfta and not because of the bread, you see, but because the rye mold smells like dysentery, and I'm working in the convent infirmary, and I'm washing Mechtilde's body, and I'm praying for her, and I can look back over my shoulder and describe the cast of light entering through the small window and the plane tree out in the garden and the cuckoo on the branch of the tree, and I can hear the cuckoo's song.

And voices can do the same thing. I hear a voice, usually it's one I'm unfamiliar with, and I get a physical sensation that starts at the back of my head and travels to the tops of my feet like a wave, and it goes down my arms to my fingers and around my head to my face. And when that happens I know that one of the recollections is about to present itself. I don't know, maybe it's that the person's voice in this world has the same tone or pitch or resonance or something as someone's in the past. It's not a thought, Laf. It's not imagination or fantasy or anything like that; it's a pleasurable physical sensation—the wave the voice sets off—like someone you love is breathing on your body, and it remains through the whole episode. The memory or whatever it is is not a hallucination. I can touch things. I once picked up a mango on a table at a wedding reception on Saint Kitts in 1782 and tasted it, and I've never eaten one in this life. I even had an allergic reaction to it and had to be rushed to Memorial two hundred years later. You see what I mean?

And this never happens when I remember my own life, my childhood, say. Those memories are vague in comparison—they are like the idea of memory. They seem so flat—that's all I can say—like clothes you hang out to dry on the line. Thin and limp. I do remember my dad once lifting me up when I fell off my bike. I remember he kissed me on the knee.

I can't explain any of this, but I know it. What I mean is that this knowing has nothing to do with thinking or articulation. I don't control this knowledge any more than I control the cells in my body. But the cells are there, and so is this other world. It's undeniable.

Me, I can remember a dream I had when I was two years and two months old. I know my age because the dream happened on the day they brought Edgar home from the hospital and told me, Here's your new baby brother. In the dream, Edgar's asleep in the crib in my parents' room and there's a christening party going on in the living room. Out of nowhere these shadowmen—two-dimensional guys with pointy heads and elbows—appear on the wall in the living room, but I'm the only one who notices them, and I'm in my room. Somehow I know they are menacing and intent on evil. Before I can alert any of my aunts or uncles, the intruders have slid along the three walls and have passed through the slit between the door and the jamb and into my parents' room. Poor Edgar, someone says, no use trying to rescue him now.

I remember the next morning, telling my mother about the dream, and being reassured that nothing like that had happened. Edgar was asleep on his back and moving his mouth a mile a minute. And then I recall almost nothing of my life for the next four or five years. I don't remember dot about my first school, Sacred Heart. My earliest memory after the dream was my first day at the new school, St. Stephen's. I was given Paula Philbin's seat because she was out with rheumatic fever. It's like I was born in that classroom and nothing of significance had happened to me before that.

I know more about Dale's childhood than I know about my own. His closest friend was Lonnie Wilcoxen, who lived behind Dale on Dal Paso. Lonnie's daddy was a public health inspector for the county. One time Dale saw Lonnie strangle a cat to death. Why'd you do that for? Dale said. Lonnie said, 'Cause I felt like it. Lonnie drank his daddy's beer for breakfast and stole his brother Kenneth's cigarettes. You get one best friend in your childhood, and Dale knew he'd got a rotten one. Lonnie lit a can of Shinola oxblood shoe polish with a match and the explosion covered him with flames. Dale couldn't put Lonnie out, but his screams brought Mrs. Wilcoxen running from the house with a blanket. Lonnie got taken away to the Shriners' Hospital in Dallas and came back in a year without a nose and with skin of various colors stretched out like gum on his body. Let Lonnie be a lesson to you, Dale's father said. And then he said, Put on Channel 4 for me, would you, son.

While my father is alive, I'm a child. If Blaise dies, then it's the slow slide to dissolution for me. I'll be next. Of course, I know the unnatural can happen—Death can enter the wrong room, can carry away the child first. Nothing could be worse than seeing your child die, nothing. Maybe the best thing I'd ever done for my father was just to stay alive. I was glad that Martha and I didn't have a child for the pain that the little death of divorce might bring.

When Judi went back to work I walked by the Chancery deliberately. Martha's car was in the lot. I looked up to her window. I kept seeing her crying in Terry's office.

Maybe it wasn't Dale's fault at all that the story was stuck. What about love? What about love and marriage? How come we have only one word for love when the ancient Greeks had three? Maybe I'd ask Terry. That would get the next session flying. A pure love is a selfless love, I could say. But can desire ever be selfless?

29.

The Harvest Is Past, the Summer Is Ended, and We Are Not Saved

DR. STOUDER LEANED BACK IN HER CHAIR, STEEPLED HER FINGERS AT HER CHIN, looked at the oncologist's report on her desk and then at Judi. The problem, she explained, is that epithelial cancers like this one are usually asymptomatic until they've metastasized. She leaned forward and put her elbows on the desk. Well, that's one of the problems. So this was it, then, I thought. This was Judi's sentencing. This was hopeless, wasn't it? Judi lowered her head and looked at her hands folded on her lap. Dr. Stouder said, As a result of our exploration, we've ascertained the progress of your particular carcinoma. It looks like Stage III-A cancer. Three-A, I told myself. I wanted to remember because I didn't think Judi would. Judi covered her face with her hands. I touched her shoulder. She stiffened. I looked at Dr. Stouder.

I looked at the egg on my left wrist, my memento mori. I ran my fingers over it—the usual soreness. Didn't Nicky tell me once that cancer doesn't hurt? Whatever it is, it had started as a pea, oh, six, seven years ago. Why didn't I get it taken care of?

Now that we've documented the cancer, our next step is what's called cytoreductive surgery, where we debulk the disease, Dr. Stouder said. Judi said, What does that mean? It meant, according to Dr. Stouder, a total hysterectomy. When do we do this? Judi said. Dr. LeClair will perform the operation. The best surgeon we have. You're lucky. We're setting up OR time now, and I'll let you know this afternoon. And then what? Judi said. I'll be cured?

Dr. Stouder took a drawing of the insides of a woman and turned it on her desk to face us. She pointed with a pencil. The disease, she said, we think, is confined to the pelvic viscera and omentum. She made a circle on the paper with her pencil. With the gross tumor removed, you will have a reasonable chance of responding positively to therapy.

Therapy? Judi said.

Chemo and, just possibly, radiation. This will be up to the oncologist, as you know, but probably you'll have about six cycles' worth of treatments. If there are no traces of the disease at that point, we'll do a "second-look" operation. And if there's no clinical evidence of the cancer, then you're off chemo.

I'll lose my hair? Judi said.

Probably. Let's take it one step at a time.

In the car I told Judi, Why don't you let me drive. She shook her head. I don't need my brain to drive, she said. I said, Let's just go home. I'll call in sick to work. I wished I hadn't said that. She said, No, you go. I'll be all right. Rain beat against the roof of the car and washed down the windshield. All you could make out of the doctor's building was the bluish-white color. Judi started the car, let it idle. She switched on the heater and the defrost. August, I thought, fucking August and fifty degrees. I said, I don't want you to be alone. Judi looked at me. Well, there's nothing you can do about that, she said. I *am* alone. Judi put her head on the steering wheel. Judi, I said. She put her head back on the seat and closed her eyes. No more pussy willows, she said. And she began to cry.

30.

The Mystery and Melancholy of Marriage

EDGAR CALLED TO TELL ME THAT OUR FATHER WAS SLIPPING AWAY. HE TOLD ME I should catch the next plane down there if I ever wanted to see the old man alive again. Look, he said, if it's money, I'll send you the goddamn money. I tried to explain to Edgar that leaving Worcester was impossible right now. I told him that I was in marriage counseling with Martha for one thing, and that Judi has cancer for another. Edgar said, You sound like one sick son of a bitch yourself, Laf. Lives get complicated, I said. Edgar asked me to hold on a sec, someone's at the door. Turns out it was the exterminator, and he needed to let him into the attic. Be right back.

Who's going to watch Spot and who's going to fill in for me at Our Lady's? And what the hell am I supposed to do when I get to Florida— stare at my father and watch what's left of his life get pumped into him through plastic tubes? Edgar said, I'm not supposed to mention this but what the hell. When Dad dies, the motel's half yours. We're partners. I said, What are you talking about? Well, Mom doesn't want it, never did. She's retiring, moving in with us. They've done all right, you know. I told Edgar I didn't want half a motel. He said, Dad wants you to have it. You don't have a job, Laf. Dad's worried about you.

Edgar asked me to hold. He had an incoming call. Edgar said he'd just landed tickets to a big wrestling match at the Miami Arena. They're calling it the Havana Jam and they got this bearded Cuban giant, El Cid, who's a grandson of Fidel and he's taking on all comers. It ought to be a war.

You've only got one father, Laf, only one in your life. You ought to be there to comfort him in his time of need. Edgar, I said, you sound like some TV evangelist. *A foolish son is the calamity of his father,* Edgar said. I said, Look, I don't want to be a pain in the ass, but I'm right here where the three of you left me. I didn't go away. This is our home. This is where we belong, not in Disneyland.

At the next counseling session, Martha wore a dress I had never seen before, black with a bold floral print, pink and yellow, cut above the knees. She wore black tights. She looked sexy. She was all smiles in the waiting room. She asked me how I liked the mobile home. I nodded. She asked me if I'd done my homework. Jesus. I'd forgotten it. I still had five minutes. I told Martha I had to go to the men's room down the hall. I sat in a stall and rewrote the list. I forgot something, but added *sexy.* I washed my hands and rejoined Martha. Why did I wash my hands? The door to Terry's office opened and the midget couple from last week walked out. He had a spot of tissue on his chin—cut himself shaving. He was crying.

In Terry's office, I noticed that the Indian statue was not on the coffee table. Martha took the chair. I wondered if Terry worried that one of us might bust the statue in our rage. Terry sat quietly, waiting, I guess, for one of us to begin. Martha cleared her throat, took her homework list out of her purse, and read it. She said I was funny, and I made her laugh. That is, I used to make her laugh. She told Terry how I used to make up some songs about the two of us, hilarious songs. I'd forgotten about that. She said I was a free spirit; she admired that and wished she could be more like me. She said she liked the way I got angry when I watched the news, the way I yelled at the anchormen. She told Terry that I had somehow never learned to tie my shoes, and she found that endearing. She said I spoke my mind; I made friends easily; I helped around the house; I was considerate. Martha went on. I didn't recognize the guy she was talking about.

I presented my extemporaneously annotated list and felt a certain tranquillity and largesse. This was going well, I thought. Terry did not allow the self-congratulatory interlude to linger. Neither one of you, she said, mentioned anything physical about the other, anything intimate. You were both in your heads—she tapped her forehead with her finger. What did we think of that? When neither of us said anything, Terry asked if we thought that might indicate a problem in the relationship. I sat on my anger. Why was Terry subverting a promising situation? I said, Yes, it might indicate a problem, or it might be that we felt sexual talk was a bit personal. I looked at Martha. Terry said that touching someone's shoulder, holding someone's hand, was not necessarily sexual. And, my goodness, she said, this is your marriage at stake here. She looked at Martha, at me. Perhaps, she said, it's time to get personal.

The timer by Terry's chair went off like a warbler's song. That meant we had two minutes left in our fifty-minute hour. Well, Terry said, we've certainly got our agenda for next week. I said, I can't meet next week. Martha said, Why? I couldn't believe I hadn't planned a response for this. I had to be with Judi at the hospital. My egg, I said. I held up my wrist. Getting my little whatever-it-is checked out. Martha said, Where? Memorial, I said, and before anyone could ask anything else, I suggested that perhaps Martha and I could get together at another time on our own to deal with the intimacy thing. I was certainly willing to. Martha said fine, but she'd have to check her appointment calendar at work. I'll call you this afternoon, I said. I wanted to throw in the business with my father, say how he was dying, how I might have to zip off to Florida at a moment's notice.

Back at Judi's, two more rejections in the mail and a letter from Aquino and McMahon, Attorneys. I called Florida. My father answered. I said, "What are you doing?"

"Working."

"Edgar says you're on your deathbed."

"Edgar exaggerates. It makes him feel important."

"So you're all right, then?"

"No worse. My left leg and arm are pretty well shot. I'll be getting therapy. No golf for a while. The oddest thing, though, he said. You figure this out. I got like instant replay going on in my head. A guy comes in and registers. I give him Room twenty-one upstairs. He asks me in French where he can rent a jet-ski. He leaves. Five minutes later the exact same thing happens again. Same guy, same room, same questions."

"You probably just think it happened before. It's déjà vu."

"I don't think so. Listen to this, then. This just started yesterday. Your mother peeled me an orange, set it on a plate. First I see the orange, then I see a bowl of oranges."

"Maybe you need to get some rest."

"Pretty strange, if you ask me. I see one carnation in a bud vase. But when I look up at the ceiling, there's a whole bouquet of carnations."

"Don't look at the ceiling."

The letter from Bart McMahon, Esquire, requested my presence in his office to sign a no-fault divorce decree as soon as possible. Why hadn't Martha warned me this was coming? What is this shit? She wants it signed, I'll damn well sign it. I leashed Spot and took him along. I wanted company. He tried to drag me into the park, but I tugged him back to the sidewalk. I figured I should get this over with before I thought too much about it. Who knows what I'd do then. This *was* the right thing to do, wasn't it? Not like this was the actual divorce, anyway. This just brought our drama to the third act, is all. Spot lay quietly by my chair, snacking on a business card, while I signed at all the *x*'s. Six months, the secretary told me. It's all formal in six months if there are no problems. I thanked her.

31.

Jeopardy!

NICKY FORGOT TO PHRASE HIS ANSWER IN THE FORM OF A QUESTION. IF HE HAD said, Who is Herbert Philbrick? or maybe even, What is Herbert Philbrick?, then he'd be some ten thousand dollars' richer, at least. No telling what he might have won on the next day's show—Nicky told me it's not the next day at all, just later that same day, no matter that Alex has changed his suit from gray to blue ("It's all illusion out there, Laf")—and the show after that. He could have become a Grand Champion, bought Our Lady of the Sea Fish & Chips from Lardo Larsen and one of those enormous big-screen TVs for his apartment. And he knew the question to the answer, that's what killed him. Alex said, Richard Carlson played this counterspy in *I Led Three Lives*. Nicky didn't hesitate and didn't stop at the name. Herbert Philbrick, he said, a real-life advertising executive from Boston who infiltrated the Communist party for the FBI. There was a pause as Alex looked off-camera at his producer and a murmur arose from the audience. Then Nicky heard this disheartening buzzer go off and realized immediately what he had gone and done. So often in this country, Nicky told me, it's style that gets rewarded, not content.

Speaking of style, Pauline's Marvin got himself arrested at Elm Park at three in the morning with two sixteen-year-old girls, a hypodermic syringe, and a bag of heroin. He'd been arraigned and released on bond. Why is Pauline doing this to herself? And still on the crime front, Edmund Prefontaine had been put in protective custody at Walpole and would remain there for the foreseeable future. And Richie Muneyhun caught on that Arthur Bositis had been pestering Stoni with phone calls. So Richie and two of his pals, Psycho and Desperado, showed up in the parking lot at Boston Beef on their Harleys during the shift change, wanting a few words with Arthur. Psycho jammed a sawed-off shotgun into Arthur's back while Richie held Arthur's head in both hands and slammed Arthur's face onto the hood of someone's Chrysler Newport seven times. Richie's few words for Arthur were that the next time he bothered Stoni, he'd get himself a bum blast. He defined the term. He showed Arthur the shotgun. See this? he said. Well, what we do is we grease the barrel of this baby and then we force it up your ass, and then my man Psycho squeezes the trigger, and it's so long, asshole. The irony here is that it was Stoni herself who took care of Arthur when he was brought into the emergency ward by a couple of the packers, who had seen it all from the plant window. He told the cops later that he didn't know who had done this to him. His nose was broken, his eyes were black, a tooth got chipped, six stitches in his forehead. He was a lucky guy, Stoni said. And I believed her.

My father called. He sounded excited by a recent development. Now I got mirror-vision, he told me. It's crazy, Laf. I haven't told anybody. My brain's turned into a circus. He said there he was, flopped on the couch, watching a ball game on TV, when the batter for the Yankees slaps a liner out to centerfield and starts running to third base. All's I could think of was Jimmy Piersall was back in the game, my father said. But he doesn't get called out; he rounds third and heads for second and slides in for a double. Then I realized that Clemens wasn't no lefty. You with me, Laf? I said I was, I thought. Weird, he said. I told him probably something happened to the polarity in the magnetic field of the picture tube. Scrambled electrons or something. I didn't know what I was talking about, of course.

My father said, No, wait. It's not just the TV. The whole frigging world is reversed. We're right here on the Broadwalk, see. I'm looking out the window at the beach. The coconut palm that used to be out the door and to the right is now out the door and to the left. If I drag myself out to the sand, I can look up to Dania pier and see it and the ocean to the south. It never used to be there. And Miami's north. Or it's left, and left is south now. I don't know. What a crazy business, Laf. And I can't read. I'm looking at our stationery here. Near as I can make out it says *LETOM ATSIVARAM*. I told him he ought to see a doctor. He said he had three doctors already. I mean for your eyes, Dad. Eyes aren't supposed to do that. He said, It's not the eyes, it's the brain. And I kind of enjoy it. Keeps me alert. The one thing I can't get used to is your mother sleeping on my side of the bed.

Judi got her hair cut very short. She looked like Jean Seberg in *Breathless*, like she should be hawking newspapers on a street corner. She said she wanted to get used to the feel of it, for when it fell out. It made her look younger, I thought. We sat on the deck watching the crew from Bowditch & Marinelli scrape and prime Mr. Lesperence's house.

Judi described Helfta. I must have made a face or rolled my eyes. She said, Don't get exasperated with me, Laf. I apologized. She said, "The first thing we did every morning, before matins, was we each took our spoon and went to the churchyard and scooped a measure of earth from our burial plot. Every day, we dug our grave."

"Do you remember any of your deaths, not the dying, but after. I mean, where were you before you came back as another person or another name?"

"In another body, you mean." She closed her eyes and shook her head. "It's not conscious, so it's hard to say. It's like potential. Just that. Energy seeking matter. It's so light, you're blinded. You spin so fast, you're standing still."

"Was Gertrude disappointed that that's all there was to heaven?"

"When that disappointment could have happened, Gertrude had ceased to be."

32.

The Hour of Lead

WE COULDN'T SLEEP. WE WATCHED A VIDEO OF *ONE FALSE MOVE*. WE STILL couldn't sleep. We lay in bed. We got up and went to the kitchen. Judi studied the contents of the refrigerator. I told her, sure, I was hungry. But I reminded her of the diet Stouder had recommended. Should she be eating like this? She ignored me. Judi made a cookie sheet full of mock pizzas—tomato sauce, mozzarella, and bacon on English muffins—and I mixed a pitcher of vodka martinis. We moved out to the deck. I lit the citronella candles. Spot woke up, stretched, joined us.

Judi and I talked about all the things that conspire to kill us. Like high-tension power lines, I said, and cellular phones and microwave ovens and beef pumped with steroids and fluorescent lights and acid rain and military leaders and miserable art. We heard the squeal of automobile brakes, winced, waited for the impact that never came. We heard an owl hoot. So did Spot. He lifted his ears, cocked his head. Judi asked me about Dale and Theresa. I told her how Dale was feeling sorry for himself these days, and he's avoiding Theresa at the same time he's missing her. He's upset that the first woman he's ever been so nuts about is encumbered with children. Children don't have a role in his fantasies. He's always wanted romance in his life, and now children are depriving him of it. He could share his life with another person, but three? He thinks he doesn't like kids, I told Judi, but he hasn't known any.

Judi said, "So what's going to happen?"

I said, "I don't know."

"So how can you write?"

"That's *why* I write them—to find out how they'll end."

She said, "Well, you must have some idea."

I said I knew how I wanted it to end—the two of them together with the kids.

"So make it turn out that way."

"I can't do that."

Spot began to lick my foot. I moved it. I told him to stop. I gave him a pizza. He wasn't sure what to do with it. He slid it on the deck with his nose. He barked at it. Then he ate it.

Judi said, "So what are you trying to say in your story?"

"This is what happened to Dale and Theresa, and here's why."

"You know what I mean. What are you trying to say?"

"I'm saying, This is what it's like to be this particular human being, and this is how it feels."

I had to remind myself that Judi was going into the hospital in the morning, that she must be scared and anxious, that she had that cunning business at work in her body. So I restrained myself. Judi said, And what about your own life? What about you and Martha? I told her I didn't know the ending to that story either. Well, How do you want it to end? she said.

I said, "Has Terry said anything to you?"

"No. She couldn't. Wouldn't."

I shook my head, shrugged. I didn't want to answer or even think about the question.

Judi said, "She called me, you know."

"Terry?"

"Martha."

"Martha? When?"

"Last week."

"Jesus. What did she say? Why didn't you tell me?"

"She called me a jezebel and a disgrace to women and feminism. She said you two were happy together until I took you away. I told her I didn't take you anywhere. You came."

"I'm sorry," I said.

"You should be," Judi said. "You're screwing up people's lives."

"You want me to leave? I'll leave."

"Don't get petulant."

"Well, what are you saying?"

"That we're not all in a story, that this is real, that you can't diddle around with people's lives."

I wished I were back inside the house now, alone, typing. The eastern sky was already beginning to lighten. Spot was asleep, his back leg twitching. Judi had fallen asleep. Birds sang. Well, I might someday be living in a stone house in Garden City, Kansas, with my new word processor and my fat book contract and Spot and who knows who all else, but today I had to get Judi to Memorial, wait around for the surgery.

In her sleep, Judi said, No, I'm not; I'm an experiment in light, and this is the hour of lead. Quietly, I began to clear the table.

33.

Pink

I GET ANTSY IN HOSPITALS. I DON'T KNOW WHAT TO DO WITH MYSELF. I FEEL guarded, tense, claustrophobic. Maybe that's why I stood at the window in Judi's room, pretending I was out there in the city. Judi lay propped up in bed in her white johnny, which she insisted on calling her hospital gown, like this was a dance she was going to. The pair of us were quiet, waiting for something to happen and hoping that instead of a prep nurse knocking, an emissary from the Surgeon General would burst through the door, all out of breath, waving a scrolled parchment over his head, saying a terrible mistake had been made—Judi's not sick at all; she's healthy as a horse, in fact.

I had a view of the clogged parking lot and of a few gray-trunked maples along Kendall Street, already losing their orange leaves. I think how we've killed off all the chestnut trees with blight, the elms with Dutch elm disease, and now we're choking the maples with cement. I hear the click of the intercom, then a call for a Dr. Perry, Dr. Robert Perry. And I hate the way hospitals smell. God, here's Judi sick, and I feel like it's me that needs help.

"I have to talk about this, Laf," Judi said.

I pulled a chair over beside the bed. I held Judi's hand. I told her, "You'll be all right."

She said, "Talk, not bullshit."

"So talk," I said and realized what a rotten thing that was to say. I stood, kissed Judi's forehead.

She said, "I'm losing part of myself." She smoothed the sheet over her stomach and thighs. "What will I be like?"

"You'll be healthier."

"One minute I think, yes, I'll be alive and all better and back to normal. The next, I think this is just the beginning of the end."

I squeezed her hand and smiled.

She shook her head. "This isn't supposed to happen."

I ran my fingers through her fluffy hair. She winced, told me that her head hurt, her eyes, her shoulders.

"Stress," I said.

"Maybe it's good you get scared like this. You realize how important life is."

I heard the squeaking wheel of a gurney approach the room and pass.

"I had a dream last night," Judi said. "I was in a kitchen." She closed her eyes. "Linoleum floor had a green border, and the rest was cream-colored with confetti flecks of red and black everywhere. A table, chrome legs, with a red and white checked tablecloth. A stick of margarine wrapped in foil on the table. It had a four-leaf clover on it and said 'Good luck.' "

I said, "Well, that's appropriate."

She opened her eyes, smiled. "Two places set with pink Melmac dinnerware, Mason jars of chocolate milk. A glass ashtray and a pack of Old Golds. I'm in this kitchen, Laf. I walk over to the window and look out. It begins to rain, and suddenly, instead of a clapboard house next door, there's a vista, you know, hills, ponds, forests, mountains, and it's raining like mad—raining all over the world. It's raining in the kitchen, water is running down the walls, down my face and arms. It's like music, and everything I see is lush and shining, and I realize in the dream what the dream is all about—that we're all like the water. All the water that there will ever be on earth was there at the very beginning—there's never any added or taken away. And it's like that with souls. All the souls that have or will exist were here at the start—we fall to earth, we're condensed by death, evaporated, I guess you'd say, and we fall as rain again."

"Judi Dubey." A nurse read the name off a pink sheet of paper. Judi raised her hand. The nurse told me I'd have to leave.

I kissed Judi, said I'd be there when she got back from recovery, when she woke up, when it was all over.

She said, "Laf, don't leave me."

I smiled, kissed her again. "I won't." I walked to the solarium. I tried to read. I guess I fell asleep.

Biff Evinrude shook me awake and told me that living inside someone else has its advantages. He introduced himself. We shook hands, and then he folded back his flannel bathrobe and showed me his catheter and his leg bag. He smiled like he'd just won a bowling tournament. We were sitting in the solarium on 4 North at Memorial Hospital. He said, They finally believe me. I'm sick again, and it could be the big one this time. He told me he already had multiple sclerosis, but it was in remission, and he was epileptic and would have dramatic and alarming grand mal seizures, especially when he didn't take his Dilantin. But why wouldn't you take your medication? I said. To have the seizures, he said. I said, Who's living inside of whom? That's one nasty-looking tooth, he told me, and then he padded off down the hall in search of a Dr. Patel.

I checked my watch. Judi was either still under the knife or in recovery. Just to make sure, I walked by 424 and peeked in. Empty. I took the elevator down to the cafeteria, sat at the counter, and ordered a coffee. I wondered what would fill the void in Judi's body when they finished digging all that mess out. Do the other organs settle? Would her abdominal cavity collapse? I didn't know why I thought Judi would be in and out of here in a hurry. I figured she'd get the surgery, wake up in recovery, dress in her room, stop down at the pharmacy for medication, and go home to recover. This was all much more complicated than I had wanted to believe. She'd be here four days minimum, according to Stoni.

The man beside me told me his wife had the Big C, was how he put it. He explained that cancer is a symptom of something else. When I just nodded, he said that the disease is a physical manifestation of sin is what it was. Well, that's one theory, I said. The guy gave me a look. I said, What I mean is it's a useful metaphor. He said, Metaphor my dimpled ass. Cancer is a hellfire in the body. He said, Tillie's up there on 5 South right now, dissolving. I told him I was sorry to hear that. I bought him a coffee and got myself a refill. I left a tip and told my friend, Tillie's forlorn husband, that I had to run. I wished him the best. I told him to hang in there.

I got off the elevator on 4 North. I saw Biff Evinrude at the nurses' station. He was demanding an enema. I went to the pay phone to call my father. He told me that for a couple of hours last night everything was upside down. But then he drank a cup of coffee and it went away. He said, Pretty soon I'll be seeing inside out. He told me people's faces looked really funny upside down, talking through their foreheads and everything. I saw Trixie get off the elevator and head for Judi's room. I told my father I had to go, said to say hi to Mom and Edgar for me. He

told me they were all on their way to Orlando for the wrestling matches.
I thought, Where the hell did I come from?

Trixie told me I looked awful. I told her how we'd been up all night.
She fished through her purse, drew out a small gold case, and tapped
out a white pill. Take this, she said. I did. She said she's always been
blessed with vim and vigor. Never a sick day in her life except for a little bit of polio when she was a child. I stared out the window down at
the parking lot. A clutch of nurses was standing by the admitting entrance and smoking. Trixie asked me what I thought about her new look.
She'd had her lips and eyebrows tattooed, the lips a Castilian red, the
brows a darker shade of brown than her hair. You look spectacular, I said.
She said she was saving up for a beauty mark on her right cheek.

Trixie shifted in her chair. She said, There's really nothing to worry
about. This morning she'd called the Psychic Friends Network and had
spoken with Shandra, who told her that Judi would come out of this better than ever. I said, Do you really believe in that stuff, Trixie? She said,
If I didn't believe, it wouldn't work. I said, It's all superstition, don't you
think? Trixie said, Well, I'm certainly not taking any chances with my
daughter's life. And then she told me that Shandra had predicted the fall
of the Soviet Union, the whole messy business with the Royal Family,
the Burt and Lonnie troubles, and that flood in Bangladesh. I said, If
Shandra's so good, why hasn't she given you next week's lottery numbers. Trixie said, Shandra wouldn't soil her powers with vulgarity.

"Is Stoni on duty?" I said.

"She's working graveyard tonight."

"How are things with her and Richie?"

"Richie's got himself a job."

"Doing?"

"He's a bouncer at the Hot Tin Roof."

"Perfect. Have you heard anything about Arthur?"

"I just got a postcard from him. He's down the Cape."

Trixie's little white pill had a lot of words in it. I told her about Dale
and Theresa and how Dale had called Theresa after a week, and they'd
had a polite, but not particularly tender, dinner out at the Cattle Baron.
Trixie said, I have a good feeling about your friends. I think they can work
it out. I told her about my father's curious vision and Spot's improbable
diet, and she said how I had quite a vivid imagination. I told her how I
thought you could always revise your life, how you could work and work

on it, finesse the details, see if what you're saying is what you wanted to be saying. That's what I loved about life, I said. You always have another chance to get it right. She said that would be so nice if only it were true. I told her about learning to ride a bicycle, about seeing my best friend in grammar school get struck in the forehead by lightning. How it lifted him right out of his shoes, incinerated his socks, and charred the bottoms of his feet.

Finally Dr. Pawlak, the oncologist, came in. She smiled, looked at a chart she carried under her arm. Well, she said, everything looks remarkably good. Dr. LeClair got it all out, it looks like. She's as pink in there as Nova lox. I think Judi's going to be okay. I really do. Of course, we'll continue to be cautiously aggressive with our therapy. Dr. Pawlak said that Judi would not be back from recovery for several hours yet, and when she got back she would be in no condition to receive visitors. Probably, we should just come back in the morning.

34.

Time Is a Test of Trouble

A. "AT THE HOSPITAL"

On the day after her surgery, Judi lay in bed fevered and incoherent. She'd been given Dilaudid for the pain and she was hooked up to IV drips and monitors. Stoni, Trixie, Hervey, and I sat in her room and talked quietly about her. Occasionally, Judi would speak a single word: *Scarlet. Baffle. Pygmy. Bouquet. Shame.* Stoni explained the treatment plan. Judi would receive six courses of chemotherapy in three-week cycles, which would begin in two weeks—time to get her strength back. Judi was sweaty, pale, and grimacing. Hervey chewed gum and dug dirt from his fingernails. He told us about an uncle of his who was digested by a slow-eating cancer. Trixie cleaned out her purse and told us all that we had nothing to worry about. The worse was over. Stoni told us to expect problems. First of all, there would be the withdrawal from the painkillers and the steroids. Then there would be the hormonal changes brought on by the hysterectomy. And then the chemo was likely to be unpleasant. There would be possible further surgery—to insert a Port-a-Cath in her chest, first, and later, to take a second look inside. Yes, Trixie said, but the worst is over. Let's look on the bright side. Stoni said, Well, the bright side is that Judi should be out of here in four days if everything goes well. The four days, it turns out, stretched into a week.

I had to deal with Judi's initial indifference to my being there and her subsequent anger. She said I was a selfish bastard, and I suppose she was right. After all, I hadn't even sent her flowers. I must have thought my presence by her side would be comfort enough. Trixie and Hervey sent a bouquet of pink roses; Judi's colleagues at work sent a blooming milk-and-wine lily; even Noel sent flowers—red carnations and baby's breath. Arthur sent a card; Richie sent a card. I just showed up. After the first day I figured, What the hell, I screwed up already. What's the point?

Biff Evinrude got discharged on Tuesday, but refused to leave. He sat in the solarium wailing and keening and cursing the nurses. A pair of security guards took him away. Stoni told me that Biff was a notorious chronic at all the local hospitals. He'd opened his abdomen one time with a filleting knife, made a lateral incision just below the navel, and fished out several inches of intestine. Then he telephoned the paramedics. Another time he stapled his dick to his thigh with four industrial staples. Get out of town, I said. Stoni said, It gets worse. I don't want to hear it, Stoni.

Layla came for a visit by herself. I asked her where Pozzo Beckett was. She told me he'd gone to Vermont with a couple of characters named Bo and Peep, who were humanoid emissaries from another galaxy. So what's in Vermont? I said. That's where the spaceship is picking them up, she said. They're going to Venus. I said, Venus? That would be impossible, Layla. They'd burn up, disintegrate. Layla said, Not if you know what you're doing. And you forget, she said, who Pozzo is. I said, And you passed up the chance to go? She told me she didn't have the fifty bucks for the ticket.

B. "AT DENTALAND"

Small world. It turned out that I knew my new dentist, Dr. Vigeant. She was the same Ginny Vigeant I went to grammar school with. She had been overweight then, quiet, and very smart. She sat between Carolyn Cupit and Carla Nettlebladt in eighth grade. She looked at my tooth and shook her head. Who did this? she said, meaning the dismal crown. I told her. She checked my records, nodded. You normally get nitrous oxide? And Novocain, I said. She smiled. I said, I'm not at all ashamed of having a low threshold of pain. She patted my arm and told me not to get so defensive. She explained how she would take this monstrosity out of my mouth, make a cast—I know you've done this all before—fit a temporary crown, and in a week and a half I'd have a tooth I could be proud of. We agreed on a discounted price. Even the temporary will look better than what you've got, she said. She said she needed me awake for some of this business today, but if I wanted, she could put me under for a while. I wanted. Very definitely. Under the gas I dreamed that Spot and I were cruising down a back road in Vermont. I was driving my father's car, the '71 Plymouth Fury. Spot was watching cows out the window and telling me that some dogs, mostly your purebreds, believed in an afterlife, but he certainly wasn't one of them. I said, Look at me when you talk. I want to see your lips move.

C. "AT THERAPY"

Martha said that her life was collapsing, that she was feeling self-destructive, that if anything happened to her, it would be my fault. I'll tell you how bad it is, she said. I'm reading self-help books, listening to self-improvement tapes. She had invested sixteen years in our relationship, and now it was not paying off. What was she supposed to do? How could I expect her just to start over? Do you know what's out there? she said. Do you? Slimeballs with hairy backs, bald heads, and groping hands. Worms, she said. Cretins. Moral degenerates. Both Martha and Terry referred to my behavior as a "midlife crisis," and it pissed me off royally, I suppose, because it made me seem both predictable and ordinary. I'd rather be on fire than be ordinary.

D. "AT 137 VANZETTI DRIVE"

While Judi was in the hospital, I left the typewriter on her kitchen table. I kept the lawn mowed, the hedges trimmed, the shrubbery pruned. I got my first real acceptance for a story from *The Quixote Quarterly*. The story was "Mr. Buttinski," about what happens when a man hears a terrible domestic dispute through the bedroom wall of his apartment. It's the landscaper guy—Mr. Greengenes, his trucks say—and his wife. The man, Al DeBettancourt, can hear the husband accuse the wife of having someone's (sounded like "Fernando's") cock in her mouth. He hears her plead with her husband. He hears punches and slaps. Something, a lamp maybe, or, Jesus, maybe her head, slams against the wall. Al yells, "I'm calling the police!" and everything goes quiet. That's how the story starts.

Anyway, I was understandably in heaven, but I had no one to share the moment with. Spot could tell I was excited when I read Mr. Robt. Coffin's letter of acceptance to him. He wagged his tail and licked my leg, but then he went right back to chewing on the plastic bedpan I'd brought home for him. I felt legitimate for the first time. Real. Valid. I was encouraged to get back to Hobbs, back to Dale and Theresa.

It was a Sunday afternoon. Theresa must have spoken with the children, or maybe they really did miss having Dale around. Anyway, Theresa and Caitlin are in the kitchen making pan-fried chicken, smashed potatoes, as Caitlin calls them, and snow peas. Dale and the boy are on the living room floor building a house of cards. When the house collapses, Peter just laughs and laughs. Dale pretends to be frustrated, and they begin again. The dinner is more than delicious. After eating and doing the dishes—Theresa washes, Dale dries—the four of them go for a walk. Dale pulls Peter in a red wagon. Dale feels proud, like he's been responsible for something significant in his life. He feigns ease, like he's so used to these Sunday walks. Dale stays the night. After making love with Theresa, he wonders is it the feeling of family he enjoyed or that warmth coupled with independence. He was, after all, uncommitted if not unengaged. He thought about Keynes, home alone, and he realized he was being irresponsible by staying over. Maybe the next time, he thinks, he'll bring the dog along. Theresa has her back to him. She is not asleep. She's staring at the clock on the nightstand.

Two days after my story was accepted, I got a rejection in the mail. This sort of thing keeps you humble. You're only as good as your last verb. The story was called "And Then the Windows Failed." The editor at the *Great Salt Lake Review,* Maurice Fields, called the characters unimportant, the language arch, and the plot pedestrian. He included a subscription form with his letter. A joker.

35.

Post-op

I WAS ON MY WAY TO PICK UP JUDI AT THE HOSPITAL. SUPPOSEDLY, DR. PAWLAK would meet us there for a pep talk. Judi had already given me the bad news over the phone the previous afternoon. The cancer was, in fact, a little worse than the tumor board had originally thought. Stage IV. I said, III-A, IV, what's the difference? Judi said, There's no Stage V. She read to me from the notes she'd taken. Undifferentiated epithelial carcinoma of the ovary. Malignant cells implanted on the peritoneum, on the surface of the liver, the stomach, the colon, the omentum—whatever that is—on the bladder, on the diaphragm. This sucks, Laf. Judi began to cry. I said, Hold on, I'll be right up. But she told me she's already been doped up and would be asleep in like five minutes, and anyways, Trixie was there, and she'd see me in the morning.

Judi was sitting in the chair near the window. She had on her blue silk shirt and her denim skirt, and she looked great, maybe because I had braced myself for worse. Judi said her throat was sore. They'd been making her cough all the time to keep her lungs clear while she was in bed. She showed me her leg and foot exercises.

Dr. Pawlak walked in, followed by four young interns, three men and a woman. Probably here to see how you deal with one of the tough cases. She shook my hand, Judi's, leaned against the foot of the bed. She gave Judi a schedule of the chemotherapy. Judi said, Is it worth it? All eyes on the doctor. What we're attempting to do is halt the spread and kill any wandering tumors, cells, that sort of thing. Six cycles. Every three weeks. We're going to be very aggressive. You'll be getting intravenous administrations of a combination of drugs. She discussed side effects. The interns took notes. All fast-growing cells would be affected: hair follicles, bone marrow, cells in the lining of the mouth, the stomach, the bowels. But all the damage—the hair loss, the sores, and so on—are temporary. So we'll see you in two weeks. And then she was gone, entourage following.

The nurse who was wheeling Judi to the front door had a guardian angel pin on her uniform. She smiled at me and said it sure looked like rain today, but we sure could use it. I nodded. Had I missed a drought or something? I ran ahead to the parking lot and pulled the car around to the pickup lane.

Judi rolled down her window, said it felt so good to breathe fresh air. She closed her eyes, let the wind blow in her face. I said, Where to? She said, The drugstore, I'm afraid. It began to sprinkle. Judi closed the window. She said, I have this feeling like the past is reasserting itself. I said, What do you mean? She said, Like this cancer is an expression of some pattern in my life. I said, You've been reading too many psychology books. She said, But I've never been sick before. I don't know.

I touched Judi's hand. I said, We're going to get through this. I had this feeling that elevated me, a feeling of insight, courage, hope, and this unwarranted but insistent confidence. I felt like I was telling the absolute truth for once in my life. And I had said *we*, not *you*. Sometimes I surprise myself.

36.

The Honey of Poison-Flowers

THEY STARTED JUDI OUT THAT MORNING WITH A BENADRYL DRIP TO PREPARE HER body for the chemo. She was cheerful, said she was relieved, in a way, to be doing something finally about her recovery. An hour later, a nurse administered cisplatin and Cytoxan. By then I was at Our Lady of the Sea dredging clams in flour. Stoni called and explained how she was prepared to be the home-care nurse for as long as it took. I hadn't until that moment even thought about the care that Judi might need or how I would have to be involved in her care and recovery.

I picked Judi up at Memorial in the morning. At first she wouldn't or couldn't talk. Just stared at the dashboard. I didn't want to say, Jesus, you look like hell, Judi, which she did. So I stayed quiet. Judi said, "My veins are full of ants." She scratched her left arm. "Burns and itches." She took a long breath. I could see that she had more to say, but she was so groggy.

"You feel like shit, huh?"

She shook her head. "Not so bad. My scalp's numb." She smiled, touched her head. "Just weak."

"We'll be home in a few minutes. I've got the couch set up for you."

"Are you going to put all this in your novel?"

"What novel?"

She gave me a look, the frown and the raised eyebrow. "The one about the aspiring writer and his dying girlfriend."

"I'm not writing about this."

"You're taking notes," she said.

I told her I had enough problems with Dale and Theresa and with little stories right now. I didn't need any other lives to mess around with.

She told me I was full of shit. And then she said, "You'll end up hating me."

"I will not."

"My hands feel different," she said. She flexed them, made fists. "Like cold, numb. Like less sensitive."

After a week Judi was just beginning to feel better—like she had the flu, a little nauseated, stiff, and headachy. But she had to admit, the chemo wasn't as bed as what she had read about. Now, if only the drugs are doing their job. Judi called the office, made plans to get back to work with a reduced caseload. A couple of days later her hair was shedding. Just what I needed, she said, another reason to hate myself. Now I'm ugly, too. I said, You are not. In a way, she looked exotic and vulnerable, and I found that attractive. I kissed her head all over. I went out and bought her a long paisley scarf, a Red Sox cap, and a black beret. She stood in front of the mirror and kept trying them on, adjusting them, trying them on again.

She told me she missed having sex. She cried. I said we could try. The experience was unnerving because of Judi's obvious physical discomfort—she couldn't lie on her side or tolerate my weight. But it was me, too. I felt squeamish about the whole business. Her fresh scars, her wincing. There was too much else there in bed with us for me to get aroused. I tried to just fondle her. She squeezed my hand to stop. It's okay, she said. I'm sore.

We lay there in bed. This must be difficult for you, all this celibacy. I figured I'd be noble about it. I said, Not really. I've never been, like, obsessed with sex. You could ask Martha. Judi said, I don't have to. Ouch. I said, What do you mean by that? I like you the way you are. She kissed my nose.

37.

The Disassembly Line

I SAT AT THE KITCHEN TABLE, MY EYES CLOSED, MY HANDS OVER MY EYES. STONI was in helping Judi, changing the bedclothes. Richie Muneyhun was out on the deck, drinking his morning beers, listening to the radio, sunning himself.

I knew what Dale was thinking. He's thinking that maybe this relationship with Theresa is fine just the way it is. Dale's finished shaving, and now he's checking his beard in the mirror. He hates mirrors. He keeps noticing things he doesn't like—how his hair is even thinner than he thought it was; how his ears are getting as fuzzy as peaches. When did this happen? And what's the evolutionary point of it, anyway?

Dale gets out his little scissors and begins to trim his eyebrows and his nose hairs. He can feel a cold sore getting ready to erupt on his upper lip, can feel that first itch. He'll put a tea bag on it before he leaves for school. Dale thinks, Where was I? What am I so upset about? Maybe I've got exactly what I want here. I live in my own house, Theresa in hers. My life is quiet, clean, orderly—the way I like it. Dale combs his hair. He's not sure he'll exactly verbalize what he's thinking to Theresa, but it all seems to make sense, doesn't it? They have each other, *and* they have their separate lives as well. In a way, Dale thinks, that's ideal. That's what Dale was thinking: *ideal*. What I was thinking was Theresa's not going to go for this at all. What I thought I should do was put the two of them in a room alone and have them talk about their futures and then stand back and see what happens. My next scene, then: let's see, Dale's living room; Keynes on his chair, Dale and Theresa on the couch, sort of staring at the television; Saturday afternoon. The kids are with their grandmother. Theresa says, Dale, what are your intentions? He makes a face probably, feigns incomprehension. But he knows precisely what she's talking about.

A couple more days of this, and then she'll feel fine, Stoni said. She poured herself a coffee, lit up a smoke. She looked out the door at Richie and said that Judi had fallen asleep. About ten bad days with the chemo, she said, and then ten better days. And then it starts all over again.

I asked Stoni if she ever thought about dying. Ovarian cancer, I'd read, runs in families. She said that she tried not to, but she was a nurse, after all, saw death all the time. So what do you think about it? I said. It cures all diseases, she said.

Stoni told me she wasn't afraid of death, but what came or didn't come after death. That's the thing, you know.

"What do you think follows death?" I said.

Stoni looked at me, at her hands, at the clock, at the ceiling. "Darkness, lightness, weightlessness, emptiness. I don't know." She stood. "I think it's out there waiting for us." Out there? Did she mean Richie? Stoni stared out the window over the sink. "Like the edge of a cliff." Stoni turned to me. She looked toward Judi's bedroom. "Every minute could be our last," she said. "How do we live with that?"

I said, "You mean death's waiting out there in the future?"

Stoni sat down at the table and fired up another Winston. "Not just in time," she said, "but place. That's where death waits." Stoni smiled. She said I was a morbid son of a bitch. Maybe so, but evidently I had hit on a melancholy streak in her. She said, "The future is fixed. There's not a damned thing we can do about it. That's what Einstein meant. Space and time is a landscape. It's there." She pointed out the window. "I'm not going to live one second longer or shorter whether I smoke three packs a day or swim through a shit storm."

I said, "You don't really believe that, Stoni. You're a nurse, for crying out loud."

You can't think long about dying without getting reckless or depressed unless you're a religious zealot, I suppose, and I'm not. Anyway, this time

I got reckless and manic. I decided that I would tell Martha the truth—that I was living with Judi, had been right along, not in a travel trailer at all. And then it would be Martha's move.

I called Martha's office. I suppose if she had answered, I would have chickened out. But I got her machine. I confessed, apologized, hesitated, said I guessed I'd see her at counseling on Thursday, and hung up. I hoped to God she hadn't been sitting at her desk, screening her calls.

In the kitchen, Richie was kissing Stoni good-bye. He was off to see his parole officer. He rubbed his gut, complained about being out of shape. He looked at me, said, Jail is discipline, man. Everyone should do some hard time. Keeps you alert, tough. Like a tiger. Then he asked me if I wanted to get rid of Spot. Of course not, I said. He said, I really like that mutt.

When Richie left, Stoni told me Judi was her hero. She said, She raised me. Fed me, walked me to school, told me bedtime stories about Dad and how he'd gone off in search of George, and when he found him, they'd come back to us, and we'd all live happily ever after. I loved her for that lie. Every night Sir Ronnie, our dad, would discover another clue and defeat a villain and almost find his son. She told me Arthur Bositis would be stopping by for lunch. I suggested that this could be dangerous, couldn't it? Stoni said, Not if Richie doesn't find out. Why don't you join us? she said. Arthur's bringing some ground sirloin. We heard Judi call for her sister. Stoni excused herself. I cleared my work off the table so we could eat.

The phone rang. It was my father. How are the eyes? I said. That's why I called, he said. The palm trees are red. Your mother's mole, the one on her forehead? Well, he said, it's a greenish purple. The ocean's orange. It's so amazing. I said, And you're okay with that? Sure, he said. But you know what it does? It changes the way food tastes. I have to close my eyes when I eat. Your mother's beginning to suspect that something's up. I hear her whispering to Edgar over the phone. Do your eyes ever hurt? I said. Not even a little, he said. They're marvelous little machines, aren't they?

I saw Arthur drive by the house once. The next time he parked a few doors down under a maple. When he saw, I guess, that the coast was clear of Muneyhuns, he got out of his car. Arthur smelled like blood. He left his white butcher's coat on the deck railing. We had beers while Stoni made salad and burgers. I got out a jar of strained peaches from the fridge and went to feed Judi. I kissed her forehead. She opened her eyes, shook her head. You don't want to eat? Sleep, she said. Okay, I said, we'll try later.

Arthur and Stoni mixed up a sauce of mayonnaise, ketchup, Dijon mustard, lemon juice, Tabasco, and a drop of vinegar and put it on their hamburgs. So, I thought, they shared intimate culinary secrets. I wondered what was going on here. Why Richie Muneyhun's name was not mentioned, why Arthur would put his life in danger, and why Stoni would encourage him to. I listened for the rev of a motorcycle engine.

I said, "How are things on the kill floor, Arthur?" I expected a joke. "Deadly," he'd say. "Stunning." Or maybe, "I can't beef about it," or something.

He said, "Puke heads."

"Excuse me?"

"Got us a load of bad cattle this morning. Puke heads. Contaminated. What we call Four-D livestock: dead, dying, diseased, and disabled. Pathetic stuff. That happens once in a while."

I looked at our lunch.

He said, "Not this. Don't worry. I know where my meat comes from, and it ain't from no abscessed steer."

"It's so gruesome what goes on over there," Stoni said.

Arthur made a face. "It's not gruesome. We just take them apart so you can eat them." He explained how the cattle get the bullet in the head and don't feel a thing. How the meat packers cut them apart piece by piece—head, guts, skin, limbs—hoist them by hooks on an overhead track, and carve away.

I wanted to ask Arthur what his intentions were. Was he planning to outlast Richie Muneyhun? It seemed to me like a pretty dangerous triangle he was balanced on. Arthur looked at his watch, said he had to be going, had some pus-filled carcasses to air out. He looked at me and smiled.

Later, when Stoni had gone home on the back of Richie's Harley, I sat beside Judi's bed and fed her baby food. She ate most of it. Her hair was falling out undramatically but steadily. I took some clumps of it off the pillow. Judi made a disgusted face.

"I'm so sick of feeling like shit," she said.

I held her hand. It felt hollow, cold.

"I don't know if it's worth it," she said.

"Stoni says there's bad days and good days. You're going to feel better tomorrow and you'll be on your feet in a couple of days."

"And then it starts all over."

"But it might not be as bad the next time."

She looked at me. "Why don't you try it." She said she wanted to sleep and would I come to bed with her and read her a story. I undressed and slid under the covers.

38.

What's Cooking

So let's talk about food. My own culinary vision, you understand, is seriously myopic. Consider that for much of my childhood our family had the identical menu every week. On Mondays we ate American chop suey, which, if you are fortunate enough not to know about, is elbow macaroni and hamburg in a tomato soup–based sauce. On Tuesdays we had meat loaf glazed with tomato-soup concentrate, baked potatoes in their jackets, and a vegetable—either canned waxed beans, canned beats, or canned peas. Wednesday was shepherd's pie, which we called *pâté de chinois*, for some reason. Thursdays, spaghetti and meatballs. Friday, tuna noodle casserole with a top layer of potato chips. Saturday, frankfurts and beans with brown bread. Sunday, pot roast, brown potatoes, and string beans. The same bill of fare on the same night every week for years. Follow that up with years of eating parochial school cafeteria food—the absolute nadir of American cuisine: sloppy joes; nachos; assorted flash-frozen, deep-fried chicken parts; alleged cheeseburgers, always well-done; instant mashed potatoes; cold creamed corn; elasticized pizza facsimile; and so on. So you can imagine that this would be a great leap of imagination for me—trying to prepare a week's worth of lunches for Judi and me and our guests. I make delicious hot chili, used to make terrific bacon and eggs until the cholesterol scare (my numbers are in the stratosphere), make beef fondue, which I could eat every day (but see "cholesterol scare"), make a decent salad ("decent" means with olives, scallions, feta, lots of onions, Tuscan peppers). And that's it. I started out the week with great hope. I consulted Judi's cookbooks. I couldn't shake the deeply held belief that the four basic food groups were indeed beef, tomato, starch, and sweet.

Monday: *Eating Our Way to Recovery.* Guests: *Trixie, Hervey, and Noel.* Menu: *French onion soup; marinated scallops en brochette served on a bed of rice pilaf; orange Jell-O.*

Judi did feel well enough on the eleventh day after chemo to consider real food, to get out of bed, to get dressed, to fret over her hair, to complain about the intense pain in her upper thighs. She sat in the kitchen while I prepared the brunch. The phone rang, and she told me to let it. She had already disarmed the answering machine. As I put the scallops, bacon, and lime strips on skewers at the sink, Judi sat at the kitchen table and read me a story from page four of the *T&G* about a million abandoned children roaming the ghost towns and the countryside of Rwanda. Judi said, It's like the world has gone insane.

We were eating on the deck if the rain held off. I set the table, put the food on the grill. Sitting outside in the sunshine with sunglasses and a wide-brimmed straw hat, Judi looked ceramic, brittle. Our guests arrived. I brought out a pitcher of beer and a tureen of the soup. Judi drank water and passed on the soup after sipping a spoonful of broth. No one would say anything, but I could tell I had overdone the salt. Judi passed on the entrée as well. Trixie kept saying how robust and lovely Judi looked, don't you think so, Hervey? Hervey would nod. He said in his opinion cancer don't activate until you open a person up. That's what gets it going. No doctor is ever getting inside his guts. Guy at work, Polack name of Kazmierczak, Pete Kazmierczak, healthy as a freaking bull, gets his annual checkup. They see a spot on his lung, open him up, in a month he's eighty-five pounds and dead. Noel said Edmund was pressing license plates in Walpole these days. Worked himself right into a good position in the plant. Every time I see a car go by with one of those new red, white, and blue plates I think of my boy. Hervey kept making sour faces. I told him he didn't have to eat the limes. They're mostly there for the flavor they give the scallops. Trixie asked me what the marinade was. Orange juice, vermouth, and vodka. Martini kabobs, Noel said. Thought it had a little kick to it. Judi ate the Jell-O. When they left, I cleaned up. Judi said, I don't know why you're still here. She paused. But I'm glad you are. Thanks, I said. Are you afraid of what people would think if you left me now? She cried. I held her. Was I? I told her, Don't be silly. I put her to bed. What people?

Tuesday: *Mexican Fiesta.* Guests: *Ron, Josh, and Mark.* Menu: *gazpacho; black bean salad; taco tots; chicken burritos; butterscotch-jalapeño pudding.*

Judi ate the gazpacho, had a few bites of salad. She and her colleagues talked about work and clients. I pretended not to listen to their talk about a certain Mr. X, who seemed to be dying from the fear of growing old, or Mrs. Y, who had four children and yet claimed to be a virgin and was fully expecting to ascend into heaven at any moment. That's why she paid cash. Josh said he was as healthy as a pig, just a little touch of AIDS.

Josh told Judi that she needed to change her thinking, had to find herself a doctor whom she could hug, not one who holds her away with test results. Honey, he said, you have to think of this cancer as a chronic disease, not a terminal one. How are you going to live with it, he said, not how are you going to die from it. And you, he said to me, you are going to have to be patient and supportive, and once in a while you're going to have to give her a boot in the ass—whenever she's feeling sorry for herself. You just call Albert if you have a problem with that. We laughed. Josh left Judi with a shopping list for foods, a bag of vitamin pills, phone numbers, books and recipes, and with hope.

When they got up to leave, Josh told Judi, You be good, girlfriend. He told me, Adios, Señor Proulx. Judi apologized for not eating more, said it really was delicious, really. Said she needed a nap, said, Laf, if you really do care about me, then why are you still doing this thing with your wife? She didn't wait for an answer, which was good because I didn't have one. I knew, however, that I'd better consider the question because it would resurface as a topic of conversation and soon.

I put on a jacket and took Spot for a walk. The lights were on in the Boninas' living room. I saw this youngish couple whom I knew only by name on their sofa staring at television, her leg over his leg. They looked so beautiful. I could see my breath in the air and the smoke coming from the Foley's chimney. I felt calm and optimistic. I thought, What a good world this is.

Wednesday: *Prince Spaghetti Day.* Guests: *Stoni and Richie.* Menu: *antipasto; garlic bread; spaghetti and meatballs; spumoni.*

If you visit Jack Kerouac's grave in Lowell—and you should if you haven't—you'll pass under a railway bridge that is painted with the Prince spaghetti logo and this message: "Welcome to Spaghettiville." That's why I buy I buy Prince and not, say, Muller's.

Because of the rain, we ate inside. Judi couldn't get over the cholera sweeping through the refugee camps in Zaire, the thousands of people dying every day. Stoni described the symptoms of cholera for us. Richie changed the subject. Said how depressing it was that you couldn't eat any of the freshwater fish you catch in New England anymore because of the acid rain—we all looked out the window—and the mercury. I tried to picture Richie with a fly rod, waders, and creel. He told me he and his dad used to fish the Quaboag River every Saturday in and out of season when he was young. Used to clean the fish, wrap them in tin foil, stack them like cord wood in the freezer, eat them all winter. You do that now, eat all that trout, you'd probably glow in the dark.

Richie could eat a meatball in one bite. He ate fourteen. Stoni told Judi that Trixie had heard from their father. She called him Ronnie. He's in Henniker, New Hampshire, she said. Just phoned her out of nowhere. Fifteen years between calls. Trixie told him how you were. Judi said, How am I? Sick, Stoni said. I'm sure he's real concerned, Judi said. Richie's beeper went off. He went into the parlor to make a call. We ate our spumoni in silence. A beeper? I thought about those fish piled in a freezer and about fathers you can hardly remember and can never forget.

Thursday: *Dining Out at the El.* Diners: *Martha and I.* Menu: *stuffed grape leaves; kibbe sandwich; baklava.*

Martha likes to talk in restaurants. I like to talk after a few drinks. If I have a few cocktails and no one brings up doctors or Republicans, I get sweet and effusive. After Martha had heard my confession on her answering machine, she left her own message. Said to meet her at eleven-thirty at the El Morocco. We'll have lunch before our session. What she said as we examined the menu was how it must have taken some courage to make that call. I was disarmed. Was she setting me up for the fall? Would there be a messy scene in the next few minutes? We ordered.

Martha ordered a bottle of retsina to go with our dessert. She poured. What was going on? I felt like a traitor to Judi, but the grape leaves were wonderful. I may not know what love is, but I know pleasure. We drank, we smiled, we ate baklava, licked our fingers, got silly, said, What the hell, and ordered another bottle of retsina. We called in sick to marriage counseling. I thought about how love and marriage are different. One is an emotion, the other a relationship. I thought, hell, maybe I do love Martha. Just can't be married to her. I took a deep breath, a sip of retsina, and didn't say anything.

I remembered when I proposed marriage. We were in Martha's backyard, sitting on a stone bench by her mother's garden. The lilacs were blooming. I told her what she already knew—that I had little to offer her except my future. I could hear my voice, could feel its tremor through my bones, but it was like I was sleeping or far away. I told her I loved her. She smiled and kissed my hand. Then she cried. I asked her again would she marry me. This was the nicest thing I ever did for Martha. For anyone. The purest.

Martha asked me how Spot was. Say hi for me, she said. She told a joke about O. J. Simpson, how he was going to take another stab at marriage. She said she heard it from the bishop. I thought maybe one joke about a failed marriage was enough, so I changed the subject to other disasters and wondered how jokes about them start and spread so quickly. We talked about Cape Cod. That's where we were when the Challenger exploded. We were eating in a little restaurant in Truro when we heard. Later we walked around P-town pointing at houses we might want to live in.

We paid the check. Martha said she'd make me coffee. We drove to her place. The apartment smelled different. I sniffed—like vanilla and cinnamon. There were messages on the fridge with names I didn't recognize. Names and phone numbers. Martha had a new stereo. She told me to put on whatever I wanted. I turned on the radio to a jazz show on 'ICN and heard Duke Ellington. We had coffee in the parlor. I noticed these little items that I had bought at flea markets and she used to hate. They were all over the house: the alligator nutcracker, the old box of Hartz Mountain canary food, the photo of Fess Parker in the old frame, the bronzed baby shoes, the ashtray from the Loveless Motel in Nashville, the Lundgren & Jonaitis milk bottle, the 1918 menu from Coney Island Hot Dogs, the Jerry Mahoney ventriloquist's dummy. Martha adjusted the venetian blinds to keep the sun out of our eyes. We went from coffee to wine seamlessly. An insouciant burgundy. Martha took out a photo album, and we paged through it. We laughed at our hairdos and clothes, watched ourselves grow older in minutes. We ended up making love on the floor. When we finished, I didn't want to be the first one to move. Ellington was into "Caravan" by then. The news came on. I didn't move. Martha smelled like buttermilk biscuits. I felt her shoulder twitch. I was free.

Friday: *Blue Light Special.* Guests: *Layla, Pozzo, and Arthur.* Menu: *grilled cheese on white; pickle chips; cole slaw; French fries; lemonade; apple pie à la mode.*

What I was trying to re-create here was the picture on the menu at Kresge's lunch counter in about 1965, back when we used to shine our penny loafers with Vaseline, back before the city fathers built a shopping galleria downtown and all the good stores and all the good lunch counters closed: Woolworth's, Kresge's, Newberry's, Grants, Liggett's, Denholm's, the Waldorf. Menus with pictures of the food. Think about it. Says something about the place, doesn't it? Pride? I don't think so. Anyway, Pozzo didn't eat meat since he came back from space. He'd become a veterinarian, he said.

Judi said I looked distracted. I'm fine, I told her, just at a crucial spot in my story, and I'm preoccupied, sort of. Spot woofed when he heard his name. I told him to hush. Judi ate her grilled cheese, but not the crust. She drank her lemonade. Her appetite wasn't much, but it was encouraging. Pozzo was pretty close-mouthed about Venus, actually. Demure, you might say. Arthur got him to open up a little bit. He wanted to know what they ate on Venus. Pozzo said, Not each other, not anymore. They eat something called *fartlek,* which is organic but not animal and not quite plant and looks like gefilte fish, like a brick of gefilte fish. Layla said, Pozzo brought some back; tastes great, kind of.

Pozzo, I said, you still the sun? Judi kicked me under the table. He nodded. I asked him if he intended for us to understand this solar image as a metaphor, like Jesus or Osiris or Adonis or one of those. He said not. So who was your father? I said. He said, Marlon Beckett from Grafton Street. Not Chaos or the Void? I said. Why was I hassling him? Pozzo said, My dad split when I was like seven or eight. Took off with the baby-sitter, Giselle Turgeon. Even though Giselle was in high school, I was in love with her, too. I saw the mythic dimensions Pozzo's story was taking on, but I didn't push him. If he hadn't already thought of tracking down his old man and exacting revenge, then I wasn't going to bring it up.

We heard the roar and backfire of a motorcycle and froze. Arthur dropped his fork and his jaw. He paled. We listened as the pitch of the engine increased—Arthur pushed back his chair and measured the height of the Devlins' fence—and then faded. I looked at Arthur. I wanted to say, Why do you do this? Why go out with a woman who wants another man, a dangerous man? Why put your life in peril? But I kept quiet. No matter, Arthur heard me. Because I love that girl, he said. I'd do anything. Love is patient, Pozzo said. Layla took Pozzo's hand, kissed it, said, Let me file these nails for you, honey.

After lunch, Stoni stopped back to take Judi in for tests at Memorial. She brought along a silk kerchief for Judi. Green and gold. She tied it onto Judi's head. This would be Judi's first venture back into the world since the chemo. She seemed apprehensive. I walked her to the car. She walked slowly, as if she were a full glass of water that didn't want to spill. When they left, I changed the sheets on the bed. Every day now I could brush together a handful of hair from Judi's pillow. I went to the kitchen and sat down to work. I didn't write about Dale and Theresa. I wrote about a boy and his father in Maine. Somehow that's what the week had meant to me. I don't try to figure it out. I just write it. When I finished the story a week later, I sent it off to *Probable Cause*. Here it is:

39

"The Wood Inside"
by Lafayette Proulx

WHEN THE EARTH FINALLY THAWED LAST SPRING, IT WAS OPENING WEEK OF rainbow season on the Big Wilson, and we buried the Easter animals that Dad had wrapped in tin foil and stacked in his freezer alongside Hector Papineau's dressed-out venison: the pair of Muscovy ducklings from the Ben Franklin's in Guilford who caught pneumonia, Mom said, from sleeping out on the back porch; Simone's cozy leghorn chick, Lulu, whose eyes leaked green syrup, and whose beak softened to oatmeal; and my Belgian hare, Jake, who'd gnawed nearly through the claw-foot leg on Mom's wardrobe before choking on a splinter, digging at his neck, tearing through his fur, skin, and sinew, trying to reach the wood inside.

Mom's husband, George, dropped us by Dad's on his way fishing. Simone and I ate Sugar Pops and watched TV at the kitchen table while Dad showered and dressed. We watched cartoons. Simone kept her mittens on. In his bedroom, Dad answered a phone call and spoke quietly to whoever it was. I carried our milky bowls to the sink and set them in an inch of sudsy, gray water beside the two glasses. I took a Marlboro from the box on the counter, slipped it in my shirt pocket. Took the book of matches, too. From the Dog Sled Tavern. We watched that coyote blow himself to smithereens again with a tube of Acme dynamite.

We buried our animals off the path in the woods that leads down to the Bowditch farm. Buried them wrapped like candies three feet deep by the speckled alders. Dad tamped the dirt with the rusted blade of his spading fork. I said a prayer to St. Francis. Simone hugged Dad's leg and sniffled. He smoothed her hair. She closed her eyes. We drove to the Dix-field Diner. Dad does all his talking in public.

We sat in a booth. Silver and blue vinyl seats. The diner smelled like Dutch Cleanser. Simone and I sat across from Dad. He wore the plaid flannel shirt we'd bought for him last Christmas. Dad joked about mud season with Mary Moody, our waitress. I could see Dad's reflection in the window, see the back of his head like the dark side of the moon. And beyond his reflection, I could see George's pickup parked across the street outside Ledoux's Olde Tyme Inn. Dad told Mary he'd have two eggs sunny-side, bacon, and wheat toast. And give the kids whatever they want. Two chocolate milks and two grilled cheese sandwiches.

Simone kicked her feet against our booth, blew chocolate bubbles through her straw. Dad hung his spoon from his nose to make Simone laugh. He saw me staring at his hand and at the space where a finger used to be. He smiled, touched the back of my hand with his fingertips, drew a circle. Dad sponged the yoke with his toast, ate the toast, clapped the crumbs from his hands. He sipped his coffee and watched Mary Moody slide a dish of apple pie from the glass dispenser at the counter. He sat up straight. And then he started talking.

After my father left, quit Sawyer's Home Heating Oil, and moved to Delaware, that's when Donny Morin told me we could have saved the Easter animals, could have stuffed them with sawdust like his old man did with the twenty-three-inch rainbow he's got mounted over the sofa in their trailer. Donny watched him do it. You scrape what's inside, all that damp and shiny stuff, and then whatever it is will last forever. That's the way it works. Donny said his old man said you only get to keep what's gone.

40.

A Literary Evening at Circe's Bar & Grille

I STILL WASN'T SURE THIS WAS SUCH A HOT IDEA. OUR LOCAL LITERARY MAGA-zine, the *Blackstone Review* (which had rejected without comment two of my stories, "Tula Baker's Face-Lift" and "Tenderness," and three ses-tinas, one with these ambitious end words: *cleave, schizocarp, highboy, neb-bish, patulous,* and *yammer,* all in the last year), was sponsoring a literary reading, featuring writers from the forthcoming issue. I had to ask my-self, Was I going to the reading for revenge?

I'm of the school that believes literature, like children, should be seen and not heard. But Nicky told me this was Victorian thinking, and I should be ashamed of myself. He told me these lumpen poets were my comrades. You think I should go and mingle, then? I said. We used to mingle, he said, now we network. He patted me on the back, winked.

I called Judi after I'd strained the fat in the deep fryer to see if she'd like to join us. She said, Thanks, but no thanks. Said she just wasn't up to it—all the barroom smoke would only make her ill. She told me to just go on with Nicky and have a good time. Stoni was bringing over a movie for them to watch. *Charlie Chan at the Opera.* I told her if she needed me for anything to call Circe's.

So Nicky and I closed up Our Lady's and walked downtown. We grabbed stools at the bar, back by the door. That way we could whisper if we wanted to be snide, could roll our eyes if we had to. And if we needed to leave, we could slip out without disturbing the patrons, dis-tracting the readers, or ruffling any metaphors. We should have recognized how we were only reinforcing our bad attitudes right off. Nicky ordered two ouzos, in honor of Homer, he said.

I recognized a couple of people. One was this bearded guy I've seen for years grilling hot dogs at Coney Island. And for some reason I think he's a defrocked priest, but I don't know why I think that. Another guy I knew was sitting with a young woman who looked familiar, probably an old student of mine.

If you're sitting home every day writing, you could get the idea that you're the only practicing writer in the city. But here they were, the Worcester literati, and they all seemed to know each other and seemed so delighted to be together. And none of them knew me from Adam's off ox. I caught the novelist at the end of the bar looking at me. I smiled. He nodded. I knew who he was from his photo in the *Telegram & Gazette*. He'd left town a decade ago and was back to sign some books at Tatnuck Booksellers. Wrote a Southern gothic novel, of all things. He sat alone, I noticed, and drank steadily. Trying to be Faulkner, I guessed.

The first reader was an English professor from Holy Cross who had several books of poetry published by small but prestigious presses. His name was Scott something, and he was quite charming in an earnest and self-effacing way. I bet his students loved him. He told us that he got most of his inspiration from the wilderness, from his love for his wife, Liz—Liz is here tonight, he said; he asked her to stand; she refused.

Scott recited a poem about fishing in the Quabbin Reservoir and hooking something profound and deep that jolted him out of his worldly cares. And there were golden scales gleaming in the sun and thunderous slaps of water and ten-pound test line tangled up in Heaven's Gate and later a meal of transcendentally poached rainbow trout. I looked at Nicky, ordered two more ouzos. Nicky said he had to pee and did so while the performance poets were setting up.

A guy who called himself Bonewheel (Hi, Mom, it's Bonewheel. How's Dad?) played saxophone while his partner, Jane Eyre, performed a long, Whitmanesque poem about a bus trip across America. The poem, "Inside/Outside USA," was nightmarishly gruesome, but the music was sweet bebop. Bats burst from storm drains, tarmac liquefied, corpses floated into living rooms on tides of radioactive sewage. Fellatio was frequently, gratuitously, and prodigiously performed in malls, at Burger Kings, and in supermarkets. Pus oozed from air-conditioning vents. The audience chuckled, nodded their heads, applauded, as if to say, Yes, yes, this is the way we live these days in America. Nicky whispered that Jane Eyre must be a Nazi.

The featured reader was a large African-American woman whose photo graced the cover of the newest issue of the *Review*. Her name was June McClary, and she was from Boston. She had just published her first novel, a tale about coming of age in Roxbury called '*Buryed Alive*. June told us immediately that she was thirty-something and a lesbian. A few in the audience barked at that, hooted their approval. Then she read a chapter from the novel dealing with the central character's first sexual encounter with a white girl after a gym class at South Boston High. It was very funny and heartwarming. It really was.

During the question-and-answer period that followed, June told us that she had been compared to Toni Morrison, Maya Angelou, Toni Cade Bambara, and J. D. Salinger, and she was quite serious. But, she added, I don't write like no one. Whoopi Goldberg, she said, was interested in the novel for the movies. Applause.

I suppose it was inevitable, the ensuing discussion of the pitiful state of contemporary American poetry. The audience for poetry had disappeared, Scott said, and it's the fault of the poets. This was another popular notion at Circe's. Poets write for other poets. It's become an elitist pursuit, he said. Not in this room, I thought. In other countries poets are honored and respected. Everyone writes poetry, Scott said, but no one reads it. One young woman suggested that rap music was the real poetry of America, and though she got no support from the peanut gallery, it was agreed that poetry needed to be more accessible, needed to abandon its literary pretensions if it ever again wanted to be taken seriously. If people don't understand poetry, it's the poets' fault, not the people's.

Nicky raised his hand, but no one saw him. I ordered two more. Nicky spoke up. He said, "You know, if we make poetry really simple, really accessible, like you say, even our pets will be able to understand it. Thank you." His pronouncement was followed by silence and knitted brows. Then he said, "In fact, we could just make endearing noises." I told Nicky he was upsetting my comrades.

June McClary announced that she and her friends were going to a gay bar and did anyone else want to join them. Scott and Liz were quarreling quietly, decorously. Nicky and I switched to beers.

41.

I Looked Up and Saw the Two of Us Reflected in the Mirror on Judi's Bedroom Ceiling

WE SPELLED *Is*. I WAS OUT STRAIGHT AND APPROPRIATELY FIRST PERSON SINGU-lar. Judi lay curled like an *s*. She was dead asleep and talking in what could have been Bulgarian, I suppose, or Klingon. Whatever it was she was saying, she was excited about it. I heard the painting crew arrive at Mr. Lesperence's and heard Spot bark twice at them. I closed my eyes and looked ahead at my day, saw marriage counseling at two. I hadn't spoken with Martha since our surprising assignation of last week, and I had no idea what she was thinking. Maybe everything will be all right between us. Maybe I should take a shower. Judi stopped her chattering. Next door, someone extended an aluminum ladder, resting it against the house.

So why had Martha and I made love? Does it signal that intimacy has returned? I opened one eye. Judi straightened her legs, extended an arm. Now we spelled *If*. Was I reading too much into sleeping positions? So while I lay pondering my inexplicable infidelity with my wife—an in-teresting concept, for sure—Judi was facing a second round of chemo or trying not to face it. Stoni would be taking her to Memorial later this morning. They'd be home before I got off work. I was hoping her treat-ment would go better this time. Judi didn't even want to talk about it. She had told me the night before not to wake her up. All she wanted to do, she said, was sleep. Sleep until she was healthy again.

When I was in the first grade at St. Stephen's, Sister Mary Timothy explained sin to our class by drawing three milk bottles on the chalkboard. Then she produced a stick of brown chalk from her desk drawer. She explained to us that the bottles were like our souls. See how nice? she said. And then she smiled. The first bottle she left as it was and said, That is your soul in the state of grace. Grace is green, I thought. Got it so far. In the second bottle, Sister shaded in a blotch of brown with the side of her chalk right where I figured the heart of my soul was. That's a venial sin, she said. And here's another—she browned in another area and then another. Then she embrowned the third bottle completely and stepped back away from the board. Did anyone know what this third bottle was called? Roy Desaulniers yelled out, Chocolate milk! Sister ignored him, probably forgave him, might even have said a prayer for him. Mortal sin, she said, and she let that sink in. And you will be going straight to hell if you die with a soul in this condition. She tapped the soiled milk bottle with the point of her chalk. We've talked about hell, she reminded us. You do remember? How could we forget? Fires, body sores, darkness, melting eyeballs, no Mom, no Dad, no candy, monsters with ice picks, buried to our necks in dung. Lasts longer than school does. Yes, we remember, Sister. I was terrified. Well, Sister said, there is a cure. Hallelujah! Tell me now. She held up an eraser. Confession, she said. Confession, I'll have to remember that and get me some. I committed the word to memory. Then Sister erased the mortal sin and the venial sins. Why was I thinking of all this now? Because that's how I imagined cancer, a spreading brownness, a corruption in the milk bottle of your body. And chemo is the eraser.

Terry sensed the tension as soon as Martha and I walked in and sat on opposite ends of the couch. She smiled and nodded hello. She waited. Martha fussed in her seat. I imagined myself far away, in a stone house with the fireplace going and a view down the hill of a quiet lake. Martha spoke:

Why did I throw him out of the house? Because I wanted him to love me. He says love is not something you control. He doesn't know what love is if he can say that. Love is not a condition; it's a behavior, a desire. My problem is I love a man who does not love me. I've parked for hours outside her house. I've seen him walk by the window running his hand through his hair. I've seen the lights go out in the house, seen the lights come back on. I've heard Spot's barking.

I said, "Yes, Terry, I heard what she said. I don't know where to start." I took a deep breath and puffed.

"He seduced me," Martha said.

I said, "What the hell are you talking about, Martha?"

Martha reached for a tissue and pulled one from the box on the coffee table. She shook her head and cried.

Terry sat up, leaned forward. "Go with it," she said to Martha.

I said, "Excuse me, but I did not seduce her."

Terry said, "Why don't we listen to what Martha has to say."

Martha caught her breath. "We had lunch and drinks, and we went to my place, and he talked so sweetly and everything."

I couldn't believe it. "How is that seduction, Martha?"

Terry raised her brow to a supercilious level, assured me I'd get my chance to talk. "Right now," she said, "Martha is in a lot of pain."

Martha said, "And now I've probably got AIDS or something from that whore he's fucking."

I looked at Terry for some acknowledgment of the lunacy loose in the room. Terry, though, was holding Martha's hand, telling her to breathe, to release the pain. "What was it like making love to your husband?" she said.

Martha finally got hold of herself. "I wouldn't call it that," she said. "It was just sex. That's all."

A breeze is coming off my lake. I'm through writing for the day. I pour myself a snifter of cognac and sit by the fire and read *The Magic Mountain*. I read until I hear the scrunch of tires on the gravel driveway.

"And how did it feel?" Terry said.

"It felt cheap and humiliating. I was disgusted. The only way I could endure it was to think of something else." She said, "It was like I wasn't even there."

I said, "I could tell."

Martha wheeled around and swung at me, caught me right on the temporary crown with the back of her hand or her wrist or something and screamed that I was a bastard. When I looked up, Terry was holding Martha's shoulders. I held my hand to my bleeding lip. Martha cried. The crown was loose. I decided just to bleed on Terry's shag carpet. She could afford the steam cleaning.

Terry patted Martha's back. Martha nodded and sat down. Terry asked me if I would like to sit back on the couch and continue. I stayed where I was. I said, "What's going on here?"

Terry said, "What do *you* think is going on?"

I said, "I think I'm getting beat up." I ran my tongue over my swollen lip. "Is this what you call appropriate therapeutic behavior, Terry?"

She said, "Well, do *you* think it is?"

I said, "You're getting on my fucking nerves."

She said, "You sound angry."

I said, "You're a genius, Ms. Freud."

She said, "Why don't you get up and sit down."

"I am sitting."

"And deal with your hostility."

Martha said to me, "Why are you here?"

I tried to talk without moving my lip or disturbing the loosened crown. I still don't know if I meant what I told her. "Because I want this marriage to be over."

"Why don't you just leave?" Martha said.

"I did leave."

Martha said, "Why don't you get off your ass and walk out that door?"

I considered and discarded the nasty answers in my head. I thought about it. I said, "I do care about you, you know." Martha began to pound her fists on her knees. I closed my eyes. I said, "I just don't think I can live with you." I could hear Martha sobbing. Terry shifted in her chair. I could hear the blood coursing through my body.

I imagined Martha and I together again in the future. Maybe that's her slamming the car door, walking across the driveway with lobsters for tonight. But I knew I wouldn't be seeing Martha, not in a significant way, for the rest of my life. What would happen, then, to all our private jokes, our domestic rituals, our secret language of gesture and nuance, our silly terms of endearment? This was a death, Martha's death as my wife. I had taken away our future. I didn't want to think I was capable of this. At that second every sweet moment we'd ever shared washed over me, every embrace, every laugh, every dream we dreamed. I knew that I would always hear her voice, that my skin would always crave her touch, that my body would always lean into her arms. I felt like I was drowning.

Martha said, "Why are you torturing me? I don't deserve to be treated like this."

Terry filled the ensuing silence. "Martha asked you a question, Laf. Were you able to hear what she said?"

I stood, took a tissue out of the box and applied it to my lip. I knew if I opened the door, nothing would ever be the same again. I would never be the Lafayette Proulx Martha had married. I didn't know if I was being courageous or foolish, cowardly or sane. I turned the knob.

Martha said, "You're just going to leave?"

I held the door.

"Just like that you're going to leave?" she said.

42.

Illness as Metaphor

A. "PAUL AND SILAS"

When I was in eighth grade at St. Stephen's School, Paul McDonald, my close friend and the inventor of Elephant Street Basketball (a full-contact sport played, if possible, on slush and ice and featuring optional dribbling, Indian rubber, and body checks) spoke up in civics class and told us all that the godless Communists in North Vietnam had to be stopped. North Vietnam, he explained, was an infectious and pernicious tumor, and it would have to be cut out of the body politic lest the cancer spread to the rest of the Free World. Sister Dominic Marie fingered her beads. Her lips trembled in silent prayer. I sat up in my seat. Paul's speech was remarkable for its passion (civics class was normally a time for dozing or staring at Rosemary Walsh's alabaster neck), for its alarming certitude, and for its stunning use of metaphor. I could see that Brian Foody was puzzled. But I was certain of it—cancer was evil.

I knew about cancer. For nearly a year or so of my childhood, around third and fourth grades, I watched my uncle Silas, my father's youngest brother, wither away with what my mother called cancer run amuck, which always sounded like a summer camp to me. (It was, in fact, adenocarcinoma of the pancreas and it metastasized throughout his body.) Uncle Silas's bedroom was off the kitchen in my grandparents' apartment. Every Sunday the family—aunts, uncles, cousins—showed up at my grandparents' after Mass, and one by one we were led into Silas's room to say hello. Mostly, he was too weak to speak or even to smile. The bedsheets were held above his body with some kind of tubular frame be-cause the weight of the sheet was painful.

Uncle Silas grew smaller and more sallow over the months until he looked like a wren. In my world, sickness was a miserable but tempo-rary condition, so I kept expecting that one of these Sundays Silas would be playing his guitar again. He'd be in the parlor doing Hendrix and dri-ving all the old folks crazy.

I remember the fluorescent ceiling light humming over the kitchen table and bulkies, cream cheese, coffee, Zarex. I remember the sticky linoleum, the black cat clock, always eleven minutes fast, whose tail and eyes moved. I remember my cousin Danny saying to my grandmother, When Uncle Silas dies, will we bury him in the garden? I remember standing on a chair by the fridge and poking my finger between the bars of the parakeet's cage and letting Mr. Peteydink peck at my fingertip. (I can't believe I remembered his name.) I remember eating Post Toasties and milk right out of the little box and hating the entire experience. I remember the mumble and drone of the television coming from the par-lor and the closed door of Silas's room, the scrolled brass door plate, the two rubber bands slipped over the brass door knob, the keyhole like an exclamation point or a tiny mouth. My uncle Silas was twenty-three when he died. Later, Silas's dad, my grandfather Henry, would die of prostate cancer in the same room, in the same bed. He'd go fast. Over that bed hung a wooden crucifix, and tucked between it and the cab-bage rose wallpaper was a holy card of the Blessed Virgin. Mary accepts the veneration of two kneeling children by the seashore. The card reads, *"O Marie, conçue sans péché, priez pour nous, qui avons recours à vous."*

B. "THE NEIGHBORHOOD"

The first time Judi and I really discussed the cancer was several days after she had recovered from the first cycle of chemo. We'd gone out to cele-brate. First to a movie, Herzog's *The Mystery of Kaspar Hauser,* which I just love and which Judi found interesting, and then over to the Boyn-ton for dinner. The film examines the inability of science to understand the mystery at the heart of our existence. My old buddy Biscuit was loi-tering out front of the Boynton. These were hard times for Biscuit. I gave him a couple of dollars and introduced him to Judi. That's not your old lady, he said. I explained. Why don't you ever call? he said. I'm still at my mother's. He gave me his number. I repeated it. The same number I called a million times when we were kids. Too good for your old friends?

he said. Hardly, I said. I asked him if he'd gone to Woodstock II or III, or whatever it was, rock festivals being Biscuit's passion. He told me how the security guards searched ticket holders. He called them all corporate fascists, meaning any artist who played there. He said that without sex and drugs and booze, rock 'n' 'roll wasn't all that interesting. I said, Well, we've got to go. I shook his hand, told him to take care of himself. His eyes followed a passing car. You won't call me, he said.

Judi picked at her Greek salad, let me steal the feta cheese. I told her I could live on feta cheese, Toll House cookies, and cognac. I felt uneasy eating steamers in front of her. Was I making her sick? When I finished, I ordered myself another beer. Judi said, sure, why not, she'd have a glass of Chardonnay. I saw Biscuit walk in, bum a smoke off a guy in a booth, and take a stool at the bar. Judi tasted the wine and sent it back. She never does that. I thought Biscuit's liver must be the size of a walnut by now. Judi said the new glass of wine was fine.

"Do you want to talk about it?" I said.

"Do you?"

"Of course. What is it?"

"I'm frightened, Laf. About more chemo. I don't want to go through that again."

I took Judi's hand. "Listen, don't get all worked up about this. The anxiety will only make it worse, you know that." I squeezed.

"You can't just dismiss me."

"What are you talking about?"

"I'm dying . . ."

"No, you're not."

"And you don't want to be agitated, don't want to deal with me."

"That's ridiculous." I let go of her hand. What did I do that for?

"You're going to hear me out whether you like it or not." She sipped her wine. Considered it. "Tastes like nails."

I said, "I know you're afraid of dying. Who wouldn't be, but . . ."

"I'm afraid of suffering, of being disabled, out of it. But I'm not afraid of dying. Dying's the least of it."

What was I going to do, argue with her? Tell her she's in denial? Persuade her to get in touch with the fear and the trembling, let me see the weeping and the gnashing of teeth?

She said, "I'll die if I want to."

"Don't talk like that."

"Is it bad genes, do you think," she said, "or bad luck? Or what? Fuckola. Does my body have the cancer or do I?" Judi rested her chin on her hand. She stared at the paper-whites in the bud vase.

How many springs, I wondered, had she put narcissus bulbs on stones in a bowl of water, set the bowl on the windowsill, and watched the miracle of the first green shoots?

"Have I become cancer?" She looked over to me, sat up, crossed her hands on the table. "Who is it that says 'I'? I feel betrayed. Oh, Laf, this is the fucking shits."

I told her that I knew things looked bleak, but she'd only begun to fight. If anybody could, she could beat this thing.

She put her hands on her belly. She didn't tell me how much I sounded like some high school football coach. She said, "I can't trust my own body. It humiliates me with pain, you know?" She cried for a moment, wiped her eyes, and apologized. Then she made me laugh. Referring to her insides, she said that the old neighborhood's not what it used to be. Bad crowd moving in. Real estate values down the toilet.

I told her she still had her sense of humor. I finished my beer and we paid the bill.

Judi said, "Laf, what would you relinquish to be healthy? to have a future free of suffering? Not pain. Suffering. Give up your job? friends? family? stories?

How intense the pain? I thought. How dire the suffering?

43.

Bad Gets Worse

As HER SECOND ROUND OF CHEMOTHERAPY APPROACHED, JUDI WAS FEELING more energetic, less anxious, and seemed resolved to battle this thing. She was back to work a few hours a day. She was sleeping through the night and was able to eat a full meal without any gastric distress. Her hair was already starting to grow back, though it felt more like down than hair. Three times a day she did these visualization exercises that she had read about in one of Josh's books. She saw herself at sixty-something playing doubles with some yachty types out at the Webster Thayer Country Club. I said, Swell, but where was I? She said, In the clubhouse lounge drinking vodka martinis and telling stories to impressionable matrons. Well, I said, at least I wasn't golfing.

Judi would imagine the medication as a platoon of marauding soldier ants devouring every tumor in its path. The next time it might be her white blood cells as a plague of locusts laying waste to her malignant fields of cancer, or her T-cells as a frenzied school of brutal and efficient piranhas tearing the flesh from this unfortunate carcinoma. She said she thought the exercises were working. And, of course, we both wanted to believe they were. I said, Well, it makes sense. You're taking control of the struggle this way. You're bringing your creative powers to bear. I told her to envision a million microscopic televangelists surrounding the tumor like hungry Pac-Men and haranguing the cancer cells into submission. She told me that wasn't working. So we tried to send in a zillion little Camille Paglias with tiny holsters and six-guns to blast away every politically and physically incorrect cell. Better. We filled Judi's body with Ahabs and Bruce Lees and jackals and a squadron of warrior androids from the planet Hippocrates in the star system Cos. We were having fun with cancer. Which worried me. I worried that Judi would ultimately pay for this affront to the illness. Of course, I also worry that if I change seats while watching a ball game, the Sox will blow whatever lead they have.

The night before chemo, Stoni came by to check on her sister. She told us about a Port-A-Cath that the doctors would be inserting into Judi's chest. She didn't know when, but it was the usual routine. This clever installation would allow doctors to administer their chemicals with an IV needle directly into her body without poking around at her collapsing veins. Judi seemed to be paying attention. I got Stoni and me another beer. I think Stoni told Judi, though I'm not sure about this—there's only so much I wanted to know—that they also used the cath to perform what Stoni called "water washes," where they flushed out the exfoliated cancer cells. Something along those lines. I opened the beers, slid one across the table to Stoni. But I kept feeling the pressure of my swollen prostate, the throbbing of the unsettled nerve in my new crown (Dr. Vigeant, bless her heart, had replaced the loosened temporary with an appropriately dishwater-gray permanent, at long last), and this dagger of pain behind my left eye. Danger made me frantic.

When Stoni raised her glass, her eyes caught mine, and I recognized pain, fear, or resignation, or something I was not meant to see. Stoni caught me watching her and shook her head, lowered her eyes, I know she did, to tell me that our brief season of hope was ending. There was a long winter ahead.

That night Judi couldn't sleep. She cried. I held her. She read a while. I tossed. She was afraid, she said, of what was going on in her body right now. She couldn't visualize. She was too distressed. She didn't know if she wanted to go through with this chemo tomorrow. I told her, Don't be silly. You have to. She put out the light, lay back. She said she had pain like a thick belt around her waist, and it was like someone was squeezing it tighter and tighter. Stress, I said. You'll be fine. Now get some sleep. At three I slipped out of bed and went to the living room couch with my pillow. I fell asleep in seconds, it felt like.

Judi shook me awake. I asked her what time it was.

"Three-fifteen. Come on," she said, "I'll make you some coffee." We went to the kitchen.

All I had to do was just smell the coffee, and I started to wake up. I could feel all my nerve cells tremble with anticipation. Fascicular junkies. Judi said she didn't know if she'd had a dream or what it was, but before, in bed, she kept seeing a buttery flower pushing up through this creamy mound of snow. Springtime, I said. Rebirth. She smiled, said, Winter first.

We ended up talking about our work. It's like we started gabbing and couldn't stop ourselves, like we were teenagers who'd just discovered that war was bad, love was redeeming, capitalism preyed on the poor. It started with sex. Judi said that as a therapist she had more privileges of intimacy than she did as a lover. There are things I can't ask you yet, she told me. But the client is asking me to open him up to find out what's going wrong.

While she talked about paying attention, I squeezed oranges for juice, fried us some eggs, toasted raisin bread. I set the table. Judi folded napkins. I kissed her on the head. I served the food and we ate together.

"Therapy," she said, "is seeing the universal in the particular—the essence. Clients are not subtle even if they think they are."

I pictured myself in Terry's office. My legs were crossed, my hands clasped on top of my head.

"You see the way they're dressed, the way they sit or stand. You hear the tone of voice, the rhythm of their speech." Judi mentioned a young woman who'd come for a session yesterday. "She was late. She wore no makeup. She looked at the floor when she spoke, worked her engagement ring on and off her finger. She didn't have to tell me she was depressed. She showed me."

And then I heard the crows in the fir tree and saw the gray light of morning out the window. It was 6:45. I told her she'd better hurry up and shower before we had to leave. We'd talked, I realized, for three hours without a breath, but we hadn't talked about cancer or chemo or pain or dying or any of that except that as she got up from the table, Judi said, Maybe the chemo will be easier this time.

It was worse. She threw up in the car on the way home. I figured it was the heater, the stuffiness and everything. She didn't have the strength to be upset about her mess. She looked yellowed except for her knuckles and the swelling under her eyes. She threw up again in the garage, all over her parka and her sneakers.

I cleaned her, changed her into a nightgown, and got her into bed. That whole time she cried. She couldn't talk. Could shake her head a little. I called Dr. Pawlak and got her machine. It's an emergency, I said. I called Stoni. She listened and calmed me down. She'll be okay. This is bad but not unexpected. She said she'd be by around three to check on her. I called Nicky, said I couldn't come to work. I cleaned out the car as best I could. I went back in to check on Judi. She was asleep, it looked like. I took her sneaks and parka out to the deck to hose them down. Of course I had to play with Spot first. He'd been lonesome. He tried to lick the vomit off the shoes. I hosed the shoes, the jacket, the dog, the deck. I set out Spot's food and water. I tossed the mess in the washer. Judi was still sleeping. Good, I thought, maybe the nausea had passed. I tried to be quiet while I mopped up in the bathroom.

I could tell when she opened her eyes and probably saw herself in the ceiling that Judi didn't know where she was. She looked around with her eyes, not her head. Laf, she said when she saw me, oh, Christ, Laf. She cried. I wiped her eyes with the hem of the sheet, made a mental note to buy Kleenex. She told me the light hurt. I drew the blinds. Her whole body, she said, felt like a toothache. The phone rang. Dr. Pawlak said I should take Judi's temp; she'd hold. And I would have if I could have found the thermometer. I told Dr. Pawlak I'd have to wait till Stoni got here. She said to call her with the temp, and if it's 106 to call an ambulance and get her back to the hospital. She said, I want you to know this is not an uncommon reaction to the chemo. These medications are extremely toxic. My guess is that Judi's over the worst of it. I said, Are you sure you didn't give her too much of it? I mean I've been reading in the *Globe* about the health reporter who was killed by the cancer clinic. Dr. Pawlak was certain that Judi's dosage was correct.

I sat with Judi while we waited for Stoni. I helped her to the bathroom to be sick again. Nausea and diarrhea. She drank a little water, but threw it up minutes later. Stoni arrived, helped me change Judi's clothes and bedsheets. I ran out to Monahan's Pharmacy and got tissues, a thermometer, some toothpaste, toilet paper, hand soap. I got an ice pack, a heating pad, Band-Aids. I was going to be ready for anything. Judi's fever was 104.9. Every joint ached, she said. Stoni cooled her down with ice on her forehead. Stoni said she was staying and maybe she should sleep in here with Judi. I thanked her. She told me, This means the chemo is working—it's knocking everything out of commission.

For the next couple of days Judi felt nauseated. She could barely eat: Gerber's strained peaches once in a while, orange Popsicles, a bite or two of Jell-O, maybe some cooled mashed potatoes. She was down to ninety-eight pounds. Leaden pounds, she said. She could barely lift an arm much of the time, slept sixteen to twenty hours. I was concerned that the disease was back in spades and was busily ravaging her. Judi told me sleep was her way of battling the illness by conserving her strength, channeling all her energies and her will to the immune system.

I decided to start doing my typing out in the garage, make the area into a sort of writer's studio. This way Judi wouldn't be disturbed by the slapping of keys and the balling of paper. As sweet as she was, Judi had already explained to me on the third day that if she could manage a rocket launcher, she'd have blown the freaking typewriter to Kingdom Come and me with it. She closed her eyes and turned her head on the pillow. To smithereens, she said. I catch your drift, darling, I told her, and I brought a gooseneck lamp up from the cellar and set it out on the workbench in the garage. I even let Spot come and keep me company while I wrote. I let him chew on old tomato crates, on a cribbage board I'd found behind a Studebaker hub cap, and on whatever else looked expendable. I wrote one story out there, "The House of Good Eats," but then the weather turned colder. I brought out the quartz heater and I was still cold. Then I brought Judi's car in from the driveway, and I sat inside it and typed with the machine on my lap and the heater on low. Still didn't smell right in there. I sprayed it with lilac air freshener. I was careful not to drain the battery. It became clear to me, however, that I would soon need to adjust my technology—I'd have to learn to write with pen and paper so I could write in the house again.

By Tuesday Judi was feeling better. She even yelled at me for being a slob. Why couldn't I have vacuumed at least once? Because your head was exploding, I said. And get your shit off the table. The paper, the notes, the books, she meant. She was still tired, however. She told me this constant fatigue was as debilitating as the pain almost. Made her depressed. I heated up some chicken bouillon and poured her a cup. We sat at the table. She blew on the spoon, sipped. Hot. I put an ice cube in the broth. She said was it going to be like this for the rest of her life? Was she going to be in pain all the time, every minute?

"It's not the cancer doing this, Laf. It's the drugs." She pushed the cup away, wiped her mouth with her hand. "I can't go through this hell again."

I explained to her what she already knew—that the chemo was temporary, and, yes, it was awful now, but in the long run she'd be better off. Chemo was hope.

"Hope for what? Stage Four, remember?"

"You have to fight this thing."

"I can't even think, Laf. Can't read. I can't work like this. I haven't been able to remember things. It's like my mind is going blind."

I said, "You know, maybe the next time will be like the first and not like this one. Maybe it won't be bad at all."

"There won't be a next time."

In a few days, when her pain was a memory, I'd reason with her, beg her if I had to. And she'd have to tell Stoni and Trixie and Dr. Pawlak, and they would all, I was sure, explain the foolishness of her decision.

44.

Love and Marriage

I BEGAN TO WATCH THE NEWLYWEDS WHO HAD MOVED INTO MR. LESPERENCE'S house. Marriage, I figured, at its best anyway, is a collaboration of hearts. The couple were the Nybergs, Chet and Maryalice. When I first introduced myself and Spot to Chet, I told him, Love is the house that marriage builds. He looked perplexed. He stepped back. I told him I was a writer. He smiled, relaxed a bit. I wasn't out for his money or his soul, he realized. Chet was a lawyer just starting out his career with Bowditch and Dewey. Bowditch, I said. Some Bowditch painted the house. Yes, he said, same family. Maryalice worked part-time at Sharfman's Jewelers. One afternoon I brought her over a carrot cake I'd baked and said, Love is not a singular affair, is it? She laughed at that and said that Chet had told her about me. You're Laf, right? She told me to have a seat, she'd cut the cake, perk some coffee. She told me she'd start a career (law, sales, public relations, who knows?) as soon as the kids they were going to have—a boy and a girl, she hoped, C.J. and Grace—got to first grade. Maybe I'll even teach, she said.

Chet and Maryalice dressed alike in chinos, oxford shirts, cable-stitch sweaters, and deck shoes. On Monday nights Chet had his buddies over, and they all watched football in Chet's den. Every week Chet invited me over for the game. I kept meaning to go even though I knew I'd be incredibly depressed. I didn't have a cap with a team logo on it like Chet and his pals. I know this sounds snotty, and I apologize. One guy they called Tubba wore a Patriots uniform every week—shirt, knickers, athletic shoes, the works. Whenever something remarkable happened in the game, the pack of them would whoop and leap. I could hear them from our house. If I looked over through the window, I'd see them laughing like mad, slapping each other's hands. They scared me a little.

Spot and I ran into Maryalice one morning. We were walking through Abbie Hoffman Park; she was jogging. She stopped to say hi. Spot sniffed her shoes, licked her salty legs. I told him to quit it. She joined our walk for a bit. She asked me what I was writing about these days. I said, Love. What about love? she said. We stopped so Spot could lift his leg and mark the hydrangea. I mentioned Theresa and Dale and how their story was now a novella and threatening to become a novel. It was a story about love trying to exist without marriage. Maryalice said, Don't you think it can? I said, I suppose so, but can it exist without commitment? She said I sounded old-fashioned. We were quiet, and then Maryalice said, So your wife's a nurse? I said, It's not my wife you've seen. Maryalice said, Oh. I said, That's her sister the nurse. You haven't met Judi because she's laid up with cancer.

And after that remark, Chet and Maryalice became less visible, less congenial. I understood. They were not afraid of contagion, but afraid to think that this is where their bloomy marriage was leading them to inevitably—the cancer ward or the trauma center or the nursing home. How do you maintain buoyancy in an ocean of grief?

Our received wisdom declares that it takes two people to destroy a marriage. But maybe not. Look at Marvin and Pauline. Marvin was married to an angel who remained devoted to him. He pretty much went out, got himself hooked on dope, lost a business and then his family. And look at me. Didn't I just walk away from a woman who loved me and needed me? And why? So I could sit around and think and write about imaginary people? Is that good enough?

I needed to start paying close attention again. And I might have gotten right to it if Richie Muneyhun hadn't had a craving for baklava. What happened was he was home watching *Mighty Joe Young* on the VCR when he found himself hungry, and all he had in his fridge was tuna and peanut butter. He got on his bike and cruised into Worcester and up to Eleni's Midnight Café. And that's when he saw Stoni and Arthur in Arthur's pickup pulling out of Eleni's lot onto Franklin Street. He followed them. And then Ronnie showed up.

45.

My Name Is Legion;
for We Are Many

JUDI'S FATHER COULDN'T STILL HIMSELF. EVER SINCE I'D SHAKEN HIS HAND AT the back door and invited him into the kitchen, he seemed ruffled and agitated. He tried to sit at the table with me, strained to hold himself down, but just bounced right up off the chair and paced the room. I thought of a fly buzzing against a lampshade. He leaned his duffle bag against the fridge. He washed his hands at the sink. He smelled his hands, palms and backs, and washed them again. He looked out the window and told me a dog was chomping on an umbrella. Spot, I said. He told me his full name: Hieronymous Ulysse Dubey. I told him mine: Lafayette Kosciusko Proulx. My father studied the Revolutionary War, I said.

Hieronymous had a repertoire of erratic, jerky little moves. He pulled up at his pant waist, reached down to tug at a cuff or a sock, scratched his ear, rubbed his eyes, wiped his nose with the heel of his hand. He did this thing where he pressed his fingertips together and held his arms out in front of his chest, then moved them back and forth like some kind of crab or insect. He rocked back on his heels, lifted up on his toes, twirled his hair around his index finger, scrunched his face like a weasel, squinted, blinked, stretched his jaw, twitched his shoulders, shook his head. I was exhausted.

"Hieronymous, can I get you something to drink or something?"

He told me to call him Ronnie.

"Ronnie, then. Some tea? milk? cranberry juice? Moxie?"

He wanted milk. I poured him a glass. He told me he was paranoid-schizophrenic. Diagnosed and certified. He drank the milk, wiped his mouth with his hands, and washed his hands. But I'm not routinely deranged, he said. No garden-variety crackpot. I've boldly gone where no schizophrenic has gone before. He explained that all his activity, his gestures, all this stage business, he called it, was part of a song, a kinetic melody he was playing. The music of the spheres, he said. I keep the universe going. I hear myself when I move, you know. Every tic is a note, every twitch a chord. Every flourish is a tone. Nothing's random, he said. I'm a new symphony every day. Every hour a new movement. You watch me, he said. You'll learn something. More milk, please.

He wore a blue and yellow plaid flannel shirt, a navy cardigan, and a powder-blue polyester suit with white stitching. It matched his eyes. Ronnie had come to see his daughter, whom he hadn't seen in seventeen years. Hitchhiked down from Henniker soon as he heard. Trixie had got hold of him. I told him that Judi was off with Stoni at the hospital. More tests. They'll be back in a couple of hours. I asked him if he'd like to shower. Ronnie said he hadn't thought to bring along a change of clothes. I was in such a hurry, he said. I looked at the duffle bag. My notebooks, he said. Flyers and things. My songs. I told him he could wear my clothes. He said, I'll need a shave. Beards are not hygienic. Facial hair traps chemical pollutants like benzene and ammonia. It's like inhaling DDT every minute of your life. If you have a mustache, forget about it. The Chinese have done a lot of research in this area. We got a lot to learn from those Reds. I set out a pair of jeans, a sweatshirt, underpants, and socks on the john. I heard Ronnie talking to himself in the shower.

When he rejoined me at the table in my clothes, I saw myself in twenty years. He'd slicked back his squirrel-gray hair. He had a wad of cotton in both ears. I said, Did you bring along any medication? He had, he said, but it made him catatonic, and he didn't like to take it. He opened his duffle bag and took out a pad and pen. He set the bag on the floor and sat on the chair. I asked did he want some lunch. He said he wanted a can of sardines, if we had any. Brain food, he said. It's got RNA in it. I said, How about baloney and Cheddar? He settled for that. As I made his sandwich, Ronnie wrote down numbers on his writing tablet. Strings of numbers that intersected on the page like words on a Scrabble board. He closed his eyes and held a hand up to quiet me, went back to his figures. When he stopped, he told me that what he was doing was translating these phrases he hears into numerical language. Here you go,

I said. I set the plate on the table. Beer? Water? A clever little Cabernet? The water, he said. Is it fluoridated? I don't know. Milk, he said.

He told me that the phrases came to him the hard way—in code and through the limbic brain. He tapped the back of his skull. He'd been forced to use the lizard brain, as he called it, because his cerebral thoughts were being scrambled by the Voice of America; the Bank of America; the Boy Scouts of America; *Good Morning, America;* and AAA. Besides, his cortical synapses were being monitored by the FBI.

Ronnie didn't eat his crusts. He asked me how Judi was doing. I said, Holding her own. It's hard for her. He asked me what any father might ask: Do you love Judi? I would have said yes, but I didn't get the chance. He handed me his business card. I would have said yes, but would I have meant it? The card read: *"Ronnie" Dubey, Pope of the H.U. Dubey Church of the Galaxy, aka Czar of Czars, His Royal Empirical Holiness, Quasar the Omnipotent, Pulsar the Powerful, Charmed Quarkmaster Plenipotentiary and Fountainhead of Atoms.* And there's a halftone of Ronnie's face being orbited by electrons.

I said, "Can I keep this?"

"What do you think of it?" he said.

I turned the card over as if the answer might be there. I looked at Ronnie. "I think you ought to take that pill now," I could have said. I said, "Interesting."

"It's a joke," he said and smiled for the first time. He went to the sink, held the counter, and did two knee bends. He came back to the table. He raised his eyebrows. "I know what you're trying to do," he said. He went to the fridge, read the shopping list held there by a Buick-shaped magnet.

"What's that?" I said. "What I'm trying to do."

"Biofeedback control," he said. "Remote video of my silent thoughts. Transistor hipster, silicon chipster."

I said, "How about dessert? Strawberries? Ice cream?"

"Your forehead," he said.

"What about it?"

"The cross on your forehead."

I actually felt my forehead, wrinkled it. No discernible cross.

Ronnie sat. He said he was sorry. He put his face in his hands.

"You want to take a nap?" I said.

"A walk." He put his sneakers on. He looked around the room like he couldn't find the door.

I walked to the door, opened it. "Don't get lost," I said.

"Is that a joke?"

When he'd gone I cleaned up the table, put his gear into the duffle bag, and stashed the duffle bag in the mud room for now. I went out to feed Spot. He sniffed me all over, sneezed, woofed.

46.

Fathers of the Fatherless

JUDI SAID, YOU MAKE ALLOWANCES FOR YOUR FAMILY. THEY MAY NOT SEEM normal to the world, but they're normal to you because you've been dealing with them all your life.

We sat relaxing in the parlor, sprawled on the couch with our feet on the glass coffee table, waiting for Ronnie to get back from his walk. Judi had spent three hours at the hospital earlier waiting for X-rays. Three hours being ignored by gossiping techs: We're doing the best we can, miss. Please have a seat. Three hours wanting to storm out of there, but worried, of course, that today's exam would be the crucial one. She had a headache. I was drinking bourbon; Judi, spring water with a twist. She told me I was drinking too much. I guess when you can't drink the hard stuff yourself, you begin to notice. I didn't want to hear this. I never do. She said, You are, you know. Better slow down. I used to tell Martha that my dream was to live like William Powell in those *Thin Man* movies. Wake up already shaved and spruced, put on my silk robe, have someone serve me eggs and vodka martinis for breakfast. But I didn't mention this to Judi.

She asked me to massage her temples. She closed her eyes. "All families are dysfunctional," she said. "That's part of the definition of *family*."

I couldn't argue. I told her, "Shush." In minutes she seemed to be asleep. I figured I'd ease her head back against the pillow, go out to the kitchen, and put away the supper dishes.

She said, "Fathers don't come off very well in your stories, Laf. Why's that?" She opened her eyes.

I sat back and reached for my glass. Of course, I knew she was right, but, in fact, I didn't have an answer. My fathers were either missing or away on business or drunk on their asses or simply nasty. This wasn't my own father's fault. Blaise was none of the above. I think I gave them problems to see what made them tick. Problems were like new clothes to them. Something to get used to; something to sport around in. What is it with men?

"Where do you suppose Ronnie is?" Judi said.

"He's got your number if he gets lost. He's got a key."

"I wonder why he came."

"To see you."

"He's had a lifetime to see me."

The telephone rang. The machine answered. Beeped. Nothing.

Judi said, "He was always around when we were young kids, but never there, you know? Always somewhere in his head. He stared at the the TV but never watched it. You could sit on his lap and he'd rock you, but wouldn't talk." Judi smiled. "He wasn't loopy like he is now, I guess. Never carried a duffle bag full of notebooks. Never called himself, what was it?"

"Quasar the Quarkmaster."

Judi shook her head. She said Ronnie was kind but ineffectual as a dad. But not crazy. A little vague and withdrawn. And she was sure he was no kind of husband for Trixie. And then he was gone.

Judi sat upright, sipped her water, held the glass with both hands on her lap and looked at it. "My poor brother." I leaned toward her. She held me off with her hand. "I was outside when I heard Trixie scream. The next thing I know, Ginger Margoupis from next door is running past me and into our house. I was on the tire swing, and something told me not to move. And then Ginger's daughter Cookie, who was like fifteen, took me over to her house and we watched TV. *Rawhide.* Clint Eastwood. And I never saw my big brother again. I did see them wheel the body out to the ambulance, one of those old Cadillac station wagons they used to use. Later, I saw the length of rope on the kitchen table, coiled like an eight."

We were quiet. Judi started to say something. Finally, "How does anyone so young get so hopeless? He always seemed a little sad, but was so sweet to everyone."

Judi said, After that Ronnie just sort of drifted away. Stoni blames it all on Trixie. Thinks her mother's a shrew who drove the quiet man on the La-Z-Boy to the nuthouse. Judi checked her watch. It was almost nine. She said she wasn't going to be able to make it much longer. She took her shower, got into her nightgown, robe, and slippers, while I poured myself another drink, cleaned up the kitchen. I saved some shepherd's pie for Ronnie in a casserole dish. I brewed some herbal tea for Judi, set her cup and spoon on the kitchen table. She came into the kitchen yawning. She said now wasn't I sweet. She kissed my cheek.

We sat. Judi said one reason people become therapists, herself included, is to work out their own shit. To continue the search that began in childhood, the search that will help them understand why things played out the way they did. She said without passion, though, you'll never get back to those memories, the ones you need. "Passion, that's the door to memory. But passion takes a lot of energy and will and persistence. And tenacity." Judi said, "Right now I don't have a lot of any of those."

"Every crisis is an opportunity. You told me that."

"Yes, it is," she said. "And every crisis is a chance to be creative, to make yourself over, to become the person you want to be." She smiled. "But if you're nauseated half the time, if you're always exhausted, if every goddamn nerve in your body is dull with pain, it's hard to be creative. It's hard to be very imaginative if you're depressed."

"Don't get pissed off."

"Why shouldn't I?"

I shook my head. "You should."

"Look at me, Laf. My skin's gray. My mouth's full of ulcers. My lips are cracked and bleeding. My toenails are loose. I've got hot flashes. My hands are red. My tongue is brown. There's a ringing in my ears. And my fucking hair's fallen out." Judi cried. I stood behind her chair and hugged her. I wanted to tell her to just go ahead, let it all out, but that sounded patronizing and false. I wanted to tell her that everything would be all right, but that sounded foolish and heartless. I didn't say anything, which may have been the right thing just then. I hoped Ronnie didn't choose this moment to come home.

Judi caught her breath. I kissed her neck. I got her a damp facecloth and some ice for her eyes. "And it's not just the cancer," she said. "It's the cure."

I didn't want to get into this discussion. I'd end up saying she had no real alternative, did she? But I knew that her night table was piled with books on alternative cancer therapies. I'd read through them. Yin foods for yang cancers. Colonic irrigations. Hypnosis. Coffee enemas every four hours. Twenty pounds of organic fruit every day. Clay packs. Laetrile. Massive doses of flaxseed oil and selenium. Glucose drips. Chelation. Ozone treatments, whatever they are.

Judi said something.

"What?"

"The cancer," she said. "It's so quiet."

I took the dripping cloth and ice and put them in the sink.

"When this is over," she said, meaning the cancer, "then we're going to work on your issues."

Did she say this to lighten the moment? to let me off the emotional hook? and herself off? Anyway, I went along. "What issues are you talking about?"

"Your anger and resentment."

"You've been giving this some thought."

"You'd better sign up for the lifetime therapy plan, bozo."

I made a face, said I was an emotional he-man. What was she talking about? "I'm practically the wolverine of the here-and-now, of dealing with it."

She said, "You're still pissed at the boy in second grade who didn't pick you on his side in some football game."

"First grade," I said. "I was in first, he was in fourth. Big stud. And it was baseball. Did I tell you that story?" I was back in the schoolyard, standing in front of the captains, hoping to get picked, punching my glove, my pathetic, four-fingered Don Buddin infielder's glove, trying to look like a heavy-hitting speed-demon. It goes down to the last pick. Paul Assad looks at me and my ripped dungarees and my torn Keds and he says, like it made any sense, "This kid's no spring chicken," and he picks Mouse O'Toole instead of me. Mouse, who couldn't catch a ball in his pocket. Today Paul Assad owns an insurance agency and his face is on billboards. I wouldn't buy an umbrella in a shit storm off Paul Asshole.

"Laf?"

"What?"

"I said why don't we go to bed. I'll talk with Ronnie tomorrow."

"Just let me walk Spot."

"I want to try to make love before I conk out."

"In that case, Spot can wait."

47.

Who Are They Who Are Like the Clouds?

RONNIE BORROWED MY TYPEWRITER AND LOCKED HIMSELF IN THE BATHROOM for three hours. I busied myself making dinner. Black-eyed peas, yam soufflé, chicken-fried steak, and cornbread. I'd been reading Eudora Welty. I heard the irregular slap of keys, the occasional toilet flush, the running of water. Ronnie emerged at last, told me it was time for a new ribbon, asked to borrow an envelope. I told him he could keep it. In the top drawer I said, and motioned with my head. How about a stamp? he said. I gave him fifty cents. He walked to the post office and mailed the letter, came back as I was heating a brown sugar glaze for the yams. He told me I should keep my eye on the mailbox for the next couple of days. It was for me? I said. Why didn't you just hand it to me? He said, No can do.

The letter arrived the next day while Judi was at work and Ronnie was off looking for old friends in an assortment of taverns. The envelope was addressed to "Lafayette Silk Fynbo" in care of "Judi Kazootie Dubey." He had printed "Confidential" and "For Your Eyes Only" in the upper left-hand corner. On the back of the envelope, in green ink, he'd written, "Who are they who are like the clouds?" I assumed I'd find the answer inside. So I made myself a cup of coffee and sat at the table. I read:

Dear LSF:
They spray me with toxic nerve gas from automobile exhausts and even lawnmowers and snow blowers and leaf dispersers,

which is why I can hardly go outside anymore. When I leave my room at the Aubuchon and descend the stairs, I usually run into a couple of "tenants" trying to look like they live in the building, pretending to chat, staging a neighborly scene for me to observe. Very clever. Many would have been fooled. When I open the door to Mechanic Street, the cars begin to cruise by, just as if they'd been doing so all morning long. This is the "Refrigerator Light Effect," which you might be familiar with. Anytime I stroll into a convenience store there's a Pakistani clerk waiting to sell me anything I want. How convenient indeed. I want you to understand my life, but this is to go no further than, well, you know what I mean: this computerized, non-evolved, left-brained, new fake urban landscape and that ersatz starry sky.

Our planet, which you call Earth, is the only one in our universe where there is life before death.

They are the nebulous, veiled, drizzly Jesuits who planted this silicon chip in my brain, which is the mark of the beast. This happened in 1977 at Monson State Hospital where I suffered electro-shock therapy which turned me into a thermonuclear reactor and sent my mind into the cosmos of infinite space/time. I operate all satellites. I refused to go to Jerusalem to be coronated King of the Earth. This foiled their neat plan all right. Which is why they began their regimen of bio-feedback beta wave control via bacteriophagia viral contamination, which is why I have been incapacitated from my life for so long and am only now re-ionizing. They have tried to erase my memories with cathode-ray oscilloscopic brain invasion therapy. This causes me to suffer tremendous cranial pain. I want you to understand this. Pain that feels like all my wetware is being ground by a Black and Decker power sander.

The Christians are getting away with it—world domination, what else? They want to control our schools, our government, want to fill our children's minds with superstitions of divinity. They've done it in the Cygnus-369 solar system. Help me to oppose their cyber-charade and fight these enemies of our civilization. We must stop the suffering. It may seem like a lost cause, I know, but remember that in the real cosmos, entropy does not exist, anything can come from nothing, sand runs up the hourglass, life begins at death, darkness is both an obedient wave and

a discrete particle. Peek around the darkness, Laf, and into the
light.

Your Humble Servant,
H. Ronnie D, Q of O
(in disguise)

I wondered what Ronnie made of me, of this house, of his ailing
daughter—the daughter he had yet to speak with—how all of that fit
into his skewed cosmology. I had noticed how he touched and examined objects in a flippy, dismissive way, like anything might hold the
answer. He might smell a light switch, hold a key to his ear, taste cello-
phane tape. I've seen him put a salt shaker against his thigh and then lift
his arm. He told me it was a form of hyperkinesiology, a method of checking his cellular chemical balance. I have to be sturdy, resolute, alert. Anything could happen, he said.

He told me about an estate auction he once went to in Saco, Maine,
and how it was nearly the end of our universe as we know it. The item
in question was an innocent-seeming gallon jug of Seroco Egg Preserver,
probably from the turn of the century. When I saw that Calderón de la
Barca from the wormhole in Betelgeuse X-9 was bidding on the jug, I
knew I couldn't let him have it. So while you were probably snuggled
up with my daughter and the rest of the world was watching *Benny Hill*
or passing gas or licking their greasy fingers, I went toe-to-toe with evil
and annihilation and won.

I said, "Your daughter's very sick, Ronnie. You know that, don't you.
Very, very sick."

He nodded.

I knew what he was thinking—why hadn't I said "dying"? I said, "Are
you hungry?"

48.

Pozzo and Richie Unplugged

Pozzo Beckett, the sun, drilled a hole in his head in order to open his third eye. The process, as you might imagine, was an arduous one. It began with a carpenter's brace. Layla told me the story on a visit to the house to see Judi. While we waited for Judi to wake up from a nap, I made Layla a black cow, and we sat out on the deck. She showed me a Ziploc bag in her purse filled with Pozzo's matted blond hair. She smiled. She said that as long as she had Pozzo's hair, she had control over him, over his love part, anyway. She said, Nobody really controls the sun.

Give Pozzo an *A* for ingenuity and an *A* for tenacity. First thing he did was fit a double-twist auger bit into the hand brace, hold the knob, and crank away. He broke the skin and he bled, but the brace wasn't doing the job. He had trouble keeping the lead screw straight, for one thing. And then the two hits of Green Daze that he had dropped kicked in, and he forgot what he was doing. The next day he designed and drew up plans for a new tool and gave his sketches to his cousin Luci Gilberg, who taught sculpture at the Craft Center. She built it for him. Essentially, the Becket Manual Trepanner, as he called it, was a simple hand drill with a very short drill bit and a hacksaw blade—a ring of serrated teeth—wrapped around the chuck. As the drill is turned, both the bit and the teeth enter the skull, cutting an easily removed disk from the bone. Layla shaved Pozzo's head. She watched. His first attempt took four hours with a break for lunch. He was left with a circular groove and a puncture that already, Layla pointed out to him in the mirror, resembled an eye. On his second attempt a week later, Pozzo fainted from the pain.

Next, he bought some clove, Eugenol toothache drops, and Ben-Gay, mixed them in a blender, and applied the anesthetic paste to his still-tender wound. Evidently it burned like hell. And then it hurt like crazy when the saw blade turned. His eyes itched, his nose ran. He tried an application of ice. The same. He got hold of procaine and a hypodermic. But the needle broke on his first stab. Speed was the answer, he decided. He borrowed a Rockwell saber saw from Hervey, who must have taken it from work.

Pozzo finally broke through, Layla said. There was this gush of blood and this stink of something burning. Pozzo said he could feel his brain pulsing, could hear babbling and gurgling, like everything inside was schlurping around. Layla couldn't hear anything. She handed him a toy dart with a suction cup at the end of it, and Pozzo wet the cup with his tongue and lifted the plug from his skull. He asked Layla to touch his brain if she wanted to. She didn't want to. She was afraid by now. It was pink, but maybe just from the blood. She couldn't imagine why they call it gray matter. Pozzo closed his eyes and saw he could still see. Said he could see an angel descending from heaven, leading a great, foul dragon, and he saw thrones and the dead, columns and columns of them, and a vast and bottomless pit, and this was not at all what he had expected, and then he moaned, whimpered, and passed out cold. Layla pressed the skull plug back into Pozzo's scalp, tamped it with a spoon. Didn't want his brain getting dirty. She got a baseball cap out of Pozzo's sock drawer and fit it on his bald head. It said, *P&D Sullivan Sand & Gravel.* She called 911.

Arthur Bositis must have caught Richie Muneyhun unawares. The police found Richie hanging upside down in the kill room at Boston Beef. He'd been drilled between the eyes with a single shot from the pneumatic gun that's used on the assembly line to dispatch steers. He wasn't dead when they found him, but he wasn't very much alive either. There he was, hooked by the tendons at the back of his legs, suspended like a sack of laundered overcoats on a dry cleaner's motorized rack. His eyes were closed, his mouth open. They found Arthur a few feet away, sitting on a metal folding chair, watching Richie's blood drip into a coffee can. Arthur had called the cops, confessed.

Judi and I have argued about life, about what constitutes a human being, and we differ on some points, but I think it's safe to say that we agree on one thing—a person is not a body. There's something else. Energy, soul, mind, spirit, whatever, something other than, or in addition to, the flesh and blood that constitutes the essence of a person. My point here, though, is this: Here at the end of the twentieth century our medical chronic wards have become repositories of bodies, but not of people. Richie Muneyhun, for example. After the violence at Boston Beef, he was taken to Memorial, hooked up to a ventilator, and kept alive on various machines and by the grace of medical technology. His mother wouldn't hear a word about taking him off life support. He may be a vegetable, Peggy Muneyhun admitted, but he's a vegetable with a soul. Miracles happen, she said.

But it would take more than a miracle to remove Richie from his persistent vegetative state. Time travel, maybe. What we know is that a brain begins to deteriorate almost immediately without oxygen, begins to atrophy as soon as the billions of cells begin to die. First the cellular fluid and the mitochondria swell. Mechanisms within the cell dissolve. Loss of energy causes the cell to lose connection with neighboring cells. The fluid expands the walls of the cell further, till it's like an overfilled water balloon. The nucleus fails, destroyer enzymes are released. Pretty soon what's left is what's called respirator brain, essentially a mass of soft, green viscous liquid, a sort of slime pudding. Picture the tomalley of a boiled lobster ladled into a bowl, and you'll have an image of Richie Muneyhun's post-abattoir brain.

But he was alive, as in "not dead," to those in charge, and that accounted for the initial delay in Arthur's trial. Prosecutors were hoping to replace the charge of *Attempted Murder* with simple *Murder One*. Arthur was pleading self-defense, an argument that was perhaps undermined by the image of Richie's suspended body that the jury was certain to see. The prosecutors got their wish. Someone pulled the plug on Richie Muneyhun's carcass in the middle of the night, some two months after the incident. All of this played out while Judi continued the struggle for her life through chemo and what would follow.

The trial resumed with the new charges. Arthur's lawyer argued that someone on the hospital staff was the murderer, not his client, who was in jail at the time of the death. There was a second delay in the trial, one which would eventually result in Arthur's release. It turns out that a half dozen of the jurors had taken to hanging around together evenings at the foreman's home. Eating, chatting, listening to chamber music. After a few bottles of wine, they held a séance and spoke through a channel (the foreman's sister-in-law) to Richie Muneyhun's spirit, who identified Arthur as his murderer. As far as these six were concerned, there was no need for further testimony. One of them, however, went and blabbed about the visitation to an uninitiated juror, who spoke to Judge Greenberg, and so on. I guess the judge doesn't believe in visitations. Arthur was freed on bond, the future of the trial in doubt.

Richie was buried with his motorcycle. When he died he weighed 150 pounds. All Stoni would say about his death was that it was an act of mercy. I wondered what she thought and felt, not just about the death, but about the whole terrifying love business she'd got tangled up in. Did she feel at all responsible for the killing? Did she feel responsible for setting the inevitable in motion?

Me, I can't excuse what Arthur did, but I understand his fear. Arthur's sin was murder. But it was an aberration. Richie's sin was his way of life, was himself and his disregard for civility, hospitality, and discourse, his belief that whatever he wanted he would have. Look at Richie, at Edmund, for that matter, and note that desire blossoms into obsession, envy into malice, greed into rage.

49.

Sea Monkeys

IT WAS STILL DARK WHEN I GOT UP. I FED SPOT, WALKED HIM TO THE PARK AND back, told him he was a good boy and I loved him. I got the newspaper off the front lawn and went in to the kitchen. I was in the mood for concertina music. I put a Giulio Regondi tape in the boom box, turned the volume low, closed the door to the living room. I heard the shower clang on. I made coffee, poured a cup, sat down to read the paper. Some Brazilian novelist had written 1,039 novels under thirty different names, as of this week. Hasn't even read everything he's written. Judi said, Good morning, sat across from me, yawned, took the Local section. We heard, "Tell Me Heart! Why So Desponding?"

Ronnie joined us. He wore his blue suit, T-shirt, no shoes or socks. "Morning," he said. "Hello, Judi." He sat down beside me, got right up, rubbed his face with his hands, took a deep breath, fished his glasses out of a pocket, and put them on.

Judi said hello, studied her dad, the crooked glasses, the damp lips, the scar on his left eyebrow, the hammertoes.

Ronnie said, "I owe you an explanation."

Judi said, "At least."

I got up to use the phone.

Ronnie said, "Are you mad at me?" He cracked his knuckles.

Judi said she was. And hurt. "But I'm glad to see you." She smiled.

Ronnie said, "Me, too." He smiled, sniffled. "Not glad to see me. You know what I mean. You."

I called Hervey, told him we'd be there in a half hour.

Judi said, "Why did you come?"

"You're my daughter."

"But why did you come?"

"I'm sorry things had to be the way they were." Ronnie walked to the fridge, back to the table.

"Did they have to be that way?"

"I came to make you breakfast, Judi. French toast with vanilla and cinnamon. The way you like it."

"I can't eat, Ronnie."

Ronnie scratched his knees.

Judi said, "You look awfully nervous. How do you feel?"

Ronnie said, "Don't do that, all right?"

"Do what?"

"Don't pull that shrink talk on me. You're not my shrink."

We heard the tape click off. I told Judi we should get going. She thanked Ronnie for coming. She went to him, kissed his head, patted his shoulder.

After we dropped Judi at Memorial, Hervey and I went to the Broadway for breakfast. Judi was in for a CA 125 blood test, a chest X ray, a CAT scan, I think it was. And she was going to tell Dr. Pawlak, No more chemo. We parked in front of Lederman's Bakery. Hervey let the car run so we could hear the end of "In Dreams." Hervey said he could remember when Water Street was cobblestoned. Rattle the screws right out of your bicycle, he said. Shimmy the teeth right out of your gums. Hervey turned off the ignition. He pointed ahead. I shook JFK's hand right there, he said. Used to be Sheppy's fruit market. I tried to imagine Hervey forty years younger. He's on a maroon Schwinn, no fenders or chain guard. His right pant leg is rolled up and he has a Lucky Strike hanging out the side of his mouth.

We sat at a booth. Hervey ordered poached eggs on toast, nice and loose, an egg cream, and a Sanka. I got the French toast and coffee. Hervey talked about the old Worcester, the one they tore down to build the galleria and the glass banks. We used to have a city here, he said. Now we got a shopping district. I don't even know the place anymore, he said. Do you realize there's not a single bowling alley left down town? Not one. Used to be, I don't know, a half dozen candlepin lanes within three blocks of City Hall.

Hervey went to the register and bought five scratch tickets and a tabloid. I saw one of the Farrells, Bobby, I think, take a seat at the counter. I waved and smiled. When Hervey didn't win any money, he complained that the lottery was a scam. The waitress freshened my coffee. Hervey perused the paper, shaking his head. Nice fucking world we live in, he said. Here's a guy puts out a death contract on a five-year-old girl that he raped, so she can't testify against him. He turned the page. Our food arrived. Hervey asked for ketchup. He went on. Mommies burning babies with cigarettes; daddies stuffing babies under waterbed mattresses. Hervey stopped, salted his eggs, shook his head. He folded the paper and set it beside him on the seat. I'll tell you what else pisses me off royally, Hervey said. Your veneer. I stopped chewing. Did he say, "Souvenir"? Nothing's made out of honest-to-Jesus wood anymore, he said. It's all cheesy particle board and fake laminated façades.

"Did you cut the Prozac in half this morning, Hervey?"

He looked at me, wiped egg from his chin with a napkin.

"Just a joke," I said.

I remembered that Bobby Farrell had always wanted to be a priest. He talked about it in the fourth grade. Last I'd heard he was in the sem. I looked up at the counter. Bobby was counting out change. He stood. His T-shirt said, "I Brake for Flea Markets." He put on his sunglasses.

Hervey said, "It's the air."

"What's that?"

"It's when they open you up, the cancer starts; when the air gets to it, it spreads."

I realized this is what Hervey had been thinking about all along, really. This open-air theory he'd talked about over supper on the deck.

Hervey picked his teeth with the edge of a matchbook. He has two deep creases by his eyebrows that lead down his nose and then arc out around his mouth so that, when he smiles, it looks like he has pliers on his face. He told me about his union steward, Porky Bourque, who went into St. V's to get a polyp scraped out of his ass. Just before Thanksgiving. What the hell's a freaking polyp doing there, anyway?

I said, "It happens, Hervey."

"With those little tentacles and everything?"

I said, "I don't think it's that kind of polyp exactly."

"You a doctor?"

"No."

"The good news," Hervey told me, "is they get the little fucker out. The bad news is they look around. What they find is a million more polyps and all of them malignant as hell. By Christmas, Porky's dead."

I tried not to think about Judi. Tried.

"You see, they let the air in where it doesn't belong. My old man, Eustache. Same thing happened to him. Doctors open up his belly and they find all his business slathered with black strap molasses, smells all rank and putrid, like a prison outhouse. All they could do was sew him right up and shake their heads like they had nothing to do with it. Dr. Carriciolo told my mother she should make arrangements."

We freshened our coffee. We weren't going anywhere. Hervey explained his aerogenetic theory of metastasis. Said we all have these dormant cellular cancer seeds in us. Hervey spooned sugar into his cup, searched for a metaphor. "Sea monkeys," he said. "You know what I'm talking about?"

I did. *Feed Them! Grow Them! Breed Them! Train Them!* I'd had my own little Ocean Zoo as a kid, full of the cryptobiotic creatures. *Beyond the Wildest Dreams of Science! The World's Only Fully Manmade Pets!*

Hervey said, "Sprinkle your package of sea monkeys into a glass and set the glass on the kitchen table. You could wait till the Red Sox win the Series. Nothing's going to happen. Right? Am I right?"

I nodded. "You're right."

"Now, you pour some tap water into the glass, add the water purifier, wait a day, sprinkle in the Instant Life, and bango, you've got a universe of sea monkeys eating and screwing their atom-sized hearts out—it's not even a glass of water anymore, is it?"

"Not so you'd want to drink it."

"No one's ever cutting Hervey Jolicoeur open."

I said, "Not everyone with cancer has had surgery."

"And that's why you see so much more cancer these days. The air's so full of shit. All the chemical pollution is like fertilizer, you know, makes the cancer bloom. You know what else tees me off?"

"What's that?"

"Those low-bred morons that spit out their gum on the sidewalk. Like I need that shit on my shoes."

I sipped my coffee.

"Nobody had polyps in them when I was a kid."

I picked up the check, figured the 15 percent.

I dropped Hervey off at the VA hospital in Jamaica Plain for his annual physical. I drove back and picked up Judi at Memorial. "How did it go?"

"Pawlak says she'll alter the dosage."

"And?"

"I don't know."

"You know how I feel. One more time. If it's bad, I wouldn't blame you for stopping."

"That's what Stoni said."

"Great minds," I said. "So?"

"I'm afraid."

"But you'll do it?"

"She said she'd put it off another week."

"So you'll do it?"

"Yes. I've got two healthy weeks to enjoy."

When we got home, I had a message from my father. His voice was a disturbing squeal.

Judi said, "Go see him. Now would be the best time."

And I saw that it certainly would be.

50.

Florida, State with the Prettiest Name

I TELEPHONED EDGAR AND ASKED HIM TO PICK ME UP AT THE FORT LAUDERDALE airport. He took down the flight information and said, Perfect. I'll shoot right over from the Rotary luncheon. He asked me to hold on a sec. He yelled at one or both of his boys. Your uncle Laf's coming down for a visit. I imagined their disinterested faces, their limpid eyes fixed on a television screen.

I dialed the Maravista to let my parents know I was coming. When Eudine picked up I told her I was coming to visit. She said, Why tomorrow? What the hell did that mean? I said, Mom, why don't you get a private line so I won't be interrupting the business calls? She said, Did you just call to complain? I apologized, but I didn't know why. You can sleep on the couch, she said. Thanks. She said, Well, you know your father's hemianopsiatic now.

"He's what?"

"Your father has lost half his field of vision. The top half. Hold on and I'll fetch him."

Blaise told me he wasn't so worried about the loss of sight, not after all he'd been going through. He said, "I just lift my head if I need to see the part in your mother's hair. An inconvenience that will pass," he said. "But this morning I couldn't find my left arm."

I didn't respond. I was thinking how you wouldn't even need to see your arm to find it. I was thinking stroke, paralysis.

He said, "And then at lunch I was eating your mother's pea soup, and

I lost the spoon in my broth. And then when I found my arm, it wasn't attached—it was just out there, floating about two inches from my whatchamacallit."

"Your shoulder."

Blaise did not seem amused by his latest afflictions the way he had been with the other peculiarities. I figured he must be afraid now.

He said, "I've seen bread. I've eaten bread all my life. I've touched bread. I've made bread. But I can't imagine it. I know it when I see it. I just can't you know, picture it anymore."

I said, "I'll be in town tomorrow afternoon."

"You will? That's terrific."

"I'm looking forward. We'll talk."

"About what?"

"Whatever. I'll see you tomorrow," I said.

Edgar smiled and shook my hand. He said, "When are you going to get a freaking haircut? Is this all the luggage you got?"

"That's it, Edgar."

As we were driving out of the airport, a minivan in the breakdown lane was engulfed in flames. About twenty yards from the van, a man leaned against the Jersey barrier, staring straight ahead into the passing traffic, pretending, I suppose, that he had nothing to do with the disaster. He was just waiting on a friend. I said, "How does that happen? How does a car just combust like that?"

"Happens all the time down here," Edgar said.

We heard sirens. I remembered how we used to pronounce it when we were young. "Sireens," I said, and Edgar laughed. Edgar looked spiffy. He wore a starched white shirt, yellow tie, ebony cuff links, gray cotton slacks, and loafers. His hair was short and brown, but his sideburns were white. I'd forgotten his eyes were blue like that, like my mother's, turquoise almost. There was a baobab tree right by the side of U.S. 1. I recognized its swollen trunk and its delicate limbs from a photo in *Peoples and Places,* my fourth-grade geography book. I pointed the tree out to Edgar. I told him if he ever needed water, he could just tap into the trunk. I said, "You now that's an African tree. It doesn't belong here."

"We got lots that don't belong," Edgar said. "We got catfish that walk. We got monkeys over here in Dania, living in the mangroves, hanging out in apartment-house parking lots. We got frogs the size of footballs. This is one strange place, bro."

Indeed. While I was there in South Florida for what turned out to be ten days, a bank clerk driving a Toyota Celica on I-95 got so pissed when he was cut off in traffic that he shot and killed a seventy-four-year-old woman who was riding in the bed of the offending pickup truck, being driven by her grandson; a school-bus driver was shot in the back of the head by a fifth-grader; some guy killed his girlfriend's daughter and they told the cops she'd been kidnapped; a teenage mother tossed her four-day-old baby out a fifth-floor window; a young couple said they were playing with their four-month-old when his neck snapped, when, in fact, they'd been holding him by the feet and battering his head against the fridge. And so on.

I said, "How's the family, Edgar?"

He nodded, smiled, turned left by a car dealership. He took a phone out of his pocket, pushed buttons, and said, "Hi, Mom, we're on our way." He handed me the phone. My mother said, "Your father's locked himself in the bathroom."

51.

Conversation Hearts

THERE'S A STONE CANNON ON THE ROOF OF THE MARAVISTA MOTEL, ITS BARrel poking through a crenel and aimed at the ocean. The motel is white with gold trim and features a four-story corner tower crowned with a pavilion. The tower, the building, the grounds, are all cluttered with plaster statues—the Virgin, saints, angels, conquistadores, Roman voluptuaries, gnomes, and lions. All this could be mine.

It turns out that Blaise had forgotten how to undo the lock in the bathroom. We got him out. We ate supper. My father wore a bib now, a white one with a picture of a lobster on it. He closed his eyes when he brought a spoonful of food to his mouth. My mother looked at him, at me, shook her head. She excused herself. We had gingerbread with whipped cream for dessert. Edgar made a phone call from the table. He told whoever it was about a new Mayan restaurant in Pompano, Chicken Eats-Ah! My mother told me that the style these days was for short hair. My father said, Leave the boy alone. Then he coughed.

After supper, my father put on a black nylon warm-up suit. Nike, the jacket said. The winged goddess of victory. We went walking, the two of us, along the Broadwalk. My father's suit flapped in the wind. We stopped at a bench advertising *L'hôpital du Sud de la Floride pour les Canadiens*. We sat. Blaise weighed 116 pounds, he told me, and had shrunk, I'd say, to five feet five inches. He smelled like warm milk. His teeth seemed too large for his mouth now. It looked like he was trying to swallow piano keys. He said, "You just don't expect this, Laf. Old age. It's a complete surprise."

A file of pelicans coasted along the shore. The sea darkened and the lights of cruise ships came up. Blaise told me he had only peripheral vision left. Can't see what's right in front of me. What's in front of me, of course, is death. Last thing I want to do is die. Joggers and roller skaters passed us, strollers and cyclists. I swear one of the skaters was someone from Worcester, an altar boy with me way back when. Drank wine from a cruet one morning. What was his name? Sister Louise Marie sprinkled him with holy water to drive out the devil. Bruno?

I said, "How come we never talked?"

"What are you talking about? We talk. We're talking now, ain't we?" He leaned forward, put his hands on his knees, cleared his throat. "You're right. We never talked. Why?"

"I asked you first."

" 'What's silent in the father speaks in the son.' Nietzsche said that."

"Why can't I remember much of my childhood?"

"You don't want to. You don't want to know the truth—that you were happy."

"What I *do* remember isn't happy."

"That proves my point. You need someone to blame for how you are."

"What was I like as a boy?"

"You were pretty regular, sort of. You played with your dick all the time. We were worried we wouldn't be able to send you to school." He laughed. "You still do that?"

Bruno skated by again. Not Bruno. Brazeau. Blaise told me I wasn't otherwise good with my hands. Didn't build anything with my Lincoln Logs, Erector set, Legos. All I made were walls. Didn't like trucks and balls much either.

"So what did I do?"

"You liked to talk. Actually, you liked to listen. 'Tell me this, Dad. Tell me that.' Talk and dig holes in the yard. You buried things. Marbles, baseball cards, plastic farm animals, money."

None of this rang a bell.

"You liked green food, but not vegetables. Lime Jell-O, green M&M's, like that. You were afraid of pencils."

We talked about Edgar. ("He's foolish enough to be content, smart enough to stay that way.") About Mom. ("She's got her shows and her grandkids; she'll be okay.") I wanted to find the topic or the question that would bring us together. "Are you happy, Dad?"

He looked at my shoulder and saw, I suppose, my face. He said, "I'm dying, for Christ sakes. I can remember right now the happiest moments in my life and none of them make up for the pain I'm feeling now." He took a breath, wiped his eye. "Knowing I'm dying hurts so much."

I wanted to touch his shoulder. I wanted to say the right thing, that he was making me happy. Something. I would remember this moment with fondness, I wanted to say. But I thought that might hurt him.

"You're happy, and you think why aren't I always this happy, and you realize why, and then you're not happy anymore." He told me the happiest he ever was was waking up in a hospital in Korea and realizing he was alive. He started to cry like crazy, he said. Like a baby.

"So what happens, do you think? When you die."

"After you die you're what you were before you were born. Only then it was going to end." Blaise reached in his jacket pocket. "Candy?"

"Sure."

He held out a palmful of small parti-colored hearts. Valentine candy. I chose an orange one. I read the message. *My Pal.* I gave it to Blaise. He thanked me. He picked one out for me. *OU Kid.*

My turn. A white one. *Tell Me.*

Blaise chose *Coax Me.*

We ate the entire pocketful.

The wind swept sand across the Broadwalk. Blaise said his patron, St. Blaise, had his flesh torn with iron combs.

"You feel like a martyr?"

"I feel like I'm blowing away."

I told him I'd hold him down and put my arm around his shoulder. He leaned into me. I remembered this moment: My father and I standing on an icy lake, fishing, watching our tilts, stomping our feet. I'm so cold I'm crying. I turn to him and bury my face in his chest. He hugs me.

On our walk back to the Maravista, Blaise said, "Here's a tune you'll remember. I used to sing it to you all the time." He started to sing "It's Howdy Doody Time," only he didn't know the words, so he made new ones, and then I joined in and we walked along the darkened Broadwalk singing:

> It's Lafayette Proulx time,
> It's Lafayette Proulx time,
> Can't even save a dime,

Can't even make a rhyme.
He's such a silly schnook
That you could fill a book
With what he don't know
So, kids, let's go!

In the morning, Eudine shook my knee until I woke. "Your father's passed," she said.

52.

Waking the Dead

My best friend at St. Stephen's was Jimmy Carrigan. When we were nine, Jimmy's dad, Rags, died suddenly. Not sick or anything, at least not so you could tell. Jimmy told me about it later, one night when we were twelve and lying on our backs in left field at Lake Park, looking up at the starry sky, hoping we'd see a satellite, or, better, a flying saucer. Jimmy said that one minute Rags is settled into his BarcaLounger, watching a Sox game on the tube, yelling at Yaz to lay off the curveball; the next thing you know, the napkin on his lap is on fire from his cigarette, and his rayon shirt's like, melting. Jimmy poured his dad's ale on the flames. He shook his father's shoulder, then he watched the next inning, spying on his dad out of the corner of his eye. When Rags still hadn't moved or snored, not even when Jimmy dropped the ale bottle on his slippered foot, Jimmy went to the back porch and called his mother in from hanging out the clothes. I almost didn't yell to her, he said. The wind was blowing through her hair, flapping her dress. She had a clothespin in her mouth. When she saw me, she smiled and lifted a pillowcase from the laundry basket. In the den, Jimmy and his mom stared at Rags and held each other. Jimmy told me he could smell his dad's flannel shirts on his mother's apron. He told his mother, When I die, I'm going to have a lot to tell him, how good I did in school and Scouts, how I took care of you and stuff, and how maybe I became a priest and what that was like. Or a cowboy. And he'll want to know how the Sox did. We'll have a lot to talk about. Jimmy told me it was funny, and he couldn't explain it, but at that moment, standing just inches from his father's cooling corpse, he felt strangely exhilarated. He understood maybe for the first time that life had meaning beyond all the crap the nuns handed you in religion class. He'd have to pay attention to the world now, knowing he'd be reporting it all to Rags in heaven.

I lay there looking at the Big Dipper, thinking how my old man was alive and how I had nothing at all to say to him. Jimmy said he'd already forgotten what his father's voice sounded like. I tried to hear my own father's and couldn't. Tone, I got, but not sound. Jimmy and his mother moved away not long after that night. Moved up to Methuen, where her people were from. Methuen might just as well have been Timbuktu. I never saw Jimmy again.

And here I was some twenty-six years later, kneeling at my own father's casket in the Burgie Urgel Funeral Home in godforsaken Miramar, Florida, and I was being nettled by morbidly obsessive thoughts. There was Blaise's head, propped up a bit, turned to the right as if intent on hearing whatever secret I might whisper to him. I wondered who had done his hair like that, parted it on the right side—the wrong side—and slicked it all back. The hair in his ears was gone. Were his eyelids closed with Super Glue, his jaw sutured shut with heavy thread or wire, his throat and butt stuffed with wads of cotton soaked in cavity fluid? The bruise on his forehead had been bleached away. I heard the click of Edgar's camcorder. I tried to summon grief, but what came to mind were the trocar buttons on Blaise's chest. Yes, there *was* one thing. I realized that when your father dies, then you're next.

I found myself downstairs, sitting in the smokers' lounge with Edgar's wife, Delores. Just the two of us. No smokers. She was tapping her foot a mile a minute. She wiped her eyes with a Kleenex and rocked on her chair. I smiled at her. She said the boys were going to miss him. She told me how the family took Blaise out to the Black-eyed Pea for his last birthday. How the wait staff all joined them in singing "Happy Birthday." Blaise had the catfish dinner. When the meal was over, Blaise decided to soak his dentures in a cup of coffee. The boys thought it was the funniest thing they'd ever seen. I said something to Delores about dignity and confusion, and I probably didn't make much sense. I didn't even know my father wore false teeth. Delores started in about her and Edgar. Out of the blue.

She said, "We had our honeymoon at the Mallory House in Key West." She shook her head, raised her eyebrows, took a deep breath. "On Whitehead Street. It's not there anymore. Anyway, we're unpacked and freshened up and in our room. Smelled like patchouli. Your brother's sitting on the edge of the bed, his hands folded on his lap. I'm on this wicker ottoman thingy. We just looked at each other for minutes. We didn't smile or talk or twitch or anything. We looked at each other, and we knew at the very same instant that we were not in love, never had been, never would be, and we should not have married."

I said, "Honeymoon jitters," and smiled.

Delores ignored me. "I don't know how we realized it all of a sudden like that or why we hadn't faced it earlier." Delores blew her nose. She looked at me, fixed my eyes. "I said it first. I said, 'Edgar, what have we done?' and I felt great relief." Delores closed her eyes. "No one can tell you what love is, what it feels like, can they?"

I shook my head. "I don't guess they can." I sure can't.

"And so it's easy to make a mistake like we did." Delores looked at the ceiling. "But, you know, there we were, the pair of us, up there in our love nest in Key West with our new outfits on, with these gold bands on our fingers. And me with a new name even. And back here in Hollywood in our new two-bedroom, two-and-a-half bathroom dollhouse was a living room full of shiny electrical appliances and dinnerware and linens and culinary gadgets and other wedding gifts. It was too late to do anything about our mistake. We weren't movie stars. We hugged each other and then went out to eat at this very elegant Cuban place, La Paloma Verde or something." Delores took another long, slow breath, smoothed out her dress. She looked at me, trying to gauge my response. We heard the creaking of the floor above us, muffled voices from the staircase.

"We treat each other well. We do. Better than most, I think. From what I gather." Someone came down the stairs and went into the restroom.

I said, "Things seem to have turned out well."

Delores said, "So now we sort of live in different parts of the house. We're scared. Scared of being the one who leaves." Delores waited for whoever left the restroom to make his or her way back up the stairs to the viewing salon. "Is it right to go to your grave without ever even once in your life feeling honest-to-God love and intense passion? Is it?" Delores began to cry. "Even with the kids, I don't know."

I held her, said how we're all tense and edgy what with Dad's death and all. While I reassured her, patted her shoulder, she told me how it's the fear that drove them to their charismatic church. Keep yourself busy and keep yourself in line. That sort of thing. Delores excused herself. Said she needed to wash her face, compose herself.

I said, "It's okay to cry. It's a wake."

She said, "I'll see you back upstairs."

If Delores ever left Edgar, would I even remember her? Would I re-call her voice? the color of her hair? her tapping foot? I thought, yes, I'd remember this exchange at least. I could say, yes, I remember Edgar's ex. Delores, right? What's she doing these days? But who on earth would I say that to?

I went back upstairs and sat beside my mother. She looked at her watch. Guy Duplessis and a man I did not know whispered together in French. What might be worse than living without love? If you are in love and if that love vanishes—that could be worse. I remembered a con-versation with Blaise. He was talking about his erratic eyesight. He told me he hoped the next trick his brain pulled would enable him to see into the future. I hoped that didn't happen.

53.

A Many-layered, Infolded Mystery

LOVE AT FIRST SIGHT IS IRRESISTIBLE AND INEXPLICABLE. I WANT TO SAY IT'S transmundane, but transmundane seems haughty, and love at first sight is not that. It arrives without warning and is earned without effort, leaving us startled and grateful. It is neither reasonable nor calculated. It is like ecstasy, like rapture, like standing outside yourself. It is apprehension not thought, gesture not word. Love at first sight elevates romance above the level of accident—the accident of geography or economics or occupation. It is, we may decide, destiny. Love at first sight is sudden, ineffable, profoundly emotional, and absolutely transfiguring. It's what we live for. It's the obliterating focus on the beloved and the eloquent shortness of breath. It is a stroke of lightning, as the French say, a blast of passion. And it can only happen to strangers.

And there I sat on my two-hour layover in that mutopolis of strangers, Hartsfield-Atlanta International Airport, thinking about love at first sight and death and time; that and studying the women who passed by Gate A-33. Like this woman—the one walking her brown suitcase like it's a dog—with her thin, straight blond hair, her ankle-length print dress, her denim jacket, her squash blossom necklace, the needlepoint carpetbag on her shoulder. What's her story? I wondered. Art school graduate, maybe. Vegetarian. Dreams of living in Santa Fe. Or this woman who looks vaguely, I don't know, Lithuanian—high cheekbones, prairie wolf's eyes, coppery hair. She notices me notice her, and so she stares up at the video monitors as she walks. Arrivals. Departures. Or this gap-toothed woman sitting across from me, reading a paperback novel, her black hair swept behind her right ear and falling across her left eye. No makeup, no jewelry, except for a thread of gold around her right ankle. I adjusted my sunglasses, watched her read, imagined what it would be like to wake up in the morning beside her.

We live in the mountains, in a log house, maybe in Colorado. I wake up when I hear the deer munching the fallen apples in our yard. I kiss her ear, nuzzle her neck. She moans. I slide out from under the covers, taking her warmth and her smell with me. I walk downstairs to the sunny kitchen, brew coffee, sit at the table with Jeffrey, our cat, on my lap, wait for her. Her name's Anna. She's pressed a Post-It note to the fridge. I can read it from here. It says, "Rejigger the cold frame hinge." I don't know what this means.

I opened my eyes, looked across the aisle. She had the cap of a blue pen in her mouth and was writing a note in her book. I felt cheated. Why wasn't I born in Cleveland or Laramie or wherever it is she's from? Why hadn't we met in junior high science lab? What was I missing without her in my life? I heard an announcement that Delta Flight 757 for New Orleans, with continuing service to Houston, was boarding at Gate A-28. I wondered who worships Anna.

How do I say this? It wasn't that I wanted to know her now, although that would be nice, if lamentably brief. I wanted to have already known her. I wanted her fears and her desires to have shaped my life. I wanted to have held her body against mine for a thousand and one nights, wanted to have traced my finger along the lines of her face. I didn't feel at all foolish thinking like this.

And then Anna stuffed her book and her pen into her backpack. Just when I was getting to know her. I was devastated. When she stood and worked the pack onto her shoulders, I saw the outline of her ribs through her Danskin top, her small breasts, her nipples. I wanted to cry, to ask her to stay. I smiled instead. She smiled. And then she walked out of my life.

I'm like this at airports. By the time I board my flight, I've usually decided that I'd like to live with every unattached woman in the world. Maybe this makes me crazy. But not dangerous. Maybe I should stay out of airports. I know this is not love, of course. What it is is a queer feeling of nostalgia for an impossible future, for what can never be: Anna and I snuggled under quilts in Telluride. That's fantasy. Love is different.

Love is anticipation and memory, uncertainty and longing. It's unreasonable, of course. Nothing begins with so much excitement and hope and pleasure as love, except maybe writing a story. And nothing fails as often, except writing stories. And like a story, love must be troubled to be interesting. We crave love, can't live without its intimacy, though it pains us. Judi told me that every person in therapy has a love disorder: never felt love, can't find love, trapped by love, unraveled by love, thinks love is lust or love is loss, fears love, loves too much, uses love for profit, jealous in love, lost in love, love affairs, unrequited love, love sick, doesn't love Mom, won't love Dad, can't love the kids, can't love the self, hopeless love, self-absorbed love, love as a crutch, love as a truncheon, love in ruins, crazy love, love that eats the heart, careless love, drowning in love, love that dares not speak its name, blind love, consuming love, obsessive love, conditional love, dangerous love, first love, last love, fickle love, love and marriage, love lost, secret love, love on the run, love that hates, dutiful love, borrowed love, thief of love, love in embers, love in vain, love in shackles, love maligned, love that warps the mind a little.

And the man who would love all women couldn't seem to love the women in his life. At least not adequately. If Proust was right, if the only paradise is the lost one, then perhaps the only love is lost love. If love means compassion and concern for another, if it means easy intimacy, comfort, security, and grace, then I was once in love with Martha. But if it means desire over time, if love abides, then I was not.

When we were courting early on, I could not be distracted from Martha. I often felt as if my head and my heart were carried away. My whole body felt lifted from the ground, and so I would ask her to hold me. I spoke her name when I was alone. I looked for her in everything, and found her. Ours was a courtly love, an attempt to prolong the passion, the aching uncertainty, to maintain the romance. This was love you read about in fairy tales. Young love. Timeless love. Immutable and true. And so it was a lie. Romance turns out to be a shallow sea. Romantic love like ours is meat to the teeth of time.

The way I had felt about Martha was sort of the way I felt about Pauline. Sometimes when I was cleaning up Judi's vomit in the bathroom or changing her bed linens, I imagined Pauline watching me, being impressed and moved by my selfless compassion, charmed by my devotion. Even then I knew this was depraved, but I couldn't stop my thoughts. Sometimes I thought that when Judi would die, I would be free, whatever that means, and I would have an attractively tragic past, which Pauline, having grown tired of Marvin, would be helpless to re-sist. Sometimes I thought I was a prick for thinking like that. Was it love I wanted with Pauline or a way out? I didn't even know her, really. She was a mystery—so much so that I had to make her up like a character in a story. And, of course, it's impossible not to love and admire your characters. I may love Theresa, say, more than Dale does.

With Judi I felt differently. If ours was love, it was accidental. It wasn't romance, and it wasn't ecstasy. We didn't need to be foolish or preten-tious. I wasn't used to such sobriety in a sexual relationship, not so early on, at any rate. Because of Judi's cancer, we were stuck in the present. I liked *her,* I realized, more than I liked *us.* And I still had the past to wres-tle with. Martha and I had constructed a life together. We had it all, a home, enduring and cherished memories, a mutual future. We had it made, and I gave it up. I failed Martha, failed myself. That's how I felt sometimes. But other days, I thought I barely got out alive.

54.

Side Effects

I WAS IN THE BATHROOM, LOOKING AT MY FACE IN THE MIRROR, WHEN I HEARD Judi come home from work. I heard her yell hello and open the fridge. I heard Spot barking out in the yard, heard the refrigerator door snap shut. I was studying these new (at least as far as I knew) lacy red blood vessels on my nose. Christ, any more surprises? Yes, I had a single, weedy eyelash over my left eye that was twice as long as the others and was gray and crooked. I snipped it off with fingernail clippers. And my eyebrows could use a trim. The helixes and lobes of my ears had gone all fuzzy with down. Jesus, I'd be shaving my ears soon. I stepped back, smiled, and admired my monochromatic mouth, my handsome crown. I felt better. I'd have to send Dr. Vigeant a thank-you note.

Judi knocked. I told her to come in. She was eating an orange Popsicle. She asked me to smell her breath. I leaned over and stole a kiss. She told me to cut it out, she was serious. Smell! I said, Your breath is fine. It is not, she said. She clicked her tongue, smacked her lips. Her mouth tasted queer, she said, like rust and like oil paint. And the Tic Tacs weren't helping. Gum's not helping. She handed me the Popsicle. I finished it in two bites. She opened the cabinet under the sink. I sat on the toilet. She swished some organic cinnamon mouthwash around her mouth, spit it out. She brushed her teeth gingerly, spit out blood.

Our bathroom had become a pharmacy. Just in case Judi started feeling healthy, the medicines were here to remind her she was famously ill. Judi had two kinds of nausea medicine—Ativan and Zofran. Three, if you count the Pepto-Bismol. She had Benadryl elixir to treat her mouth sores. If that didn't work, she used Orabase salve. She took acyclovir for her cold sores, Nizoral for mouth fungus, and Mycostatin pastilles for some other oral problem. When she couldn't eat, she took prednisone or Marinol marijuana capsules, which I had not yet sampled. (I was waiting till I had several hours to waste.) And that's not even counting the chemo drugs and the hormone-replacement drugs and whatever else they were giving her at the hospital. It's a wonder she could stand up. And it's not counting what we kept in the fridge—the Ensure and the Nutren, the Easter basket full of vitamins and mineral supplements. We froze nystatin in plastic medicine caps that Judi would let melt in her mouth.

Judi washed her face, dripped Visine into her eyes, put on Chap Stick. She looked in the mirror. She said, "I look like a raccoon."

We took Spot for his walk. Judi put her Red Sox cap on backward. I tied her sneakers for her. The Nybergs were washing windows. We waved. Spot peed on their hedge. Judi told me that people with multiple personalities sometimes have physical symptoms for one personality and not for the others. Like Cain could be a total diabetic, let's say, takes his insulin and everything. But Abel is perfectly normal. Abel doesn't need insulin because his pancreas manufactures it.

Spot barked, tried to go after a passing motorcycle. I gave him a tug. I said, "So you're wondering does the process extend to carcinoma."

"Sure. But it's more than that. It's like there are aspects of the mind that are outside of matter. That's what I mean. Same body, different person. Helen has anemia. Leda's blood is normal. Same body, different personality."

"So what do you want to do, fracture yourself into a few personalities, find a cancer-free one?"

"I would if I could. But here's the thing, Laf. Something in the mind, the brain, whatever, something that's unaffected by the body is controlling the body, is telling the body to be sick or healthy."

"But the brain is physical."

"I don't know how to explain it. Probably because I don't understand it. It's obvious that the spiritual, the nonphysical, must exist in the physical somehow. Anyway, I think we can learn how to program the brain to wipe out our illnesses. Spontaneous remission. Miracle. Whatever you want to call it." Judi stopped. "Something like that." She told me she was tired.

We walked into Hoffman Park and sat on the bench by Abbie's memorial. I let Spot off his leash. First he stood there like he hardly believed it. He looked at me. I stamped my foot, and he took off and ran like a fury, like he was going somewhere. But all he did was make big circles. Whenever he bounded by our bench, Judi applauded. Spot seemed to run even faster.

I asked Judi if she was going to her support group meeting tonight. She said she didn't feel up to it. I asked her if that was any way for a therapist to talk. How could she expect people to come to the groups she led if she wasn't going to her own cancer-patient group? Because they're all Barneys in the cancer group, she said. "I love you, you love me. Blah blah blah." It's not honest. We should all be screaming.

I changed the subject. I told her that Ronnie was talking about leaving. She said that's what he does best.

"Don't you want to talk it out with him?"

"Not unless he can give me back the years he stole from me."

"Give him a chance to help you. He wants to."

"He doesn't even know what planet he's on."

"He's in pain."

"Well, I didn't fuck up *his* life, Laf. I didn't condemn *him* to a life of screwed-up relationships."

"Excuse me."

"Nothing personal."

"Think about what you're saying."

"One disastrous relationship after another, starting with Daddy."

I suppose I should have been upset about this. The fact that I wasn't may have been proof of Judi's assertion. I wanted to think harder about this, but I kept drifting away. Spot was playing soccer with some kids. He's a natural. Judi laid her head on my shoulder, closed her eyes. After a while I said, If we're so disastrous together, then why are we together?

Judi opened one eye, looked at me without moving her head. Closed it. She said, Well, I'd better love someone before I die. You'll have to do. She said *love*. Judi loved me? I didn't ask if she was serious. I said, Do you think love is a choice? She said, For me it has to be.

"Is that going to scare you off?" she said.

"What?"

"Don't act stupid."

"Love, you mean? No."

Judi opened her eyes and sat up. She stared at me. Squinted. Tried to read my face. She said, "You're one angry man."

I said, "Don't start this again." She was always trying to find out what

I'd done as a kid that made me so afraid of my own anger. She said the fact that I didn't seem to care about conventional success and security was tied up with anger. That it was my childish, irresponsible way to strike back. At whom? Myself? Dad? Mom? Martha? All of the above? Why wouldn't she tell me?

She said, "What's for supper?"

"Bananas Foster."

"For supper?"

"Ronnie's idea. A whole meal of desserts."

"And you went along with him?"

"Stoni's coming, too. Bananas Foster, blueberry cheesecake from Lederman's, baklava from Aris's, and an apple pie made with Macouns."

"Laf, I can't eat that stuff."

"And I made you some onion soup."

"Bananas Foster. Really?"

We cut through Hope Cemetery, and we were halfway through before I realized where we were. I had Spot on his leash now and had to keep tugging at him to keep him from lifting his leg against the headstones. I was sure some custodian would come driving up any second now in his golf cart and start screaming at us. I picked up the pace.

Judi said the worst result of all the chemo and medicines was that she hadn't been able to regress to her past lives since a week after it all started. She felt empty, she said. At loose ends. More than just her insides were gone, she said. I put my arm around her shoulders. We leaned into each other and walked. Out of the corner of my eye I caught a name on a tombstone: *Hallelujah Amen Korner.* That's going into a story.

We stopped so Spot could sniff the wrought iron entry gate, pee on the scrolling. Judi tugged my arm. I asked her if she was feeling okay. She nodded. I said, "What is it?" She cocked her head, raised her eyebrows, and I knew. Spot sat. He looked at me, let his tongue flop over the side of his slack jaw. I said, "Martha?"

"What about her, Laf?"

A landscaping truck pulled by us into the cemetery, the driver slapping the steering wheel in time to music. I scratched Spot's ear. He closed his eyes. "That's over."

"Were you keeping it a secret?"

"I guess I was. I was afraid to think about it. I haven't loved her for a long time. I didn't realize that until she threw me out. But I miss her. Every time I try to tell myself it's over, get on with your life, the past comes rushing back, and I get nostalgic and I have regrets and doubts. It's crazy."

"Do you love her?"

"I've got every logical reason to. For who she is. For our history. All that. What I don't have is an unreasonable desire to love her." I felt like I was betraying Martha, but this was the first time I had tried to articulate my thoughts, and I needed to continue so I could hear what I said, know what I felt. "I did love her," I said. That's all I needed to hear. I began to cry and couldn't stop, couldn't catch my breath.

Judi said, "Let it go, Laf. Your grief isn't going to hurt anyone." She took my face in her hands and kissed my eyes.

55.

Just Desserts

WHILE I CARAMELIZED THE BUTTER AND BROWN SUGAR IN A SAUCEPAN, RONnie stood by the stove with a book of matches in his hand. Matches from the Standish Café, a shot-and-beer joint on Main Street, glamourless, dark, stale, quiet, a place where folks come to drink, not to socialize. Not much of a bar really, but it is ninety-five years old and does have one distinction. It is on the street level of the Standish Hotel, directly below the very room, 213, where Sigmund Freud stayed when he made his only visit to the United States in 1913. Carl Jung stayed down the hall in 210, already a little perturbed by the master's stubbornness and his sickening cigars, we're told. Jung sat on his cane-backed chair in his black suit, reading Goethe and running the back of his hand along the tufts in the chenille bedspread. The fact that Freud disliked America and Americans, then, has something to do with the Standish and with the fine citizens of Worcester, Heart of the Commonwealth. But I digress.

Ronnie wanted to be the one to set the dessert on fire. I assured him he could, but first cut the bananas in quarters. He did. We had the radio on to *All Things Considered*. Alex Chadwick talking to a playwright who'd written a play about Newt Gingrich and his first wife. *Contract with Jackie* opens in a hospital room and begins with Newt entering, presenting his ailing wife with divorce papers. It's a farce. The Trinity Square Rep is putting it on. The wonderful thing about it is that the playwright, Peter Someone, got an NEA grant for the project.

We put the bananas in the sauce, added the cinnamon and banana liqueur. Ronnie poured himself a glass of the liqueur. He liked the color. The smell reminded him of those orange candy peanuts you used to get for Halloween. He took a sip, drank the rest in a gulp, poured himself another. He said it was tasty but made his teeth hurt. Then he started in about radio cybernetic cybergation biofeedback control and nonfact talkage. I stopped him. I said, Set the table. I heard the phone ring, heard Judi answer. I looked at the clock. I said Stoni would be here any minute.

Ronnie said, "Sometimes I don't know if I'm crazy or if I'm just making it up, putting on an act, you know."

"Why would you do that?"

"Well, that's how it started. I just made believe I was bazots. Didn't have to deal with the dead boy that way, or anything else." He looked at me. "But I lost control of the pretending." He shook his head. "I suppose since I don't know if I'm crazy or not, then I'm crazy." He shrugged, scratched his crotch.

I asked Ronnie to get the ice cream out of the freezer and the scoop out of the junk drawer. He asked what I thought. "Am I nuts or what?"

I said, "Well, I consider you eccentric, Ronnie. And, like you said, you're schizophrenic. But crazy, that's a little strong."

Judi came into the kitchen, said hi, opened a cabinet, and took down wineglasses, set them on the table. She said Trixie would be joining us later. She's in the neighborhood, getting a manicure over at Get Nailed. She opened a bottle of sherry. I finished stirring, added rum. Ronnie looked out the window. He said, "Spot's eating a bicycle tire."

Stoni knocked and entered. She'd been smoking dope—smelled sweet and loud. She kissed her sister and her father. I said, Don't you kiss the cook? She said, Not until I've tasted his food.

Judi scooped ice cream onto our plates. Ronnie lit the sauce on his third match. I poured the flaming sauce over the vanilla mounds. Ronnie said it reminded him of napalm. Thanks, Ronnie. We followed the bananas with apple pie, which Stoni had à la mode. She was so hungry, she said, she could eat her family.

Ronnie can be either very withdrawn—so much so that you wonder if all his senses haven't closed down or something—or very animated and chatty. Tonight we couldn't shut him up. And he spilled his wine twice. Once with a sweeping gesture of his arm. The next time he set the glass down on the edge of his plate. He was lecturing us on the apple conspiracy being directed by the Washington State Apple Commission and the Department of Agriculture. He said a hundred years ago there were eight thousand varieties of apples in the country. Eight thousand! Apples used to be a fruit. Now they're a product. So we're down to apples that travel, a dozen or so varieties, and all of them insipid. Tasteless, acidless mush. Eventually, if the powers get their way, we'll have two choices, Delicious and Golden Delicious.

Stoni said, Do you think it's a good idea, all this sugar? And she glanced over at Ronnie and raised her eyebrows. Now he was talking about soap. I missed the transition. About Dr. Bronner's castile soap and how the label represented the most profound yet accessible philosophical writing we have in America today. He quoted Dr. Bronner, soap maker and Essene rabbi: "If I'm not for me, who am I?" Judi rolled her eyes. Ronnie, she said, take a breath. He told us that UFOs weren't vehicles at all. They were intergalactic aerospace macrobacteria. Stoni cut herself a slice of blueberry cheesecake. Ronnie said if we blasted a rocketload of antibiotics into space, we could begin to eliminate the bacteria.

Judi asked Ronnie about the place in Henniker. I gave it up, he said. I'll be going back to Portsmouth, maybe. Or Nashua. You never know. Why New Hampshire? I said. Live free or die, he said. It's better you guys don't know my whereabouts. That way if they interrogate you, you know nothing. He winked.

Stoni put her hand on his, forgot what she was going to say. He looked at his plate, stuck a finger in the pie, licked it. Stoni said, Dad, you've been here four days, and you haven't talked with Judi about her cancer.

Judi said, "Ronnie, you don't have to if you don't want to. I'm just glad you came."

He said, "I saw a lot of UFO activity in Nam. At My Lai, Calley took his orders from the UFOs hovering over the village."

I said, "I thought you said UFOs were bacteria."

"You don't think bacteria have brains?" Ronnie looked at me, leaned toward me, finished his chewing. "Bacteria run the whole ball of wax." He held up his fork and made a circular motion.

Stoni poured the Turkish coffee while I served the baklava. We heard Trixie's car squeal to a stop. I set another plate, cup, saucer, fork, spoon. Ronnie fished a bottle of pills out of his shirt pocket. He swallowed one, washed it down with sherry. He closed his eyes. I answered the knock at the door. Trixie came in with a box of doughnuts tied with string. Her fingernails were as red as litchis. I took her jacket. She stood there and looked Ronnie up and down. This was the first time they'd seen each other in, it must have been, sixteen, seventeen years. "You're still easy on the eyes, Ronnie," she said.

He blushed. "How are you, Trix?" He stood, touched her arm with his fingers, kissed her cheek.

"I haven't had any complaints," she said. We all laughed. Trixie sat between Ronnie and me, asked Judi how she felt.

For a while the family reminisced. About the time Ronnie tried to repair the toilet with a cold chisel and split the bowl in half, flooded the bathroom. That was on Christmas. Or Thanksgiving. No one was quite sure. The plumber cost a mint, though. About a vacation to Lake Winnipesaukee when their motorboat sank. About another trip, to Ausable Chasm, when they all got carsick from the hole in the exhaust. Especially George. Things became subdued after that. Trixie asked Stoni about Arthur and Richie, how she was handling all that. I wondered why it was some families seemed to attract damage. Stoni said she was still angry at both of them. She opened the box of doughnuts and took out a chocolate raised. She told Ronnie he didn't have to go to Portsmouth or anywhere. He could stay right here. I knew what was going through her buzzed little mind—the trailer. Poor Hervey.

Ronnie shook his head. "Impossible. It's dangerous for me here. They already know my whereabouts."

"They?" I said.

He put his finger over his lips to quiet me. He pointed to the light fixture over the table. He winked.

Judi said, "Why did you leave us in the first place?"

Trixie said, "It was a husband-wife thing."

Judi said, "Let him answer."

Ronnie started jabbering about nuclear alienation testing and disposal, about what he called Nosferatu Eyesight TV and the Kryptonite Earphone Transistor Radio and the Worldwide Cyberkinetic Cellular Monitor, all of which I was anxious to hear more about, but Judi cut him off.

She said, "It's obvious you haven't cut through your bullshit yet. Save that psychocrap for your social worker. I'm not buying it."

Nobody said a word. Trixie took out her compact mirror, smiled into it, wiped flaking mascara off her eyelids with a napkin. Ronnie held his hands up in front of his chest as if he were checking for rain. I looked at my hand, at the dry skin where my wedding band had been. Judi said she was tired and was going to bed. She stood. She apologized to Ronnie. I had no right, she said. She excused herself.

Trixie said, "She's under a lot of stress."

Stoni checked her watch. Said she'd better get going. She gave me a kiss. I packed a bag for her—baklava and cheesecake. She told Ronnie she'd see him tomorrow, told Trixie not to wait up for her.

When I got back from walking Spot the Wonder Dog, Trixie was gone and Ronnie was at the table, scribbling in his notebook. "I should get a dog," Ronnie said.

"Well, Ronnie, they can be a royal pain in the ass."

Ronnie poured another shot. I asked him about his teeth. They hurt, he said, but that means they can't be tapped. I let that pass. He said, I don't have any friends.

"You have a family."

"Don't you think I want to work at a shop? go out after work for a drink with my pals? Don't you think I want to join a bowling league? mow the lawn on Saturdays? watch football on Sundays? Don't you think I want someone to call me on the phone? And don't you think they would just love to have me do just that? And then where would we be? Civilization, I mean. Without my vigilance, we'd all be slaves tomorrow."

"Ronnie, don't get pissed, but this is your paranoia talking."

"I used to be crazy. I admit that. I used to think that Mussolini was my high school baseball coach."

I said, "Maybe you shouldn't worry so much about the world and everything. Take a day off and see what happens."

He said, "You think it's easy? Look, I've got no family life, no love life, no social life, no work life. I have become emotionally independent. No one's there for me. Sometimes my head hurts so much from the noise, I have to slam it against a wall and then I go into convulsions. I want to believe it's all in my imagination, what's going on, but I know it isn't." Ronnie closed his eyes, put his head in his hands.

He said, "I want the suffering to stop. All the suffering."

I finished my beer.

Ronnie said, "I'm just going to sit up and finish my song."

"Good night."

"One thing, Laf."

"What's that?"

"Judi. I just have the feeling I know her from somewhere. Not my daughter, but this woman. And I keep thinking it was a long time ago and we lived in a small town and traveled with the same crowd. Maybe we spoke French. I wanted to tell her this as soon as I saw her, but she's so practical, this one, so down-to-earth, she'd just think I was silly."

"I don't think she would. I'll tell her, though, what you said."

Ronnie smiled. In the morning he was gone.

56.

When the Deep Purple Falls

WHILE JUDI WAS UNDERGOING HER THIRD BLAST OF CHEMO, I WENT TO PIER 1 and bought the last six of these Indian print cotton sheets, the kind of thing you might use as a bedspread, tablecloth, curtain, shawl, furniture covering, or whatever. They were purple with black woodcut illustrations. I bought a staple gun, staples, and tacks at Jerry's Hardware. I went home to cover the mirrored bedroom ceiling. I'd been reading about cancer recovery and self-esteem. Mirrors are taboo. Besides, I'd never liked it in the first place. It was here, Judi told me, when she bought the house from a cop. It made me feel uneasy, like I was being watched while I slept, being graded while I made love. Anyway, I should have examined the sheets a bit closer than I did. Five of them were fine. They all depicted this dancing Hindu god wearing a tiger skin. His third eye was open. The sixth cloth, however, featured this gaunt, five-foot skeletal goddess, I suppose she was, wearing earrings fashioned from corpses. Serpents and skulls adorned her body. Charming. I fastened that sheet on the window side of the room and hoped Judi never noticed.

When I finished with my interior decoration, the canopied room was darker than it had been. I hadn't counted on that. The sheets billowed down. The room seemed temporary somehow, yet liturgical, the ceiling now a baldachin, the bed an altar. The point was that Judi would not have to look up at her unhealthy self.

I drove to Avant Gardens and bought a potted gardenia plant to brighten the room. I swung by Todd's Medical Supply and picked up the egg crate mattress pad I'd ordered. I remembered how the last time the room got to smelling like I don't know what. Like seaweed left out in the sun. Like sweat and cork and must and cider vinegar. And now, with the end of Indian summer, we wouldn't even be able to crack a window to air out the room. So I stopped by Humboldt's Gifts and bought incense—sandalwood, myrrh, and lilac. I wondered why no one made sautéed garlic incense. That's the best smell in the world, isn't it? Or baking bread. Or pot of simmering chocolate. Or the smell of Pauline's neck. I could start a business. *Commincense. DollarsIncense. Incenseitivity. Incensual Adults.*

Stoni came by in the morning to get the house, the sickroom, in order. The plan was for me to pick up Judi at the hospital in Stoni's Jeep. Nicky was coming along to help. Stoni emptied her plastic bag on the kitchen table. Two plastic bed pans, each initialed with a laundry marker: one *V*, the other *B*. I didn't ask. One bottle of Dr. Bronner's castile soap. Bar soap harbors bacteria, she said. She unfurled a banner she'd had printed on computer paper. It said, *Welcome Home, Judi,* and had fireworks before the sentence and a yellow ribbon after it. She handed me the tube of something called Astroglide.

"What's this?"

"It's like supersonic K-Y jelly." She smiled and started to tell me how she once used it at the hospital to extract a—

I stopped her. I said, "Thanks."

Stoni told me she'd spoken with Judi. "You must be awfully horny."

I said, "I wish you hadn't brought it up."

She said, "Did I?"

I blushed. I set the Astroglide on the table.

"This stuff could slip a camel through the eye of a needle."

"One hump or two?"

"You *are* horny."

"I'll be on my way," I said. I put on my jacket, thanked Stoni for her keys.

On my way to Nicky's I thought about my season of chastity. I mean, I understood it completely, but abstinence does serrate the edges of life. For one thing, I was lately far too aware of my groin. I'd find myself squeezing my thighs together a lot. Celibacy, I figured, was probably not doing my prostate any good either.

The thing of it was this condition wasn't so different from circumstances of my recent past. Martha and I could go weeks without doing it. Sleeping in the same bed, acting civilly, affectionately, to each other during the day. I don't know why we did that at night, why we behaved like two little magnets that repelled each other.

I read once that Flaubert would become aroused when he wrote a sex scene, would even masturbate at his writing desk. I never went that far. I have gotten up, splashed my face with cold water. I have taken walks. Maybe it's the Catholic schoolboy in me. We used to call it the "sin of self-abuse."

As a result of my discomfort, Dale and Theresa were enduring a cool phase in their relationship. They pulled back a bit when I started to get all too familiar with Theresa's body—the little mole just to the left of her navel, the tiny bump on her hip bone. And then I'd spend long minutes watching the sophomore education major in the front row in Dale's macroeconomics class. She was a runner. You could tell by her calves. Why does she sit like that? Well, I thought we all needed a cold shower.

Nicky had a box of plain doughnuts. On a health kick, he said. No more honey-dipped, no more chocolate raised, no more jelly. I had one. Nicky told me he hadn't been to a doctor in his adult life. He said, I got a knee that locks up on me. I got plantar warts, hemorrhoids, allergies. I get wicked leg cramps, but vitamin E usually takes care of that. He scarfed his doughnut. Break out with fever blisters if I get too much sun. Sinus headaches. Sometimes I feel like my whole body's a bell and I'm ringing with pain. Never been inside a hospital, he said. Until today.

I told him he didn't need to go in. Wait at the door. They'll be taking her down in a wheelchair. We'll help her along from there. Nicky seemed relieved. He offered me another doughnut.

Nicky sat in back with Judi's overnight bag. Judi wore sunglasses, but kept her eyes closed. I could see that her mouth hurt, the careful way she moved her tongue, the way she kept her jaw open a bit. She swallowed cautiously. Her lips were cracked and scabby. Her skin had broken out in little red dots. Her neck was bruised. She took deep, slow breaths. I watched the traffic and watched her. She told us that every joint and muscle in her body ached like they'd been pounded by a hammer. I could see she was crying.

We pulled into the garage. Nicky and I eased her out of her seat, got her up the couple of stairs and into the house. Stoni took over and led Judi to the bedroom. Nicky and I stood in the kitchen. I leaned against the fridge, Nicky against the stove. We looked at each other. He said, "What are you thinking?"

I shook my head. Shrugged. "She's got that bewildered look. Jesus."

And then we heard Stoni call for us.

Judi had thrown up. I took the mattress pad out to the deck to hose it down, let it dry out. Nicky stuck the ball of sheets in the washing machine. Judi sat on the bathroom floor. Stoni said, "Don't worry, this is all normal."

I sat on the edge of the tub. Judi was chilled, shaking. She said, "Who am I?"

I said, "You're Judi."

"Who the fuck am I?" Her body spasmed, and with her head locked against the wall and her face to the ceiling, Judi threw up again, the vomit a furious green spray that shot ahead several feet.

I held her. Stoni came in with the bedpan marked V, held it in front of Judi. We'd need to change her again. Nicky watched us from the bedroom door. He asked if he should call a doctor. I told him maybe he could get a mop and pail from the cellar stairs. Judi vomited until everything in her stomach was gone. She threw up bile and then sheets of her own tissue and then clots of blood that looked like globs of gelatin. Nicky brought in plastic sandwich bags filled with ice that Stoni held to Judi's forehead. Judi was crying; Stoni was crying. I could smell all the crap sweating out of Judi's pores, all the poisons. And then, when it seemed that all her strength was gone, that her body was too limp to convulse, Judi lost control of her bowels. Watery diarrhea began to seep from her. Judi screamed that she just wanted to fucking die, and all we could do was sit there on the floor with her and tell her it was all right, it will be over soon. Stoni told Nicky, still by the door, to go ahead and call an ambulance. She gave him the number. Judi called me a bastard for making her do this. And then she fainted. We washed her quickly. Washed ourselves. Nicky cleaned up while we helped the paramedics. Stoni rode in the ambulance, said she'd call us from the hospital.

Nicky and I finished the cleaning, then showered. We put on old sweats while we washed our clothes and dried them. I poured us each a glass of Hennessey. We sat on the couch with the bottle between us. Jesus, Nicky said, I've never seen anything like it. We put on music. Allison Krauss. Steeleye Span. We listened to Stoni's phone message: Judi's fine, sleeping like a baby. She's going to be fine. They'll run a CBC in the morning. She's sedated. She's fine. Hope you two are all right.

I didn't care how cold it was. I opened the bedroom and bathroom windows. I wanted the smells of chemicals and vomit and fear and death and festering flesh and emptied bowels out of there. The wind blew my ceiling cloths loose. They hung, flapped, fell like parachutes. I didn't care. I could put them up again.

57.

The World of Dew Is
A World of Dew, Yet Even
So, Yet Even So . . .

THE JAPANESE POET ISSA WROTE THIS HAIKU AFTER THE DEATH OF HIS ONLY child. Why do we need to die? Why must we suffer? This is what I think about while Judi recovers from the horrible reaction to her chemotherapy, while the oncology team tries to devise a new and less devastating strategy, while I smile at customers, take their money, wish them a good day at Our Lady of the Sea, while I walk home through the cold and quiet city, while I scratch Spot behind his ears, let him clatter through the fallen oak leaves in the park. All I know about death is you don't live through it and you're not here anymore. *Here* is where I am. But I don't know why this dwindling away. Where is the tenderness in that kind of world? When I visit Judi, she is asleep, and I am relieved. Her vital signs are splendid, they tell me. Encouraging. These things happen. Sleep. Deep and dreamless sleep? Sleep like a little death? I leave a card, a flower. I sign my name and Spot's to the card. I leave a book. Alice Munro's stories.

Death, I think, is not a moment. It's a process. The body is a gestalt. It's more than the sum of is parts. The cells can be alive when we are not. This must have something to do with energy. When does the process begin?

I go through the mail. Judi's subscription to *Martha Stewart Living* has run out. She is invited to receive the next ten issues for just twenty-four dollars a year—a 39 percent savings over newsstand price.

In second grade, Sister Mary Michael told our class that dying meant going to heaven. Henry Belch wanted to know how far heaven was from Worcester. Sister said, Heaven's wherever God is. Henry said, Where's God? God's everywhere, Sister said. Henry looked around the room. Thank you, Sister. He smiled.

In the schoolyard, the jump-rope girls sang:

> *Mother, Mother, I feel sick,*
> *Send for the doctor, quick, quick, quick!*
> *Doctor, Doctor, shall I die?*
> *Yes, my dear, and so shall I.*
> *How many carriages shall I have?*
> *One, two, three, four . . .*

Sister also said that the body is a tabernacle of God.

Death seems imaginary, abstract, speculative. Perhaps, then, we should not reflect on death at all, but on a person who is dying. Decomposition is singular enough, actual, concrete. It insinuates itself on the senses, and it will desecrate your tabernacle. Reflect on that. Is this what we mean by death—this necrosis, this atomization that begins when gravity seizes the heart and the pumping stops? when tissues spoil and trillions of nuclei fail? when enzymes within the cells break loose and consume their hosts?

When I can't sleep, I sit up watching evangelists on the all-night Christian network, wondering what it is they do to get their hair to hold such sinuous shapes. I'm surprised when I see Smokey Robinson sitting on a gold brocade sofa, chatting with the host about Jesus Christ, his personal Lord and savior. I don't know why I'm surprised.

Christian TV is full of beautiful young, blond, ministerial couples. They schmooze with zealous guests, they sing, they testify to God's mercy and love. I have my favorite couple, the Lovings. He's the Reverend Wayne Loving, a preacher with exquisitely tailored suits and feathered, longish hair. She's Recie, and she's as pretty as her husband. She wears neo-Victorian long-sleeved dresses, blue ones, lacy and shapely, and she wears, perhaps, too much makeup. I detect this glint in Wayne's blue eyes, a message meant for the gentlemen viewers, meant for me, saying, If you believe in Jesus, you too can get you something just this sweet, someone with a dove's eyes, with breasts like roes that feed among the lilies, whose lips are a thread of scarlet, whose love is better than wine, under whose tongue lie honey and milk. And I think not someone *like* Recie, but Recie. I want to talk with her in the morning before she puts on her armor, before the mascara and the stiff hair. Recie, I want to say, what is it with this prosperity theology, with your trips to the mall, the seamstress, the car dealership? When I say this, I touch her hand. She'll step toward me, rest her cheek against mine, and say, "You shall lie all night betwixt my breasts and my jeweled thighs in our green bed." I must be out of my mind.

One night Wayne and Recie bring their baby girl onto the set and hold her so the camera can get a close-up. They have dressed little Paige in a frilly pink getup, which disappoints me. I figure this must be Wayne's idea. They have put what looks like a garter belt on Paige's head, and it's like the baby's whole life flashes before my eyes. I don't know why, but I think about Martha then. Strange. When I snap out of it, Recie is telling me that Christian women are the most liberated women in the world. She says, We're liberated from having to work for a living, liberated from civic responsibility. We can devote ourselves to the House of the Lord and to our own houses. Amen. Praise Jesus. She says, You can't be halfway with the Lord. And I think, I'm too late to save her.

Dostoevsky's Kirilov said there are only two reasons why we don't kill ourselves: pain and the fear of the afterlife. I realize that an overdose of morphine would be painless. Even a gunshot to the temple would hurt less than chemotherapy, than cancer. As for the next world, that's never been a fear of Judi's.

I turn off the TV. I decide to write. I brew coffee. I sit. I get up and look out into the blackness. Judi. I want to write about Judi. How do you tell a story about a smart, beautiful, young woman who is taken by surprise, who has her body attacked and her future snatched away? And if you tell it, what is it about? I want to write about this so that I can understand it, knowing I will never understand it. I decide I should shower, shave, dress for work, this writing work.

In the shower, I think how my life has changed so much so recently after so many years of sameness. I think how painful change can be to the brain. I feel lucky, and I feel sad. I miss Martha. I hope I'm smart enough not to call her.

I sit at the kitchen table with my writing tablet, my word finder, my dictionary, my clutch of pens. I try three of them before I'm ready. Blue, fine-point rolling ball. Somehow I understand that this narrative about Judi will not be a short story.

Where to begin? It's winter—the cold, the damp, the tattoo of sleet against the storm windows, the world reduced to grays and browns and white. How about a title? *Breathing Through the Eye of a Needle* or *We Shall Not All Sleep, But We Shall All Be Changed.* Maybe begin with a hallucination induced by pain and medication: Judi sees a helicopter outside her bedroom window. The helicopter gets louder, but not larger. It enters through the window and circles the bed. The noise is deafening. The helicopter begins to drop little people onto the bed. People from Judi's past and from her past lives.

What if Judi tells her own story? She might begin with this: "Death is in my house, in the air I breathe. Each day he sings to me. Each day he sits closer to my bed." I knew I could start anywhere, with anything, with a pair of salt-stained boots tucked under a radiator, with the click of the lock on a cellar door, with a fluff of cottonwood seed dropping from a tree, lighting on a sleeping dog. I could start with anything because in anything, everything is implied. I knew I could start anywhere, but this was becoming unbearable.

I imagine Judi in her bed, on her back, eyes shut, wearing a cotton pajama shirt, green with darker green piping around the collar. I hear what she thinks, and I write it down: *He has made my bed away from the windows. He reads to me at night, slides his hand under mine. Now I smell soup, onion, his favorite. He's on the phone to someone, whispering. I open my eyes and see the gray light in the window. This makes me happy, the daytime, I mean. I'll sleep with my eyes opened.* This gives me the creeps. I stop.

I begin to yawn like crazy. I pour myself another cup of coffee. I open the dictionary and pick four nouns and a verb at random and let the words guide my writing for the next, say, ten minutes. I check the clock. I chose: *sansevieria, panic, chrism, chlorophyll, genuflect,* and immediately I see my grandmother Agnes, my mother's mother. I see her standing by her desk, on the phone, chewing her Clorets gum with her front teeth, listening, tamping the soil of the sansevieria that's planted in a ceramic St. Francis of Assisi planter. When she reaches to the floor to pick up a bit of vermiculite she's dropped, she genuflects because of her bad back, the rheumatism. And then she's in St. Vincent's Hospital after her second heart attack, and she's weak, and her voice has changed alarmingly—

it's thin, reedy, high, like a flute—and it seems to come from somewhere else, and she doesn't recognize me, but she recognizes Father Hulot, who has come to anoint her, and she screams at him to get out, get away, don't touch me, you bastard, and the nurses have to come and lead us out. And that was the last I saw of her, and I realized then that someone dear could die, that for the rest of my life my grandmother would be away.

I snap out of it. I wipe a bit of drool off my lip, chin. I hear Chet Nyberg start up his car. He's a go-getter. It's ten of six. Chet has a secret life. Just like Judi. I think of Chekhov's Iona Potapov and his little horse. To whom shall I tell my grief? Let's say you had a girlfriend, and that girlfriend died . . .

58.

Archaeology

I WANTED TO FIND JUDI, TO KNOW MORE ABOUT HER. I LOOKED FOR JUDI IN the cellar, rummaged among the artifacts for biographical evidence. Some of the detritus, I supposed, was abandoned here by earlier civilizations, the red bean bag chair, for example, the yellow awnings wrapped in blue canvas, the Naugahyde club chair, the orange life jackets, the Flexible Flyer. Against a wall was an upright roll of nursery rhyme linoleum. Someone had planned a baby's room. There were several old tin lard cans, a carton of uncapped Mason jars and an iron dumpling press that were probably older than the house itself.

On and under a workbench were the following appliances: an unused, still-in-the-box electric wok, a green enamel fondue pot, a steel fish poacher, a Mr. Coffee machine, a food processor. Wedding gifts, you would think. But I knew that Judi had never been married. (Martha and I once owned three fondue sets, two toaster ovens, six electric blankets, four irons, three electric carving knives. We gave the extras away as, you guessed it, wedding gifts. We also had a hot dog steamer, of all things, and an electric ice crusher.) No, not wedding gifts, I decided, just the Dubey family fondness for domestic conveniences. A fondness, I knew, that was grounded in hope.

In one corner by the bulkhead door were garden tools—a small hand cultivator, a pitch fork, a spade, a bulb dibble, a trowel, a green hose on a white trolley, a galvanized watering can, and a metal lunch box designed to look like a suitcase with facsimiles of old travel stickers on it. Inside the lunch box were packages of flower seeds: gold-laced primroses, Dark Beauty asters, Imperial Blackberry Rose pansies, meconopsis, hollyhock, and dicentra, whose bloom looks like an icy-white, comical heart. Once, then, Judi had wanted a garden. I decided I'd plant the flowers in the spring. I wondered, would Spot eat them.

Mostly old clothes in the attic. Overcoats in storage bags, boxes of blouses, slacks, and sweaters. Handbags, tote bags, shopping bags. A stack of old forty-fives, Motown mostly, Beatles, Monkees. There were two aluminum tennis rackets. The most interesting attic find was an accordion in its case. The accordion was jade-green with a white fingerboard and a filigreed grille.

In the bedroom, in the top left-hand dresser drawer, a jewelry box, and in the box a silver charm bracelet with four charms: a heart, a four-leaf clover, a Statue of Liberty, and a seashell; Judi's class ring from UMass, 1979; and a pair of earrings made from Frostie root beer bottle caps. In the right-hand top drawer was a plastic basket with wave clips, hair rollers, and bobby pins. I came across a familiar silk camisole, smelled it. Nothing unusual.

I hunted through Judi's jacket and coat pockets and discovered a single business card for one *Leah Rose Ditmore-Gordon, L.M.T., Massage and Aromatherapy.* There was one surprise in her address book, an entry for Kris Kristofferson, with a phone number, Nashville area code, but no address. I dialed the number. A woman answered. I asked for Kris, please. She hesitated, said, May I ask who's calling? I said, Lafayette Proulx. I'm with Apocalypse Records. She had me repeat what I said, asked me to hold on a sec. I heard her say, Kris . . . I don't know. Some guy named Proust. I hung up. Judi and Kris. There's a story there.

Judi's high school yearbook, the *Messenger,* sat on a shelf in the linen closet. Holy Name High School, 1975. There she was, between Edmund Doyle and Vincent Druzialio. Judi was the only student in the senior class who did not face the camera for her portrait. That's just the kind of gesture that can get you in deep trouble at a Catholic school, get you labeled as rebellious, intractable. I wondered was it Judi's idea, turning her right shoulder to the camera, or was the photographer feeling rambunctious. Judi looked off to her right without a smile, but with a look of benevolence. She was quite serene and stunning, and quite out of fashion with her short, wavy hair. I imagined that Doyle and Druzialio cried themselves to sleep over their enormous good fortune. Beneath her photograph, this: *Senior Religion Project, Ushers Club 3, Cheerleading 2, Spring*

Musical 4, *Health Careers Club* 2. She was in one other picture, a candid, with a boy named Ludy Bukys. The two of them are in chemistry lab, staring at a petri dish. The caption reads: *A new love potion for Sister Monica John.*

Judi kept no photo albums in the house, but she did have a White Owl cigar box crammed with loose photographs. A black and white print of Judi and Stoni in a playpen, both of them clutching the bars with hands and mouths, looking into the camera while brother George, in a white shirt and tie, watches them. Judi with Santa Claus. Judi with the Easter Bunny. Judi's First Communion. Judi at a prom in a blue gown with a boy wearing a madras tuxedo. Judi on a beach blanket with two girlfriends. Judi at ten or so, sitting on a picnic bench looking sad. Behind her on the table are a plate of hot dogs, a jar of tea or juice or something, and a large white bowl. There's a photo taken through a car windshield of a cow lying on an asphalt road, another of the St. George's Church fire on Wall Street, flames curling out from under the eaves. I was at that fire, and I wondered if I'd seen Judi there. I wondered if she was one of the girls standing on the roof of a tan Chevrolet. There's a black and white snapshot of five-year-old Judi wearing a straw bonnet, holding a tiny box purse in her gloved hands. She's standing in a patch of dirt in front of the Quonset hut. She's smiling or she's wincing.

59.

Constant Companion

JUDI SAID, I'VE THOUGHT ABOUT THIS, LAF, AND I KNOW I DON'T WANT TO SPEND however much time I have left trying to avoid what's, after all, inevitable and natural. I'm not being brave at all; it's not that. I just can't stand being so tired all the time that I don't know who I am, can't remember my own name, so sick that I don't care. I'm not giving up. I'm not.

I said, I understand. I touched her knee.

She said, I can't fight this cancer if I'm wasted with poison. I'm not afraid of dying . . . well, all right, I am. But I'm more afraid of the pain. I'm afraid of not being able to think clearly, afraid of not knowing what's happening around me and to me.

And what was I afraid of? I had the expectation of a future, at least. Let's say it's ten years from now, twenty, and I get sick like this. Who'll sneak the cognac into my hospital room? Shit, I didn't want to think about this. What will you leave behind, brief candle? Heat? Light? Smoke? Ashes?

We were sitting on the living room couch, Judi and I, eating bananas—good for the recalcitrant digestive system—and drinking vodka martinis, Judi chasing hers with a glass of milk of magnesia. We had the heat jacked up to eighty. The radiators clanged. Judi asked me if I would bleed them in the morning. I didn't know what she was talking about, but I said I'd take care of it. Judi had wrapped herself in a pink blanket, put on two pairs of wool socks.

Trixie and Hervey had gone home, Trixie in a huff because Judi had told her no more chemo, no radiation, no immunotherapy, no more experiments, no nothing. Trixie cried, said, You can't just lay down and die. Judi explained that her chances of surviving even five years were less than seven percent *with* the chemo. Not much worse without it. Trixie said, But the doctors told you forty percent. They lied, Judi said. It's easy to lie. I've done my homework. I know the score. She told Trixie how the chemo drugs, heavy metals, were damaging her heart, her lungs, her kidneys, her liver, and God only knows what else. Trixie said, You'll come to your senses in a few days. You're going to be all right, I just know it.

Judi said, Wonderful martini, Laf. She kissed my cheek. I asked her how she was feeling. Not bad. Her jaw hurt and her fingers; her fingernails were tingling. And, of course, her mouth was still ulcerated, sore, and her throat was raw. A little queasy, but not bad. Just normally sick. We were waiting for Stoni to drop by. Judi said, I'm afraid of the dark. You can fool yourself in the daytime, but not at night. She looked at me. Why is that?

I didn't know, of course, but I guessed. You can't distract yourself so easily at night, in the dark, I said. It's so quiet. All you're trying to do is slip away into dreams. It's just you and yourself. And maybe you haven't listened to yourself all day and now it wants to be heard. I said, Shouldn't you be explaining this to me? You're the therapist. Anyway, it's good you don't live in Alaska.

Judi wondered what blind people made of the night. Can they feel the darkness out there approaching? The end of the light? Do they even understand light?

The phone rang. It was my brother. I said, How's Mom, thinking why else would he call me. He said, Who the hell do you think you are, Laf? Huh? You fucked up your life, so now you're going to fuck up mine. I said, Edgar, what are you talking about? I heard our back door open. Stoni waved to us from the kitchen, took off her coat, boots, gloves, scarf. Edgar said, Don't give me that shit. You know what I'm talking about. I swore to him I didn't. Delores, he said. I said, What about Delores? Stoni kissed me on the cheek. She smelled like outdoors, like leaves, I guess, and like clothes drying on a line. I could feel the cold air around her body.

Edgar said, Did you hear what I said? I got off the couch and Stoni sat by Judi. I sat on the floor, leaned back against the Morris chair. Judi and Stoni chatted. I listened to my brother tell me that Delores was leaving him after all these years and all because of a little talk she had with me.

He said what right did I have to interfere in his marriage. I told Edgar I was sorry, but I did not tell Delores anything. I gave no advice. I listened to her. Edgar said, That's not how she tells it. I said, I don't know what to tell you. Edgar was quiet. Stoni lit up a joint, passed it to Judi. Judi made a silly face at me and inhaled. I said, Edgar, are you still there? Edgar?

I found out that Delores was in their bedroom, that she had not, in fact, left Edgar at all, that they'd had a family meeting after supper where Delores laid out her feelings in front of him and the boys. She said she was unhappy. This was news to Edgar. One of the boys said, So what, we're all unhappy. What's the big hairy deal? She told them she was going to look for a place to live, and the boys were welcome to come along if they wanted to. I said, Where are the boys now? Edgar told me they were watching TV. He was out in the garage on the cellular phone. I told Edgar that it sounded to me like Delores was giving him a chance, that she wanted him to stop her from leaving, to give her a reason to stay. Edgar said, You think so? I do, Edgar. Why don't you go talk to her now. He said, What if she's packing her things? I said, Talk to her. He said, I will. I said, How's Mom? Edgar told me she was fit as a fiddle.

Judi handed me the joint. Primo Chemo, she said; I don't feel nauseated anymore. I took a hit, went and made three more vodka martinis. Stoni turned on an oldies station. Judi started to laugh. Said she just remembered something she wanted to show us. I got her purse. She fished out a folded paper, an ad she'd torn out of a medical journal at the hospital. The ad was for a machine that looked like a drill press and was called the Polytron. The bold print in the ad said, *Only the Polytron reduces an entire mouse to a soup-like homogenate in thirty seconds.* Stoni got hysterical. Mouse soup, she kept saying. Great for cat owners. She said, Listen to this: *Unique tissue disruption by mechanical shearing and cavitation.* Judi shook her head. Pretty sick, she said. I was stuck on the words *homogenate* and *cavitation.* I was thinking of milk and teeth and coal mines. What interesting words. I meant to get up and get the dictionary, but I forgot.

Stoni dialed the 800 number in the ad. She spoke to an answering machine, told it she was a Dr. Maggie Siddiqui from Memorial Hospital and she would like to order a Polytron, but what colors does it come in, and do they have a machine that deep-fries. She hung up and took another hit. She said that today, driving past Chevalier Furniture, she'd seen a sign in their window: WE HAVE YOUR STOOL. You see, they must mean bar stools, she explained to us. Then we laughed.

Judi wondered why furniture stores were always going out of business, but then never really did. Like we'd forget they had a gigantic final close-out total liquidation sale two months ago. And why do all car salesmen put their photographs in their ads? What's that about? I said, Why are all Chinese restaurants red and yellow?

We were quiet. Marvin Gaye sang. *"I guess you wonder how I knew . . ."* Then Judi started to talk about simple, annihilated souls and about living a blind, annihilated life, about those who live without a why and those who expect revenues from love. She said she saw a light brighter than the light that shot from the sun, a light that shadows the light of love. I looked at Stoni. Her eyes were closed. Judi stared at a spot on the ceiling. I looked where she looked, and I noticed that the cracks and dust and shadows had composed a face. It could be a man or a woman. It's eyes were closed, its jaw set, its hair slicked back. It could be a corpse. It could be Dale getting out of the shower.

When I tuned back in, Stoni was gone and Judi was talking about stars and planets. I heard pots rattle in the kitchen. Stoni was hungry. My dope-addled insight was that Judi wasn't talking about the universe at all, but about her body. I smiled and listened attentively. Cancer cells, as I understood her metaphorical rap, were the billions of stars, and the tumor was this galaxy spinning out of control in the darkness. Judi's afraid of the dark. What is all that darkness in the universe? It couldn't just be the absence of light, could it? It can't be nothing. It's got all these stars in it, all these suns, all these planets, all these creatures in it, with creatures inside them. Darkness must matter. This was fine dope.

Stoni returned with a bowl of popcorn, the best popcorn, we all agreed, that we'd ever eaten. Popcorn sprinkled with Romano cheese, cayenne pepper, and garlic salt. Magnificent popcorn, Stoni. And then it seemed while I was doing it that it took me an hour at least to mix three more vodka martinis. First, I had to find the vodka, which was camouflaged in the freezer. Then the vermouth. Then I had to read the vermouth label. *The Dry you are looking for . . .* What did that mean? Did we want our drinks on the rocks or straight up, with olives or with twists? When I got back with the drinks, Judi and Stoni were staring at the bowl of glorious popcorn. For a second, I thought maybe I hadn't gotten up to make the drinks, but there they were on the tray in my hands.

Judi said, You can try not to be in love with someone if you want to, but that's like trying not to be afraid. I just smiled knowingly. I felt some pressure to wax philosophical, but I was having a hard time. I was still smiling. My face hurt.

Judi said, I don't want pain or fatigue or doctors or hospital wards or tests. I want sunshine and company, friends, music, my home, my room, my pal. I want a miracle, she said. But I'm not going to hell again for the hope of a chance of one.

Stoni said she needed to hit the road, but we convinced her she couldn't find her keys, never mind drive. We were right. She agreed to sleep on the couch. I said I was taking Spot for a walk. Judi said she'd be waiting for me. I needed to clear my head. A starless night. Halo around the moon. Spot visited all his favorite trees and hedges. I could not conceive of my own death, of nonexistence. This is the kind of thinking that leads to religions, I told myself. Be careful.

I thought about Dale and Theresa and I felt guilty like I always do when I haven't been working. Dale's out camping this weekend. Drove out through Weed into the Sacramento mountains. He's found an old antelope hunter's campsite, a circle of stones. Something occurs to him while he's gathering firewood. He knows that when you're afflicted with love you never recover. I realize that Dale has happened onto the spot I had fantasized going to die.

Back home, Stoni was snoring on the couch. I covered her with Judi's pink blanket, turned the heat down to seventy-five. Wasn't I going to do something with the radiator? I got undressed, took the tube of Astroglide, and slipped under the covers. I snuggled up to Judi's back, slipped my hand into her pajamas. Judi turned to me, kissed my nose. She was crying. Everything hurts, Laf. I'm sorry. It's like the vandals are inside demolishing the neighborhood. Soon, she said. Promise. I want my life back. What if I don't wake up? I said, It's okay. She said, Tell me a story. I said, What kind of story? About a woman at the end of her rope, a woman who makes a remarkable recovery.

60.

Gastroenterology

Judi gained back some of the weight she had lost in the hospital and on the chemo. She looked less diminished. Her hair grew back a shade lighter, thinner, and curlier. She said she didn't feel so old, now that people weren't doing everything for her and to her. She was back to work, gradually building her client load, and back to her visualization exercises. She was taking vitamin and mineral supplements that she bought at Mr. Natural's. Pauline had become like Judi's pharmacist. Judi was also seeing Pamela Bibaud again, back to visiting her past lives.

We were in the waiting room of Dr. Lankau, a gastroenterologist she'd been referred to. We'd been sitting an hour already. Judi told me that in Poland, in seventeen-something, she was the mistress of an itinerant musician. She was sixteen or so and three months' along when she was taken in by the nuns at a convent in Czestochowa. Her name was Magda. She learned from the abbess that the convent was to close after three hundred years. One frosty morning, Magda woke up, prayed, went to the kitchen to stoke the hearth fire, and saw the sisters out in the churchyard. She watched them exhume the bones of all the nuns who had ever served God at that convent. They would carry the bones with them to the Mother House in Bohemia.

Judi told me that none of the deceased nuns had a headstone. They all had names in life, she said, but not in death. Judi said something went wrong with her delivery. She lost the baby—she would have named him Kazimir—and died herself minutes later. I asked her did she remember what it felt like to die. I thought that was the point of this particular regression. She told me no. She could recall the excruciating pain of labor. She remembered biting down on an iron nail until her teeth broke. An hour and a half after we had arrived, Judi was admitted to the doctor's examining room, where she waited another hour.

Judi continued to see Dr. Pawlak and to get her blood work, X rays, CAT scans, and what not. You could see, though, that Stouder and the others had emotionally removed themselves from Judi's case because she wasn't playing by their rules. They didn't care as much about her as about her disease, and she was keeping them from it. It seemed curious to me that doctors thought they could win this battle with death anyway. What are they teaching in medical schools these days? A lot of ego goes into cancer treatment, but precious little compassion.

While we waited for the car to warm up, for the windows to defrost, I asked Judi if she were ever reborn into the past. Like, is *now* a long time ago? She hadn't thought about that. She couldn't, though, remember living in the future. She told me about the results of Lankau's tests. There seemed to be some activity in the intestines. Another reason to hate myself, she said.

61.

In Full Guimpe and Wimple

It was inevitable in this town that I would run into Martha. It happened like this. After work I thought I'd grab a beer, sit there, and write. I would have gone to the Boynton, but I was afraid I'd run into Biscuit, and he'd rag me about not calling him, and I'd end up in some long unwelcomed conversation, and I'd get nothing done. So I stopped into the Leitrum Pub. Usually there was enough chatter in there to drown out the television. I got a pint of Bass and took a booth. I wrote.

My plan was to get back to Theresa, see what she might be up to while Dale's away camping. I scribbled some notes about them. Dale thinks love is voluntary, none of this fate business for him. You love someone, he thinks, so you can get to know them. I watched a woman at the bar get off her stool, walk to the jukebox, play some Stones. She was smoking, tapping her foot, singing to herself. She pushed the sleeves of her black sweater up to her elbows. She made a phone call. When she hung up, she shook her head, took a deep breath, burped. She went back to the bar, grabbed her glass, sipped, sat up on the stool. I wrote a kind of outline for a story about such a woman as I imagined her to possibly be, a woman with salt stains on her boots, hair that she can't do anything with, and five, maybe ten, extra pounds at the hips. Like all the women in her family.

And then I heard someone behind me say, "I'll just have a sparkling water," and I knew it was Martha, but I couldn't prove it because the booth was too high to look over. God, I thought, our backs are up against each other. Whoever she was with returned with the drinks. He said, "Cheers!" She thanked him. Martha, for sure. I wanted to sit there and listen, find out what she was up to. And I wanted to run out of there as fast as I could. I did something unusually forthright. I stood up, stepped to her booth, and said hello. She looked at me. Maybe she'd thought I'd died or moved to the Failed Writers' Home. I turned to the gentleman, said, I'm himself, the one she's told you about. He told me his name was Frank. Frank O'Connor. Father Frank O'Connor. Three sentences to get that out. This was good. Martha and the Right Reverend in a tavern. This was dangerous enough to be encouraged.

"I won't ask you to join us," Martha said.

I told her I was just leaving. I asked if I might come by someday and collect my clothes. She told me she'd gotten rid of them. "My rayon shirts?" I said.

"Burned them."

"Everything?"

She smiled.

"Not my books?"

"Gave them away. And your tapes."

"Did you enjoy that?"

"At first." She looked into her beer.

I kind of admired her spunk. She would have needed a backhoe to clear the shed of books and magazines.

I looked at Frank. "Just another reason not to get attached to worldly possessions, Father."

"Then it got kind of sad," she said. "But I don't really want to talk about it."

"I'm sorry. You shouldn't have to."

Father Frank said, "Maybe I'll leave you two—"

I said, "No, Father, sit." It seemed odd calling my wife's date "Father." What was I thinking—"wife," "date"?

Martha said, "I did save the wedding photos. Sentimental, I guess. Maybe someday I'll look at them again."

I could see she was going to cry.

"You want them?" she said.

"No. Well, if you don't . . . You keep them."

On that day I got my story "Splice of Life" back from the *New Dixie Review*. It arrived with a note from Dr. Knox Hinton, editor, professor, and director of the Center for Southern Culture and Literature at the University of the Deep South.

Mr. Proulx:

While some of my esteemed colleagues are mildly amused whenever a misguided Yankee with literary pretensions presumes to write about the South, I am personally furious and highly indignant at your feeble and affected meddling in the lives of people about whom you know less than nothing. This story is drivel, sir. Furthermore, you have no right to invade the South with your arsenal of northern clichés and stereotypes. Why don't you, instead, ridicule the pathetic souls who inhabit that cold and sooty burg you call home?

Sincerely,

J. Knox Hinton, Ph.D.

I could be flip and say it was Dr. Hinton's lugubrious adverbs that saddened me most, but, of course, it wasn't that. It was his contention that I was poking fun at my characters that upset me. Why would I make fun of a person in pain? Why would anyone? I don't think despair is funny, or divorce is funny, or child abuse if funny, and the idea that someone would think that I did made me almost sick. So what was so mocking in the story? The phone call from the unfaithful husband? The beer-slurping dog? Is living in a motel somehow ridiculous? I tried calling Knox Hinton twice to ask him to explain himself. Twice I got the answering machine. Once I said nothing. Once I said, Good morning, Dr. Hinton, you don't remember me, but I was in your class one time, and I'd like to speak with you a moment, if I could. Please call me at your convenience. I left Judi's number.

I wrote Knox a letter, which I mailed, and in which I told him I had lived in Milledgeville, Georgia, Jackson and Yoknapatawpha County, Mississippi. I admitted I was not born in Louisiana, but asked if Bradbury were born on Mars? Conrad in England? Shakespeare in Verona? I asked him if he thought André Dubus ever got a letter from the editor of the *Brahmin Review* telling him to write about Louisiana and leave Massachusetts to the natives? I tried to explain that there is a geography of imagination, that there are many worlds we live in, that art is not life, that my Monroe, Louisiana, is not the actual Monroe, Louisiana. I know because I've been there. The Bayou Motel is not on Louisville, for one thing. I've stayed there. I told Knox he sounded like a very intelligent man who probably had his life and his literature all figured out, which meant he'd be successful, no doubt. But, and pardon me for lecturing the professor, your attitude could prove a flaw when something comes along that doesn't fit neatly into your scheme of things. You might ignore the unexpected, castigate that which challenges your notion of the world, and this might keep you from winning the Nobel Prize for Editing. I told him I'd sold—and I use the word loosely—the story in question to one of his amused colleagues. He could read it next fall. I told him how New England was taking on a Southern flavor, how they were building a Wal-Mart in Marlboro, how I could buy Sweet Georgia Brown ale at Mullavey's Package Store, and Quaker grits at the Stop & Shop. We've even got a country music station out of Worcester now. I told him I thought all the important regional differences were spiritual now—except for kudzu. I told him I was a Catholic boy who grew up practically a mystic, but I'd lapsed. Sometimes, though, I still need to explore the spiritual. Problem is people up here don't take the soul to heart. Transgressions here are crimes, not sins. That's when I go south. I asked him, What's the housing situation like there in Hinterland, Alabama?

That night Judi told me that Josh was in the hospital and he probably wouldn't come out this time. It turned out that he was dead by the time Judi told me. That's all we said about it. That night I dreamed I was back at St. Stephen's in Sister Sylvanus's class, and we're all kneeling on our chairs reciting the Angelus when Sister comes up out of nowhere, slaps my face, and pushes me to the floor, kicks me in the side. She screams that I'm the one who will abandon his faith. And it was all eerily like the way it happened in real fifth grade because I refused to watch a holy movie at lunch in the church hall, only in the dream it was not Sister Sylvanus at all, but Martha who was standing over me in full guimpe and wimple, her rosary beads clacking against my desk.

62.

To Cure This Deadly Grief

THE FIRST THING DORIE MARCELONIS SAID TO US WAS "THERE'S NO SUCH thing as terminal cancer." She said this and smiled. I held my tongue. I wanted to like her. She was so cute and all. I hoped she wouldn't keep making ludicrous statements. Dorie wore a long blue plaid jumper over a white T-shirt, turquoise bracelets on both wrists, and dangly silver earrings. Each earring was a dancing man playing a recorder. Her auburn hair was pulled back from her forehead and tied in a pony tail. She was thin as smoke.

Judi and I sat with Dorie in her parlor. Dorie was the healer Pauline had raved about. Dorie had healed the Dalai Lama's bodyguard of Sjogren's syndrome, Pauline told Judi. Judi and Dorie sat on this enormous mohair sofa like people had in the thirties, black with floral cushions and a scrolled walnut frame. I sat across the room in a matching button-backed chair. The springs had lost their tension. I sank into the cushion. I felt tiny. That may be why I was thinking this little cottage was so much like my grandmother's apartment when I was a kid. That and the dark Persian carpet, the doilies and antimacassars, the potted ferns on the radiator covers, the Swedish ivy in a macrame hanger, the mahogany lamp table. Dorie told me to just shoo the cat off my lap if it was bothering me. She said, "Get down, Na'pi, scoot!" The cat whined, hopped to the floor, and pranced toward the kitchen with his tail straight up.

We heard the tea kettle whistle. Dorie got up. When she stood she kind of leaned back from her hips. I noticed the Day-Glo Band-Aid on her ankle, as orange as a detour sign. I said, "Do you know Booger Marcelonis?" She looked at me like this was a trick question. I said, "Booger. Lives on Shays Road in Worcester. About, oh, thirty-fivish. Walks everywhere."

Dorie said no, she didn't know any Booger.

I said, "You look familiar."

She said, "I have one of those faces."

We were here at Dorie's for introductions and assessment. I mean, Judi was here for all that. I was along for support and because I was curious. The actual healing sessions would begin with the next visit if everything went smoothly between Judi and Dorie. Dorie returned with a tray on which she carried a teapot, three mugs, a creamer, and three spoons. "I know I know you from somewhere," I said. She smiled, set the tray on the glass-topped coffee table.

Dorie asked Judi if she'd undergone an MRI ever? CAT scan? ultrasound? X ray? Yes. Yes. Yes. Yes. Well, that's not good, Dorie said, but at least I know what I'm dealing with. What she was dealing with was severe disruption of Judi's *prana,* her auric fields, something like that, something about DNA not healing or replicating. I thought, I've seen her somewhere before. Just then Dorie looked over, scrutinized me, cocked her head like she thought she heard distant bells or screams. She seemed to deflate, as if her whole body were frowning. She turned back to Judi and explained how the medical procedures interfered with her mental, emotional, and etheric auras, made the healing more problematic. Judi didn't question this, so who am I?

Dorie said, "Judi, tell me how you feel about this cancer you have."

Judi folded her hands on her lap, looked at her hands. She shook her head. "It scares me. I think it's killing me." Then she looked up, smiled. She cried.

Dorie touched her own heart with her right hand, closed her eyes, took a breath. What was this about? I wondered. She moved her hands along her body as if she were fingering notes on a flute. What was she measuring? She opened her eyes. "Judi, what do you want to happen here? What are your expectations?"

Judi said, "What I want to happen is that I get healed of this cancer. What I expect to happen is that I won't be. I'll just get sicker and then I'll die."

Dorie was quiet. She explained what she would be doing, trying to locate the source of the cancer, not the biological source, the symptom, she called it, but the real source, the damage from difficult relationships or other emotional trauma in this life or another. I looked out the window at the slate-blue pond. I saw a rowboat tethered to Dorie's dock. As I watched, the wind picked up, rustled through the pines. The rowboat turned into the wind and faced me. I wanted to be in that boat. I wanted to drift away. I wanted to look down into the water, watch the sunfish school through the pickerel weed. I wanted to lie back, close my eyes, listen to the water slap at the side of the boat. Set the typewriter on the rowing thwart, get myself a little camp chair. Why not? But where would I get money to buy a boat, a house on a lake? I heard something about a thousand-petaled lotus, and I tried to pay attention.

Dorie told Judi, "You've kept your legs crossed for a half hour now. You kept covering your sacral *chakra* while we talked. Look at yourself."

Judi's hands were on her knee, and her leg was pulled up like a shield. She smiled, sat up straight.

Dorie said, "It's as if you were protecting this cancer." She reached toward Judi's stomach, held her hand six inches from Judi, and stroked the air like it was a cat. "Your aura should be glowing with vibrant colors. It's brown here."

I thought this was interesting. The eyes won't work for this kind of seeing, obviously. I didn't believe it, but I admired the imagination at work. Brown like maple syrup? I wondered, or brown like cinnamon? I wondered if Dorie could see the tumors through the skin. So I asked her.

She told us that every disease, every condition, has a specific vibration which she can tune in to like a radio. And each has a particular temperature, a unique texture, and each a precise brilliant tone, a red or a violet, most of them. She said also what happened was each ailment presents itself to her as a symbol. Like ulcers are pots of boiling pudding; lung cancer is a coal bin; MS is a gray sheet of rusting metal. Cancer in the reproductive organs is usually bees.

She explained this to Judi. She would work her third eye and her heart *chakra* on Judi's second *chakra* where there are blocks in the energy field. We need to discover the cause, the root cause, for the sickness. It's manifesting in the body, but it has come from elsewhere. Dorie let that sink in and then added, "This healing is not just for now, Judi, you know that. This is for all the lives you will ever live."

I wanted to say, Hello, girlfriend, we're all adults here, are we not? And we all know that what we are hearing is cruel and fatuous bullshit. It would be funny if it weren't so monstrous. Repeat after me: Cancer does not germinate in outer space, and it does not travel through time. So let's conclude the buffoonery and get back to the real world. We're dealing with a human being here, with her life. Well, that's what I wanted to say, but I didn't say anything. Perhaps even groundless hope is better than no hope at all. And maybe hope would make Judi resilient enough to fight the cancer. The placebo effect. Who knows what I'd be doing in Judi's position. Crawling to Lourdes on my knees, no doubt; sitting in the lobby of a Tijuana cancer clinic, sucking on laetrile lozenges, waiting for my turn to get secret and ancient Egyptian drugs pumped into my veins for the next eight hours.

There isn't much difference, is there, between Judi's reincarnations and Dorie's brave new world and between them and what the Catholics believe or the Muslims or any of them? The prospect of dying is so horrifying that we need to deceive ourselves or we would be paralyzed. So in the face of everything we know about nature, we simply deny our death. Everything else in the universe dies—dogs, worms, the sun, trees—but we live forever. Our brains have programmed themselves to accept the supernatural. The brain is not so reasonable after all. It wants to live forever. Every time we say a prayer, put our finger on the planchette of the Ouija board, chant our mantra, the brain rewards us with the release of soothing endorphins. Just enough to make us want more.

Let's face it. None of this supernaturalism can be true. But believing in it does seem to be essential. I'm right, aren't I? So what happened to *my* faith program? What am I left with? Words. Questions. Dale and Theresa. Fear. Enough.

Judi excused herself, went to the bathroom. Na'pi returned, hopped to the warm spot Judi had just vacated, sat and licked his paws and then his chest. Dorie said, "Your blue is all muddy," meaning mine. "Your third *chakra* . . ." She stared at my stomach. "The cord of auric light is tangled."

I said, "And . . ."

"There's someone, a woman . . ." Dorie shut her eyes. "I see blond hair, freckles. She's hurt."

This was Martha she was talking about. But how could that be? Did Judi tell her?

"She follows you. Does that make sense?"

I said I knew a woman like that.

"Be careful," Dorie said.

"I will."

"You have a young soul."

"Should I be insulted?"

"You are skeptical."

"I am."

Judi came back. I stood to go. Dorie said, "I've seen cancers that go away. I don't know why. I've seen miracles." She stood, walked us to the back door. She asked Judi not to drink alcohol or take any medication. Judi agreed. Judi would start in two days. At nine, back here at the house. Dorie told Judi she needed a hug. They embraced. "And you, too," she said. We hugged. She stepped right into my awkwardness and squeezed. I said, "Thank you."

She said, "Edith Piaf."

I let go of her shoulders. I knew now where I had seen her. "The library!"

Dorie smiled.

I told Judi how I'd been listening to Piaf at the library when I looked up and there was Dorie staring at me, looking puzzled. She didn't even look away when I caught her.

Dorie said, "I knew we'd be seeing each other, but I didn't know why until this morning."

63.

Wheel at the Base of the Self

DORIE SAID THAT WHAT SHE HAD HOPED TO SEE WAS THE IMAGE OF A SIX-PETALED vermilion lotus, spinning and radiating light. She was talking about her meditation the night before. What she saw instead were those bees, countless bees, swarming around a pulsing, throbbing ball of orange light. This was disturbing, Dorie said, but helpful.

The plan this morning was for me to wait out back in the yard, read at the picnic table, nap in the hammock, row in the boat, whatever. But it was raining, and I didn't offer to go for a drive. Judi said she didn't mind if I watched. I could see, though, that Dorie minded. Call me psychic. She asked if I could sit quietly in a corner. I said I could. She asked if I could keep an open mind. I said yes. She looked at the top of my head. You could learn something today, she told me. I nodded. She sat me on the floor near the fireplace, handed me two large pillows. I smiled. Thank you, I said. Consider me your apprentice.

Judi lay on her back on a massage table in the middle of the room. Dorie snapped a cassette on the recorder. Peruvian flute music. At least that's what it sounded like to me. Dorie opened a decoupage box and took out a crystal attached to a gold chain. She told Judi she was going to measure her *chakras*. She held the crystal over Judi's body. She began at the head and moved to the hips. Each time Dorie stopped, the pendent crystal spun in slow, tight circles. Dorie sat on a stool at the head of the table. She placed her hands on Judi's head and remained quiet for several minutes. Dorie said she was going to energize Judi's body through chelation, which apparently does not mean what I thought it did—removing metals from the body. Dorie held her hands about six inches over Judi's feet, palms down, fingers extended, and began to move them as if massaging the air. She told Judi she might feel heat or a tingling or a tightening of her chest. Dorie worked her way to Judi's head. Occasionally, Judi moaned, flinched.

Dorie said, "I'm lighting you up, Judi. I'm pushing energy through the blocks."

Judi looked to be asleep. Her mouth was open, her arms and her legs jerked. This is how she sleeps normally, with all her nerves harmlessly misfiring.

Dorie said, "Judi, let whatever happens happen." She held one hand a foot or two over Judi's heart, then brought it down to six inches. Now with both hands she moved to Judi's head and began to move toward Judi's feet. Her hands dipped in places, rose in others. At moments Dorie seemed to be kneading ethereal dough. At other times she seemed to be smoothing fabric. She said, "You may feel hot; you may see inside your body; you may feel as if you're in another place or imagine you're being visited by people from your childhood or from a preincarnation; you may feel my hands on you, inside you. That's the *chakra* funneling the healing energy into your physical body, cleaning and balancing. You may feel nothing. Just let it flow."

Judi writhed. She cried briefly. Dorie worked at Judi's abdomen like a potter throwing a ball of clay. "Can you feel the cold, Judi?"

"Yes."

"You've been blocked here for a long time," Dorie said. "A century, maybe longer." Dorie closed her eyes. "Do you see what I see?"

Judi said she did.

I saw Na'pi, the little prince, step down from the windowsill and then leap from the floor to the fireplace mantel. He looked at the women.

Dorie said, "What do you see?"

Judi said, "The river, the road, the sky, the light emerging from the smoke."

Dorie said she was going to seal the aura. She held her hand over Judi. Judi opened her eyes. I think she said, "Hope and control," but I'm not sure. Dorie told Judi that now she, Judi, would be taking a journey through her body. She said the doorway was the forehead. "You are seeking knowledge," she said. "Now, I want you to move to your belly. Nothing can stop you. Now look around you. You're looking for the tumors, for the cancer. Do you see them?"

"Everywhere I look."

"Now I want you to listen."

I heard the recorded flute, which I had forgotten about. You could hear the note the flutist played and the breath the flutist exhaled. Then I heard tires on the gravel road out front.

Dorie said, "What do you hear?"

"A humming like a machine that's high and then low, loud and then soft."

"You're hearing the note that fractures structure and the note that smashes chaos."

"And now the sound is color," Judi said.

"Violet?"

"Yes, from mauve to black."

"I want you to use all your senses now. Touch, taste, smell." Dorie waited. "And be aware of how you feel right now. The you on the inside. The you on the outside."

I don't ever want to smell any of my internal fluids. The thing about being healthy is that the body kind of disappears. But now I was aware that my eyes were itchy—probably thanks to Na'pi—and my wrist-egg throbbed. My feet itched. My nose was stuffed. I had to pee. I was beginning to feel a little queasy. I heard Dorie say, "What is it that you need in order to get healed."

Judi said, "They won't tell me."

Dorie told Judi to come on back, to return through the brow *chakra* and to relax and to imagine herself back in the womb, where it's all warm, soft, quiet. "Just float there," Dorie said. "Your body is whole and pure and miraculous, and nothing can touch you."

And that's what I did. Without evoking an image of my actual mother, which would have ruined everything; I ensconced myself in her womb. I was upside down because that's how I liked it, the blood rushing to my enormous head. I opened my little fist, closed it. I touched the umbilical cord, my first love. I thought, Wouldn't it be wonderful to live our lives backward? Like suddenly you open your eyes in a hospital room and you're aware of tubes in your nose and wires in your arm, but you don't know where you are or where you came from. Like Frankenstein's monster. You're frightened and you cry a little. In a few days, you're feeling better. The people tell you that for eighty-four you're doing as well as could be expected. What does this mean? In a week you're brought home. You are disoriented, but you settle into idleness. You read, fish, and go to restaurants with your wife for about twenty years. You suffer the usual childhood illnesses—arteriosclerosis, cancer of the prostate, Alzheimer's—but they get better, as they always do. You decide there's more to life than loafing around. So you sell the Florida condo, move north to be near your brother, get a job. As the years go by, you like the job more and more but you make less and less money. It's okay. You need less. You're happy. The world seems less complicated. You decide there's more to life than work. You're not maximizing your potential. You're using only a tenth of your brain power, a quarter of your abilities. So you retire and go to school. College is great. You make all kinds of friends and everyone has so much energy. For a while there it's sex, sex, sex. You do all your thinking with your dick. But as you get younger, you understand that even though intercourse is amazing, especially with Margaret Nugent, there must be more to life than indulgence. There is. Running as fast as you can. Toys. Sugar. Cartoons. You get tired easier these days. You begin to take naps. Soon you're sleeping whenever you can. Your mom has to wake you up to eat. You're not interested. The food's bland. You can't see that well. What you can smell is unappealing. You can no longer discriminate sounds. It's all just noise. You end up sweetly dreaming your life away. And then you're unborn and you spend nine months or so floating in a warm ocean, all your needs taken care of. And then you die.

When I snapped out of it, Judi was talking. She told Dorie that she could see a light at the bottom of the river and she was walking toward the light. And now her knees were wet and now her feet have been swept up, have lost their purchase on the rocks. She could hear him yelling, coming for her. And then she allowed herself to rest, to ride the current, and she was carried away. Judi cried. Dorie cried. What had I missed exactly?

Dorie asked Judi to sit up. The session, apparently, was over. I was sure we'd been there for hours, but it had been fifty-one minutes. Dorie and Judi sat on the couch. I stood, hesitated. I went to the chair and sat. Dorie said it would take her a few minutes. Judi stared at the ceiling. I was exhausted. Dorie told me she was clairsentient and so could feel the pain that Judi felt. But she would recover in a few minutes. When she did, she told us what Judi evidently knew, that it was worse than we thought. Dorie was sure that there was involvement with the lungs and the head.

Dorie took Judi's hand. "Of course there is reason to hope. We know where to work now. We have discovered the source." She looked at Judi.

I said, "The river?"

Dorie nodded. "Judi can tell you what went on if she needs to."

I said, "Why she was trying to kill herself?"

Dorie said, "Yes."

Judi rested her head on Dorie's shoulder. She smiled at me. I tried to picture Judi with her head on Dr. Pawlak's shoulder. Any doctor's shoulder.

64.

A Coincidence of Opposites

DORIE'S HUNCH ABOUT THE SPREAD OF THE CANCER WAS CONFIRMED BY THE radiologist's report on Judi's most recent X rays. A constellation of specks on the left lung, a blemish on the right hemisphere of the brain. Bad news that for some reason offered Judi hope. Her trust in Dorie had been validated. I suppose that was it. I was more alarmed by the news than she was, and I phoned Dr. Pawlak to try to, I don't know, get some kind of insight into how we might convince Judi to undergo radiation therapy if nothing else. And I guess I wanted to know if it was already too late even for that. I left three messages, one on a machine, two with the receptionist who wore the heavy perfume. Dr. Pawlak did not get back to me.

I read through some of Judi's books on *chakras* and auras and Tantric healing and all. I liked the flowers and the colors and the provocative images of the Jeweled City, the Soundless Sound, and so on. But I wondered was this so different than a novena to St. Francis? a prayer to St. Jude? Well, there was this idea that every *chakra* was connected to a gland in the body, the pituitary, the thyroid, and so on. But that just seemed to unsettle the elegant aesthetics more than anything else. East or West. *Prana* or Grace. Soundless Sound or Unmoved Mover. My impoverished materialist self couldn't buy either.

As children, we all watch clouds, and we notice that that one there looks like a dragon with glasses creeping over a mountain. And this one's a bowl of fruit. There's Alaska. Like that. A knot on a beech tree looks like the Knapps' cocker spaniel. We might spill a glass of wine, now that we've grown, turn our heads a bit, squint, and see Van Gogh's *"Starry Night,"* or we might stare at an inkblot in Dr. Rhadymanthus's airy sanctum, blush, and confess to some naughty adolescent indiscretion that will never, ever happen again. A shadow on a hedge reminds us of the Quaker Oats man. We see Jesus everywhere: on a tortilla, on a freezer door, on a billboard, in the snow on the TV screen. Everywhere but in church. What we're doing is taking random stimuli and giving them meaning. We're not comfortable with the undesigned, the disordered. We're forever organizing our experience into coherence. Well, some of us are.

And some of us take this denotation too far. Ronnie, for example. I took him to lunch one afternoon when he was visiting. Took him to the café at the Worcester Art Museum. He ordered watercress on a kaiser roll and a bottle of domestic spring water. He asked me why I'd taken him to this place out of all the places in Worcester. I said, You can't get fresh hearts of palm at Hot Dog Annie's. He didn't laugh. He looked around. Every gesture that anyone made in the room, Ronnie interpreted as a hand signal to himself. Occasionally, he would glance past my shoulder and touch his ear or hold up a palm like he was balancing a tray. He told me that the blackboard menu was a coded communiqué advising him that certain human operatives would be attempting to implant fictitious memories in his brain. That's what I mean by taking signifying too far. You could find yourself in a William Burroughs novel.

I was not invited to Judi's ensuing sessions with Dorie. I could drop her off, and I could pick her up an hour later. Evidently, my energy fields were interfering with the magnetism in the room or something like that. And I was probably inhibiting Judi and Dorie. But the real reason for my exile, I would learn, was that I was the source of Judi's cancer. Well, the I she'd met in that former life, the I who was called Père Berard and who knew Judi, who was then Marianne, a hundred and something years ago up the St. Lawrence in Québec, knew her, it turns out, in the biblical sense as well as in the social and pastoral, caused her to be with child, to despair, and to drown herself. And now, a century and more later, Judi has still not come to terms with her remorse, her shame, her regret, and it is killing her.

And Judi was, in fact, beginning to feel better. She had more energy these days and more strength. She told me she could actually feel the tumors shrinking. I said, Let's get an X ray and confirm it. She said, No

X rays until I'm recovered. I said, One or two X rays can't hurt. She said it would be like sucking plasma off a high-tension line. She told me what had become clear to her only recently, that the universe—actually, she said "universes" and explained that the earth's universe is just a single bubble in a vast boiling cauldron of universes, and that that multiverse is just a fractal in a landscape of multiverses, and so on—that universes, then, are not composed of dead matter, insensible duff, but constitute a living organism, a presence. What I know now, she said, is not that I will possess eternal life, but that I already do. And I didn't argue with her. Hope is hope, I thought. It's not true or false, it's just hope.

65.

The Secret Life

DORIE HAD TOLD JUDI THAT SHE COULDN'T EAT ANYTHING WITH A FACE. SO NOW Judi was preparing a vegetarian supper for Dorie's visit. Salad, focaccia, manicotti, spumoni. I reasoned with Judi. I said clams don't have faces, and I don't think you could call what a shrimp has a face, either. Judi said, I think what Dorie meant was if it tries to get away from you when it's alive, then you shouldn't eat it. She smashed a clove of garlic with a mallet. Oysters, I said. Mussels. Judi shook her head no. I realize that your favorite animal is the brisket, she said, but tonight we're eating meatless, and you'll like it. Now set the table.

Dorie arrived with a house gift, two black rocks about the size of softballs. Boji stones, she called them. The scarred one with the ridges is a male, the smooth one a female. She told Judi they were healing stones. They helped close holes in your energy fields. Judi gave her a big hug and a kiss. Maybe it was the idea of gender-specific rocks that set me off. I don't know. It might have been a troubled day of writing. Anyway, I felt confrontational, haughty. I wanted to engage Dorie Marcelonis in battle. So I poured myself a martini—I had a pitcher of them ready in the fridge. Dorie said, No, thank you, but she would have a glass of red wine. Wine it is.

Dorie and I went out on the deck while Judi finished the cooking. We would take advantage of the unseasonably warm early spring weather. I introduced Dorie to Spot. Spot licked her sandaled feet. He has a thing for salt, I said. Dorie kissed Spot right on the mouth. Spot, she said, you're a monkey.

We sat at the table. I lit a citronella candle. I cleared my throat. We raised our glasses. To you, I said. She smiled. To Judi. We drank. I said, "You know, I don't like this idea that cancer is a symptom of some emotional sin in this life or in another. That's blaming the victim, it seems to me, and it's kind of sick."

Dorie smiled. She fiddled with an earring—a silver hand with a star in its palm. "I understand your skepticism," she said. "We're not blaming anyone. We're just searching for causes."

I quoted Oscar Wilde (who hasn't?). I told her, " 'It is only shallow people who do not judge by appearances.' The secret of life is the visible, not the invisible."

"That's very wry," she said. "But also ironic, don't you think?"

I apologized. "I didn't mean I thought you were shallow." But, of course, that's exactly what I'd meant. "How come if I was involved with Judi's suicide and stuff back in Canada, back when I supposedly was this Berard person, how come I'm not screwed up from it?"

"Who says you're not?"

"I don't have cancer. I'm not dying."

Dorie raised her eyebrows; she sipped her wine.

I said, "You think I have cancer?"

"You may be physically fine for now, but emotionally? spiritually?"

"You think I have emotional problems?"

"Do you?"

"Doesn't everyone?" I wondered when I had started my retreat. Wasn't I trying to confront Dorie on her frivolous spiritualism?

Dorie said, "So tell me about this life."

"What do you mean?"

"What are you afraid of?"

"Heights." I meant this to be a smart-ass answer even though it's true.

Dorie raised those eyebrows again. "When you look down, do you think the ground is pulling at you?"

We heard Judi call us in. We pushed back from the table. I saw myself on the ledge of an office building about ten floors up. There's an open window about thirty feet away. My hair's blowing in my eyes. I look down without moving my head. I'm petrified.

The meal was delicious. It made me wonder why I thought I needed to eat meat at all. Then I remembered the smell of bacon frying, grilled hot dogs on toasted rolls. Sure, I could live without prime rib, but without fried baloney? We're talking quality of life here.

Dorie asked me what my stories were about. I hate that question. It would take every word of the story to answer honestly. Otherwise, you can give only a stupid answer, which I did. I said, Life and death, because what else is there? But as soon as I heard myself, I knew I didn't want to stop on that word, that phrase, so I said, I write about ordinary people in extraordinary circumstances, but that wasn't right unless you consider falling in love extraordinary, which maybe it is.

Dorie took a bite of spumoni. She said, "I mean, what themes do you try to explore in your stories?"

"Well, loneliness, grief, separation. Like that." I didn't think we should be talking like this with Judi sitting right here drinking her herbal tea. I didn't want her to get depressed.

Dorie smiled. "I wonder where your obsessions with those issues come from. Do you know?"

I knew that I was on my second martini and that I was gabbing away with a psychic healer and a psychotherapist and that I should probably be more circumspect in my revelations, be a little more cautious. But instead I said something offensive, something about wanting to keep the mystery in life and creating art out of what I couldn't understand. What an asshole.

I guess I was lucky. They found me pompous, not hostile. Dorie laughed. Judi told me I'd have to clean the kitchen for my penance. I apologized. I apologize a lot. All my life I've been apologizing. For spilled milk, for hurt feelings, for being late, for being on time, for expressing opinions, for spacing out, for being in the way, for not being around. "I'm sorry"—a motif in my life that I hadn't realized before then.

Judi and Dorie took their teas and retired to the deck. I cleaned up—put all the leftovers into a bowl and brought it out to Spot. He cleaned his plate. I did the dishes. I was afraid of losing Judi. I remembered when I was about five I got lost at a carnival. I looked up and my family was gone. I couldn't even yell. I just started running. I tried to stay in the lights, I remember. I was so panicked that I guess I didn't hear the PA announcer call my name, ask me to come to the carousel, but I couldn't have found the carousel anyway. I just ran until I tripped over a dog, I think it was. I lay there in the dirt and cried. A man picked me up, held me in his arms, and started walking. He smelled like gasoline. I thought he was carrying me away to his house, and I thought that would be fine, any house would be fine. When he handed me to my sobbing mother, I wouldn't let go of his blue sweater.

When I went out to join Judi and Dorie, they were talking about Pauline. I said, Pauline from Mr. Natural's? like I knew a dozen Paulines. Dorie nodded, said Pauline was moving away soon. She's met this terrific guy, a carpenter. He's great with the kids. I said, Isn't she married? They both just looked at me. Uh-oh. Dorie said, Marvin's sort of out of the picture. And anyway, I don't think Pauline's getting married yet. They're going to move up to Phillipston or Templeton, somewhere up there.

The phone rang and Judi went in to answer it. I wondered if Pauline had ever mentioned me to Dorie. I wasn't going to ask. I told Dorie about the carnival episode, said I thought it was such an insignificant event to be the source of a lifetime's inappropriate and antisocial behavior.

Dorie said, "Well, maybe you think everyone's going to leave you. That would make you cautious in relationships. You'd be reluctant to commit yourself."

I thought about that. I said, "But no one has left me," which wasn't quite true.

"Because you leave them first."

I made a face, tried to express incredulity.

"Your wife?"

"I think it was a little more complicated than that."

"Girlfriends?"

"Well, look, there were things on their part that might have accounted for the breakups."

"Of course. We're just speculating." Dorie rubbed her arms like she was cold. "It's interesting that you would go with the gasoline man. You really need someone to take care of you."

"Let's say that was all true. Let's say my parents abandoned me for real at a carnival. That would still not be an excuse to hurt people or hurt myself."

"Theoretically, you're right. I agree. But you can't ignore your past. Better to understand your fears, so you can deal with them, prevent yourself from hurting someone or yourself."

Judi returned, said that was Trixie calling to tell her about Layla's new tattoo. She got a big radiant sun on her back. Judi said why didn't we get in out of the chill. We went to the parlor with our freshened teas and martini. Judi sat on the couch. Dorie sat across from her on the chair. I put some Charlie Parker on the stereo and joined Judi. We talked about odd things, extraordinary things that had happened in our lives.

Dorie said she'd been married once and that on her honeymoon cruise to Nova Scotia she saw Johnny Mathis at the captain's table, introduced herself, and he sang "No Love (But Your Love)" to her. And once on a trip to Machu Picchu to witness a UFO landing, she ate monkey brains and chilies with Shining Path guerrillas.

Judi's turn. When she was fifteen, she went on a retreat with the girls in her parish to Nantucket. While she was there she saw a rose bush with blue roses. Then, in eighth grade, she made it to the finals of the national spelling bee in Washington. She was one of the ten best spellers in the country. She lost when she misspelled the word *quinonoid,* which she spelled for us. I didn't know why Judi had never mentioned the spelling bee before. I asked her to spell *xanthous, psephology,* and *coelacanth,* which she did.

Judi said, "You're up, laughing boy."

All right. "I met Mother Teresa in New York when she came to America for some kind of surgery. I drove down with Martha and the auxiliary bishop. We went to a reception. Mother was tiny, talked incessantly in several languages, gave me a holy card, and asked for donations.

"When I was fifteen, I was standing outside the Central Building when I heard people start screaming. I looked up to see a man in the air, seventy feet up. I couldn't believe it. A man in black trousers and a white shirt. One of his shoes flew off. I turned away. He sounded like a watermelon hitting the sidewalk, and, I saw, his skull was opened like one."

Dorie said she'd better be going. Judi walked her out to her car. I told myself that Pauline wasn't abandoning me. In fact, I thought that whole abandonment theory Dorie worked out wasn't right. It didn't feel like the truth. But she was right that there was something back there in my childhood. I could sense that now. When Judi and I went to bed, I lay there thinking about my parents and about our life at home when I was young. I remembered listening to them make love in their room across the hall. Edgar was always asleep. I always wanted to be, but my anxiety kept me awake. I wanted to be able to close my ears like I closed my eyes. My mother would give directions. My father would grunt, squeal, snort. His lack of language appalled and frightened me. I didn't know what I thought then—that Mom was Circe and Dad was her pig or that he was a beast and Mom the savaged waif. I just knew I was uncomfortable.

I thought about sex with Martha, how polite it all was, how methodical, pleasant for the most part, but not ecstatic. Dutiful, you could say. Because I feared becoming a swine? losing control?

I remembered another scene from childhood. I was about eleven. My parents had had a bitter quarrel during which my mother threw a dish of spaghetti across the table and hit Dad in the face. We didn't see him for a week. When he did come home, Mom stayed in her locked bedroom. Dad made coffee, sat at the table. I asked him how he was. He said, Fine. He motioned me over, hugged me. He was crying. I thought maybe they'll get a divorce, and I found the thought comforting. This would be a quiet house. I wouldn't get bossed around so much, wouldn't have to listen to his jaw crack every time he chewed. I'd be a special child somehow, the man of the house. I sat at the table and poured myself a coffee. I'd never tasted it before. I burned the roof of my mouth.

"So, Dad, did you come to get your stuff?"

"What are you talking about, Laf?"

"You leaving us?"

"I wouldn't ever leave your mother. Couldn't. She'd die without me."

I remember thinking, Never? Stuck forever? You're nice to someone and they expect you to stay where you are for the rest of your life?

66

How I Saw You, How I Fell in Love, How an Awful Madness Swept Me Away

DALE'S CONFLICT ISN'T WITH THERESA AT ALL, BUT WITH HIMSELF. I THINK I understood that all along, but I hadn't really felt it. Dale doesn't want to be alone, but he often wants to be left alone. He wants to love Theresa, but he's not sure he wants her to love him. Interesting, isn't it? In fact, he already loves Theresa, which means that he has relinquished some control over his life. That's what he thinks, anyway. But is this love he proffers or adoration? And if the latter, does he think of Theresa as an object? an idol? All his life Dale has worshiped women from a distance. Whenever he got close to a woman—and that happened only three times—he found that she did not live up to his expectations. They were as flawed as he was. So how could they save him? Poor Dale. Wherever did he acquire these addled notions of love? Surely not from me.

I caught myself thinking about Daphne Engdahl, wondering if she'd remember me if I stopped by one afternoon for coffee and a botany lesson. Two in the morning. I looked at the clock. Two-sixteen, actually. I made coffee. I wondered if it was the right week to plant the flowers I'd found in the cellar that time. I poured my coffee. I checked to see that Judi was still sleeping quietly.

Dale and Theresa are driving through the West Texas night on I-20, coming home from Abilene. Maybe Dale had an economics conference at Hardin-Simmons. Maybe Theresa has an old friend from nursing school living in Potosi with her second husband. I don't know; I'll figure that out later. Dale's driving the pickup; radio's playing a Mexican waltz. Theresa's staring out her window. Sign ahead says SWEETWATER, NEXT EXIT. They've been quiet for fifty miles. Theresa says, I was in Sweetwater one time.

She tells Dale that when she was nineteen she ran out of gas on a Sunday afternoon in Sweetwater on Highway 70, coming from San Angelo. Dale doesn't ask her why she was in San Angelo, whom she might have known there. She walked, saw a house sitting alone about a hundred yards off the highway. She was invited into the house by a young woman and given coffee and sweet potato pie. The woman's name was Maryprice Hodge. Her husband, Meachum, came in from the field and joined them. He said he'd be happy to run into town to Donnie Jenck's Citgo station and fetch some gasoline.

Suddenly, the whole kitchen shook, dishes rattled, a platter fell off the shelf and landed on the counter. Earthquake, must be. Maryprice rolled her eyes. And then another shock. Maryprice said, Meachum, please tell the boy to cease and desist while we have company. She told Theresa that her son Val had mounted a basketball hoop right to the side of the house. He's out there now shooting free throws.

When Meachum left, Maryprice told Theresa that she worked in town at the Sack 'n' Save. Said the oddest thing happened. About a month back she started finding these mysterious and romantic love notes. In her lunch sack, in the mail, stuffed inside her cigarette pack, on the car windshield. Just all over. They were sweet, not fresh, if you know what I mean. Things a woman wants to hear. She assumed they were from the new fellow in the meat department, Gene Killeen. Thought it was him from his eyes, the way he watched me, from what he said on breaks, how he sat near me, lit my cigarettes like a gentleman. I felt like he was reading my thoughts. And I don't mind telling you he was a sharp-looking man and single. Turns out, though, the notes were from her adoring husband, Meachum. Meachum doesn't talk much, Maryprice said. Yes, she was disappointed when she learned the truth; all the romance just leaked out of her. She did have a new appreciation for Meachum, though.

Dale is disconcerted. Theresa's been places he hasn't. He considers telling her a story about that time in Shamrock when he got caught in a blizzard. But that would be a story about himself and not about other people, as hers was. And where is the mystery in a snowstorm? He asks Theresa if she wants to drive into town and find the house, visit the Hodges. She says she doesn't. Says that wouldn't be right.

When we were in seventh grade, Dale tells Theresa, Spivey Wilhite, who had stayed back twice, and was fourteen, murdered his parents because they wouldn't allow him to listen to Little Richard records. One day he stayed home from school, dyed his red hair black, waited till his mom headed to County Market before he'd come out of the bathroom. He loaded his dad's deer rifle with cartridges, and when his mom came in through the back door, he fired. The first bullet blew the sack of groceries out of her hands and drove a carton of milk against the wall, leaving Randa Wilhite with a very confused look on her face. The second bullet wiped that away. When Spivey, Sr., got home from work, he yelled for Spivey to shut off that nigger music once and for all. His boy stood up behind the sofa, where he'd been hiding, lifted the rifle. Who are you? were the last words his father spoke.

Spivey got sent to reform school. And then overnight, it seemed, he was back on the street, and he seemed much older than we were and he had tattoos and his hair was thinning, and he took a job at Phalco Plastics, and people kind of left him alone. Sometimes you'd see him at Bevis Drugs drinking a chocolate Coke or a coffee. He tried to join the army to go to Nam, but they wouldn't take him because he'd killed people. I'd see him walking along Broadway with a book in his back pocket, a cigarette, unfiltered, in his mouth.

Theresa said, Jesus, does this Spivey guy still live in Hobbs? Dale told her he washed dishes at the Cattle Baron. She'd no doubt seen him around. He's kind of fat now. When they turned off I-20 in Big Spring and drove past the asylum on the way to Lamesa, Dale told Theresa the truth. Spivey killed his parents because they wouldn't let him listen to Charlie Pride records. Sorry, but that didn't seem important enough to kill over. What am I saying? And the war was over before he got out of the reform school. I don't know why I said that about the army. Theresa said, You're way made more sense.

That evening Dale sat on his couch with his lap desk and wrote Theresa a letter:

Dearest T.

I have held my love and my kindness in reserve all my life. Right now, at 3 A.M., I don't understand my caution, what I thought I was saving affection for. I'm writing to you because I could not say what I have to say. I'm embarrassed by this admission, but I know I'm right about it. I thought I would be giving something up if I were to commit myself to you and the children. But now I can't recall what that was. Time? Could that be it? As if I could hold on to time. Freedom? Independence? But why? So I could sit with Keynes and read? I know that I have quiet and contentment (a little) in my life, and order, routine, tranquillity, and I know that I will have to give these up to be with you, and that seems a small price to pay for your love. So, if you are willing, I am eager, at long last, to saying let's go and get married and make it all official. So what do you think, Theresa? I'll be a wreck until I hear from you. I don't want to get morose, and so I'll close.

Love, Dale

Dale put on his slippers, got Keynes's leash, and they walked to the mailbox at the Allsup's. He knew that if he didn't post the letter tonight, he likely would not in the morning. Not that he would feel differently about Theresa, he just might not be able to handle the truth in the clear light of day. Dale in his parlor at four A.M. had this insight: Every act of loving affirms the goodness of the lover just because he is capable of loving and of being loved. And if you're not convinced of your goodness, well . . . Dale thought how this rationalization seemed pretty self-serving. I put down my pen, wondered if I had enough energy to take Spot for a walk.

67.

Your Molecular Structure

JUDI YELLED FROM THE BEDROOM. SHE'D BE READY IN FIVE. WE HAD PLANS. I schlepped the typewriter to the mud room, stashed my papers on the shelf over the coat hooks. We were going to a flea market up in Hollis, New Hampshire. Judi thought there might still be bargains left in New Hampshire. Fiesta ware dishes for fifty cents a piece, metal lunch boxes for a buck, that sort of thing. Judi wore her denim jacket, blue jeans, her black Harley-Davidson boots with the zippers, and a black White Sox baseball cap that she had on backward. She looked like a fourteen-year-old headbanger. She kissed me on the nose. She took the cookie jar down off the fridge and took out an envelope with cash. I wondered, Do I need my gloves? I looked out the window at the sunny yard, the bare trees, their swollen buds, at the brown grass. It could be seventy out there or twenty. I watched Spot watching a squirrel cross a telephone wire. I couldn't see Spot's breath. Better take the gloves anyway.

Judi drove. I watched the miles glide by. I switched stations on the radio. I could listen to oldies so long as the Supremes weren't on. Judi's rule. We listened to a call-in show about restaurants for a while. Some station was playing Mose Allison, but it faded out halfway into "Your Molecular Structure." *Car Talk*. I hate cars, but I love those guys. I told Judi, take a left, any left. We'll drive to Oregon. I was joking, but I meant it.

I said, "Why don't we do it? Take a long trip."

"Where to?"

"Across the country."

I could see that Judi was considering the idea.

"This summer," I said.

"Two problems, time and money."

"Yes, they'll stop you if you let them." I told her we could take the trailer, camp everywhere. Rest areas are free. Judi said she doubted the trailer would make it. It hadn't moved from its spot in thirty years or more. I said we could try it. She said, honestly, she wasn't the camping kind of gal. She said the Miata wouldn't be big enough to tow the trailer, anyway. I was momentarily discouraged, but I wasn't planning to drop the idea. I said, Let's think about it. She said, Okay. I said, We'll take a month off, see the U.S.A. I already saw us cruising through the steppes of eastern Montana, so I was surprised by what Judi said next. She said we needed to talk about her dying. She turned off the radio.

I said, "What do you mean? You're feeling better, aren't you? You said these healing sessions were working. You look great. What are you talking about?"

"I'm feeling better, but that doesn't mean I'm going to survive."

"None of us is going to survive."

"You know what I mean."

I stared out the window. We were near Townsend. I could see a familiar restaurant up a long hill. Yes, the Olde Mill. I'd been to a wedding reception there with Martha. Rob and Donna. Good friends who moved away to Kansas or somewhere. Haven't seen them in, Jesus, twelve years. Maybe on our trip, we could stop in on them. Or would that be awkward? Martha and I had words, I think, at the reception, took one of our famous long walks. I threw stones in the mill pond. Martha cried. We always seemed to fight at public occasions.

Judi said, "Death is your life affirming itself by consenting to die."

"Is this some of Dorie's New Age wisdom?"

"No. Dorie said, 'Death is the opposite of love.' "

"Horseshit."

"I want to take this seriously. Death, I mean."

"What kind of goal is death?"

"Inevitable."

"But not necessarily imminent."

"For you."

I wanted to say, almost said, "Stop feeling sorry for yourself," but I thought, Why shouldn't she?

"Where does all this anger come from?"

I looked at her. "What?" I don't think of myself as angry. I said so. I said, "I'm impatient sometimes. I get frustrated."

Judi laughed. "You use your impatience to keep you from the anger. You're afraid of it. You're afraid it's so huge and powerful that it will hurt someone. Well, it's not."

"Do I have to pay for this session?"

"Angry?"

"I'm being attacked."

"Are you?"

This wasn't pleasant, but it beat talking about death by a mile. "Have I ever yelled at you?"

"You think if you don't yell, if you don't smash the furniture, then you're not expressing anger; you're controlling it."

That made sense.

"But it's controlling you."

The sign said six miles to Hollis, and in those six miles Judi said I had stored up more anger and resentment than I knew what to do with and maybe it had something to do with feeling powerless, inadequate—a perception, she said, that was inaccurate (thank God)—which feeling probably goes back to my childhood. She said I probably thought life was spontaneous, but it isn't. We develop patterns of behavior, habits that are habits because they've worked for us in the past. My guess, she said, is one time when you felt hurt, you didn't cry or scream; you shut up about it, and you found out that Mom and Dad got off your back. Maybe they admired your stoicism. Maybe even you did. That's how they trained you, shaped you into a quiet, resentful boy.

So, I thought, does she want me to get pissed now? to yell at her? Is that it? Well, I wasn't pissed, so there. I'm doing what she said, aren't I?

Judi said this habit was appropriate for childhood, but, then, I wasn't a child anymore, was I? Even if I was irresponsible and childish at times—my cavalier attitude toward security, employment, success, I guess she meant. She said if I could stop this habit, then the reasons for it would surface—the impulses, the emotions, the perceptions. And then I could deal with them.

I gave Judi a dollar and she gave it to the parking attendant. I said, Well, if it's a problem, I should deal with it.

Judi said I should say the first word that pops into my head. Okay?

I said, "Shoot."

"Is that a joke?"

"What?"

"Never mind. Ready?"

"Ready."

"*Rage.*"

"Dylan Thomas."

"*Dog.*"

"Food."

"*Dark.*"

"Space."

"*Death.*"

"Defying."

Judi laughed, pulled into a space.

"Am I sane?"

"No."

"Thank God."

We browsed the tables and stalls. A lot of flea market vendors are horrendously overweight, and a lot of them smoke. You see plenty of dandruff and skin rashes, too. This could be the most dangerous job in America. And was there really this big a demand for Nazi paraphernalia? I bought a coffee, ate some fried dough. Judi tried to make a deal on a Fada Bakelite radio, butterscotch-and-cherry-colored and shaped like a bullet. I love all this old stuff, but in order to save things, you have to have a place to put them; you have to settle into a domicile. Nomads don't buy floor lamps with beaded silk shades, lacquered with powdered glass, or silver streamlined turnover toasters or official Gangbusters "Crusade Against Crime" toy machine guns. Bowling shirts and postcards, maybe, and the occasional Bokar coffee tin. In fact, I bought old "Greetings from . . ." hand-painted postcards where they spell out the name of the featured place in pictures. Cooke City, Montana: "On the Red Lodge–Cooke City Highway"; Denver; Fort Worth; North Platte, Nebraska; Prescott, Arizona. I even got one of Hobbs, New Mexico. Oil wells, parked cars, and the Bevis Drugstore. I showed them to Judi, said these were the places we'd go on the trip. It was fate. She said, Why don't you write a story about the trip. Like what we did and how much fun we had. I said, Judi, you got this whole time and space thing screwed up.

Judi bought a wood and glass tray with a design of parrots on it. The parrots were made out of blue and orange butterfly wings. She talked the lady down to twenty-five dollars. Did I think we needed a 1935 calendar with Joan Crawford's photo on it? Any year but '35, I said. I bought an ashtray stolen from the Green Derby restaurant in Jackson, Mississippi. I was going to use it for paper clips.

Judi told me she was tired. She wanted to leave.

"Are you okay?"

She shrugged. Then she began to cry.

I touched her shoulder. "What is it?"

"What you said about time."

"Before?"

We walked back to the car. Judi told me to drive. "What you said about the space and time thing. Well, in the last session with Dorie . . ."

"I'm listening." I backed out of our spot, drove across the rutted field. "Go ahead."

"Well, I had this experience." She looked at me. "Do you want to hear it?"

I said I did, and she told me the whole story.

68.

Time Held Me Green
and Dying

"I BRUSH MY HAIR IN THE SULFURED LIGHT OF THE OIL LAMP. I SET THE BRUSH AND *the mirror just so on the bureau. I arrange the basin and jug, smooth out the doily. I wait for you. I hear Madame Lussier in the yard, breaking the ice on the pump, scolding her dog, Genghis. Madame has told me that you have secrets. All the other young priests that she knows, she told me, are like sisters to her. But you're not one she can fuss over and giggle with. She has advised me to stay away from you. I sit in my chair. I smooth my dress over my belly. I fold my hands on my lap. I stare at the orange flames through the grate in the wood stove. That was the trigger, that's what carried me back—the pine-scented disinfectant at Dorie's. Isn't that funny? It brought me back a century to that morning, to my room, my resinous fire, my waiting for you.*

"When I walk to the door to answer your knock, the floorboards creak. You stand in the doorway, steam rising off your bald head, and I recognize you immediately even though you are older and have grown thick in the waist and the neck. I ask you why you've done this, come back to me from the future on this day of all days. You ask if you might come in. You take off your cape and drop it on the bed. You touch the crucifix on the wall, the sprigs of pussy willow in the garden basket—I'd forgotten all about that basket. You pick up the seed box where I keep my needles, thread, and buttons. You lower yourself into the chair, wince. You're old, and time is all mixed up.

"That's when I realized—there in my room and there in Dorie's—that time is not out there but here in us, and we measure it with dreams and memories, that time is not a river we drift in, but a sea that we swim in, and we can swim

in any direction. I understood then that history is an empty notion. History is what happened. Memory is what happens. There is no now, no then. There is only the everlastingness. Eternity. An absolute. It's hard to explain this. We need a language without tense.

"I ask you what you have in that sack on your lap. You tell me that you never got your own parish, never made monsignor. You say that in time you came to feel like this place—lonely, desperate, leaden. You know that I'm close to death—both on that day and now—and you tell me how the last thing I'll feel is a pressure on the chest like it's caught in a wine press and how the pressure builds until the heart is pulped.

"You tell me you want to confess, and suddenly you're young again. 'I chose God,' you say, 'and I chose wrong. God,' you say, 'is cold comfort to a bitter heart.'

"I think how when you leave, I'll put a log in the stove and stoke the fire with your several letters, your little gifts: the heron's feather, the hat brush, the floral band box, the hair ribbon. I'll sweep the floor, smooth the bed where you sat. I'll leave the door unlocked. I'll tell Madame Lussier I'm off to Monsieur Plouffe's for lye. I won't let on. I'll walk to the river.

"You tell me that freedom means doing what we ought to do, which is to choose the spiritual over the material. Freedom, you say, is inescapable. You say you had always believed that you could rectify your life until you got it right. That notion, you say, died the moment they dragged my body out of the river, my body with its lacy mantle of moss and algae, bloated, you tell me, and bluish. You look at me and say, 'If you had only told me.' I tell you the child was not the point. Love was the point.

"You open your sack on the bed. You show me the bony unborn with his bulbous head, translucent as a cave fish, and his pearly monkey's face. You say, 'The atonement is mine; I am not reconciled.' You cry and kneel at my feet. You say, 'Willful love I have; natural love I have none.' You do not ask for my forgiveness. You say you have an instinct for death, have altered but not grown; you have merely become. By now I am looking out the cloudy window. You say, 'I go down to death with indifference and ignorance; I am one to whom nothing can be added.' "

69.

Purgatory

FOR A WEEK IN EARLY MAY, JUDI HAD BEEN AWARE OF A CONSTANT FEELING OF nausea, just a touch, nothing serious, not pain so much as a reminder. She never did throw up. She ate a little, worked, but always felt uncomfortable and enervated. She could close her eyes whatever she was doing, wherever she was, and just drop off to sleep, or, if not actually to sleep, to a kind of foggy dreamland. I told her she had spring fever and what she needed was a cross-country drive. Those amber waves of grain will perk you right up. She agreed to a picnic in Purgatory.

Purgatory Chasm is this curious geologic fissure a quarter mile long and fifty feet wide down in Sutton. The vertical walls of the chasm are as high as seventy feet. The feature was formed, geologists think, when a deep glacial lake drained all at once and poured out of this single rocky outlet. What remains are canyons, caves, and overhanging rocks, all out here in the middle of the woods. I came here as a kid on a family outing and got sick in the playground riding around and around on this— I don't know what you call it—this spinning disk. Martha and I came here early one spring to hike and pick mushrooms. I remember how the place seemed cold, gray, disappointing that day.

On the drive down, I asked Judi if we come back, if we're reincarnated, is it always to this planet? this universe? She raised her eyebrows. Are you making fun of me? I said, No. She said she thought we did. That's been her own experience anyway. I guess I was just trying to make conversation, trying to get her to relax. I said, Do all the ants come back, too? She said, Yes, all living things. Well, then, how do we recognize each other when we come back? We usually don't, she said.

Judi and I walked to the grove, found a picnic table we liked. We were alone, this being a work day. We walked to the chasm. Judi wasn't up for exploring, said she'd watch me climb. We just sat on a rock, looked up at the graffiti. On June 14, 1952, someone named Leo stood on a narrow ledge sixty feet over the chasm floor and wrote his girlfriend's name on the rock: "Joyce," then signed and dated the inscription. They'd be old now, Leo and Joyce. I wondered were they married and did they live nearby, like in Douglas, and did they drive over here and look up at Leo's declaration? Or maybe Joyce married someone else and it didn't work out, but she'll come here sometimes, look up, and find solace and also regret. The deFusco Gang signed the chasm wall in 1935; Barney on July 27, 1941. Did Barney make it through the war?

It's interesting, this impulse to leave your name in public places, to say I was here, I was alive. Is it the name or is it the deed that compels? Will future anthropology students write papers about spray paint and rock, compare graffiti to petroglyphs? Would the reincarnated Barney recognize his old handwriting?

Back at the table Judi looked at her potato salad and said she just couldn't eat. She felt bloated, unsteady. She pushed the plate away from her. The smells, she said. And then she vomited on the bench, on her shoes. She cried, apologized. She put her head on my shoulder, punched the bench, and screamed. Fuck it all, she said. I think of that moment in the mottled light of the pine grove as the beginning of the end.

When we got home, I called Stoni. For the next several hours, Judi vomited bile and fecal matter. We drove her to Memorial, admitted her. They suspected and subsequently confirmed a bowel obstruction caused by an encroaching tumor. She had a mercury-filled tube inserted in her nose and down her throat into her intestines. Later, an operation, an anastomosis, attached the small intestine to the colon above the obstruction.

When she came home, Judi was at first too weak to sit up. We got her a hospital bed. Stoni moved in, set up a cot in Judi's room. I moved Judi's bed into the spare room and slept there. Stoni said our job now was to make Judi as comfortable as possible. She had a morphine drip in the back of her hand that administered a dose every hour or so. She slept a lot. When she was awake, she vacillated between hope and despair, between alertness and confusion, between comfort and pain. She told me that sometimes nothing stopped moving until she closed her eyes, and she felt like she was lying on a bed of needles. I asked her what her pain was like. She said, Like someone is slicing me up with a razor. Judi knew that something more important than anything else that had ever happened in her life was happening.

Those weeks of May and June blur together for me. I'd help Stoni with Judi, bathe her, feed her, sit with her. We had hospice nurses come in daily to help. I'd go to work and stay away longer than I needed to. Nicky and I would stop for beers or I'd go to Tatnuck Booksellers and browse, drink coffee. The smells of the house were getting to me. I was always wanting to open the windows, but Judi was always cold. People would visit regularly. Dorie always hugged me when she left. Trixie pretended everything was going to be all right. She'd keep talking about the future even when Judi told her she'd used all her future up. Hervey always brought a bottle and always made me share it with him. Every visit he'd resurrect some old pal of his who was dead, tell funny stories about what the old pal and he had done. Layla wore a nose ring now and had pierced both her eyebrows. I thought she looked cute. She told me Pozzo was reading again and talking to strangers finally, and was going to enroll at Quinsigamond Community College as a history major in the fall. Once he got his associate's degree, they'd be getting married. She told me about their married friends, Joe and Debbie, who have a baby and they're not even on welfare. Too proud for that. They're making it and are kind of a model for Layla and Pozzo. Joe sells crack is how they do it. They get by. He doesn't use himself. Albert, Ron, and Mark dropped in on Saturdays. I hadn't seen them since Josh's memorial service. And, of course, I was trying to write every day, but all I could write about was dying and illness. Even Theresa was sounding cynical.

There are a few moments during those weeks that I remember clearly. One morning Judi said she wanted to see Spot. I said, Are you sure? I could picture him now, chewing on the morphine tube. Well, Spot the Omnivorous waddled into the house and became immediately sedate. He stood in the kitchen a minute, and then, with his head lowered, he clicked his way across the kitchen and followed me to Judi's room. He put his head on the bed and let himself be patted, his tail wagging like crazy. They have no control over that, do they? He did try to step up on the bed. Judi cried in pain and that kind of spooked old Spot. I got his front paws down. He never tried it again. Judi said she wanted him to stay. I told him to lie down. He sniffed a scatter rug, circled it, and plopped down. So then every morning I would let Spot in and he would trot to the bedroom, lick Judi's face, and lie on the rug.

Another day she grieved over her loss of mobility, energy, stamina, sexual appeal, sense of self. She said, A year ago I played golf and tennis and made love all night long. Not with me, I thought. I remembered Puusepp. She said, What have I given to the world? to you? to my family? to my love? to myself? She asked me has anyone reached Ronnie yet. Not yet, but we're looking. She said, No habits, Laf. Think about everything you do. She asked me to take a letter.

Dear Richard:
I dreamed about you when I was delirious with morphine and blinding pain. I always knew you loved me, but in the dream I felt your love. You kissed the palm of my hand, remember. Now my heart understands what my mind already knew. I am always thinking of you.

Love, Judi

She told me to mail the letter to Richard. Richard who? Richard You-know-who, she said. I let it drop for now. The next day I asked her about Richard. She said, Who? I guessed: an accordion player. Judi looked at me. Richard is dead.

One morning she felt fine, she said, felt terrific. She said she knew she'd never be cured, never be back to normal or anything, but maybe soon she'd get back to work. The next day she was fevered and delirious. Stoni told me what to do. I gave Judi a tepid sponge bath and covered her with a light blanket. She was so out of it, she thought we were out at the El Morocco having dinner. I went along with her. She ordered lamb and pilaf. I had shish kebab and salad. All the time we're doing this, Judi's eyes are open and she's looking right at me. She didn't pretend to eat or anything and neither did I. We were like actors reading through the script. She looked at the window. Is that your ex-wife with the Pope? I turned and looked. I said, I can't tell from here. She said, Don't be coy, Laf. She ordered dessert. She said, You can tell from his hat he's the Pope. I looked at her and thought, This isn't Judi. This is her brain refusing to admit that it's in mortal danger. I wanted Judi back. Spot lay on his rug, his front legs twitching. I heard the tick-tick of Puusepp's watch. I opened the night table drawer and took it out, put it on.

70.

A Place of Cool Repose, the Blessedness of Quiet, the Brightness of Light

JUDI WAS SHAKEN OUT OF SLEEP BY HER DEATH, RATTLED AWAKE BY A TREMBLING cough into a final, brief consciousness. Spot heard her, woofed thinly without raising his muzzle from his rug. He lifted his eyes to me—I closed my book, lowered the music. I wished Stoni were back already from the pharmacy.

Judi was sweating, crying, gasping for air. I wiped her brow, her cheeks, her neck with the damp washcloth. "I'm here, Judi. I'm here. Spot's here. It's all right." Her skin was pucky and blotched. Something at the surface had started its work. I remembered her telling me once how the chemo made her skin feel like it was covered with electric ants. Her body jerked in its effort to breathe. Her eyes pleaded with me to carry her back from this precipice. She sucked the air, every breath a gurgle of laryngeal juices, every exhalation a moan. I held her hand. She squeezed mine. Even if death is a release from misery, even if death is a passage to another life, a better life, we have such a difficult time in the letting go, life being the devil we know.

Judi's legs began to kick. I looked around, expecting, I think, to apprehend death's visage, feel his chilly presence. I saw that it was 4:37 P.M. I listened for the back door to creak open. I wished Judi could have someone other than me here with her. Someone she deserved. Someone wild with love, love unadulterated and ferocious, who would whisper to her now, "Your death will take my life." Someone whose grief would fissure into madness, whose keening would pierce the stillness of this hollow house, whose screams would crack the vaults of heaven. Someone who would hold his god accountable for this abomination. Instead she has this stranger here who just wants her to stop this struggling.

Judi thrashed, tossed her head to the left, the right. I told her, "Judi, you can let go." And she did. She let go of my hand. I touched her face. Judi stretched her neck. I thought maybe she wanted to say something. She closed her eyes. The only sound in the room was the long hiss of her last breath. And I thought, So this is how it comes, this is how light ripens to darkness, how complexity shutters to simplicity. This is how knowledge is stilled, how fear is quenched. This is how rest becomes the long and dreamless sleep. This is how love becomes irrelevant. I sat there. I didn't know what to do. I waited.

"Death's a hard job, Laf,' she had told me that morning. "This is taking an eternity." Then she told me about her pain, how it had changed, or how her perception of it, at least, had changed. She said that now she knew the pain was the presence of God passing through her body. And I thought, Where did this enlightenment come from? And I knew, well, I didn't know, but I guessed that today, the summer solstice, the longest day, would be Judi's last.

She said the Lord had pierced her soul with the fire of his love—as with a sword—drawing his heart into hers. I said, You sound like Gertrude of Helfta. She smiled, nodded. It's the same all over again, she said. It was Gertrude, I thought, some of it was. And some of it was the morphine, and some of it was fear. This is what we do with what frightens us and what we can't understand. We fashion it into something we can live with.

She said, It's not the Lord's blood flowing in my veins, mixing with my blood, that hurts so much, but it's the pain of not being with Him, not being a part of Him, that does. She told me her ears were ringing, and there was an echo to every sound, even to her own words. She smiled, seemed amused by this, distracted. Sometimes the pitch changes, she said. I wonder if this is the music of my body, she said.

She talked about her dad. "Take care of Ronnie at the funeral," she said. "I don't want people laughing at him."

"I will."

"So, tell me what you're going to do, Laf. Tell me about your future."

"Oh, I don't know," I said. I shrugged, looked at the Indian cloth sheets riffling on the ceiling. "I'll write. That's all I know."

Judi closed her eyes, may have been asleep. What I realized at that moment was that Judi and I had never had the chance to imagine a future together, to see ourselves in another time and another place, to consider our lives as intimate friends do. We lacked a shared past. How did all of this affect our continuous present?

Judi opened her eyes. She said, "The air will be full of space where my body used to be, where it was going to be." She wet her lips with her tongue. "What's air?"

I said, "You should get some rest now."

Judi smirked. "Rest for what?"

"Want some water?"

She shook her head. "I'm totally useless."

I understood this as a statement of truth, as Judi felt it, not as an indulgence in self-pity. I said, "Judi, a person's worth isn't measured by her utility. We're not tools. We're here to think. To feel. To be good to each other."

She told me how the ringing in her ears was now a song of God and that now He was speaking to her in Latin, and she understood Him. And then she said, "Am I making sense?"

"Yes."

"I'm so tired. I'm at the point where I'm seeing faces. Everywhere. In the wallpaper. The front of the radio. The wrinkles in the sheets. In the lamp with the hat on. In the vase and the shaggy-haired flowers. Everyone's watching me. How do I look?"

"You look lovely and tired."

"We had fun," she said. "Maybe we'll do it again." And she smiled.

I smiled.

She closed her eyes. "I got what I came for," she said. She fell asleep. Those were Judi's last words.

There's a form of energy that seems to leave the body at death. Some might call it the soul or the mind or consciousness or the life force. Whatever it is, it takes the body's warmth with it and its personality. Judi was gone; something unique had passed, and I sat with what remained. Judi would have it that her soul is somewhere waiting for another body to enter. I hope she's right about all this, but I believe she's wrong. Our being here is a fortunate accident of chemistry, I think, one we've exploited about as much as we can, and one unlikely to reoccur. I hope I'm wrong. Nicky told me what he thinks is that whatever you believe in comes to pass. But I'll stick with Job: "So man lieth down and riseth not: till the heavens *be* no more, they shall not awake, not be raised out of their sleep."

I heard the back door. Stoni came into the bedroom. She nodded. "I knew it," she said. She cried. "I was at the red light at Heard Street, and I felt it." I tied up Spot outside, came back in to do whatever we had to do. We must have to call someone.

Stoni scooped up Judi in her arms, asked me to strip the bed. I did. We put on new sheets. Stoni brought in a basin of water, soap, a washcloth. She bathed her sister and then covered the body with a sheet. I drew all the shades to darken and cool the room. Stoni took an identifying tag from the mortuary pack and filled it out. She fastened it to the great toe on Judi's right foot with a twist tie. We went to the kitchen and sat.

"I'd like a drink, Laf."

"Me, too." I got a bottle of vodka out of the freezer, two glasses. Yes, I drink too much.

We drank to Judi.

I said, "What do we do now?"

"Wait."

"For?"

"About an hour and a half."

"Why?"

"We don't want any eager paramedics trying to revive her."

"She's dead, isn't she?"

Stoni nodded. "When they get here in a couple of hours, *liver mortis* will have set in. They'll see this, the red fruit of her death. They'll leave her alone."

Stoni made phone calls to relatives and friends. I puttered about the kitchen. I remembered Judi putting out her cigarette in the sink. I smiled. I took all the appointment cards off the refrigerator door. Then I emptied the medicines and vitamins out of the fridge, dropped them into a plastic grocery bag, and tossed the bag into the trash can under the sink. I dried the dishes and glasses on the drainer and put them away. I cleaned the counter and stove top. I dry-mopped the floor. When the washer stopped, I put the sheets into the dryer. I couldn't remember if I had used soap or not. I sat. I heard Stoni thanking someone. I poured myself another drink. I looked at the clock that has always been five minutes fast, daylight and standard time. I looked at the silver canisters lined up on the counter between the cookbooks and the bread box. I am the only one, I realize, who knows that inside FLOUR are red kidney beans, and inside SUGAR is rice, and inside COFFEE are coupons, most of them probably expired, and inside TEA, M&M's.

Every day of my life I think about dying, have since I was ten years old or so. Maybe this started with bedtime prayers, I don't know. And every time I think of dying I become frightened and depressed. I think about how I'll die—in a plane crash, with none of my faculties intact, of a cerebral hemorrhage; I think of where I'll die—in a rooming house, in Skowhegan, Maine, in a nur-nursing home, ba-babbling to myself; I think about when I'll die—in my sleep, at seventy-two, or before I finish this sentence. And wonder what will happen after I die. What I mean is, what will I be missing? The existence of existence and the existence of nonexistence. When I think about this at night, I can't sleep.

I remember friends who've died: Jackie Gannon, struck by lightning on a golf course the day after we graduated from college; Mal Terranova, carved his throat open in the shower; Kenny Allen, burned to death in an apartment fire; Richie Legendre, suffered a single, massive heart attack when he was twenty-nine; Butchie Gingras and Tommy Trudeau died in automobile accidents; my cousin Andy Proulx overdosed on heroin; Karen Harper had breast cancer; Frank Bauer was shot while hitchhiking in Oregon; Margie Greenwood, whom I was crazy about when we were fourteen, though she never knew it, fell or was pushed out her fifteenth-floor dorm room at BU. I imagine what these friends might be doing now had they lived. Like, say, I bump into Mal on Shrewsbury Street and we duck into the Wonder Bar for meatball sandwiches and beer, and we catch up on old times. He tells me how much his life has changed since the Prozac, how he's not so depressed as he used to be. Got a sweet little family now, a house on Solomon Pond, and a sporting goods store in Northborough. He looks good, trim, gray at the temples. Or I imagine that I called Jackie up around nine on the morning after graduation. I told him golf is for old men with funny pants. Let's drive out to the quarries and go swimming.

There will come a time, I like to think, when I might welcome death. *Welcome* could be overstating it. When I would at least receive death with courtesy. That would happen when I am old and when my family and my friends have all gone. Who would I be without them, anyway? I would realize that this is now someone else's world, and I would feel uncomfortable loitering in it.

Stoni walked into the kitchen, poured herself another shot, asked me how I was doing. I said, Fine. She told me Trixie and Hervey were on their way. She sat down. We didn't say anything. Then the doorbell rang. Stoni said that would be Mike, her friend and a paramedic. Mike came in carrying two large pizzas from the Boynton. He put them on the table, hugged Stoni, shook my hand, introduced us to his partner, Buster. Buster's two front teeth were missing. He took a bridge out of his pocket and put it in. Stoni said we'd eat and then call Dr. Stouder and have her meet Mike at the hospital. Mike took his two-way radio off his belt, put it on the counter. We heard it crackle, heard the dispatcher send a team to an accident on Institute Road. I got dishes. Stoni closed the door to the bedroom. Mike offered his condolences. Buster asked if we'd mind if he looked around. Go ahead.

Trixie and Hervey arrived with beer and a tray of lasagna. Trixie put the lasagna in the oven. Hervey said, So our little girl is gone. Stoni took them to the bedroom. Buster returned to the kitchen. He told me, You know that old Silvertone radio in the living room, that's worth some money. He said he'd leave a card. He took one from his wallet, put it on the counter. I deal in collectibles, he said.

While we ate and drank, Trixie called Morin's Funeral Home, tried to reach Ronnie with no success. Buster and Mike took Judi's body out to the ambulance. Neighbors looked out their windows. Soon I was alone in Judi's house. The phone rang, Judi asked the caller to leave a message after the beep, but the caller did not. I went out on the deck. I let Spot off his run, held the back door open for him, but he wouldn't come in the house. Spot, you've changed, I said. He wagged his tail. So we sat on the deck, the pair of us, and I thought about how we all can deal with the fact of our vanishing. Is it even possible? I thought, What do you do when your lover dies? I said to Spot, Why don't I know what to do? He woofed. Why do I even have to ask the question? Other people were making arrangements and preparations. Trixie would be deciding about casket, flowers, services. Stoni would be seeing to the death certificate and the certificate of disposition and whatever else governments require. All I was doing was talking to my dog about mortality.

I felt the need to be kind to someone, and I didn't know why exactly. Kind or polite, solicitous, noble. Something like that. If someone were with me now, I wouldn't talk about Judi or me or sickness or suffering and death. I'd get them something cool to drink, something to eat, something I would make. And I'd say, Tell me all about it. I felt sad, like there was a hole in me from my throat to my stomach.

I thought I'd clear my head with another drink. Spot wouldn't come inside, so I got the bottle and a glass and came back to the deck. I said, Am I going to have to sleep outside tonight? It was dark by then and clear. I stared at the stars and knew that some of them weren't there. Just their light was. Memory is like that light. The body is gone, the center of the world disappears. I closed my eyes. Gone.

71.

A Fine and Private Place

A. "REQUIEM"

We held Judi's funeral at Our Lady of the Angels, the burial at Hope Cemetery, and the party at her house. I've always suspected that mourners are not so much saddened by the deceased's passing—though that is certainly true—as we are comforted by the fact that we did not die ourselves, and we display our relief in a quiet ritual. We lucky ones, we bite our lips, lift our brows, fix each other's gaze. It's a tender moment.

I walked to Morin's Funeral Home. I passed the old Hood's dairy warehouse on Cambridge Street, and that made me think of Mr. Quinn, who drove a milk truck, wore checked overalls and a visored cap. I would see him most summer mornings when I was a kid. I'd ask him for ice, and he'd reach back into his cases and hand me a hunk of clear, smooth, black ice. Was he still alive? He'd have to be eighty by now. Maybe he's puttering around his house this morning, watering his tomato plants or something. I thought about checking for his name in the phone book, but I knew that widows often keep the listing under their husbands' names for years after their deaths. A small memorial, I guess.

I remembered Bill Duchesne, our neighbor, who seemed to have it all, in a middle-America kind of way. Worked out of his house repairing small appliances. A Mr. Fix-it. The New England archery champion, of all things. He water-skied, snow-skied, scuba-dived, climbed mountains. He had an elaborate model railroad in his cellar that he let the neighborhood kids play with. He was a Boy Scout troop leader, a block-party organizer, a civic spokesperson, had a wife, Jan, three kids, Ricky, Paulie, and Verna, a station wagon, a camping trailer, a power mower. And then he drives to a lovers' lane and fires a bullet through his brain.

I rode from the funeral home to the church in a black limo with Ronnie. That was my first surprise. Somehow Ronnie knew that his little girl had died, and he showed up at Trixie's house—his old house—with his blue suit on. His duffle bag was out there now in the trailer.

When you ride in a funeral procession, people watch you: the guy smoking a cigar in front of the Diamond Café, the two ladies in the Buick Regal, the kid sweeping up trash in the Burger King lot. And maybe each onlooker would be more pensive, reflective, today because of this. Maybe the man will call his sister in Duxbury, no reason, just wanted to say hi. Maybe we should have hearses cruise through neighborhoods like milk trucks used to. God, I was beginning to sound medieval.

Ronnie said what happened to Judi was the least worst thing. She could have just lingered in pain, could have rallied strength and then just had to go through it all again. He told me he kept hearing this same speech lately, over and over, and he didn't know if it was a warning, a curse, a promise, a theory, a papal bull, or what it was. He recited: "Whereas the accused *Homo sapien,* being of dubious merit and euphonious expression and having undergone exquisite torment, to wit, he has sacrificed his ego to ether, has attained release without a body to speak of. Let them all ask who would cast the first stone." What do you make of it? he said. Ronnie, I think you should ignore it.

My second surprise was the priest who celebrated the Mass—Father Frank O'Connor, Martha's old drinking buddy and confidant. Turns out he's an old and dear friend of the Dubeys. His father fished with Ronnie's brother Rembrandt or something like that. Worcester is such a small town you could just scream. "Also their love," Father Frank said, "and their hatred, and their envy is now perished . . ." I was impressed. "But not *our* love, which is their immortality on earth." Such as it is, I thought. Ronnie nudged my shoulder. Death is just a phase, he said. You get over it. And then Father Frank quoted John Donne: " *'She, she is dead; she's dead; when thou know'st this,/ Thou know'st how dry a cinder this world is.'* "

B. "NECROPOLIS"

This city of the dead called Hope. I read somewhere that very few cemeteries in the world are more than three hundred years old. So much for an eternal resting place. Stoni and Trixie sat on wooden folding chairs by the grave. I stood behind them with Ronnie and Hervey. Ronnie whispered, Death is a flirt. The sky was cloudless, the morning already beginning to heat up. Father Frank prayed for Judi's soul. I could hear traffic from the expressway. Across from me, Layla cried and held on to Pozzo's arm. Pozzo stood with his eyes closed. I thought, Life is an art, not a science. But what did I mean? That there is no progress because truth, beauty, and mystery are absolutes? Could that be it? We don't learn all that much from anyone else's life. It's like we live for the future, but not our own future. We learn all our valuable lessons too late. It's just so goddamned sad, this being here and not being here.

And then the casket was lowered. Trixie tossed a bouquet of roses into the grave, Stoni a handful of dirt. Father Frank announced that everyone was invited back to Judi's. We began to drift away, down the hill toward the line of cars. I looked back, saw the grave, the dirt pile covered not so discretely with an Astroturf mat, saw two gentlemen sitting in a pickup truck, smoking, watching us. Ronnie said, "Death is liquid." What the hell did he mean by that? You can convert it to cash? It flows? I didn't ask.

Francis X. came over and shook my hand, offered his condolences. "Come to the house," I said. "I'll buy you a drink."

"I've got to work this afternoon. Summer school."

"You're Irish. This is a funeral."

"Can't."

"One drink."

"No."

We shook hands. He asked me what I was going to do now, said he could arrange it so I got my old job back. He said, You think about it. Give me a call.

I saw the Nybergs get into their car, thought it was sweet of them to come. I wondered if they quarreled about this, Chet saying they hardly knew us, Maryalice insisting this was a neighborly obligation. Maybe she said, Get used to it; people will be dying all around us for the rest of our lives.

C. "COMPANY"

Trixie had cooked for two days and two nights, whenever she wasn't at the wake. And so had her neighbors. We had tourtière pies, ragout, little hot dogs steamed in beer, Buffalo wings, Vienna roll sandwiches—tuna, egg, ham. We had cold cuts from Shrewsbury Street and bulkies from Water Street. We had lasagna and moussaka, macaroni salad, potato salad, corn salad, green salad. We had cakes, pies, puddings, and peach cobbler. We had coffee and decaf, tea and soft drinks. We had booze. I bought plenty of booze.

I greeted people at the door, took the men's suit coats and hung them in the bedroom. I made sure whoever wanted a drink got a strong one. Nicky volunteered to tend the bar in the kitchen. Trixie had a buffet table set up on the deck. Spot was in heaven with all the attention and scraps he was getting. I mingled. I heard one man, a friend of Trixie's I think he was, or a cousin or something, tell another: Around six my girlfriend's husband calls—he's my golf partner—and he's drunk, and he tells me he thinks his wife is having an affair. I don't tell him that's absurd—I'm no hypocrite. I tell him to meet me at the club for a drink. So we meet and he wants to know how he can win her back. I tell him flowers, candy, a weekend in Vermont, blah blah blah. He feels better. Then I go home to his wife.

People around me ought to be aware that they are in constant danger of becoming characters in a story. I wondered if these two would recognize themselves. Probably, I thought, they wouldn't be caught dead reading fiction. But that was a nasty and arrogant appraisal. You never have to search for characters. They walk right up and introduce themselves. Happens all the time. Like last week at Our Lady of the Sea, in walks Dee Dee Wondolowski, whom I hadn't seen in a dozen years, I bet. The Wondolowskis were neighbors on Warner Avenue when I was growing up. I played with Dee Dee's older sons. I said, Dee Dee, how have you been? She said, The kids are grown now; we're just waiting for the dog to die. And then she smiled. An hour or so later, this guy from a road crew comes in and orders a seafood platter. Nicky asks him what he wants on it. The guy studies the menu, says, Just make me one with everything. Nicky yells out, One Buddhist platter to go! You keep your eyes open, your ears unplugged.

My third surprise was Arthur. He'd gotten his release from jail a week earlier when the mistrial was declared. He told me Stoni's still touchy about, you know, Richie. I said, Well, that's understandable, right? I mean, you killed him. Didn't you? Arthur said, Yes, I did, but it was self-defense. Then he said, Killing a man changes everything. I just don't have the zest for life that I used to.

Dr. Stouder wasn't here. Neither was the oncologist Pawlak, the surgeon LeClair. But it seemed like everyone else was. I saw Terry Cundall chatting with Ron, Mark, and Albert over by the apricot tree. When I spied her alone later on, I asked Terry about Martha. Terry said, I'm still seeing her in counseling. She's doing quite well. Quite well. That's all I can tell you. Actually, I can't even tell you that. Terry said she was sorry about Judi and all. I thanked her. She didn't say I still owed her money for our sessions. I didn't tell her I'd never pay it. She told me, Grief really saturates the air, doesn't it? Grief keeps the dead alive, she said. Nothing wrong with grief.

I saw Pauline and her carpenter, talking with Dorie. I sat on the steps with Noel, who told me he was thinking of moving back. Nothing he could do for Edmund in Walpole he couldn't do here. He told me he missed Hervey and Trixie. I tried to imagine Noel and Ronnie sharing that trailer. Noel told me his health had gone south on him. Emphysema and a bollixed liver, he said. Bilirubins in the stratosphere. He was smoking his Camels, drinking his Miller High Life. Stopping's not going to do me any good now, is it? he said. He told me Edmund's some kind of Holy Roller Christian now. He's going to be a preacher, after all. He said, What time you got? I checked Puusepp's watch. One-twenty. I went inside to freshen my drink. Ronnie winked at me, whispered, Death is the final order.

The indomitable Trixie told Father Frank that Stoni and Arthur would be getting married and presenting her with a grandchild. She hoped it was a girl. Father Frank stared at me. I could see him out of the corner of my eye. Had it just occurred to him where we'd met? I wasn't going to give him the pleasure of introducing myself. Dorie touched my elbow. She said she needed to leave and would I walk her to her car. We stood in the driveway.

"Are you okay, Laf?"

"I'm okay. Thanks."

"Judi never allowed herself to be a victim."

"In a way, I think we're all victims."

Dorie shook her head, pulled car keys out of her purse. "Only those who won't change are victims. Of themselves."

I could buy that because it made me not responsible for Martha. One of the dangers in life is how we keep ourselves the same. With the big change always at the back of our minds, the small changes seem more obvious. I opened the door to Dorie's little station wagon. She got in. She told me I'd been good for Judi, did I know that? I thanked her for saying so. I mean it, she said. Well, I wanted to believe her, but I felt like a lug. Dorie said, You were there.

I saw Stoni and Arthur in Arthur's pickup. And then Pauline walked out of the house holding hands with her fortunate carpenter. The opposite of being loved is being ignored. I watched them. They didn't see anybody. Why is it that we crave passion in our lives, but we need stability and comfort? Passion implies suffering—what faulty synapse leads to this end? Pauline and her craftsman looked like they would live forever if they didn't wander off into traffic. Mr. and Ms. Natural. Dorie drove away. I waved.

Once when I was single—eighteen years ago, I guess—I found myself in bed with a woman of my acquaintance. Not a friend, really, but a woman I knew socially, hung out with on occasion. This lovemaking was a surprise to both of us, I think. We had fun and cuddled ourselves to sleep with smiles on our faces. In the morning, she was gone—off to work, her note said. Thanks for last night. Call me. I didn't. And though we continued to see each other, we never mentioned our tender and delightful indiscretion, and never slept together again. And soon we lost touch. When I think of her now, I wonder how our lives might have been changed if she hadn't needed to fly off so early or if I had felt her stir in the bed, had touched her, tempted her to linger. I hope Pauline finds herself as wistful one day when she recalls the edgy guy with the funny tooth.

Nicky stayed around and helped me with the cleanup. We watched *East of Eden* on the television. My God, I thought, I've lost my chance ever to be James Dean. I called Edgar. I said, Aaron, this is Cal. He didn't get it. I told him about Judi. Jesus, Laf, he said, I'm sorry. He told me he'd bought himself a Pollo Tropical franchise in Boca Raton. I said, What does Boca Raton mean? I think it means "Rat Shit," he said. You sure you're okay, Laf? Said he and Delores were getting along better than ever. No, I told him, I didn't want to manage a chicken franchise or a motel. He told me he'd be sending me a big fat check for my share of the motel. I could use it. I figured I could live for three years on seventy thousand dollars. Long enough to get that first big sale to Pink Carnation Press. Edgar told me that Mom was seeing a man, a retired military officer, in fact. Lives in Century Village. I thought, Will I ever see my mother or my brother again?

Nicky fell asleep watching a rerun of *The Newlywed Game* on cable. I went to the bedroom closet to get him a blanket. I saw my green plaid suitcase on the shelf. Fate is not subtle at all. I covered Nicky, switched off the sound on the tube. My life, all of a sudden, was very simple. I went out to the deck and sat. I said, Spot, what are we going to do? He said, Woof—his answer for everything. I looked up at the night sky. Ten thousand years ago Greek shepherds looked up and saw scorpions, hunters, water bearers. Me, I look up and see discrete specks of light. I feel impoverished. Good thing human development wasn't left up to me. I can't change a tire. We'd all still be gathering leafy plants, feeding them to the dogs, watching to see if they went into convulsions. All I can do is make up stories about made-up people. The world, I'm afraid, could get along without me. No child, no wife, no dad, no girlfriend, no certitude, no career, no prospects, no home. Jesus. Well, I had Spot. I had Dale and Theresa. I had, I hoped, a sympathetic reader somewhere. I could expect to die. Everything else, I knew, was a choice. I looked at those stars again, all of them, for the moment, burning for me.

72.

The Only Worlds We Have

Time bears away all things. That's what Dale's thinking this morning. Carries away pain and loss and dreams and youth. Concentrates the heart, but muddles the mind. It's 6:15; he's into the third day of this cycle of insomnia, and he feels like a trembling machine. He's exhausted, but he knows this too will pass. These mornings, Dale keeps a thermos of coffee on the nightstand so that he can drink a cup before he steps out of his bed, walks to the kitchen, and perks another pot of coffee. Dale sits at the kitchen table, sipping, scratching notes. Keynes sleeps on the braided rug in front of the sink. Dale has his caffeine, his solitude, and an hour to prepare a lecture on stock markets, as if a single cowboy or bowhead in his class gave two sweet shits about emerging markets and global investing. And why should they? It's boring. Face it. Boring and irrelevant. Twenty years ago he had to select a major at UNM. He loved geography, thought about political science, figured it would be impractical, he can't remember why, and wrote down *Economics* for some reason. Dale sees Keynes lift his head, and then he hears Peter walking down the hall toward the bathroom.

On the day that I cleaned out Judi's office on Irving Street, brought home the few items that Stoni or Trixie might want (a photograph of Judi, Stoni, and a friend, all about ten or eleven, all in pajamas, and all sitting on the hood of a car at the drive-in; an ashtray that said *Nick's Colonial Grille;* a stack of business cards; a crystal bud vase; an address book; and a silk paisley scarf), cut up her Memorial Hospital ID card, and burned her sickness clothes (the woolen robe, the flannel pajamas, the slippers, the sweat suits), on that day I was sure Theresa was going to die. Ovarian cancer, automobile wreck. Or maybe not die, but find out that living with Dale was harder than she had imagined it. Or maybe Peter's father came back, and Theresa remembered why she had loved him. Or she would have a nervous breakdown. But none of that happened.

When Dale asked Theresa to marry him, or decided to ask, my story was over, I suppose, but I couldn't stop writing about these two. I'd been with them every day for more than a year. I wanted to find out what happened in their lives, not just in the courtship. The story may have been over, but their lives were not. Of course, I knew that if I continued to write about them, then one day I would have to write something like, *One morning Dale awoke with a numbness in his right arm and right leg. Perhaps it will pass, he thought. He crawled to the kitchen.* And so on. What I knew was that in fiction, the only false ending is *And they all lived happily ever after.* So where and when do I stop?

Judi told me that what she tried to do in therapy was simple—get the client moving. Inertia was always trouble. Her goal was this: to help the person realize how he was keeping himself the same, and then to help him understand how he could change that situation. She said, Habit stifles perception. To act habitually is to act without thinking. If you stop the habit, you get to start your life again, and one good way to do that is to fall in love. Love is change. It is not a condition, but a behavior. Routine is death to love. A marriage might stall and remain a marriage, but love stilled becomes something else. Two things, she said: Love is always a surprise, and you never get it right.

Me, I used to believe that love and happiness were synonymous. I was a fool. Love intensifies *all* emotions. Nothing is so painful or so sweet, so thrilling or so desperate. Judi and I had much love, I think, but little pleasure. And that's okay. Pleasure is, after all, a luxury. It's love that's essential. You are never so alive as when you love, never so alert, intuitive, attentive, never so smart or so compassionate. But death is the price you pay for this privilege.

Because I still love Judi, I want to be with her, and I am. I sit here at the table and close my eyes and see her clearly—her cobalt-blue silk T-shirt, her black tights, her hair in spikes—and I wonder what she's thinking, what she'll do. She closes her book—she's reading Stendhal, I see. Curious. She comes to me. She touches my hands so I'll stop this typing. She kisses my right eye, my left eye, my ears, my chin, my lips, the tip of my nose. She holds her cheek against mine. I feel her hand at my neck, the flush of my skin, the purring in my brain. I wonder what I'll do now.

Dale pours Peter's Froot Loops into a bowl, splashes in the milk. He pours Peter a glass of orange juice. When Peter sits at the kitchen table, Dale pats the boy's head, ties his shoes. Dale brings a small radio to the table and tunes in an oldies station that Peter likes. Magic, Peter says. Magic 102. Dale walks down the hall, knocks on Caitlin's opened door, says, Time to get up, sugar. School. Keynes limps along behind Dale. His arthritis is so bad that the vet suggested putting Keynes down. The animal is in quite a lot of pain, Mr. Evans. But he's alive, Dale thought. He can't bring himself to do it. In their bedroom, Dale looks at Theresa sleeping. Dead sleep, he knows, dreamless sleep. He wonders why she has seemed so unhappy for so long, a couple of years now. She loves him, he knows. But she has regrets that he knows nothing about. He can sense this in the way she sleeps so profoundly, at such length, sits so quietly at night, in the way her easy smile masks emotion. He touches her shoulder. Honey. Sweetheart. Wake up. Come on now. Theresa. It's morning.

I called Francis X. We met for drinks at Moynihan's. Francis X. told me the oldest daughter, Fiona, had moved to New York, New York, with a college boy. He told me that the offer of the job was still open, but I would have to let him know by the end of the month. August would be too late. I told him I'd think about it, I really would. He said, And what about the rest of your life? Meaning Martha? I said. He nodded. I shook my head. He said, Well, maybe it's all for the best. John Joe set us up with two more shots of Jameson's. We drank, watched the Sox get slaughtered by Baltimore, fall from first, and start their inevitable slide to oblivion. You have to love them.

   Nicky said, You can live to work or you can work to live. We sat in his room eating Vietnamese out of boxes and watching *Andy of Mayberry* and *You'll Never Get Rich* simultaneously. He said, Writing stories isn't frying fish. Give yourself another twenty years, he said. Write every day. Then, if no one wants your stories, give yourself another twenty years.

Dale sits on the couch at midnight, TV on to the late news, but mute. He tries to read the newscaster's lips. He pages through his collection of presidential buttons, wondering when he lost his enthusiasm for the hobby. *All the Way with JFK*. He has students who haven't heard of Kennedy, who think that anything that happened before their births is irrelevant. Maybe narrowing the world is one way to survive. Keynes whimpers in his sleep. He's so medicated these days, he's stupefied, inert. Tomorrow, Dale will drop Peter at the Training Center, Caitlin at the high school, and Keynes at the vet's. He closes his book. What did his fifth-grade teacher call it? His *Permanent Record*. Your past will follow you for the rest of your life as a public document. What to do? Once he'd wanted his face on a campaign button. What happened to all that? Lost heart somehow, never tried. He wondered how many other erstwhile political leaders were sitting alone tonight with their secret. Dale takes his nightly walk, but this time without Keynes. It's what you don't do that haunts you the most, he thinks. When he reaches the corner of Dal Paso and Navaho, where they always turn around, Dale stops, stares at the bright lights of the Allsup's.

Back home, Dale brews his coffee and fills the thermos. He checks the locks, checks the children, cuts the lights. He undresses and slips into bed beside Theresa. She's awake, but pretends not to be. He kisses her head. It's just beginning, he tells her. Theresa doesn't know what he means. The beginning of the end? What? You mean there's more? More and more getting up, trudging to work, putting in the hours, coming home to cook, clean, iron, argue with a daughter who dates a boy who beats her, curses at her? More of that? What happened? Caitlin will be pregnant soon, and Theresa knows that if the monster ever lays a hand on her grandchild, she'll see he's put away, kill him if she has to. God, here she is at forty-one thinking about murdering people. Is it Peter she wants to kill? Is that why she can't sleep? Murder the boy who won't grow up? They'll be seventy, she and Dale, and they'll be shackled with this lumbering child. She hates herself for feeling this way. Why can't she be noble, holy, like the selfless people they profile in the paper—couples who adopt houses full of handicapped kids? She regrets she'll never have a romance with Dale. They'll always be distracted from each other. She hears Peter open his door, walk toward their room. She tenses, she can't help it. Dale tells her, Go to sleep, I'll get him.

I'm living on the first floor of a three-decker on Grafton Hill. Spot stays inside mostly. I write at the kitchen table. Nicky and I just came back from a tour of the South in a rental car. Nicky took photographs; I took notes. I'm writing a novel about love and death in Mount of Olives,

Louisiana, a small town in a Delta parish. We've got weddings and fu-
nerals, senility, genius, lust. Love. It's all about remembering. There's a
boy named Adlai Birdsong in it and a child named Bergeron who can't
forget anything. In Mount of Olives there are thirteen cemeteries, a store
called the Black & Lovely Grocery, three Baptist churches, a Holiness
Church, and a Catholic church. There's a movie theater, the Bijou, that
runs one night a week. In summer, Lavelle Spencer sets up a huge fan
by the ticket booth that blows mosquitoes away from the entrance.

I had dinner with Stoni and Arthur at the Thai Orchid. They're en-
gaged. Being with the family keeps Judi in my life, and I like that. Stoni
looked great. She was calm. Arthur couldn't do enough for her. Pulled
out her chair, unfolded her napkin, kept asking if she needed anything.
She told me she saw Ronnie on a TV talk show. All the guests claimed
to be from other planets. Ronnie was the only one who looked normal,
who wasn't dressed in some *Star Trek* costume. But he was the craziest
of them all. Stoni smiled.

You'd think I'd run into Martha once in a while. I'd like to. I try to. I
walk up Elm Street past the Chancery for no reason at all. I can do this
because I know our lives are separate now. I'd like to talk to her, see how
she's doing, tell her I care about her, and like that. It's probably better
for me that I don't see her—keeps the shame, guilt, and regret right there
on the surface like a rash—and it's certainly better for her.

I've sold three stories in three months for a total income of six copies
of three literary magazines. Sometimes I feel foolish, and then I remember what Judi told me—better to be hungry and foolish than fat and
complacent. I don't even understand complacency. It's like a sinister force
from the planet Quark. I write every morning from seven till noon.
Then I go to the King's Head Pub for lunch. They've got a new woman
behind the bar who drives me crazy. She could be anorexic, she's so thin.
She looks like a boy, now that I think of it. I go to work at Our Lady of
the Sea, come home around eight or nine, and write some more. And
when I sleep I dream about my characters. In one dream Dale and I were
in field of switchgrass and sagebrush and saw two coyotes catch a house
cat and eat it. Dale put his arm on my shoulder, said not to worry, that's
just the world and how it works. Don't turn away from it.

PLUME **DUTTON**

GREAT MODERN FICTION

☐ **FREE ENTERPRISE by Michelle Cliff.** This potent and lyrical novel tells the remarkable story of frontier legend Mary Ellen Pleasant and other extraordinary individuals silenced by the "official record." Brought to life is the passionate struggle for liberation which began in America not long after the first slaves landed on its shores. "Provocative, strongly imagined, bold and inventive." —*Essence*
(271223—$9.95)

☐ **LA MARAVILLA by Alfredo Véa, Jr.** The desert outside the Phoenix city limits is a world of marvels spilling out of the adobe homes, tar-paper shacks, rusted Cadillacs, and battered trailers that are otherwise known as "Buckeye." *La Maravilla* is the embodiment of belonging to two worlds, and being torn between love and fear of both. "A vibrant and colorful tale of magic, history, and human sorrow." —*San Francisco Focus* (271606—$12.95)

☐ **PAGAN BABIES by Greg Johnson.** This powerful novel traces the turbulent, but enduring relationship between a man and a woman, growing up Catholic in America, spanning three decades, from the fleeting optimism of Kennedy's Camelot to the fearsome age of AIDS. "Thoughtful, engrossing . . . Combines deeply serious intent with compulsive readability." —*Washington Post*
(271320—$11.95)

Prices slightly higher in Canada.

Visa and Mastercard holders can order Plume, Meridian, and Dutton books by calling
1-800-253-6476.
They are also available at your local bookstore. Allow 4-6 weeks for delivery.
This offer is subject to change without notice.

PLF7

Contemporary Fiction for Your Enjoyment

☐ **THE SUN, THE SEA, A TOUCH OF THE WIND by Rosa Guy.** The time is the 1970s. Jonnie Dash is an orphan, survivor of Harlem's gritty streets, ex-factory worker, and, finally, a successful and recognized African-American artist. Now, flight from a brush with madness has brought her to Haiti. Jonnie is seduced by the overwhelming beauty of the place. However, she finds herself an outsider in several ironic and unexpected ways. (247807—$22.95)

☐ **ABENG by Michelle Cliff.** This book is a kind of prequel to the author's highly acclaimed novel *No Telephone to Heaven* and is a small masterpiece in its own right. Here Clare Savage is twelve years old, the light-skinned daughter of a middle-class family, growing up in Jamaica among the complex contradictions of class versus color, blood versus history, harsh reality versus delusion. "The beauty and authority of her writing are coupled with profound insight."— Toni Morrison (274834—$11.95)

☐ **ANNIE JOHN by Jamaica Kincaid.** The island of Antigua is a magical place; growing up there should be a sojourn in paradise for young Annie John. But as in the basket of green figs carried on her mother's head, there is a snake hidden somewhere within. "Penetrating, relentless . . . Women especially will learn much about their childhood through this eloquent, profound story."—*San Francisco Chronicle* (263565—$9.95)

☐ **OXHERDING TALE by Charles Johnson.** One night in the antebellum South, a slaveowner and his African-American butler stay up to all hours drinking and playing cards. Finally, too besotted to face their respective wives, they drunkenly decide to switch places in each other's beds. The result is a hilarious imbroglio *and* an offspring. "Memorable . . . a daring, extravagant novel."—*The New Yorker* (275032—$11.95)

☐ **MIDDLE PASSAGE by Charles Johnson. Winner of the National Book Award.** "A story of slavery . . . a tale of travel and tragedy, yearning and history . . . brilliant, riveting."—*San Francisco Chronicle* (266386—$11.95)

☐ **COPPER CROWN by Lane von Herzen.** The story of two young women— one white, one black—sharing a friendship amidst the divisive and violent racism of rural 1913 Texas. "A fresh, poetically evocative and down-to-earth novel."—*The Washington Post* (269164—$10.95)

Prices slightly higher in Canada.

Visa and Mastercard holders can order Plume, Meridian, and Dutton books by calling
1-800-253-6476.
They are also available at your local bookstore. Allow 4-6 weeks for delivery.
This offer is subject to change without notice.

PL117